Paleon: Echoes of an Empire

PALEON: ECHOES OF AN EMPIRE

Memoirs of Brother Alfanas — Book One

Kregg Gábor

PaleonEchoes Press
Poughkeepsie, New York

Paleon: Echoes of an Empire
Memoirs of Brother Alfanas — Book One
First Edition

Published by PaleonEchoes Press
https://paleonechoes.com

ISBN (Paperback): 979-8-9937564-0-0

*Dedicated to my wife, Laura,
and my daughter, Emma—
You are my constant source of love, strength, and inspiration.
This journey through the echoes of an empire is for you, who remind me every day
of the enduring power of family.*

Author's Note

This novel begins with a dramatized account of the last hours of Constantinople in 1453. The fate of Emperor Constantine XI Palaiologos remains one of history's great mysteries: eyewitnesses place him at prayer in Hagia Sophia and then in the thick of battle, but his body was never recovered. Over the centuries, legends grew—that he cast off his imperial robes to die as a common soldier, or that God transformed him into the "Marble Emperor," sleeping beneath the Golden Gate until the city's restoration.

In *Paleon: Echoes of an Empire*, I have woven together the historical record, Byzantine folklore, and imaginative fiction. Where history falls silent, legend whispers, and where legend is uncertain, the storyteller steps in to speculate on the question of "What if the legend could be right?" An appendix at the end of the book dissects the prologue scene by scene, distinguishing fact, tradition, and invention.

This account is informed by historical research, by Byzantine traditions preserved across centuries, and by the imagination required to bridge the gaps between them.

Essential Prologue: The Emperor's Farewell

New Rome: a title coveted and debated. Throughout history, Old Rome sought to redefine itself, reshaping governance and ideals to maintain its relevance and allure. Foreign powers, yearning for the legacy and prestige of progressive Rome, vied for the throne, each claiming legitimacy. Yet only when Constantinople shed Byzantion's shadows did a true Roman heir stand in the world.

Constantinople became a radiant center, drawing together the wealth, laws, and philosophies of the West into a unique synthesis of Roman and Greek traditions. The city embodied a harmonious blend, standing at the crossroads of East and West. Its culture, architecture, and spirit were a testament to this remarkable fusion, shining as a beacon of civilization that bridged two worlds.

The opulence and regalia of the Byzantine court made appearing before the Emperor an intense experience. But the court was more than just an impression; it was a theater that aimed to convey power and mystery.

Played out in magnificent splendor, the drama at court involved the divine and mysterious right of rule by God's chosen vicar. The throne room was not a building, but an apparatus. The emperor made sudden appearances. Guests arrived at an empty throne room. Then, in full display, Constantine emerged as if from nowhere. Miraculously.

Such a production relied on clever gears, levers, pulleys, and ropes. Together, they facilitated the mysterious machine of imagination and theatre, elevating the emperor and throne from the palace's bowels to full display in what would make the most modern entertainment artist envious.

Amidst the grandeur and mechanized wonder of the Byzantine court, peace was but a distant memory for the city and its sovereign. The burdens of rule pressed on Emperor Constantine XI Palaiologos, especially in the darkness before the coming storm. Each rare instance of calm reflection only intensified the gravity of his duty, reminding him that the fate of Rome, and perhaps Christendom itself, rested upon his shoulders.

On this fateful night, as the Emperor of the Romans, ordained by God, completed the sacred rituals, he gazed out over his besieged city. Across the darkness, he could make out the fires of the enemy. In his heart, he understood the imperial title, bestowed by divine providence, was likely to follow him into death.

The city, as much as possible, was ready. Constantine's last task was more intimate: to set his soul in order for his Creator. He wondered if God would abandon God's Holy City? Might a miraculous deliverance still come at dawn?

Outside the city walls, the fires of the besiegers lit the night, reminding all within of the peril to come.

The image of burning brought to mind a recent conversation Constantine had had with Demetrios, a trusted advisor.

"It is not cowardice to continue the fight from foreign shores," Demetrios argued.

"Demetrios, get behind me. Do we not trust and have faith in our deliverance? And if not in our deliverance, then in judgment? All things are in the hands of God, not us. I may not have been born in the *Porphyra*, but I am still the emperor under the weight of the royal purple. I cannot forsake my responsibility, my throne, my destiny. I can do no other." Constantine had then clapped Demetrios on the back and corrected, "We can do no other."

"Demetrios was a good man." Constantine reflected with sorrow on what was to come. He moved back into Hagia Sophia, up to the emperor's private entrance, and back into the Balcarnaria, the palace. If Constantine needed to die, it needed to be with as clean a soul as possible. He knew that even as God's appointed ruler, he had not always acted with the full weight of his faith. His soul felt heavy. Everything needed to be ready for any event.

He gathered all the household, embraced them, and asked them to forgive any harm he may have caused them. The night was running out. Too soon would come the dawn, and with it, the city's defense.

With the title goes the authority. While the Emperor lived, Rome lived. While Constantine breathed, God's power to redeem the horror of the recent tragedies of the Holy City was possible.

It was still not too late. Merchant ships and trading vessels still made it through the blockade. One ship might still pass unnoticed. One ship loaded with the emperor and the holy relics of his office. Previous invaders and sympathizing friends carted or carried off the most valuable and important relics, plunder of ages past. But the city had not given up everything from its coffers. Even now, laden ships left harbor not with trade but with imperial and holy salvage against the fall.

He, too, might sail to other shores. The fight might go on from foreign shores. In exile, Constantine might rally support from the rest of Christendom, a support that had long been absent. He would not be fleeing out of cowardice but out of hope for the future. Yet, he recognized the sound of desperation when he heard it. He didn't think fleeing the city was desirable.

No, that time had passed. He had resisted the temptation to preserve himself. Constantine secured the crown and scepter in the throne room. He put his sword about him and walked from the palace to the land walls for the last time, even as the dawn broke.

Knowing it would be his first and possibly last stop, he could hear the engaged battle at the main gate.

Men barked out orders, and chaos reigned. The Sultan's cannons boomed incessantly as their payloads smashed into walls and ripped into human flesh. Men defended the gates with every effort of their will, only to succumb to the enemy's steel. It was unrelenting horror.

In the thick of it all, Constantine fought courageously. Legend had him all over the city simultaneously, yet he was only a man, not a god. When he had done what he could, he moved from the Rhegion Gate to the Golden Gate. In the early hours of the morning, the Sultan's men breached the walls, and Constantinople lay open, helpless and hopeless; the defenders had lost all.

"The city is lost," Constantine yelled, his voice rising above the chaos. "But I live. Long live Rome!" In those words, he carried not hope for himself but for the ideal of Rome, his Rome, so Rome might somehow endure beyond the walls now crumbling around him.

He pulled his robes off and all imperial regalia and joined the fight as a common soldier seeking solidarity with all who would die that day. Some say that Constantine was last seen alive outside the Golden Gate. Living or dead, he seemed to be swallowed by the earth itself, vanishing into legend. The sultan's men never found his body. Leaving the attackers to assume his fate. Legend claims Constantine XI Palaiologos lies turned to marble beneath the Golden Gate, awaiting the angel who will summon him to deliver the city once more.

But for now, it was over. Constantinople had fallen. The carnage echoed for generations, Byzantium's faith reduced to mere tolerance, its vibrancy extinguished.

Chapter 1: Cathedral to Transit

Centuries later, far from the crumbled walls of Constantinople, another man, burdened by decisions he hadn't wanted, actions he hadn't planned, felt the crushing weight of them.

"I'm not prepared for this … I … I'm over my head. I just killed a man. I just let him go. I …" Nick finally sobbed. He could count on one hand the times he had killed something bigger than a bug. Nick felt guilty for days after hitting a squirrel with his car. Life has a right to live, and people should not waste it.

And human life. Well, that's a whole other level. He killed a man who had hopes and dreams. A consciousness in the universe, a one-of-a-kind creation never to be again. A man who should have fallen in love if he had not, had a family, and … well … lived. Potential died because he chose to let go.

Nick felt her hand rest lightly on his leg as she leaned toward him, eyes fixed on his.

"Don't, don't do this to yourself. He would have killed both of us if he could have. You have a right to live as well, and what of me? Do I not have a right to a future? No, he chose not you. He chose and gave you no choice. He chose, and now you must bear the hurt if you must, but it is not your fault."

"I want to go home. I want this over. This isn't supposed to be part of the adventure." Despaired Nick while avoiding her stare.

Her grip tightened on his leg. The marks of the struggle they had both been through visible on her face, softened now by an anxious compassion for him.

"You don't get to choose the script all the time. Sometimes, you must read the lines given to you and do the next thing. This doesn't end here, you know that."

Nick drew a breath, letting the silence settle, recalling the journey that brought him to this. Life had been simple, ordinary, and predictable back then. A typical sunny morning in New York, now as distant as another lifetime.

He emerged from the shadows into the bright morning sunlight with a bit of a blink, as he always did. As he came through the doors, he embraced another habit; he turned and looked at the grand façade of Grand Central Station. He never tired of it. So large, so magnificent, like a grand cathedral, raised to the gods of transportation, commerce, and economy. And him? Merely one among the thousands of devotees who daily paid homage to those lesser gods of the capitalistic pantheon. *"Yeah, why not, a cathedral to transportation, grand enough. After all, the builders built divinity right into the façade as a sub-pantheon looked down from above on the bustling city that had no time to return the glance!"* He reflected.

For the last four years, Nikolai "Nick" Paleon commuted into the city every day of the week. In his thirties, Nick liked his current job well enough. But Nick saw it more as a means to an end; he really loved the idea of not having to commute into the city every day. He really wanted to move up the ladder, not solely in his career, but in a deeper way, in life itself. Even though the commute bothered him, Nick would endure his current situation until he could earn more money elsewhere.

Nick honestly admitted his motivation to himself. He turned his love of classical history and archaeology into a profession in architecture, as few can make a good living in these fields. History and archaeology lead to an existence, not a living. But they held his affection, from which architecture emerged as a career. Did he compromise? Maybe, but if his dream future required him to make a compromise or two, well, why not? *"Put in your time, do the work now,"* he resolved, *"and later you can pursue your passions."*

He loved the path of human history, the inventive spirit of ancestors who met challenges with ingenuity and grace. Digging into the earth revealed their minds at work: walls, mosaics, flying arches, sprawling villas. Much of archaeology amounted to forensic architecture, but architecture paid the bills while keeping him close to what he loved.

He looked back up at the façade, designed in the Beaux-Arts style. The city's architecture—that was the one thing he liked. New York had it all. He could visit the classics and contemporary styles. Museums and galleries abound.

He had never visited the city as a child. His parents worked hard during the week with little time for weekend pursuits. It always seemed that more important tasks and errands required the family's attention. The city, along with other travel, would have to wait until his parents had more time and money. Nick paused and considered, *"They are still waiting."*

Nick didn't see himself as a high-maintenance child. He mostly stayed to himself. His sister and brother were more involved in sports and always running here and there, taking up more of Mom and Dad's limited time, but he enjoyed spending his time reading and dreaming.

Nick lived in Stamford, where he was born, raised, and schooled. A New Englander at heart, he crossed the cultural borders to New York City because work made it worthwhile. The city was impressive, yet somehow empty. The crowd of people made you notice how insignificant you are. You could literally rip all your clothes off and go running buck naked down the street, and only a duty-bound cop, paid to deal with your issues, might notice you. Beyond that, the city ticked along at a steady hum, uninterrupted by almost everyone. Cold in its way, the city still offered an anonymity he liked.

Nick turned and looked away from Mercury, Hercules, and Minerva, who gazed down from the massive cornice of Grand Central Station, to lose himself in studying the sidewalk and traffic on his way downtown to the office.

Ah, the office. He was really lucky there. A mere five years out of Yale's School of Architecture, and now overseeing projects and teams. Due to a massive health scare, people walked away from their careers and homes, fearing a general meltdown of those lesser gods of finance and capital into more practical goods. Professionals simply up and left their jobs. However, they also created opportunities for those left behind, such as Nick. And he had swooped in at the first opening.

As he walked along, he clicked back to a time when work was less pressure-filled but also less financially rewarding. Not coming from a wealthy family meant he had to be off to work early in life if he wanted to spend money. His parents had instilled in him a very rigid work ethic. Nick's mom and dad had worked hard to bring the family out of Bridgeport to the more upwardly mobile Stamford. His parents didn't believe in giving him an allowance, but they would buy him what he needed. He had to ask his parents for additional money, use his birthday money, or get a job to cover life's extras.

Once old enough to get working papers, he worked after hours, sweeping the local drugstore floors and doing miscellaneous jobs, from shelf stocking to garbage removal. The bike ride from his house wasn't bad, and the job allowed him to save up for his first car.

In high school, he gained his first experience with architecture and drafting. Part of the industrial arts program, it introduced him to drafting. He had four years of mechanical drafting and one year of architectural drafting. The time and interest paid off early, as he won awards for his skill in pencil-and-paper drafting before learning Computer-Aided Drafting (CAD) systems.

Nick loved to breathe life into his vision of living spaces and buildings. While flying buttresses were beyond his skill, he designed homes that promoted fuller lives and interaction. He would then render them in three-point perspective to leap off the page into mountainous landscapes or sprawling suburbs, over which the balconies and decks of his imagination could look. It was a transcendent experience for him to bring his drawings to life. His instructor had such confidence in his ability that he found a paying project for him to draw up plans for an addition to the house of one of the local merchants. What a thrill, even as a senior in high school, to allow him to work on authentic architecture. His creation would come to life: what a rush, and he'd get paid to boot!

Upon going to college, he moved from the drugstore to working at the Avery Architectural and Fine Arts Library at Yale, where books and architecture intersected. Not only did it provide him with gas money, but it also fueled his curiosity and artistry. Yale was a wonderful place to study architecture. The campus buildings ran the gamut of styles and textures. The red brick and Collegiate Gothic style of the Divinity School, with its rough surfaces and monastic feel, gave him a sense that the red brick arms of the quad leading to the chapel were embracing and drawing him in. To the more Modernist style of the Beinecke Rare Book & Manuscript Library, with its translucent smooth walls and sharp corners of thin marble that let through a sublime light that added to the warmth and solemnity of the assembled collection. So many buildings, so little time, he mused. How wonderful life felt, bringing him to this place at this time.

After college, he had one or two minor internships and eventually landed an assistant position that grew into a full-time role. He sometimes speculated that one had guided the opening and closing of his life's doors. A great Master Architect, laying out lines, building in doors and windows, connecting the various themes of his life. He laughed despite himself as he almost walked out into traffic. *"Now, back to the real world, dude, or you'll wind up as a hood ornament!"*

So what if he is now managing projects, a job that has removed him somewhat from his creative attachments and expressions of design? This job offered a terrific opportunity. Perhaps he could retire early and pursue his genuine passion, such as digging up history in an exotic location overseas. *"Keep your eyes on the prize,"* he told himself. Architecture became his compromise with the world; it paid the bills while nodding at his passion.

Yet, in his levelheaded moments, he could feel the years slipping by. *"I wonder,"* he mused to himself, *"if everyone feels like there is just something more in them that needs the chance to breathe, live, and be born into reality?"* He didn't remember getting on the elevator. *"Nick, you've been on autopilot again. The last time you did that, a car nearly ran you over! Get your mind in the game, boy."*

"Hey, Nick," he heard as he walked off the elevator. *"Oh great, here comes Howard. Bad enough, the guy takes a week off work and throws my schedule for the Barren's project out the window, but he is now stalking me as I get off the elevator. Really!?"* he thought to himself.

But what came out of his mouth was, "Hey, Howard, rough week for you, huh?"

"Yeah. My wife is still in Florida, taking care of her mom. I have the kids, but we are working things out, and I hope not to need more time off. It's tough getting them off to school and making it here. Not to mention food…"

"Yeah. It must be a challenge. Hey, can you get to those new drawings as soon as possible? We are behind on the Barrens project, and it doesn't reflect well on the entire team."

"Sure, Nick," Howie replied with a sigh that almost said, *"It doesn't look great for you either."* But he thought it best to leave that unsaid.

Nick had settled behind his desk and checked his schedule for the day. He had a project review with one of the firm's partners today; hmm, that was always fun, and, thanks to Howie, he had little to report since last week. As he embraced his coffee, the cup so nicely warm, wrapping both hands around it, he felt a chill go up his spine. He may not be senior enough for his own window, but he had his own space with a Keurig in tow. *"Life is good when you have your own source of coffee,"* he reflected as he took a sip.

Coffee would always bring him back home, even from the city. He imagined that if he traveled anywhere in the world, a warm cup of strong black coffee would put him right back in Mom's kitchen, at the table with his family, or out at Dunkin' Donuts with his friend for one of their late-night talks. Oh, the smells and sounds of a coffee shop are like riding down a road in Pennsylvania and suddenly knowing that you are on holiday because there is the chocolate of Hershey's in the air. The smell of freshly ground coffee held the same allure for Nick. Most people pull back to comfort food. For Nick, a cup of coffee and the world would change without the calories.

Nick hit the "any key" on the keyboard of his laptop, and as it sprang to life, he wondered about how much time he spent hypnotized by this screen. It had been years since any modern architect had sat at a drafting table or worked with real blueprints and ammonia. Everything was digital now. Nick spent his time working with spreadsheets. Rows, columns, cells, wow, "cells" — he knew days when that moniker aptly fit the office environment and its tasks. The numbers began with dollar signs, rounded to two decimal places, rather than being expressed in feet, inches, and tenths.

He was following the year-to-date costs on one of his projects when his desk vibrated, a sure signal that his cell phone had sprung to life from its resting position, much like a neglected child that was seen but not heard at work. The vibration was usually enough to pull him back to the land of the living and away from the drone of numbers.

Nick shifted his attention away from the work on his desk and turned the phone over to look at the number and the caller's ID. A smile came to his face as he read the name "Chris."

Nick had always led a relatively sheltered life. As the oldest child, his parents expected him to be the responsible one. Now that he was on his own, he was okay with a bit of distance from the family dynamics. He had lost no one close to him, so he had yet to feel what that was like.

Nick knew little about his family history, yet probably as much as everyone his age. He knew his great-grandparents had immigrated from Ukraine because that was what his father had told him. In 1930, they came through Ellis Island. They settled in the city of Bridgeport, Connecticut. It was Nick's dad, Mike, who moved the family from Bridgeport to Stamford. The third generation had become a little more upwardly mobile, and Nick was the first of the family to attend college. Nick's aunt and uncle had moved their families out of state years ago. The family still exchanges Christmas cards every year but never see each other.

While he dreamed and felt the urge to do more with his life, the feeling seldom stirred him to action. He was a nice guy who would help when asked but had a clear sense of duty, especially at work. Yet projects came and went, and had fast settled into the routine of daily life.

Nick had never really developed strong friendships. His introversion played a part, but the 45-minute commute to New Haven meant he spent little time on campus. When he looked back at college, he really could not remember much more than that he felt a sense of relief when it ended. Driving, working, sleeping, and studying left little time for social engagement.

Then he began his career. He committed himself to advancement. He would delude himself into believing that he had no time for serious relationships, but, truth be told, he always looked for more in a serious relationship than the women he met and dated.

He settled on expecting only an occasional diversion and nothing serious. Nick dove increasingly into work, feeling that the right person—a suitable mate—would have to find him.

Nick swiped open the call and put the phone to his ear, and greeted the caller: "Chris, how goes it with my private IT consultant today?"

"Hey Nick," Chris' words rushed back, "just a quick check-in to hear all the new and wonderful things you are up to!"

"Great. How much do you need, and are you on Venmo?"

"Always the comedian. No, I am not calling to ask you for a favor."

"Ah," Nick said suspiciously, "not that you need a reason to call my friend, but I don't think that much in my life could have emerged into blooming flowers of newness in a matter of a little over a week since we last spoke. So, what's up?"

There was a slight pause on the other end of the phone as the smile left the voice somewhat. Chris weighed his next words, trying to inject joy, or at least ease, into his voice as he responded.

Chris had started a committed relationship about a year ago, and now he was a relational zealot, especially with his oldest friend Nick. Initially, Nick cut Chris some slack over his enthusiasm. Chris had his "the one," and Nick appreciated how happy that made Chris, but he needed to stop pushing Nick.

"Did, uh, you get the email about the reunion?"

"Yeah, I did," Nick returned cautiously.

"Oh, nice, did you respond? Are you going?" Chris's voice hesitated slightly even as he asked this.

"Not sure. Work's pretty full, and I don't keep up with people from high school. You?" Nick responded honestly.

"I'm not going," Chris said with genuine disappointment. He really was an extrovert who loved a crowd. "I can't afford either the money or the time away from life down here. But guess who picked up the phone when I called?"

Nick now took his turn to pause. He thought to himself, *"Here we go. 'Zealots R Us' in action. Chris doesn't think I am complete without someone on my arm!"*

"Who," robot Nick heard himself respond as he hopelessly encouraged Chris.

"It was Sheryl. You remember Sheryl." Chris's tone became more animated.

"Oh yeah. Hope she's doing well," Nick tried to back off his interest.

"She sounded good, disappointed that I could not make it, but was happy that things were going well for me. Sheryl was always a nice girl. She asked about you and whether she would see you at the reunion."

Boom, that's why Chris called.

"Oh, she must be desperate," Nick shot back as if Chris had fired a cannonball sailing over the private walls of his life.

"Just stop it, pretty boy," volleyed Chris's return, "she's liked you since junior high school. God alone knows why. So, stand down. I'm not trying to get you engaged, married, or committed, though that last is probably not far from where you should be. I want you to get with someone who will put you back in circulation. You've got more in you than work and spreadsheets. She'd be good for you."

Nick knew he had crossed the line. Deep down, Chris' dedication and care deeply touched him. He knew he could count on Chris, and Chris wasn't wrong. At heart, he wanted a lasting relationship with someone.

A partner? *"What kind of partner?"* he thought. He had his list of what he thought he wanted. But with the type of passion and militancy that Chris exhibited in his relationship, he wanted Nick to taste and see how wonderful Chris's life had become. Nick also understood that Chris worried that his old friend had lost the romance of living; a full life involved more than a bank account and student loans. From Nick's perspective, Chris's enthusiasm scared him more than a little.

Yet the question haunted him: Was he missing something? Something his self-protective, shallow encounters with women had not prepared him for? He disliked this feeling of self-doubt; *"Everything's fine,"* he convinced himself, *"just fine."* He also knew that Chris, innocently, wanted the best for his friend.

With all sincerity, Nick de-escalated the encounter: "I know. I get it. I'm fine. I'm just not interested in anything new right now. I am grateful for your concern, and I am happy for you."

Chris paused again. "I'm not going to stop trying."

"Thank you. But I am not going to give in until I feel it's right."

Chris's smile returned. "Yup, got it. My best to your family. I will give you another call when I get another lead on a date for you." Chris quickly hung up the phone, not waiting for a response.

Nick chuckled to himself as he put down the phone.

"All right, back to the numbers," he said to the universe, and then added, "Speak to me, numbers. Speak to me."

He spent the morning reviewing the plans, budget, and next steps for a storefront remodel. It was a minor job, but he enjoyed being on the curb in the city. More people would see the company's work at eye level, rather than towering above them. He grabbed a cab, received the final sign-offs, and returned to the office just a little after noon.

When Nick returned, Rick was still in his office. Rick, also a project manager, had more years of experience than Nick. He and Nick were not that close; they were working acquaintances who would occasionally set out to lunch together.

Rick, a family man in a different place in life than Nick, spent most of his time talking about his kids or wife and complained about having to be a taxi or deal with a "honey-do" list. But he was safe. When Nick shared parts of his life, Rick would listen with empathy and insight. Rick seemed to have already figured out pieces of life's puzzle for himself, but not zealous enough to work them out for Nick.

Rick's life seemed complete and satisfying, comfortable in a way that Chris's life did not, not quite a father figure, more like an older, settled brother. There was a nice Italian restaurant they liked to go to, and after Nick's exchange with Chris, he thought it might be good for him to deepen some of his cursory relationships. He filed the signed agreement in his office and headed down the hall to Rick's office.

Poking his head in the open door, "Hey, can you break away? Feel like Italian for lunch?"

"Sure. Give me a minute to settle some stuff, and we can head out."

"Great. I will wait for you downstairs in the lobby."

As Nick shut his laptop, Chris's voice echoed: 'I'm not going to stop trying.' Nick shook it off, but it clung anyway, following him to lunch.

Chapter 2: Whispers of the Past

It didn't take long for Rick to get to the lobby. He reacted like a dog invited for a walk when it involved food. His step became a little quicker, and his focus shifted from work almost immediately. Ah, New York for lunch. Many folks came to take tours of the building and sites in the city, but Nick wanted someone to offer a tour based on the smells, tastes, and textures. From Chinatown to Little Italy and all the stops along the way. A smorgasbord for the senses. Nick self-identified as a moderate vegetarian. He thought twice about killing a spider in his apartment. Never having met a cow he didn't like, not to mention that he quickly found out that when most vegetables turn green in the refrigerator, you can't tell.

Rick expected a routine lunch, unaware of his coworker's growing feelings. But Chris's conversation had disturbed Nick. Nick couldn't figure out why. He and Chris had talked about his personal life for as long as they had been friends. Chris's nudging had never affected Nick before. Why should it now? He was successful and comfortable in his skin, right? Yes. Why change something that works … right?

But deep down in his heart, Nick had questioned the well-worn track of his life goals as he held them up against the lives of his parents, siblings, and the expectations he self-imposed. Chris's drip, drip message of the one who left the hometown, went south, and found a stable life, the one who took risks, now made Nick's safe track seem more like eroded ruts than a path to happiness. The rock of Nick's life formula showed the weathering of that constant flow of internal and external forces. Unknown even to himself, Nick was cracking under the strain.

Once a foreign concept, new directions began to have a fresh appeal. Perhaps his solid nature needed some spontaneity. Possibly, dare he even consider it, he needed a change, a risk injection into a far too predictable life?

"Hey Rick," Nick spoke to the universe more than directly to Rick walking beside him. Perhaps he hoped that by the very act of speaking, he might break out of the funky thoughts filling the void of conversation. "Any plans for the weekend?"

"Not much. It promises to be a quiet one. Beth's away visiting her mom. The kids are home, but they don't have anything happening, so pizza, a beer, and probably a little catching up on sleep.

Commuting from Katonah can get old and wear you out after a while. It seems odd not to have to run someone somewhere to do something while you wait. But I can live with more oddness in my life." Rick said with a smile.

"I hear you," responded Nick, now more engaged in the present. "Sometimes, it's good to cave dwell for a while."

"How about you? Oh, to be single again," Rick sighed.

"Yeah, I don't know. I think I am in a rut with life. A friend of mine has gotten under my skin. Not in a bad way. He just keeps trying to push me out of my comfort zone. Why do people think they have to fix you when you insist that you aren't broken?" The moment the sentence left his mouth, Nick felt both embarrassed and surprised. He had never opened up to Rick before; Nick's trust list did not include Rick's name to get vulnerable with. When it came down to it, his list lacked anyone who he considered comfortable sharing his feelings with. He wanted to change the subject.

Rick's pace slackened a bit as his brain's CPU cycles diminished, not being able to switch from food, walking, and what to say next fast enough.

"Oh, I guess it is hard to be single today. There aren't many places to meet compatible people. But if you aren't looking, then it makes it even harder to hold on to something when it comes your way. I think."

They reached the restaurant. Nick felt like a fool. *"Don't say any more."* He advised himself, *"Get some food and caffeine in you, and it will disappear; Nirvana returns!"*

"Yeah, we'll take the table by the window today," Nick said to the server before she got the menus in her hand. *"I feel like being in the light today, plus I can see folks passing by and those seated near us."* He felt.

The server seated them on either side of the table as she catered to menus, drinks, and orders.

Nick's internal security compass always pointed its needle to being able to notice people around him. He enjoyed observing how people expressed themselves and often wondered what their lives must be like.

The facial expressions of the old guy on the bench, reading the Wall Street Journal, and grimacing. *"I wonder what that's all about. Maybe I'll pick up the paper today,"* Nick considered.

The voice of someone who must be a mother advising her adult child at the table next to them suddenly rose above the din for a moment. "Darling, I told you he was a bum. He's just not worth it. Listen to your mother. You deserve better."

The mom had hair matching her voice, big and loud, that bounced with too much hairspray as she gesticulated to emphasize and support her worried tones in her daughter's defense.

"Mom, keep your voice down," her daughter implored with a cringe and hand instinctively pulling one of the waving arms of her mother down to the table as if it controlled her mom's volume.

Nick smiled to himself. *"Everybody has relational advice today. At least I can hang up on mine!"*

He liked the food, and the vibe was nice too. Some places you go to feel like you have entered a freezer: Folks are busy eating, and the staff are doing a job hoping for 20% of the bill, and it shows. To an introvert, all the nonverbal cues screamed the unspoken tone of a place. Nick had never felt uncomfortable here. The staff handled difficult customers with kindness and empathy, more than Nick himself felt they deserved at times.

'Big Hair's hands were going again as advice flared about another part of her poor daughter's life.

The expression on the daughter's face said it all as she tried to glance around the room naturally and inconspicuously for a clock before risking the power button on her phone. "Hey, Mom, it's getting late, and my lunch hour is almost over. Look here's our food; let's eat."

Her mom's arms came to rest on the table. Her daughter placed a gentle hand on the volume control this time and, holding her mom's gaze, said, "It is so nice to have lunch with you."

Nick's mind returned to the end of the conversation with Chris, and he considered, *"Yeah, they drive us crazy, but it is nice to realize someone, in the end, has your back."*

"Hey, earth to Nick. Come back to me, Nicky, come back…"

Nick started a bit and looked across the table in response to Rick's voice. "The server is going to come back, and you have paid attention to every other table in the room except this one! Pick out your food, man! We have only an hour!"

"We're middle management and salaried. Stop pushing me. Besides, you know that I usually order the Spaghetti al Pomodoro with a side salad. You get the veal marsala. I have water because I'm cheap, and you get a glass of Pinot Grigio because you're rich and lead a dull life!" Nick retorted.

"Oh, look who's talking, little mister early midlife crisis," Rick shot back. "What, no coffee?"

"Eh, I'm coffee'd-out for the day. Even I can get saturated." Nick had just enough time and said as their server sallied up comfortably to their table, smiled, fully attentive to take their orders. "I'll be right back with some bread. We are a bit busy today, so there might be a bit of a wait."

Nick and Rick acknowledged the smile and the wait with returned warmth and grace.

Rick discussed his current project, which involved a small addition to a store in the Bronx. Their lunches usually went like this; there would be a little back and forth on the walk to the restaurant, and they would work as they ate. But at their experience level, one building addition being the same as another. They jumped through the hoops, put together the drawings, made the budget proposal, and usually, with these smaller jobs, talked the client down from the ledge. Most of the time, they would need to return to hold the client's hand as plans needed to be changed and projects ran over. It had all become routine.

Nick stayed only mildly engaged. People familiar with Nick were aware of his creative and rich inner world. He could eat, listen, respond, and scan the room, all simultaneously and in an instant. On good days, this would happen without him missing a beat, but today, he continued to be off, a bit out of control, making him more cautious than ever. Nick now had an eerie feeling, as if someone had walked on his grave.

He would have loved to talk to Chris or even Rick about his feelings, but he could not put his finger on it himself. He realized he had lost his balance and that fate would use the opportunity to change or destroy his ordered world.

They ate as soon as their meals arrived. Quiet for the moment, 'Big Hair' and her normally haired daughter had moved on to having a cup of coffee while waiting for dessert. Nick took his attention away from his plate when the door to the restaurant opened; a brief puff of chilly air passed by the table.

As usual, he studied the woman who entered. She didn't fit in with the New York crowd. She carried herself confidently but seemed a bit hesitant about where to sit. *"Tourist,"* thought Nick as he sipped his water. Rick had made quick work of his veal and his wine. He was going on about having an early afternoon conference call, which had him a bit worried that he would have to leave lunch earlier than usual. Nick didn't mind finishing up alone with his thoughts as company.

The tourist took the table right behind 'Big Hair'. Nick glimpsed her when 'Big Hair' reached for her cup. Rick made his apologies again, paid his check, and headed back. Nick could now focus on the room.

Nick had grown comfortable in the city after all this time working there. All kinds of people come to New York for varied reasons. He was a handsome young man who frequently kept to himself. Women, and sometimes men, would hit on him, and he would just ignore the stare or run away from the conversation. It was part of life that you just got used to.

'Big Hair' reached for her coffee, and Nick glanced around her to see 'Tourist' staring at him. He held her gaze briefly and focused back on his food. *"Shoot,"* he realized, *"that was dangerous. That glance was a tad too long. She's sure to get the wrong idea."*

Nick pondered the situation he faced. He feared glancing up again. Helpless, a victim of his instinct. Like that speck of a pimple on your face that nobody notices until you pick at it and blow it up into a red Target bull's eye, he realized that the moment he glanced up from his plate, he would have to risk a glance to see if she was staring at him. *"Oh well,"* he resolved, *"I know that I have to find out."*

He glanced up. 'Big Hair' had shifted a little in her chair, and he could more easily see around her. 'Tourist' glanced up, and Nick responded immediately by jerking his head back to stare at the diminished pasta on his plate. The introvert in him intuitively knew his fatal flaw was the stiffness of his shifted attention. He acted as if he had been caught peeping in at a window and then pretended that he was only trying to find the front door. *"Oh shoot, oh shoot. She now knows that she has disturbed me. Darn. Where's that server? Stop taking orders from customers. Doesn't she know that her tip hangs in the balance of getting me out of here?"* Panicked, he scanned the room for the server.

It was too late. 'Tourist' moved her coffee to the far side of the table, where there was a clear eyeshot around 'Big Hair,' who had received her bill and was waiting to pay and be gone. Nick sighed as he stared at the door to the restaurant, but watched 'Tourist' in the periphery, looking him over as if he were a roast in the supermarket, or so he thought. She didn't appear to be the type to give up, either. *"On second thought,"* he sighed, *"she doesn't look like my type."* But there was nothing to do now. Even if he ran out, she would probably follow him. Crazy people. It is better to get this over in public than to wind up as a headline after meeting a violent end in some back alley. After all, you never know.

'Tourist' picked up her coffee and headed to his table. Nick immediately mentally dropped his tip to 5%.

"Hello, I noticed you from across the room. I hope that you do not mind my sitting with you for a few moments," said 'Tourist,' with a bit of an accent that Nick could not place.

A thousand thoughts, moving with the speed of what he imagined a near-death life review to be, rushed through Nick's mind. She struck him as mildly exotic, familiar in a city that attracted visitors from around the globe who were interested in a one-or two-night stand with American culture. He was not interested in fostering international tourists. He wanted someone as a package deal with no character or financial remodeling necessary.

She just didn't fit the bill. What if he just said, *"No. I'm done. Lunch over, back to work for me?"*

Surprised to hear himself, he said, "Sure, Nick. My name is Nick."

"Shoot," he thought, *"why not just put sucker or idiot to that!"*

"What a nice name. I am Elena. I come from Türkiye."

Elena had chestnut brown hair, deep brown eyes, and skin to match her Mediterranean heritage, which contrasted with Nick's paradigmatic American stereotypical image of the modern male: young, well-dressed, physically fit, nicely styled hair, and roughly coiffed facial hair. Elena would have to be forgiven for any cultural unease or discomfort, after all, Americans like Nick have a rather simplistic reputation for foreigners, especially in culturally orthodox countries, and Nick was sending all the signals of superiority and sophistication that would send anyone running.

"Well, that explained the accent," Nick thought. *"Now all I need is the 'why' and the why-me component."*

"Wow, Türkiye. I have met many people in New York who come from all over, but Türkiye, that's a first for me. Did you come here on vacation, for work, or with a working visa?" Nick had his prejudices as well.

Elena kept her thoughts to herself, betrayed only by a sigh and a slight shake of her head that betrayed a mild irritation she sought to keep under control.

"No, no work, vacation. I have heard a lot about America and how different American men are: kinder and nicer. I thought that it might be nice to experience your openness and hospitality for myself," she said with a bit of a giggle and a smile.

"Hmm," Nick's early warning system had kicked in again. *Why is she really here? Is it a husband she's after? Is that her game? Why did I even start down this road? Darn you, Chris!"*

"Yeah, well, nice meeting you. Server, here's my credit card. I need to go."

"Oh, don't be that way," Elena protested. "We have just started to get to know one another. I would love to hear about what you do and what sports teams you follow. I could come to your place tonight and explore." Even for Elena, it was bold, but she believed American men welcomed such directness. She'd given him what she'd gathered men in the West wanted: focus on themselves, sports, and suggestive talk about 'exploring,' which she had left intentionally vague.

The server put down the plates around the table a few rows back and came to take Nick's card. Elena must have seen her opportunity closing. Her expression of desperation belied that she seemed to want to reverse the direction the encounter seemed to be heading. Her eyes darted in panic. She needed to quickly figure out what should come next, which drove introspection further away from her controlled cadence. "Where do you live?" she blurted out, and immediately, she winced as if the words even surprised herself.

Now, Nick had been propositioned by some of the best, but this bordered on crazy. To Nick, Elena acted aggressively—almost like a stalker. Nick had no choice. He responded by going on the offensive.

"You come here, assume the worst, and think every American guy will jump at the chance. Do you even know us? If you think that we are all that shallow, you know nothing about Western men, our hospitality, or our culture. We are not all a YouTube or Netflix reality show." Nick, by now, had raised his voice above the din of the room, oblivious to people starting to stare.

Had Elena been typical of her own culture and gender, she would have slunk away, embarrassed and cowed by Nick, but Elena was not typical. She didn't blush easily and had been insulted by far harsher and angrier men in her own country than Nick could ever imagine. She felt a deep, generational anger, a millennial rage welling up in her over people being mistreated, misunderstood, and silenced. True, she wasn't from this culture. Yes, she didn't understand what American men wanted. No, she had no clue what Nick expected from her or what to do in this situation. She simply wanted him to give her a chance, and she needed him to talk to her. Why was he being so nasty?

"You idiot," flew out of her mouth, "I know more about the West than the West knows of itself. We in the East have millennia of experience of the West trampling us underfoot, like when the Crusaders sacked my city, Vienna robbed our soul, and then both abandoned us like some harlot they used and ignored our plight. I know about the West and 'me first' as you trade in oil, and my family lives in squalor and the heat of the day; you complain while you turn down your thermostat on your air-conditioned homes and preach to us about carbon and global warming. I endure in one day more shame and burden than you in a lifetime, and here you sit sucking your noodles and judging me."

Nick was stunned. He could not fathom her intense response. He just wanted to pay his bill, crawl to the door, and escape. This was too out of the norm for a suburban Connecticut guy who hates conflict. But she stood between him and the safety of the door and the street. He would need to win the beachhead if he wanted to leave.

"I have done nothing to your country. I don't even care about your country." Yeah, that wasn't good. Nick realized he lost control and simply wanted to land shots, cheap or otherwise, not caring that they hit him as much as wounding her. By now, everyone who had not even noticed the 'Big Hair' exchange with her daughter was uncomfortably stealing glances and trying their hardest to look like this was all a part of the dining process and not at all uncomfortable. But it was awkward.

An eerie silence settled over the restaurant that generally bustled with activity and voices, as the sound of glasses and silverware clinking. Now Nick picked up on muted table noises and hushed whispers. Nevertheless, the dinners became silent observers of the situation that placed the reluctant introvert onto center stage.

While there was a lull in the bullets, the server, smile gone, snuck the slip and card in front of Nick, gave him a furtive sympathetic glance, and hurried off to fill someone's water. Nick didn't dare glance away from Elena long enough to fill out the tip, sign the slip, and take his card; he had never experienced such emotion and hurt in his life, even when he broke off with a steady girlfriend.

"Look, lady, I didn't move my glass to your table, and you were looking my way with me in your sights all the time. I didn't ask you to sit down. You did that. Not every man is looking for a one-night stand."

"You jerk. Sleep with you!? Not every woman is trying to pick you up. Look at me right now. I would not have spent the night with you if you were the last man in New York. No, no, make that the world. Oh, and my view of American men hasn't changed. You are a pathetic little boy who has no idea what a woman wants. Grow up. Just grow up. Life is not all about you." She broke down and cried. Her fists clenched. Her red-rimmed eyes fixed on her frozen face. After a long pause, she turned and ran from the restaurant, humiliated. Nick could rot in hell as far as she was concerned.

Once in the safety and anonymity of the street, Elena leaned exhausted against the wall, hung her head, and covered her face with her hands. She realized she had a temper, which had gotten her into trouble before, but he had humiliated her. She was a stranger in his country, and he couldn't spare the time to get to know her. Now, now what? She wanted to replay the scene, but it was too late. Her chance was gone. Nick would be like most men, not eager to give a strong woman who fought back a second chance. As she walked away, she tried to shake off the encounter.

"Well, there's always a Plan B," she mumbled, her hand still trembling with frustration and disappointment, as she pulled out her phone and dialed.

After a moment, she spoke softly in Greek, "Hello Papa. I do not belong in this country. Americans ... they are so rude." There was a pause. "I know, I know, I will try to be strong and as wise as a serpent while being a gentle little dove. I will still hold on to why I am here." There was another pause. "Yes, I will take care, and my love to both you and Mama. Neither of you is to worry; I am having a good time despite the rudeness." She put the phone in her purse as she continued to walk away.

Nick didn't look around him. He hated conflict, and to lose control of himself like that meant that he was running on pure emotion, which was never a good thing for him. He also didn't like to hurt people. Nick consoled himself with the thought that her stereotypes and presumptions violated him. He had qualities beyond his finances, athletic abilities, physique, or even sex.

Nick felt bad for the server as he looked at the credit card slip. He left her a 25% tip. At the door, he turned around and took one last inventory of the battlefield. His face must have betrayed the tension he felt as more than one person cast a sheepish glance his way before quickly turning back to their plates. He let the door close silently and sighed. The hurt in her eyes followed him out the door, lingering with a weight and a curious feeling that he couldn't shake: had he missed an opportunity?

Nick didn't need to go back to work. He had nothing pressing at work, and a return appeared useless. His mind felt tired, absorbed by what he'd recently experienced. He wanted to feel justified, but Elena's tears lingered. *"I am a jerk, I guess,"* he mused, but the words stung; this wasn't him, not really. What happened? He wondered as he sank into his seat.

The train's familiar rhythm, clunk-clunk — clunk-clunk, clunk-clunk — usually lulled him into drowsiness on the way home. Not now. Each clunk seemed to hit harder as Elena's image replayed in his mind. He wished for another chance. Tears moistened his own eyes as the train pulled away into the dark tunnels under Grand Central Station.

Chapter 3 Shades of Legacy

Nick emerged from the shadows into the bright morning sunlight with a bit of a blink, as he always did. He looked around him to see who might be in the crowd, looked down at his feet, and hurried to work. As the doors to the lobby closed, he sighed with relief. *"Safe again."* It had been about three weeks since the Elena thing, and he still felt uneasy.

Nick got himself off the elevator without any encounters. Howie returned in full force and caught up on the Barrons project. This had many folks pleased with both Howie and Nick. He had a meeting across town this afternoon. He would take a cab for that. Nick tried to keep the Zoom thing to a minimum. No experience compares to a face-to-face meeting with a coworker or customer. He put a pod in the Keurig, and the smell of coffee filled his small office. The sound of the water signaled that it would soon be ready.

Rick passed by, stopped, spun around, poked his head in the door, "Hey Nicky, what about lunch today?"

"Naw. I have peanut butter and jelly. I'm trying to save money."

"Peanut butter and jelly! When pasta calls, you answer, 'No, I want peanut butter and jelly.' Really!? Come on. It's been weeks."

Nick winced, knowing he couldn't stay away forever without giving Rick a reason.

"Okay. You're on. Italian it is!" Right after the words left his mouth, his anxiety eased.

The morning passed predictably, and that was a good thing. At noon, Rick collected him for their walk to the restaurant. For the first time in weeks, he enjoyed the journey, not merely because of the walk's destination. Rick and he caught up on the different projects they had been working on. Nick believed time had moved backward a month or more. He was back to feeling good again.

They walked through the door, and the same server greeted them with a bright and sincere welcome. If she remembered the incident, she didn't give even the subtlest of clues. Nick asked for a table in the back; he enjoyed being able to see anything that might happen long before it did. However, everything remained peaceful, including his inner voice. He decided to join Rick for his customary glass of wine. Around the middle of the glass, the alcohol's influence began, utterly calming him. He saw his colleague in a new, considerate way. Nick smiled to himself as he raised the glass to his lips.

On the return trip, their conversation trailed off into distracted silence. Nick settled back into his norm of people-watching on the way back. *"That must be a girlfriend"*, he thought as a young woman pulled the back of a young man's shirt as he almost walked out into traffic as he followed his phone. *"Been there, done that,"* he thought.

The wine buzz lingered, making the city's chaos feel almost amusing. The city's vibe entertained him more than bothered him. He was back to one day blending into the next in an almost seamless cycle that had become his stable life.

On Tuesday, Nick ate at his desk.

Snail mail is still the staple of legal business exchange.

Nick had lost track of the interns' names; they came and went so frequently that he had given up trying to keep track of them. But one of the newbies stopped in with the mail, putting it down on the edge of his desk. Nick looked up briefly, made eye contact for a second, nodded, and took another bite of his sandwich.

Nothing exciting about the pile. Just ordinary mail. Nick finished his lunch and pulled the pile closer. As each piece filtered through his hand, he would quickly classify it into a category: junk, bill, notice, junk. After the junk, he needed to process the express envelopes.

Typically, they only needed a signed final 'okay' on plans. Nice. Client-produced art for a remodeling concept. Okay. "Hmm," Nick quietly verbalized, "something from Bridgeport. We have nothing happening in Bridgeport."

Nick flipped the express mail envelope over several times curiously. He pulled the red tab to unseal it. Peering inside, he found two photographs and one piece of paper. A map of the Mountain Grove Cemetery in Bridgeport, with a bright red "X" marked on one area. The photographs showed two sides, front and back, of the same gravestone. One side, written in some Eastern European lettering, Василь Палевич 1888-1955. *"Russian,"* Nick thought. The text on the other photograph seemed plain enough: "Paleon."

Nick shivered at seeing his own last name on the stone. Did this pose a threat?

"What on earth?" he said and repeated, "What … on … earth?"

Nick's great-grandparents, Alexander and Katherine Paleon, arrived from Ukraine and made their home in Bridgeport. He had visited their graves, along with the graves of his grandparents, in Stratford at Saint John the Baptist Russian Orthodox Cemetery.

"This grave makes no sense." Nick whispered, "Who is this guy? Who do I know who can speak Russian? Oh, Google, right?"

Nick fumbled for his phone. He opened Google Translate, tapped the camera icon, and clicked the picture. Soon, "Vasyl Palevych 1888–1955" appeared on the screen.

Nick glanced at it. *"'Vasyl Palevych.' Oh yeah, that clears it up. Not! Who the hell is Vasyl Palevych? What does he have to do with the Paleon family? Why am I getting this in the mail?"*

Nick enjoyed making the pieces fit. Welcome to history, archaeology, and architecture — a puzzle and an adventure in one. This stimulated his inquisitive nature, and the unsettling fact was that somebody purposely gave this to him. Why?

He pictured inspecting records, churches, and memberships, and playfully imagined a legacy might result from it. The excitement surprised him. *"Must be the wine still talking,"* he thought. Still, the idea of getting started excited him.

He had done nothing like this before. Sure, he had studied history and done limited work with primary sources, but putting the spade of research into the actual ground of primary records in a real-world problem was new. *"Oh, yeah,"* he smiled, *"Google or even ChatGPT could help."*

He logged onto his laptop and typed: "Hey, ChatGPT, I need to find information about someone who died in the Bridgeport area around 1955. Where do I start?"

In an instant, ChatGPT responded with a list of research resources. It looked like a game plan, a mix of online databases and local records he could check on weekends—a pleasant armchair detective diversion.

But the potency of the wine was wearing off. *This could take a lot of time and effort, and talking to folks; none of those things are in my wheelhouse.*

He decided to call and consult his old friend Chris. After a few teasing remarks, Chris said, "Look, what's the big deal? Some time. Some effort? You got a glimpse of passion. I say, feed it."

Apart from relationship advice, Nick valued his friend's discernment. Looks like he had a new project without a blueprint, budget, or goal. It scared him a little, but deep down, he couldn't wait to start. The trip home flew by as he thought about the next steps. He meant to wait until the weekend to begin, but by nightfall, the thought of that gravestone was obsessing him. His anxiety told him he did not have time to lose.

In the morning, Nick took a deep breath and called in to work. He had taken a couple of personal days. It was a small leap forward for him, like stepping off a dock into unknown waters.

Nick started his research with the Connecticut Death Index. Result—nothing. Then FamilySearch and Ancestry—still nothing. He fired off emails to a few Bridgeport churches and funeral homes. Days of searching, emailing, and scrolling through old records all led to dead ends. Frustration simmered, but curiosity kept him going.

Nick called his mom and went over for dinner one night. During the meal, he asked his dad about their Ukrainian roots. His father shrugged. "We were told to forget the old country. It was a fresh start here." Nick let that sink in.

Days later, after more follow-ups, Mountain Grove Cemetery confirmed that Oleksandr Paleon had purchased Vasyl Palevych's plot. It was the first solid link between his family and the stranger Vasyl.

Then came the second express package. Inside: a Sitka death record for Vasyl, more photos from a different cemetery of a gravestone for Василь Палевич 1888-1955, and an image of a marble crypt with the name "Paleon" carved over the door.

Most intriguing was the third package, which contained a set of letters. They were not in English. "It looks like Greek," he said aloud to himself.

While he could not read them, he could make out the dates 1930, 1935, and 1936. But what do they say? He didn't know anyone who spoke Greek. Maybe an Orthodox Church in town? "No," he said aloud again as if the silence cared, "no, I need to know now or I will never sleep."

Nick opened his laptop, plugged in his scanner, and soon all three letters were on the desktop of his PC. ChatGPT rescued him once; maybe it could help again?

He started the app and dropped the images of the three letters onto the text box, and then said, "I need to have an English translation of these three letters. Please read them and create three separate documents with the contents translated into English."

ChatGPT thought for a few seconds and then returned the following translations:

Letter one:

May 5, 1930

Father Vasyl,

My dearest friend,

I am greatly distressed to hear of the tragic death of your family. I cannot express how defeated I felt when the news first reached me, but now, having learned all the details, that sense of hopelessness has settled into grief. I cannot begin to imagine what you are enduring. Know that we continue to lift you up in prayer, day and night.

Though I cannot come to you myself, I am sending a trusted mutual friend, Oleksandr. You will know him when you see him. He will speak of things we dare not write.

These are dark days. Yet perhaps we may still dwell in the cracks of light that pierce through the clouds above us. Our people have known darker times. Since the fall of the Great City, we have searched for homes and echoes of light in foreign lands. And still, God is good. Be strong, my friend. Take heart. All is not lost.

There is hope, son of Ukraine, bearer of the memory of the City. May the Theotokos be your comforter and guide.

We will continue to pray and to plan, even if, for now, we must do so at a distance. I will write again soon.

In shared sorrow and unshaken hope,

Theodoros

Letter two:

August 17, 1935

My dear and blessed Theodoros,

I have only just arrived in New York. Our shipment is already en route by rail to Bridgeport. I thought it wise to enter the country through quieter means than the formal ports of entry. It has taken time to work my way down from Alaska, but my time there was not wasted. It has given me perspective and prompted a few adjustments to our plans, which I will make on the return journey.

For the first time in over five years, I sense an end approaching. Perhaps soon, both my family and I may rest peacefully, at least at the far end of this dark chapter. The seeds are almost all planted. Let us hope a new spring yet lies beyond the winter we continue to endure. Such is the hope of our generation.

I have received word from the Patriarch: I am welcome to return to Ukraine. I believe I may serve our people best by standing firm, faithful to my call, and loyal to the land that bore me, even in the face of the Soviet occupation.

Before I take up a parish, I intend to visit Istanbul. There are things we must speak of in person, and matters that must remain sealed in silence thereafter. Let hope rest in peace … until the trumpet shall sound.

Blessings upon you, my son in spirit, loyal co-laborer, and dearest of friends. May the Most Holy Theotokos shelter you and your house under her mantle of grace.

Faithfully entrusted,

Vasyl

Letter three:

October 12, 1936

My dear and blessed Theodoros,

I am now on my way from Sitka. Thank you for your last correspondence. I will indeed be careful. That I have survived is not being well-received. The Church may welcome me home, but I wonder about the State. The Soviets may regard me as a mere nationalist, but I suspect they know better.

I fear that the weight and size of our parcel, as well as its origin and destination, have drawn attention. I had to take great care in Bridgeport to ensure privacy. Nothing is safe unless it is hidden in plain sight.

I have chosen Sitka as my final resting place. I have secured a modest plot and stone. If God allows, I will continue to live and serve back home. But should that not be my lot, I ask only this: see that I am brought back here when my earthly journey ends. I will explain why when we meet next.

For the first time in many years, I feel the weight has lifted. Now, life and death seem as one. If God grants me many more years, it will be a blessing. If only one remains, that too shall be enough. All is gain.

Blessings upon you, my son in spirit and dearest of friends. May the Most Holy Theotokos shelter you and your house beneath her mantle of grace.

Faithfully entrusted,

Vasyl

There was so much here that Nick did not understand. But all of it made him more nervous than ever. "Oleksandr, my grandfather. Bridgeport, the grave. Alaska, the grave. Vasyl," he murmured to himself. The names were about all he knew. What package? What does "he will speak of things we dare not write" mean? Who died, and what does it mean to him? Alaska? Everything was pointing there.

He stared at the closing line again: "Faithfully entrusted." They weren't just letters. They were instructions. The life he'd built felt small now, fragile. Temporary. Whatever lay buried in Bridgeport, in Sitka, in the shadows of these pages, he had to know. He couldn't just walk away. And he couldn't do that as Nikolai Paleon, lead designer for Midtown Concepts. He closed the last file and leaned back, palms flat against the table. None of this could fit into the life he'd been living.

Nick took his dad to the Bridgeport grave. Pointing to the Paleon inscription, he explained the discovery. His father offered to hire an investigator, but Nick shook his head. "This is my shadow."

Within a week, he'd quit his job, packed essentials, and booked a ticket. At the airport, exhausted from the lack of eating and sleeping, anxious about where the road was taking him, he felt the shift; whatever this was, he knew there was no turning back.

34

Chapter 4: Beneath the Surface

Nick arrived in Anchorage in the early hours of the morning. He had hoped to get some sleep on the flight, but dozed. With no plan for where to spend the night, let alone how to get to Sitka the next day, Nick felt exhausted, appearing physically and emotionally spent. He figured he would get a cab to a hotel somewhere and figure out the next step.

Nick collapsed into one of the airport seats, his backpack and one checked bag at his feet in front of him, entirely focused on his phone, searching for a place to spend the night. From behind him, so close to his ear that he felt the warmth of the speaker's breath, he heard, "Hey sexy boy, come here often?"

With its heavy Turkish accent, Nick recognized that voice. A chill ran down his spine. Jolted back to the world around him, he jumped up and spun around, and there, in front of him, laughing, stood Elena, the woman from the restaurant in New York, whom he had dismissed as another tourist. Nick had no clue how to make sense of this new encounter.

She had tricked him. This psychopathic tourist had lured him here to get him alone, far from home, tired, and now trapped. He fell for it! What was her game? Yet how would she have known about the grave in Bridgeport, and about Vasyl and the Paleon name? How could it be a trick close to 100 years in the making? His mind raced as he frantically tried to figure it all out. Confusion and anxiety overwhelmed him as he deteriorated into pure fight-

or-flight mode. Nick anxiously scanned the room for exits and airport security officers.

Elena saw the fear, panic, and confusion on his face, now drained of all color. She felt very sorry for him. She had always lived life on the edge of nonexistence, but Nick led a sheltered existence, like a little boy, not in a negative sense, the way she meant earlier, but in an innocent way.

In an instant, she felt the urge to protect him. Elena empathized with Nick—out in the world now, felt vulnerable, alone, afraid, and clearly exhausted, and all because of her. Her light attempt at humor, intended to disarm his anxiety, backfired. It brought back the pain of their last encounter as a stab in the dark.

Elena wished to run up and throw her arms around him, cradling his fear-filled face against her, putting him at ease. Now, like a scared animal looking in the eyes of a predator, Nick would see every overture as a threat, and any attempt at physical comfort would increase his apprehension. As she comprehended the reality of Nick's vulnerability, Elena let her smile fade as her face became serious but soft and comforting.

Elena's true nature emerged in the compassionate and calm tone her voice now took; "Let's start over, you and me. Okay?" she suggested, extending a hand toward the Starbucks sign as though guiding him gently. "You're tired, but there's a Starbucks right here. It's public, neutral ground; we can talk." Her voice relaxed, as if sharing a secret. "I have information about Vasyl, and trust me, you've found him," she continued, her eyes holding a glint of something between certainty and sympathy. "Nick, he is your great-grandfather. You're a Palevych, not a Paleon; the Paleon family never existed."

Nick felt the world spin as the details of the room receded into some kind of weird ZOOM background blur. The raw emotion, lack of sleep, and food had chosen this moment to wrest control from him. His knees buckled, and he slid down into the silent darkness. He had been running on pure emotion, caffeine, and adrenaline for the last few days, and it was catching up with him, as he felt himself go down. His fight-or-flight response collapsed into sheer surrender to chaos, disorder, silence, and darkness, his old foes claiming a victory they had long sought, and he had held off. Nick no longer had the strength to fight.

Too late to keep him up or ease his landing, Elena climbed over the chairs between them as soon as she saw Nick's roll back as he fell hard, legs sprawled over his suitcase. He hit the floor with the full weight of his upper body, his head striking his backpack, which cushioned the impact from the hard floor.

Elena might not have been able to ease him down, but she would not leave him. She curled up next to him on the floor, cradling his head in her lap as security and medics came running. Her background blurred as her attention centered on the collapsed form of Nick. She felt so bad and responsible.

The airport medics and the tug of a security guard brought the background into focus again. Elena had brought him here, so the responsibility for Nick's safety fell on her, especially now that he could not protect himself.

Nick's darkness lifted into a haze of figures and vague silhouettes of the people around him. He gasped as if he had hit the surface of some unknown lake of cold, dark water. Nick's focus honed in on Elena as the closest person to him, most clearly seen and understood. The medics had brought a wheeled gurney and attempted to lift him onto it.

Nick let out a weak plea, "No, no … I'm okay."

"He said no. Leave him. He does not want the bed," Elena's powerful voice megaphoned. "Give him some time, some space. Look, he is beginning to come around."

One of the medics offered Elena a water bottle, which she uncapped and placed in Nick's hand. She raised his torso slightly onto her lap, cradling his head in her arm to elevate him so he could drink.

Elena looked down at him as he took a drink, and she suddenly saw her father's face and heard his voice:

"Elena, pay attention. You may not be a son, but you are the eldest and the one who cares the most. You must know what I know. You must carry on with what I have received from my father, as he received it from his. Do not fail. You are now the steward and protector of a great heritage and promise for our people. Listen." That heritage now struggled to get into a chair as she helped him half crawl up the front and into a seated position. "Yes, Papa, I will protect him," she whispered.

Now upright in one of the chairs, Nick took another sip of the water. The medics wanted him to go to the hospital. Elena sat next to him, eyes fixed on him. He could feel the warmth of her hand on his shoulder. His eyes still could not focus on anyone or anything. Desperately, he tried to assess the situation. All he needed to respond was, *"Yes, take me to the hospital,"* and he would have been away from Elena and potentially out of the game.

Exactly what to do next eluded him, but if he said nothing, his opportunity would be lost. He finally looked at her and found her face drained of all amusement, but worry remained. *"She stayed,"* he considered as his brow wrinkled. *"She stayed. She didn't have to. If she meant me harm, she wouldn't have."*

Suddenly, he came to himself and, finding his voice, said, "No … no hospital." He looked into the eyes of the medic and clarified, "I just need some food and rest. It was a long flight. It was a passing spell. Please, I'll be fine." He turned helpless eyes to Elena, and they said, *"Help me."*

Elena's eyes hardened immediately, and she fixed them on the medic as if he were an opponent she was about to engage. She had dealt with powerful structures and men before; these medics did not intimidate her. "He's fine. I will get him food and take care of him. Thank you, but we are done. We will go to that restaurant," she said, waving her hand at one of the vendors in the airport. "We will rest and eat there. All will be well."

The medic tried his best once or twice more, but Elena's eyes and Nick's helplessness convinced him that in the current fight, he would lose. Nick had leaned back in the chair and closed his eyes as his pit bull struggled on for him. He simply wanted to rest and summon enough energy to get up and walk away when the time came.

The medics retreated to one of the desks, appearing to fill out paperwork while ensuring Nick could walk away. He and Elena sat alone in the row of chairs. Elena dared not speak. She didn't want a repeat of his fainting, and Nick still had his eyes shut. She no longer watched him but fixed her gaze on the darkness outside, just waiting for him to define what was next.

After about 20 minutes, Nick stirred and declared, "I think I can stand now. I don't know what came over me. I need some food."

He made a move to stand and felt the firm grip of a hand under his arm, helping him up, and Elena's voice said, "Careful, you are still weak. Lean on me if you need to. There is a place to eat over there. We will walk slowly." Nick swung the backpack onto his free shoulder, twisted off balance for a second, and recovered. He saw Elena out of the corner of his eye as she reached for his suitcase, and as they walked slowly off, Elena encouraged Nick, "It is just over here, a small place that has food. Sit, rest, eat, and we can talk about what comes next, but what comes next for tonight. You need to sleep, and we will talk more when you wake up. Eat and sleep. That is enough for now."

Nick, unsure how to respond, pondered a series of questions: should he consider her a friend or a foe? Did she have an angle? In the end, he didn't really care. Nick needed her for now; that's all he realized. He settled into being content for the moment and cautiously trusted her: *"Any port in a storm,"* he silently observed.

By the time they entered the cafe, Nick felt more like himself, even if still shaky and not thinking straight—a state of not 'firing on all cylinders,' a favorite saying of his father. As he slipped into the booth, he sighed, shut his eyes briefly, looked at Elena, and smiled for the first time. Elena, recognizing the change, offered a genuine smile, not amused or fake, but a sincere smile that conveyed the feeling that everything was okay.

The server came, and they both decided on the same thing. A simple breakfast of eggs and toast with a glass of milk. It was now a couple of hours after midnight. Still too fuzzy to even worry about doing the math of what time it would be in Stamford, Nick texted his sister, "I'm in Anchorage, but I'm too tired to call, but tell Mom and Dad I'm here and safe." With the necessities out of the way, looking across the table at Elena, Nick said, "I need to find a room somewhere. I didn't make any reservations. Do you know where I can find a place?"

"I prepared for your coming," Elena confessed. "I had been watching you, and when you didn't go to work after Monday, I went in and asked for you. I was told that you no longer worked there. I suspected that you were planning on coming soon. So, on Wednesday, I flew ahead of you, booked two rooms at a motel down the road, and waited at the airport until you came. Here is the key for your room; my room is right next door in 218." She slid a green keychain with a large golden number "217" on it. "When we are done here, I have a rental car we can take to the motel. You will turn off your phone and go to sleep. You don't need an alarm anymore."

The food came, and Nick cleaned his plate. Those two eggs and toast had been the most food he had eaten in days, and the milk just put it over the top. He felt like he could sleep for days, but this was a different type of weariness than the one that took him down. He struggled to get to the car and stay awake until they reached the motel. Elena helped him to his room and lifted his suitcase onto the top of the dresser. Nick collapsed onto the bed. She unzipped his suitcase, but when she turned to wish him "good night" and leave, Nick was already asleep on top of the covers. Elena found a spare blanket to throw over him. She removed his shoes, turned off his phone, locked the door, and quietly shut it behind her as she left.

As she walked next door, the evening outside was quiet, chilly, and dark. "Well, he is safely here," she said and audibly sighed, "that's more than you thought you could accomplish after the first meeting. He will sleep all day tomorrow. And then we will talk." Elena didn't open her door immediately. She walked to the rail that looked out over the backyard into a small strip of woods. She reflected briefly on her accomplishments.

"Where is this all heading?" she finally asked the surrounding darkness. She had the part of the story that Papa told her and a few legends, but what happened after Sitka? She wished she understood the mystery of what lay beyond Sitka and the graveyard. They would visit the grave and the crypt, trying to find a clue as to why Vasyl had led them there, but she did not have that part of the story. She turned, unlocked her door, and closed the chilly night out.

Nick woke up at about 6 P.M. the next day to darkness already settled over Anchorage. He threw on a coat, walked to 218, and knocked on the door. Elena opened the door to let him in. Nick remained tired, but his appetite, gone since the second letter, had returned.

"Hey," he said as she opened the door, "can we head out to get something to eat? I don't want to talk right now. I just want to eat and crawl back into bed." He paused and added with a wry little smile, "Alone."

She smiled back. The little boy appeared again! A happy, funny, carefree American. But Nick, she observed, seemed a little older.

"Yes, food. There is a Greek place down the road. We will go there," Elena answered as she grabbed her coat and keys.

As Nick followed her to the car, he thought, *"She's in the driver's seat in more ways than one."*

Nick still didn't want to talk. Not only still recovering from all that he had been through, but also jet lag settled over him as he tried to adjust to the new time zone of Alaska.

"I hope that by tomorrow I can begin to get my feet back under me and wits about me," he said as he picked at his spanakopita. "I have a lot of questions."

"I know," Elena replied as she plunged her fork into her salad. "I have some answers and can explain why I wanted to talk to you in New York so desperately and then messed that up so terribly," she said.

"I don't think I need to remind you that there were two at that table, both filled more with culture and pride than talking with each other," he asserted. "I didn't make it easier for you. But let's call a truce on the recent past." Nick, once more grinning, suggested. *"It's amazing what raising your blood sugar level will do for you,"* he speculated.

Nick ended up sleeping until after eight the following day. He was up, dressed, and had opened the curtains to let in the precious warmth of the ever-decreasing hours of sun. He was sitting at a small table in front of the window and feeling okay, even about the in-room coffee he was enduring, when there was a knock at his door. It was Elena.

"Good morning," he said cheerily, "want a cup of, well, the package says it is coffee?"

"Sure," she smiled as she replied, taking off her coat and sitting at the table opposite Nick, who soon returned with her coffee. "You have questions," Elena continued, "but before you ask them, let me tell you what I know, which is very little and comes out of the distant past."

Nick wrapped his hands around his coffee, which always sent a warm shiver down his spine as his whole body relaxed into a feeling of being at home. For maybe the first time, Nick realized that the smell and taste of his coffee were secondary to him. The sensual warmth of the cup in his hands had an almost sacramental effect on him. He leaned back in his chair, now ready to receive what Elena had to say.

"My full name is Elena Sakellaris. As I said, I am from Türkiye. My family line is old. Very old. We lived in the city before it was Istanbul: in Constantinople. We were close to the imperial family, served in their household, and fought in their wars. A pledge to the emperor was a pledge as if to God, binding not only a person but also a house, a lineage. Such a pledge binds our two families, the Sakellaris, and the Palevych, who are now the Paleon family. It was my great-grandfather who helped Father Vasyl Palevych avoid the NKVD, or secret police, after the Russian Revolution. The state wanted to infiltrate and control the Russian Orthodox Church from within."

She paused with a vacant look and in a softer, wistful undertone added, "As they still do."

Her voice once again in the present, she continued, "The NKVD sought out pure religionists to be re-educated for state police service, informing on the life of their parishes. Your Vasyl resisted. But there was evidently more that he never told my family. Something else bound our families, and he took it to his grave. It was something that my family had known for millennia but, over time, had forgotten. All that remains are whispers and hints of what it might be and half-truths."

"But how did I get the name Paleon, and why did you seek me out? How do you know all this?" interrupted Nick.

"This is all Papa remembered: in 1930, Father Palevych, your biological great-grandfather, sought to protect his family, a wife and two sons, by taking them to America. He had to work secretly, for he was constantly being watched. He managed to slip his family onto a train headed to neutral Switzerland.

They arrived safely in Switzerland. Vasyl had made plans to sail first to England and then to America to get his family far away. Once his family was safe, he planned to sneak back into Russia through Alaska and continue the work of resistance. But as the family was getting off the train, a man opened fire on them. The newspapers got the story wrong and said that all but Vasyl were killed. This was not the case; the young seven-year-old son, Ivan, escaped the fate of his mother and brother. Vasyl saw this as an opportunity to protect the last surviving heir of his family by confusing the trail. He reached out to my great-grandfather, who knew of another family in Switzerland escaping persecution."

Elan paused to take a sip of her cooling coffee. The muddle of names and the revelation of a previously unknown family history overwhelmed Nick.

"That family was the Mykhailenko family," continued Elena. "My great-grandfather knew his oath and duty, so he spoke with Oleksandr Mykhailenko about taking the young boy as one of his sons, and the whole family should now be known in America as the Paleon family. Your great-grandfather, Oleksandr, was not a Paleon by birth and had no biological relation to you or your family. You are a Palevych. Oleksandr Paleon, my great-grandfather, and Vasyl set up the whole fake grave to leave clues to point to the truth that they all swore to take to their graves to protect the next generation of their families."

Nick shook his head. Things finally made sense. Of course, his adopted great-grandfather would never be able to share his family history and pass it along, as he had not learned it. That history was intentionally forgotten, not to be remembered until someone put the pieces together, someone like Elena and him?

"But why now? Why me?" Nick asked.

"That is a bit selfish on my part. Life is hard. My people are demoralized and oppressed. Our population dwindles, and the young move away. The Rum, the last of the Romans, are dying. We lived in the city when it was the capital of the Roman Empire. We culturally remember times long past. It is our city, and we have suffered much over the last 600 years. We need hope. We need help. We need an enfleshed whisper from the past.

Without this belief in what can and will be, our story fades into nothingness, and we lose more than our names; we lose everything we are: we die. The oath and legend of my family point to your family as leading to the hope we need. I am the first woman in our family to steward this secret. It's a sign, maybe, that we were meant to be. I can't help but believe that this is our time. I don't understand how it will happen, but we have been duty-bound, trusting that it will. Protecting the Palevych family is a sacred pledge, and a secret known only to my family."

Elena watched Nick closely to see how he would take this vague news. She recognized the West did not ascribe any worth to mystery, let alone belief or wonder. Nick had to decide now to risk even more on these intangibles. Duty, legacy, and pledges based on old stories and legends might not hold him here or whatever came after 'here.' The longer the silence, the more anxious Elena became.

"Well," she finally had to ask, "what are you feeling?"

"I guess it fits. The grave in Bridgeport is a fake. Wow, I wasted all that time…" Nick exclaimed, "and my own ancestors plotted against me and my genetic predisposition for curiosity and tenacity." He didn't quite know what to believe about one generation willfully seeking to obliterate and keep secret the truth from generations down the line. He had always taken pride in his lineage, but now, learning it was fake by design, even if the deception protected his family, seemed like a high price. Who was he, after all?

"Yes, but you can't blame me for that. That was what the deception was supposed to do: get a descendant hooked to follow the leads. And my family could help when the time came if there were a roadblock," Elena paused for a second and continued, "And that's where I came in."

Nick sat silently. His coffee had gone cold. He looked down at the cup and thought of his dad and all he didn't know, then looked out the window. Nick could hear Elena shifting next to him. He could see her reflection in the window as she exchanged glances between her coffee and him. He knew she was nervous. Had she alienated him yet again? Would she need to pick him up off the floor again? Nick was calm. The score between him and Vasyl was even now, and he would make good on his promise to be coming after him tomorrow, but today, he could land a couple of digs at Elena. He turned from the window and looked over at Elena, and he just stared at her until she could no longer stand it and blurted out, "What?!"

Nick grinned, loving the suspense as slight revenge before teasingly he said, "I guess we are now on an equal footing for the first time, my little puppet master! Tomorrow, we will be heading to a grave and a crypt, and neither of us has any idea how they will work their magic to change our lives or the lives of those we love. Our quest is not for names, places, and dates but for the identity of past, present, and future, about destiny controlled from the grave and beyond."

The following day would be Sunday. Nick took out his phone and purchased two tickets to Sitka, with a layover in Juneau, online. They would arrive in Sitka in the afternoon. They would need to settle in, get a car, and book a couple of rooms for a night or two. That would mean that they would hit the graveyard on Monday. Nick and Elena had their last meal in Anchorage at the Greek Diner down the road. They must be up and out to the airport early the following day.

Arriving at the airport with time to spare, Nick and Elena enjoyed a leisurely breakfast. With some time to kill, Nick reached out to his friend Chris. He hadn't heard from him in a while, and he figured Chris might get a kick out of hearing he was suddenly "Mr. Alaska." As he waited for the call to connect, Nick thought, Chris will flip when he hears this.

The phone rang and went directly to voicemail: "Hey, this is Chris. You get the beep thing, right?"

Nick laughed and left his message: "Hey, fine time to be out to lunch. Just checking in. No big news, just calling from Alaska. Call me back if you want me to ship you some snow." Grinning as he hung up, he turned to Elena. "I'd love to see his face when he hears that. He won't believe it."

"Who is he?" she asked, amused.

"One of my oldest friends. He's always trying to set me up with someone. Knowing I'm in Alaska with you would freak him out! Oh, the places I could make his mind go."

"You are so bad," Elena laughed.

Nick just smiled.

The trip to Juneau took about two hours. With over an hour to wait for their connecting flight to Sitka, they settled into the terminal's seating area. Nick tossed his backpack onto the chair beside Elena.

"Coffee?" he asked.

"Sure."

As he headed toward the coffee stand, Elena settled into her seat, picked up her phone to read a book when Nick's phone rang in his backpack pocket. She glanced at the phone and recognized the name "Chris" on the screen. Hesitating briefly, she decided it might be fun to play along. She answered, but didn't get a chance to say a word.

Chris's enthusiastic voice came through as soon as Elena answered the call. "ALASKA, WHAT!? You didn't call and tell me! You've taken this getting-out thing to a whole new level!"

Stifling laughter and putting on her heaviest accent, Elena replied, "Heh-loh, this is Elena Sakellaris. Nicky is away at the moment. Oh, yes. We are in Alaska. We stayed in Anchorage and are now in Juneau. We go to spend the night in Sitka."

The line went silent, then clearly thrown, Chris responded, "Oh … uh … sounds like fun. I, uh … can't wait to hear all about it. Take care."

Elena smiled, slipping the phone back into the backpack as Nick returned with two coffees. She took hers, trying to hold back a grin. "Chris called," she said casually. "He mentioned something about picking up women in Alaska. I told him we'd be spending the night in Sitka tonight."

Nick raised an eyebrow, then laughed. "And I'm bad? I can only imagine what he thinks now!" He raised his cup to tap hers, took a sip, and said, "Welcome to the club."

Nick, who had only been on a handful of planes, was now getting somewhat comfortable with the airport and crowds. Traveling with Elena seemed to add to his confidence, helping him relax into this new rhythm.

On the other hand, Elena had never been on a plane until her journey to America to find Nick. Money had always been tight, and splurging on herself, on a 'holiday', had always been out of the question. It wouldn't have felt right, not when her aging parents continued to struggle. She counted this trip as an investment, not a holiday. Elena trusted the old legends and stories she'd grown up with. She had walked through the ruins where the robes of emperors once touched the stones. The ghosts of Istanbul felt tangible to her in the physical reminders of past glory, of hope deferred and liberation promised. And now, somehow, she sensed, she and Nick were part of the same story.

She looked over at him. His eyes closed, phone resting in his lap. *"He's dozing from boredom now, not sleeping because of exhaustion as before,"* she reasoned, *"but there's a peace about him now that wasn't there before."* Nick, apparently trusting Elena's motives more, encouraged her.

And what did she think of him, her little boy from New York? She smiled to herself, recalling her initial impressions. She did not view him as a spoiled American; she would manipulate and deceive. Had he ever really deserved that, or was that more about her than him? *"Whatever,"* she thought, *"'Plan-B' got him here!"*

"Alaska Airlines Flight AS 342 to Sitka is now boarding at Gate C5. This is a pre-boarding announcement for customers needing extra assistance or traveling with small children; all other guests may board at this time. Thank you for flying Alaska Airlines." Came over the airport speakers. Elena gently placed her hand on Nick's arm and said, "Nick, we need to go."

He stirred and stretched as he came back to his surroundings. He wondered what had drawn all those other folks to Sitka, Alaska, so close to winter. Not knowing how long he would be in Alaska and wanting to pack light, he brought only his lightweight coat. The nights were dipping into the twenties even now. As they made their way to the gate, he thought to himself, *It is probably not going to be a very comfortable experience to be in a graveyard in the chill with the sun rising and setting earlier and earlier. I want to be home for Christmas, if not Thanksgiving.* And with that, they were off to Sitka.

Chapter 5: The Crypt Speaks

The trip from Juneau to Sitka took about four hours, just long enough for a nap. By early afternoon, they had made it through the airport, rented a car, and were on the way to a hotel down the road. Nick was driving and thinking that this adventure was not turning out half bad. He had never been to Alaska before, and now he had traveled all over it!

They might have a couple of hours of daylight left, which gave them enough time to visit the Russian Orthodox Cemetery this afternoon. That would give them a head start on tomorrow's deeper dive and investigation. Once they settled in, Nick followed the directions to the Russian Orthodox Cemetery in Sitka on his phone. The city was small when compared to the populations of New York and Connecticut, but it was decent for Alaska. He read that Sitka had been essential to the immigrant Russian community during the Revolution. Before selling Alaska to America, Sitka had been the unofficial capital. There remained a small but tight Russian Orthodox community centered around the religious life of the downtown cathedral.

On the city's outskirts, the cemetery lay nestled in the wilderness of Alaska. Elena and Nick hoped that finding the graves would not prove too difficult. Google Maps brought them right to the spot, or did it? Nick searched out the window and saw woods with tombstones peeking through the undergrowth. It was not at all the type of highly ordered, over-fertilized, obsessively manicured cemetery he was used to. Finding a grave here would be a challenge. He hadn't wanted to get involved in stopping in at the cathedral, where he would expect the records to be kept, but he might have to now.

He turned to Elena. "So, where do we find Vasyl's grave?"

"I don't know. I have never been here before."

"You sent me the photo."

"Yes, but I did not take those pictures. My father was given them by my grandfather, who must have visited the graveyard and taken them."

"Hmm," Nick paused and glanced out the window to the forest again, "up for a hunt?"

Elena followed his glance and noted, "I don't think we have much choice. But let's say we are going on a 'hike' to explore Alaska, not search for a grave. There is always luck, right?"

She, too, had considered the cathedral and burial records. But on a Sunday, if anyone were around the cathedral, they would be worshipping or resting, not wanting to search through records. Tomorrow, Monday, they might have a better chance of finding help.

"Sounds like a plan," Nick affirmed.

In its way, the cemetery exuded mystery and organic harmony. The graves, crypts, and markers blended seamlessly into the landscape of rustic nature. Instead of trying to keep nature and the organic convergence of life and death at bay, it blended the spiritual reality that "you are earth, and to earth, you shall return," almost a natural mantra over the centuries.

Instead of fields filled with symmetrical stone outcrops visible by the acre, here, mixed in, were the markers of lives waiting to be discovered. An earthy scent, mixed with the aroma of pine and fern, welcomed family and friends, combining with memories of loved ones past—each bush or tree, potentially pregnant, with a mystery to be explored and revealed.

Nick and Elena wandered and enjoyed the wonder and magic of the cemetery, knowing that the leisurely 'hike' would turn into business tomorrow.

Unprepared for wandering in the woods at night, as the last of the natural light all but faded in the shortening days of the Alaskan fall, they returned to the hotel for dinner and an early night. They wouldn't need to start too early, as the cathedral probably wouldn't open until later in the morning.

As they drove back, they stopped at a fast-food restaurant and picked up a quick meal to take back to the hotel room. It would be the first time they would share a room, if not a bed. They felt it made little sense to spend money on two separate rooms when they were both adults, and they did not know how long this adventure would last. Money was not yet tight, but they needed to be careful. Both of them were determined to build trust between them, committed to wherever the path of this mystery might lead them to follow.

Nick knew that if he ran into trouble, his mom and dad would step in to fill the gap, but he didn't want to ask for help. They were the backup plan. No, he had savings and a 401 (k) that would probably see them through.

Now, in early November, Nick didn't think he would meet his wish to be home for Thanksgiving. He wondered whether Elena had ever experienced an American Thanksgiving, but an invitation from him would have to wait for another year. *"There's always Christmas,"* he silently consoled himself.

Monday dawned cloudy. Their next 'hike' in the cemetery would be chilly and damp. Not as enjoyable as the day before. After a carbohydrate-soaked complimentary 'Continental Breakfast' in the hotel lobby, they headed to St. Michael's Cathedral. The woman behind the desk in the cathedral office greeted them warmly.

"Yes, I hope you can help me," Nick responded to her offer. "I am looking for someone's grave in your graveyard."

"Yes," the woman responded, "I can help you. Most of the records have now been entered into our computer. It was an Eagle Scout project. What is the name?"

"Vasyl Palevych 1888—1955," Nick said, and even as he did, he perceived a slight shift in the woman's eyes. Did she take a second glance at them? Though it could have been Nick's imagination, the secretary's reaction to the name seemed to suggest familiarity.

"Ah, here he is. Let me put a dot on the map of the cemetery so you will not get lost." The secretary took out a red marker and placed a dot on a hand-drawn map. "This should get you there. Are you family?"

Under ordinary circumstances, her question seemed quite natural. Still, with the way she posed it, her body language, and the lack of eye contact, Nick felt she tried to act casual and nonchalant, as if hiding the fact that there might be more to the question than she had disclosed. He didn't want the secretary to learn the genuine answer.

"We don't know, actually. It is part of a research project for a paper I am writing for school. His name came up in a web search and in an old family Bible, and I thought he might be an interesting character who would help me get that 'A.' I need to bring my grade up."

"Oh," the woman replied, "well, best of luck." She handed him the map.

As Nick and Elena left the office, Nick nearly wiped out a little older lady sweeping the floor. "S … sorry, ma'am," he stumbled. She smiled at him and returned to her work.

"Nicky, I want to peek in at the church," said Elena, taking his hand to drag him into the sanctuary.

"It may not be the Greek Orthodox Church of Istanbul, but we share some things like icons, the iconostasis, and the theology of architecture and space." Nick studied Elena as her eyes darted over the vast space. She was beaming.

"In its way, it reminds me of home. I think of this space, and a warmth spreads through my soul, and I am with Papa and Mama again." Tears filled her eyes. For the first time, Nick connected with her love of home. She might be a minority there, and it might be challenging to live there, but home is still home.

"We have to get going," he finally urged. "We don't know what we will need to do at the graveyard. This might be the end of the journey, and we will both be able to go home." Nick turned and once again nearly tumbled over the same old lady, no longer smiling.

She clutched his arm and, pulling him closer, her voice holding a sense of urgency, "Be careful, the graveyard is watched. Always watched," she whispered, then turned and scrambled away as quickly as possible.

Nick didn't follow her, but now he sensed a resolve to be done with the graveyard and out of Sitka as soon as possible. "Come on, we need to go," he implored Elena, and this time, sensing the altered tone in his voice, she joined him in leaving.

Once in the car, Nick told Elena about the cleaner's warning. Elena shook her head. "What could she mean? Watched by whom? Why watch dead people?"

"I don't know. This is getting above my pay grade and risk tolerance," Nick admitted. The image of the quaint gentleman's journey he had planned in Connecticut had not quite panned out; things had taken an ominous direction.

In the late morning, they pulled up at the graveyard again. Looking at the map, they needed to hike through the center of the cemetery and head north. Then, the hunt would begin. It took them the better part of an hour to locate the tombstone. Despite the moss and overgrowth, the tombstone matched the picture.

On one side, it read 'Василь Палевич 1888—1955.' The other side was blank. And in the back, behind the blank side of the tombstone, stood the Paleon crypt.

Nick walked over to inspect it. It had a single, small iron door with a lock on one side. Elena joined him. The door didn't even wiggle when Nick tried to open it. They both threw their weight at it, hoping it might have rusted just enough to break it loose, but not a budge.

Nick stepped back and looked at Elena. "Well? What's next?"

"Would the church have a key?"

"I don't think so. More likely, the family would care for it. I could call my dad, but I don't think that would help. We must remember that this was built to sit here until a descendant found the riddle and came here to solve it. Vasyl could not have known how long that would have taken. This might have had to stand for hundreds of years before someone tried to get in."

"It could be what we are looking for is not in the crypt itself but is outside of it?" Elena reflected.

"Maybe there is another way in? Or maybe I'll bring a chisel and hammer tonight and do some masonry!" Nick was getting frustrated. "Let's hunt around and see what we can find. You take that side and the front. I'll take the other side and the back."

They spent over two hours scouring the crypt and the surrounding ground. Nick and Elena worked together to remove the moss from the lower sections and examined all the joints in the stones, but found no other clue how to get in, only solid stone. If there were any other way to get inside, it would have to involve dynamite.

They sat with their backs against the iron door of the crypt so that the back of Vasyl's tombstone was in front of them. Elena stood up, crossed over to the moss-covered stone, and began scraping away the moss. It had grown deep and thick at the base of the stone. Elena stopped suddenly and called over to Nick, "Nick, come here, look at this."

When Nick stooped to examine the base of the stone, he saw that underneath the grime and moss, a 3-inch circle of another kind of stone had been built into the headstone. Elena spat on the sleeve of her coat to wipe away the grime. The circle had a distinct purple hue and resembled marble.

"This is Imperial Porphyry. My cleaning seems to have loosened it." She gasped.

"Let me take a closer look." Nick drew down and wiggled the stone, but he was unable to get a grip to remove it. He took out his pocketknife and patiently pried the stone free, revealing a small compartment carved into the back of the headstone and then down. Nick put his hand in to feel around, but there was nothing. He felt the dirt at the bottom of the cavity, and his fingers touched something hard. He awkwardly pinched it between the sides of his fingers and pulled it out.

The sunlight revealed an old key. Nick looked around and surreptitiously handed it to Elena. "Hide it while I replace the stone. We have no idea who might be in the woods. Let's go back to sitting in front of the crypt."

No sooner had they regained their place in front of the door at the crypt than they heard footsteps moving through the underbrush toward them. Nick was 5'8" tall and weighed approximately 150 pounds on a good day. The man who approached them now with a shovel in his hand must have been over 6' tall and twice Nick's weight, not in fat but in muscle. He appeared to be in his 40s. *"More like a bipedal tank than a human,"* Nick assessed, but then cautioned himself, *"We're here in the middle of the woods alone."*

"Allo," the obviously Russian bipedal tank greeted them. "My name is Viktor. You can call me Vic if you like. I care for the cemetery."

"Care for the cemetery?" Nick silently questioned. *"How do you 'care' for a forest?"* But he heard himself say, "Well, it is a very pleasant place." He felt he did not want to insult a piece of military hardware.

"Hmm, are you a relative of Vasyl?" Victor said curiously, showing no interest in compliments.

"No. We are visiting Sitka. We stopped at the cathedral and heard that the cemetery was unusual and worth a visit." Nick wasn't good at lying and immediately understood his error if Viktor checked with the secretary.

"Hmm. It is a nice day for a walk in the woods. Be careful. It is easy to get lost in the woods or to get into trouble. Good day." Viktor replied without missing a beat.

"Good day," Nick and Elena responded in unison, both relieved to see him disappear into the undergrowth.

As Viktor plodded off, Elena leaned over to Nick and whispered, "Do you think he saw us take the key?"

"I don't know. But I do think that we are done here for today. It might be a coincidence that he is here when we are, but my heart suspects that he has had news from the cathedral secretary. We need to get into this crypt, and I would prefer to do it during the day. I would not fancy meeting Vic in a dark crypt at night. No, I should have said I would prefer not to meet Vic at all. We will need to be careful. We now understand what the cleaner meant, and we are being watched."

The next morning, they arrived at the cemetery just before sunrise. An October chill settled over the woods, filling the shadows, making their task even less enjoyable. They parked the car away from the edge of the cemetery, making them feel discreet and less conspicuous rather than accomplishing any actual effect.

They made their way quietly to the crypt. Nick fitted the key to the door, which, after years of corrosion, turned hard, but it turned to unlock the crypt. Once unlocked, the door swung easily into the crypt.

"You stay here," Nick told Elena. "I will go in and see what I can. If someone comes by, raise your voice to let me know."

Nick, key in hand, went in and pulled the door shut. He hated to close himself in the dark unknown, but Viktor undoubtedly still prowled about, even more so since yesterday, watching for their next move, and if he chanced by, everything needed to seem in place.

Nick turned his phone light on. The crypt was large. The casket, the only object in the crypt, sat on an elevated slab to the left side behind the door. Nick had plenty of space to walk. *"Too much space,"* he actually bemoaned. *"It's too mysterious."*

The interior walls were blank, with no apparent compartments or places to hide anything. *"Well,"* Nick disappointedly concluded, *"the casket is the only thing left."*

Nick looked at the casket with trepidation and wondered how one opened it. He didn't want to. He had not dwelled on the end of life, apart from the last couple of months, and now he spent most of his time in graveyards. Yet, up to this point, he had yet to meet directly with a corpse. Now, it seemed, having an introduction to some long expired family member he had no desire to meet was in the cards.

Nick went up to the lid and tried to lift it. To his relief and surprise, it yielded to his push on the lid. *"Of course,"* he thought, *"Vasyl would want the person who found the key to be able to get into the casket without having to destroy it, and someone who could force the iron door would have no problem rendering an old wooden coffin to splinters."*

Slowly, the lid creaked open on decades-old hinges. Nick had to shove his phone in his pocket to use both hands to lift the lid, which plunged him back into a dark room with not even a sliver of light coming in from around the door. The lid rested on the sidewall of the crypt with a bang. Nick could see the welcome glow of his phone through his pant pocket. He took a step back.

He liked family, especially during the holidays, but this unplanned reunion did not fill him with joy. In the still night of the crypt, Nick imagined himself going through the pockets of a corpse and rummaging around the casket and liner for a hint, a clue. And then there would be the bugs and maggots. Flashes from the "Indiana Jones" movies came to mind.

Nothing for it! "Get in the air and into the water, Nicky boy," he encouraged himself as he pulled the phone from his pocket and stepped forward to examine the inside. There in the center of the casket was … a gray box; only a gray box. He let out an audible sigh. The box was heavy. *"Must be lead,"* he reasoned. *"That's good. My pocketknife will be able to pry the seam loose enough to see what's in it."*

Indeed, his pocketknife made quick work of the lead seams. He soon had enough of the seam open to peer inside. There he found a book. That looked to be bound in silver. He loosened more of the lid and pried it back enough to pull the book out. It appeared to have been bound in silver and ornamented with gold. Set in the four corners of the cover, precious stones glimmered in the pure white light of his phone, and tucked underneath toward the center four different images accompanied the stones.

Putting it aside, he looked back in the box. A thorough exploration confirmed that no other clues remained in or on the box. He did a quick search of the casket, but it, too, had nothing more to reveal.

Nick's phone was down to 15%, so he needed to leave before the darkness forced him to go feeling about for the door. He didn't want to walk out into the sunlight with the book glinting with gold and silver in his hand. He didn't know who was looking on, and he felt that their amateur deception with the car would not fool Viktor for one moment. The forest could have unseen eyes just waiting for him to emerge.

Nick opened his jacket, loosened his belt and pants, untucked his shirt, and slid the metal-bound book next to his bare skin beneath his undershirt. He shivered as the cold silver and gold contacted his warm torso. He hated being cold! *"My own polar plunge,"* he mused. Nick then tucked himself back together. *"It will be safe for now,"* Nick reasoned. *"If I have to run, I won't need to worry about it slipping out of a loose coat. The jacket over everything will make it appear like we took nothing from the crypt."*

Elena walked about and busied herself by the grave to draw any eyes away from the crypt, while remaining close enough to watch for any unexpected company. Nick exited the crypt. He locked the door, put the key in his pocket, and joined Elena at Vasyl's grave.

"Let's go. You drive," is all he said.

Nick wanted only to return to the car's safety. He would wait until they returned to their hotel room to pull the book out for a close inspection.

As they both suspected without certainty, Viktor watched from the woods, following their every move. His heavy frame could pass unnoticed in the background when it suited his purpose. Yesterday, he wanted them to hear him coming. Today, he needed to watch unseen from the shadows of the wood. *"Hmm, the Paleon crypt,"* he wondered, *"I had not made that connection with Vasyl before. What is the connection? Why did they go in there? What did the little man find? Who is this Nick?"* Watching them drive off, he said to himself, "Nick, I think we need to talk. You and I need to be friends; we WILL be friends." Viktor smiled.

Chapter 6: Evangelion

Nick and Elena left the cemetery without detours on their return trip. After looking at the book from the Paleon crypt, they would have plenty of time for things like food. It was their only link to the future and what would come next, if not the journey's end. Either way, Nick kept the mystery securely tucked close to him.

As Elena drove them back to the hotel, Nick recounted his experience in the crypt. With Nick's description of what he found, Elena speculated on the identity of the book that Nick concealed. Having grown up with the traditions of Eastern Orthodoxy, coupled with Vasyl's role in the church as an Orthodox priest, meant that Nick discovered an Evangelion, but she kept her suspicions to herself until they were back at the hotel, where she could look at it.

Nick scanned the parking lot before unlocking the car and getting out.

He felt certain that Viktor allowed them to leave the cemetery because of uncertainty about how they fit into … *"Well, that's the question, isn't it?"* Nick reflected silently. *"Into what?"* He cautiously left the car and hurried to the hotel entrance.

With the closing of the lobby doors, they felt protected with the first level of security closed behind them. The elevator doors opened, and they were on their floor. A door suddenly opened on Nick's right. He started and jumped aside. A laughing woman and man stepped into the hall from the doorway, and he nearly ran into them. "Excuse me," he apologized.

"Excuse us," they said unfazed, "so sorry to have startled you!"

He didn't even turn to see them head off down the hall. He and Elena were now safe in their room with the door firmly locked. Nick untucked his shirt, and the book fell out onto the bed. Elena took it in her hands, warmed by Nick's body. She ran her fingers over the cover, touching the engravings and the stones in the corner.

"It's a special book," she told Nick. "My people call it an 'Evangelion.' This one is ancient and very pretty. It contains the Gospels we read in our services. Vasyl himself held and read from this in worship throughout his life. But it is not his. It is older than he was."

Elena took the Evangelion to the table. Before setting it down, her hands caressed the cover. She wondered about the prayers this cover had heard, the hands that had held it, the lips that had reverently kissed it in adoration. The adoration of the faithful had consecrated it, and they continued to hallow it spiritually. After placing it on the table, she opened the curtains to let in as much light as possible. Both she and Nick thumbed through the pages.

"Is this Greek?" Nick asked.

"Yes, Byzantine Greek," she explained. "My people still speak a form of it. I can read this with no problem. Everything seems to be in place. I do not remember the Gospels well enough to catch if they are all in order, but I can see no apparent clue. The only odd thing is that it has a list of names in the back. On the surface, it looks to me like they are the names of priests and the towns where they were born or officiated, I think."

"I don't understand Greek, so this one is up to you. As you read the names and towns in the list, is there anything that stands out to you?"

The list of names was three pages long and handwritten, so Elena was silent for a while.

"Yes, what is he doing there?" She pointed to a line, Ολεξάνδρ Παλεόν–Μυστράς.

"What does it say?" Nick asked.

"It is the name 'Oleksandr Paleon' followed by the town 'Mystras.' That is a town in Greece. But he cannot be part of this list. Paleon did not exist until 1930 when your adopted great-grandfather took on the name Oleksandr Paleon, or the American version, Alexander Paleon."

"It must have been Vasyl who wrote the list in the book," Nick couldn't remember what she called it. "It would only be a descendant of the Paleon line who would notice the out-of-place piece of wheat in the haystack. But what does Mystras have to do with it?" Nick was silent for a minute before he continued, "Well, the next leg of our journey is pretty clear: we're off to Greece!"

Elena's eyes brightened.

While not her home, they were heading back near where she had been born and spent all her life. A ferry ride or a manageable drive, and she could be in her own room again. Moreover, there would be more resources at their disposal. Nick would enter her world. The Rum may be small and powerless, but dedicated and duty-bound to the community.

"I will reach out to my father. Maybe he can help," she said with excitement.

"Good. We still don't get why we're going there, and I suspect there is still something this book needs to tell us, but there lies the problem. We have customs hoops to jump through. The moment we try to get this book out of the US and into another country without a legitimate bill of sale, we run the risk of it being confiscated. It can't go with us. We should also avoid the risk of putting it back in the crypt. Viktor is still out there somewhere. We need it with us, yet it's too risky to take it out of the country."

Nick sat considering a resolution to the problem. As he did, he played absent-mindedly with his phone as it recharged. Suddenly, he stopped with a look of resolution. Elena, not surprised, having now experienced the multiple expressions her traveling companion held in his repertoire, as Nick, looking at her, cheerily proclaimed, "I've got it." She shook her head and smiled at his self-satisfaction: "We will photograph every inch of this book …"

"Evangelion," Elena interjected quickly.

"This book," continued Nick with a smile, "on our phones, both of our phones, just in case. We will then take both the Bible," he hoped the compromise word would please her, "and the key to a safe-deposit box. I will mail the safe-deposit box key to my father and ask him to hold on to it until I ask for it. If we need the physical Bible or to re-access the crypt, they will be safe here, and we won't have to worry about them.

Not seeing Viktor is more unnerving than knowing where he is. I feel that every action risks all, as every next step hangs on the edge of disaster because he could be anywhere doing anything and we won't catch on until it is too late."

"I like the plan, especially because it helps us protect what others have sacrificed for in the past," Elena affirmed as she once again stroked the cover of the Evangelion.

Nick and Elena took turns photographing each page, front cover, back cover, and spine of the Evangelion. They then set out with the Evangelion tucked safely on Nick to a local bank. On their way back to the hotel, Nick wrote a brief note to his dad, slipped it and the safe-deposit box key into the mail express packet, and … paused. He held the sealed packet and thought back to his desk; it seemed like a lifetime ago when he opened that first express envelope from Elena. He believed it would be a gentleman's pursuit of a couple of days, a trip to Bridgeport and back, no more, and look at him now, Alaska, and about ready to book flights to Athens. An old life from not that long ago. With that, Nick handed the envelope to the clerk. In no time, it would be safe in his dad's hands.

On the way back to the hotel, Nick went online with ChatGPT and laid out the next leg of their journey:

To travel from Sitka, Alaska, to Athens, Greece, here's a general outline of the steps they would follow:

1. Fly from Sitka to Seattle
2. Fly from Seattle to Istanbul
3. Connecting Flight to Athens, Greece
4. Arriving in Athens

Elena drove as Nick read the list off. When he hit number two, which read 'flying into Istanbul,' she couldn't help herself as she exclaimed, "Home. I will need to tell Mama and Papa. There will be a layover. They will love to see us, and you will have real coffee, as only the Turks can make it! We want to ask for his help anyway."

"Sounds like a plan. When we return to the hotel, you call your folks and set everything up. I will make the flight arrangements. We should aim to depart tomorrow, which would put us in Istanbul sometime on Wednesday and Athens late Wednesday or early Thursday morning. But wait, you don't need a visa, but I do. How long will that take?"

Elena sheepishly confessed, "My father is an academic with numerous connections and is well-regarded in Byzantine studies. Thinking that you would return with me, I had him arrange a visa for you as a visiting scholar invited by the University. You can get into Türkiye, but we'll need my father to handle the visa issues for both of us to go to Greece."

Once back in the hotel room, they swung into action. Nick lay on the bed booking flights while Elena called her dad at the table."

Elena spoke little about her family. Nick didn't press her on the issue. He never heard her talk to her father and mother on the phone, but she occasionally would have private conversations out of Nick's earshot. The truth of the matter is that as part of a minority population, you guard what you reveal about your family and protect them through walls of privacy. Of the three children of Niketas, or "Papa," and Despina, or "Mama," Sakellaris, Elena was closest to her parents. Her brothers, Andreas and Kostas, had distanced themselves from their background to achieve upward mobility. Elena felt sorry for Kostas the most; by seeking acceptance in another family, the military, he would have to bury his Rum identification, taking on the trappings of the Islamic culture of the state.

Elena now phoned Papa with Nick present and listening to one side of the conversation. She knew Papa would be so happy to help them. Papa, a historical records clerk at the Boğaziçi University Library, did not teach. Still, he had access to scholars and clerics worldwide who came to access the library's rare works and historical archives. Papa especially loved working with academics who were part of the Byzantine Studies Research Center on campus. In other countries, Papa would have been a professor, but not here, not now. Niketas modeled for his children that integrity and honoring your values are as important as the titles and honors others give.

Nick watched as Elena's face lightened with a smile as she spoke at first in Greek: "Hello, Papa," then she hesitated, looked up at Nick, gave him a wink before speaking again in English, "No, Papa, in English from now on. Nick needs to hear and understand everything now if we are to trust each other."

"Papa," she continued, "we are coming to Istanbul and then on to Mystras. We have a couple of clues that we need help with, and we will explain more when we see you. Can you and Mama meet us at the airport? Can you come with us or find someone to help us in Mystras?"

There was a pause as Niketas considered Elena's request. Niketas was a cautious man of modest means. Like all minorities, he walked in the shadows, wanting peace, to get along with his neighbors, to raise his family, and to enjoy the heritage of which he was proud.

"I see you can't come to Mystras, but you can meet us at the airport. I understand," Elena paused. "We don't know when we will get to Istanbul right now. I will text you when we have more information. But what about finding someone who can help us with Mystras?" Another pause in the conversation: "Good. Try. I pray that you and Mama are doing well."

There was another lag in the conversation.

"Give her my love and tell her I am well. I am so eager to see the two of you. I love you. Take care of yourself. Goodbye." Elena's eyes filled with tears. Home had its challenges, but the family leaned on each other, and it was … after all … home.

Elena hung up and turned her attention to Nick. "Papa said there are a couple of visiting scholars at the University, one of whom is also on a pilgrimage to Hagia Sophia and has met with the Ecumenical Patriarch. He will quietly see if anyone can travel to meet us in Athens. You are coming to my part of the world, Nicky! Oh, that you will meet Mama and Papa. I am so happy."

"What's with the 'Nicky' thing?" Nick wondered. *"Where did that come from?"* Only Chris used that name for him, and then only playfully when he wanted to underscore familiarity and affection. He had never had another friend or girlfriend call him 'Nicky.' It was cute, and it felt right when she said it—natural and affectionate. Accepting the new familiarity without comment, Nick responded, "It will be great

to have another set of eyes on the Bible. I must confess that if there is another clue here, I don't know what it can be."

Things were now falling into place. They would:

- Tomorrow, Tuesday, fly out of Sitka early, reach Seattle by around noon, and fly out of Seattle for Istanbul.
- The next day, Wednesday, arrive in Istanbul by noon, have a 3-hour layover, and then take an afternoon flight from Istanbul to Athens. Arrive in Athens later in the afternoon.

Elena texted her dad that they would be in Istanbul at noon on Wednesday.

Nick looked at Elena and laughed. "We are getting too efficient at all of this. Do you realize it's nearly time for supper, and we've had nothing to eat? Let's head out someplace for our last Alaskan dinner."

They decided on a nice Italian restaurant they had passed earlier. The restaurant had a packed parking lot, a sign of quality food. The moment they walked through the door, the smell of tomato sauce and garlic mingled with the low lighting, soft music, and clinking of glasses. Nick closed his eyes. He did not need to take a leap of imagination to feel like he had returned to New York and now stood in any number of fine Italian restaurants. It would not take too active an imagination to keep his eyes closed and convince himself that he had daydreamed all of it. Rick would shortly nudge him to place his order, and when he opened his eyes, he would be home.

"Sir, sir …" he heard a strange voice and felt a gentle touch on his arm as Elena stirred him back to reality. "Can I seat you?"

Nick took a deep breath, exhaled, nodded, and followed her to a table in the busy center of the room. Once they had placed their orders, Elena excused herself. "Papa texted. I am going to step outside where it is quieter so I can call him. I will be right back." Nick nodded.

He was looking at his phone when, from the other side of the table, he heard, "Nicky, did you miss me?" But it was not Elena's voice that said it. The sound of the word "Nicky" rang hollow and cold. Nick didn't look up; he knew that voice. It was Viktor.

"You and I need to talk, my friend. You see, I have a problem: the people I work for pay me money to know what people like you do not want them to know. So, we have no choice but to become friends. We will spend time together, probably considerable time together, as long as it takes."

Nick had the presence of mind to text Elena immediately the word 'Help' before he looked up from his phone. He slowly looked at Viktor as Viktor's eyes studied Nick, trying their best to intimidate him. Nick, now aware of every movement he made, even drawing breath, became intentional so as not to alert Viktor to his fear. Hyperaware of where his eyes were going and how he was moving his body. Outside, he was blank, even as existential terror consumed him. His mind raced, but he was at a loss for how to respond. "What…" he blurted out numbly, trying to buy some time to think. "I…" not much better, "I don't understand Vic," he uttered. He needed time to develop an improved plan than his failed conversational model.

"Okay, let's play then," chuckled Viktor. He felt in control and didn't mind playing a little. "I think you have a connection to a very valuable secret that many people like me have tried to work out for nearly a century. A valuable mystery that Vasyl Palevych took to his grave, a grave the Soviet and now Russian loyalists here have watched since 1955. I did not consider the connection to the family of Nikolai Paleon," Nick felt a chill as Viktor used his full Christian name. Nobody, not even Chris, knew that Nick stood for Nikolai, "or the Paleon crypt in the graveyard. A crypt, I might add, that you went into. I need to know what was in that crypt, what you learned, and where you are off to next. Indeed, I propose that, as friends now, we go together. My friends and I can be particularly useful and powerful allies. But we can also be terrifying enemies. Come, let's be friends together. I think now would be a wonderful time for us to leave and take a pleasant walk, as best buddies do, yes?"

As Viktor spoke, Nick saw Elena moving into the room. He dared not even glance directly at her, fearing to betray her efforts to Viktor. But in his peripheral vision, he could see as she began moving with the intent of a border collie herding sheep. She didn't make eye contact with him. She observed the movements of the servers and the patrons in the room. Indeed, she figured they stood no prospect of directly confronting the professionally trained and experienced Viktor.

Elena wove around the busy room, blocking one server and sending him down a long aisle to a roadblock of a table of guests ready to leave. He turned and had to reverse. But Elena planned that he would have to, and she had pulled back and redirected another server to cut him off. Happy with her shepherding of the flock of servers and guests, she moved in Nick's direction.

"Nicky," the chill voice of Viktor repeated, "time is up. Please do not make a scene. It will not help you to make me angry. Come along like a nice little man…" Elena had reached the table, and so had the server. Elena 'accidentally' caused him to stumble, upsetting his tray, whose whole contents hit … Nick!

Everyone stopped eating as Nick and Viktor's table took center stage. Nick, now covered in fine dining, smelling of tomato sauce and garlic, sat without moving, but wishing to crawl under the table. Horrified, the server tried to pick food off of Nick and moved large blobs about with a much too small napkin. The maître d' ran over to the table, as were bussers with mops, brooms, and buckets. Viktor didn't escape entirely, requiring a wipe here and there. The maître d' ushered Nick off to the kitchen to clean him up. On the other side of the kitchen door, Elena pulled him as fast as she could out of the restaurant's back door and into the car. They were off.

Viktor sat at the table for a few minutes. *"Let the worm wriggle on the hook a little longer, as if he thinks he can escape from the hook. I have time. This was a delay, not a problem."* He found their little tricks amusing.

Nick and Elena wasted no time planning and driving their way back to the hotel. They would pack and leave the hotel at once. At the hotel, she parked right in front of the lobby doors. The sign said, "No Parking," but she figured they would be out of there before any tow truck would arrive. Elena would get everything packed as Nick cleaned up, changed his clothes, and wiped down. They would check out and head to the airport to spend the night until their morning flight. The airport would provide them with public cover and plenty of security. That might not stop Viktor, but he had one weakness:

Viktor did not want Nick dead. Nick needed to be able to answer his questions. So long as they leveraged that weakness, Nick would stay alive and free.

Safely at the airport and through the body scanners, they slowed down and assessed their current situation. Nick settled Elena into a row of seats with his backpack and headed off to the lavatory to clean the rest of the sauce and cheese out of his hair. He ended up washing his hair with hand soap in the sink. Exhausted and hungry, he collapsed in his seat next to Elena.

"That was close," Nick finally said to her. "I thought for sure I would be forced to change partners for the last part of this dance. Thanks to your quick wits and acting, we managed to get away for now. Viktor said that Vasyl's grave had been watched since 1955. He said that he had taken a valuable secret with him to the grave, but he didn't tell me the secret. I don't think I want to go back and ask him," Nick ended with a wry smile.

"It might not be good for our health. Papa has arranged to meet us at the airport. Even though it would be better for our prospects to stay on the airside of security, Papa, and Mama will take us to dinner on the airport's landside when we get in. He also mentioned speaking with an interested visiting scholar, who would meet us in Athens. He is going ahead of us on other errands and working on obtaining visas for us to enter Greece. Papa said he is visiting from a monastery in Uzbekistan but has connections in the Orthodox Church, academia, and the government. He has been in Istanbul for months and worked closely with Papa. He will be at the Athens airport when we land in case there are any issues. Papa will tell us about him in Istanbul."

They had snacks from a vending machine and dozed on and off. The night passed uneventfully, though not very restful, but they consoled themselves with the reality check that a sleepless night and making it to Istanbul without a run-in with Viktor was better than being his guest for the night. They were not naive enough to trust that they had shaken him. Yet every day they put him off, the universe might step in with new information and trajectories.

Viktor stood in the shadows of the airport watching Nick and Elena's every move and now waited at the gate for the flight to

Istanbul. *"Let them run to Istanbul,"* Viktor thought. His eyes were everywhere. He would be told of their movements. Let them run. He would be close behind. But there were still details he could not guess at this point and so called for finesse and patience on his part: What were they after? What have they taken? He had been able to get into the crypt, but except for the remains of the lead box, it was empty. He needed more to go on. Dare he involve others? At this point, would they care? Would they credit him, or cut him off yet again for their own gain? Perhaps this might be of greater worth to keep to himself and rely on others only for bits and pieces of information.

Viktor's deliberations evoked his own ghosts and memories that brought him to these shadows, where he watched and hoped.

The fall of the Soviet Union had taken everyone by surprise—more people than just him had careers ended, while others had flourished from the chaos.

This Paleon thing had been the first real action for him in a long time. *"It is a fork in the road,"* he felt. *"Yes, I must handle it with all the skill I can. But it is mine. And it will either win me back into Moscow's trust, or free me from it forever."*

As Nick and Elena dozed off, Viktor stepped outside. He had time. He would wait until they were on their way, and then he would follow them. Once outside, he took out his phone and dialed. He would call the shots for now and see where they led.

"Ah, allo my friend," he said once the call connected. "Yes, it's been a long time. I need a favor, one that will settle old debts." There was a pause as the other responded, "Good, good. I have a package coming your way that I need to know about. I will send you a photo and the flight information by text." Another pause for response. "Oh, oh, no, no, nothing big," Viktor said as he lightened his tone in diversion, "just wondering and having nothing else to do, you know." He gave a slight off-the-cuff laugh. "I will be coming on the next flight … no need to involve anyone but yourself. I will see you soon."

Viktor faded back into the shadows.

Unaware of Viktor's brooding nearby, Nick and Elena boarded the flight without a problem.

Before taking his seat, Nick scanned the plane and was relieved Viktor was not on the flight. Thanks to the last-minute booking, Viktor couldn't have known where they were going. But Nick felt Viktor's eyes watching him, even though he could not see him at the airport. Victor waited for them to board the plane, and then he would follow them. Nick realized it was an act of self-deception to think that their luck and feeble calculations would continue to be a match for Viktor's brawn and experience.

Viktor looked up at the empty gate. *"Yes,"* he thought, *"go ahead and ditch poor Viktor. Have a nice flight, and I will see you in Istanbul, where we shall all talk."* Viktor walked over to the counter to buy his ticket on the next flight.

Chapter 7: The Choreography of Brother Alfanas

Now in Istanbul, Nick and Elena disembarked from the plane a little after noon. Elena's parents were waiting at the "Revolve Restaurant and Bar" on the airport's landside. They planned to be outside of the secure "airside" area of the International Terminal for a couple of hours. This would give them a buffer to board the flight to Athens and limit their exposure to the insecure landside. Nick appreciated not being asked to go off the airport as they had had no intention of exposing themselves to either a chance or an arranged encounter with the unseen Viktor.

Niketas and Despina were waiting outside the restaurant. All three of them collided in a mass of arms, kisses, and tears. Nick hadn't thought about how much this trip had impacted Elena as well as him. Throughout all of their encounters, Elena kept herself composed, for the first time Nick saw her cry. He hung his head to give them privacy. While thrilled for her, he felt this aching space in his own heart as he thought of home and his parents.

Elena saw Nick from the corner of her eye and remembered that she considered him part of her family now. "Mama, Papa, I want you to meet Nikolai Paleon."

Nick felt awkward meeting them, which meant that his faulty language skills kicked in. "Yeah, um, hi, Mr. and Mrs. Sakellaris, it's nice to meet you." He stuck out his hand, and Despina brushed it aside to hug and kiss him on the cheek.

"Such formality—you call us mama and papa while you are here."

Niketas took the still-extended hand and shook it firmly. Then, keeping hold, he pulled Nick to him, throwing his free arm around his back and slapping him while hugging him.

"Welcome, my boy. It is a blessing to meet you."

They hurried to get a table. Two hours would fly by, and they had a lot to talk about. Nick felt relaxed, the most relaxed both he and Elena had felt in a while. Joy, food, and information passed around the table as they ate. The conversation did not dwell on their adventures. Nick and Elena only offered a brief sketch of what they had done, without going into details.

Elena's parents did not ask for more. It was as if Mama and Papa knew the kids needed a break, a sabbatical for a couple of hours before they returned to the game. Nick and Elena, as mature as they were, appreciated the embrace and care of being parented over the meal.

They mentioned nothing about Viktor or their anxiety. Not only did they not want to worry them, but they also wanted a couple of hours when he didn't exert control over their lives. Nick stopped even scanning the room for him.

The meal, over too quickly, exceeding their two-hour deadline, meant that they had to hurry to the security check-in. Elena called time over first.

"Mama, Papa, thank you so much. It was such a refreshing joy to see you. Keep praying for us, and I will let you know when we get to Greece."

"Now," said Papa, with renewed focus, "when you get to Athens, Brother Alfanas has promised to meet you. He needed to be there yesterday anyway, but he said that he would make arrangements for your arrival. So, look for a wandering Russian Orthodox monk, and more than likely, that is him. He is about my age and height. He is very personable and approachable for a monk, that is."

Elena and Nick exchanged quick, concerned glances with each other. Niketas noticed the discomfort. "What's the problem, daughter?" he asked.

Elena had never questioned her father's judgement. That is simply the cultural way of showing respect, but the memory of Viktor in Alaska unsettled her.

"Papa," she began slowly, "you know him well, this Brother Alfanas?"

"Very well," the other said firmly, "you can trust him implicitly, if that is your concern. We work together at the university. He's a respected Byzantine scholar who is visiting our collections, and he is very knowledgeable. From what I understand, he was born in Ukraine but cannot return. I've spoken to him about our family's shared burden with the Paleon family. He's read all the letters, every one of them." Niketas gently reached out and squeezed Elena's hand as he said this. "He's not only intrigued, Elena, but he understands why you felt you needed to go to New York. The riddle of the unknown … it draws him. I trust him, and so should you."

"Very well, Papa," squeezing his hand back as she spoke, "it will be good for us to have someone helping us." She looked over and gave Nick a quick, reaffirming smile.

As they entered the security line, they gathered for a last huddle of four; hugging, kissing, and saying goodbye. Nick and Elena returned to their next gate just in time to board. They were now off to Athens. As they settled down into their seats, Nick turned to Elena.

"Your folks are very nice. I felt like I had known them forever. It turns out that amid the challenges of this trip, there are moments beyond price."

She smiled at him and reached out to hold his hand, but said nothing as she turned to look out the window.

They arrived in Athens ahead of time. By mid-afternoon, they were on the airport's landside and began their hunt for Brother Alfanas, hoping he was there watching for them. They didn't have to worry too much as his long black robes and veiled cap made him stand out as the only obvious choice in the crowd. Nick guessed that his build was medium, neither thin nor heavy. He held a black walking stick with a solid silver cap on top.

Nick approached the stranger and asked, "Are you Brother Alfanas?"

"Indeed, I am, and you must be Nick." He shook his hand and then, holding it out in Elena's direction, said, "And you must be Elena."

Elena shook his extended hand but said nothing.

"I have made reservations for you at one of the area hotels. I have been staying with the brothers at one of the monasteries. Now let's get you settled, make plans for tomorrow, and I will head back to the monastery. I rented a car to explore Athens and drive to Mystras. Let's get your luggage so we can be on our way."

Once in their room, they used room service rather than be in the crowds again. But the conversation could not wait for the food. The three of them sat around the small table to plan.

"All right." Looking at them intently, Alfanas began, "There is fear in your eyes. You looked like hunted animals in the airport terminal. You must tell me everything."

They began with the dark cloud named Viktor and quickly recalled the events in Alaska. Alfanas did not just listen. He studied them as they spoke. Nick wondered about him. He read them like a book, hearing them like a story. When they finished the incident at the restaurant in Sitka, Alfanas, furrowed brow, elbows on the table, eyes staring at the surface, leaned back in his chair, reached for his stick with one hand, exhaled heavily, and said, "Leave him to me. Tomorrow, you will remain here in Athens. He is not to follow us to Mystras, but it will take me a couple of days to deal with him. Now tell me why you think we must go to Mystras."

The monk's calm determination and confidence gave Nick a sense of security, like having an acting parent who could take charge and help them on the next leg of their journey. It felt nice not to be the one responsible and in charge. Nick took out his phone and located the pictures of the list of names in the Evangelion as Elena placed the food on the table. Alfanas took Nick's phone and studied the list.

"Hmm, that was a good catch," he confirmed. "Now let's look at the rest of the Evangelion itself. It is too bad you could not bring it here, but also smart not to risk trying. We do not know if we will need to reference it again before all is over. I do not think any clues will be found in the text. That would take too long and require in-depth knowledge of the Greek Gospels. No, let's stick to the covers and blank pages."

He scrolled through the photos again, and when he came to the cover, he smiled and said, "Curious. Let's see if you can spot it." He passed the phone to Elena, knowing Nick would never pick it out, but Elena had grown up with Orthodoxy her whole life. "There is something out of place on this cover. What do you think?"

Elena inspected the image. Nothing looked out of place to her. Passing the phone back, she said, "I give up."

"The stones are correct and represent the Gospels' four writers: Matthew, Mark, Luke, and John. But the four images are mistaken. In other Evangelion, they should be a winged man or angel, a lion, an ox or calf, and an eagle. But what do we find? The double-headed eagle of the Byzantine emperors is in all four corners.

A monk in the sixteenth century would not do such a thing. This is a holy book, not a political tool, or even for private devotion; it is sacramental. But there is even more of a clue. The image is distinct in its border and design. It perfectly represents something called the 'Coronation Stone' embedded in the floor of the Church of St. Demetrios in Mystras. The stone, therefore, is most probably the place of the next clue."

Alfanas took some food and a sip of water and thought for a second, "I have just come from presenting a gift from my monastery to the Metropolitan of Sparta. Although the Church of St. Demetrios is primarily a secular site, I believe I can leverage the Metropolitan's influence to arrange a prayer vigil as part of my pilgrimage to Istanbul's holy sites.

While I pray for the night, you can explore the stone for clues. This will take me time to set up. I am afraid you will be in Athens for at least a week. I cannot expedite the delay.

Okay, enough for tonight. Thank you for the meal. We have our tasks, and I will chat with you tomorrow. Do not move from this room until I phone you. I have resources in Greece, and I believe I'll have a solid plan in place by mid-afternoon tomorrow, but I need to confirm a couple of things first. Use the peephole in your door to verify your visitors."

Brother Alfanas left without another word, but once outside the hotel, he looked about him and stared down at the pavement in front of him.

"There is work I need to do before bed. Unless I am far from my mark, Viktor is here and may even be watching me now," he intimated silently to himself. *"Well, let him get a good look. Let him wonder about the old cleric. It might dissuade him from making any sudden moves. Unless I am mistaken, we will meet soon, even as soon as tomorrow, if I have my way."*

With that, he got into his car and headed off into the night.

Alfanas correctly assumed that Viktor looked on, keeping out of sight. He had indeed been intently watching as the trio walked into the hotel together. And yes, he wondered who this new monk was. It certainly looked like Nick had taken him into his confidence. He had known that, at least historically, the church was a part of the grand deception that interested him, but what did this cleric know? He would find out in time.

Nick and Elena had no intention of wandering off sightseeing in Athens until they had news of Viktor. They felt safe enough in the hotel room with a locked door between them and any intrusion. Breakfast and lunch were once again room service. And they waited. It was not until early in the afternoon that Brother Alfanas called them.

"There is a cafe not more than a 10-minute walk from the hotel. I will meet you there at 2:00. Be precise. Sit outside and order your coffee. Do not go inside. Go quickly directly to the cafe and nowhere else. No window shopping or pauses. Please wait for me there. Everything will be well."

At ten minutes to two, they set out. Passing through the hotel lobby doors, they suddenly felt vulnerable and exposed. They went down to the cafe, where Brother Alfanas would join them. Nick and Elena wondered why he would risk moving them from their place of safety to such an exposed location as an outside table at a public cafe, but they trusted him and his judgement.

They didn't know they were being observed walking down to the cafe. Viktor had taken up an almost permanent residence in the shadows of the hotel, now following them down the sidewalk. He felt certain he would have another conversation with Nick today, and didn't plan on letting the couple out of sight as he blended into the crowd. Viktor had no way of knowing that black blends into the dark shadows better than any other color. He did not expect that the monk kept Viktor's surveillance under scrutiny and Alfanas' eyes followed Viktor down the road.

Brother Alfanas had been in Eastern Europe all his life, which had begun in Ukraine, where he had lived for many years. He knew firsthand the mind games Russia played on the Ukrainians and its petty jealousy of Kyiv's actual place at the center of the history and culture of the Kyivan Rus'. Alfanas had not always been a contemplative. He would hide Nick and Elena in plain sight. In the dazzling sun and the thousands of eyes of downtown Athens. Viktor had a lot of experience, but Alfanas had lived in the shadows for most of his many years; he had walked there both physically and spiritually all his life.

Now he could see Viktor. He watched his every move. *"Predictability,"* Alfanas considered silently, *"that's his weakness! I know you, Viktor. I have yet to meet you, but I know you."*

Brother Alfanas kept an eye on all three as they neared the cafe. Nick and Elena did not pause but continued straight to the cafe. Viktor would not be able to intercept them until the cafe. For his plan to work, Alfanas must pick the right moment to emerge from the shadows.

Nick and Elena had made it to the cafe. They sat at a table near the street. Had they been real tourists, they could not have asked for a better day; temperate and sunny, busy, joy-filled tourists flowed through the outdoor cafe, adding to its ambiance. The smell of coffee and baked goods filled the air as servers walked about waiting at tables. Yes, they would have coffee, but no, they would have nothing to eat.

Cuddling up with a nice cup of coffee between his hands, completely disarmed Nick. He shut his eyes as he turned his face toward the warm sun, relaxing as he leaned back in his seat. Holding his cup of black coffee close to his chest and letting the smell fill his nostrils drew him away from every care.

The feeling of a hand placed heavy on his shoulder jarred him back to reality, nearly upsetting the coffee in his hand.

"Ah, what a nice day for coffee outdoors," it was, of course, Viktor. He had one hand on Nick's shoulder and the other on Elena's. "I think that you will *both* stay for our talk this time. I would not want poor Nick to have to change his clothes again."

Viktor moved around and seated himself opposite the two young travelers. His eyes were studying their every movement and action. He saw fear in their eyes, and that pleased him. Fear would now drive their choices and actions, helplessly betraying Nick and Elena. He felt he would soon get the answers he wanted from them, but he would not underestimate them again.

Viktor focused on Nick as he said, "I have been very patient with you, Nick. This will be the second time I have invited you to talk with me. I promise not to harm you if you tell me what I need to know. No harm to either of you. No harm to either of your parents as well." He paused, letting the threat sink in before he continued, "I don't want them to have to be my next stop. So messy, so long. But if we do not talk, then I cannot promise to avoid unfortunate things coming to any of you," he shot a glance at Elena. "Now, what did you find out in the crypt, and why are you in Athens? Where are you going from here?"

Viktor leaned back in his chair, briefly scanning his surroundings. He had been so intent on Nick and Elena that he had not noticed the dark shadow move across the street and sweep into the cafe. It was Brother Alfanas.

Alfanas walked casually with an air that appeared more focused on the letter he was holding than on the table and its occupants. A naïve monk, the image everyone who thought the best or the worst of the world took him for. In every way, detached from the world's reality, and somewhat superfluous.

Viktor stood up as he watched him approach, more out of surprise than any real threat from the cleric. Viktor had been too lax in concentrating on Nick and Elena and did not like being surprised. Brother Alfanas continued to draw up to the table with no betraying reaction, but as he reached the table, he looked up from the letter and greeted Viktor with a smile.

Alfanas warmly extended his hand out to shake Viktor's with the salutation, "Ah, another friend, how nice. I am Brother Alfanas. It is good to meet you. Please sit. I am sorry that I must steal Nick and Elena away, but I promised to show them the sights in Athens today."

He turned to Nick and Elena with the same smile and cheerful innocence with which he greeted Viktor. "Good news, my friends, we will be able to view the Parthenon today. And on that other bit of research you wanted me to investigate, I received this note this morning." He placed the paper he was reading down in front of them. Written in Greek, with a prominently visible hand-drawn double-headed eagle of Imperial Byzantium. "Nick, I know you don't read Greek, but it simply says that I will meet my friend in the Elaionas district this evening. Come, we are late. Let us go."

Brother Alfanas pulled around behind Nick and Elena and, with a hand under each of their arms to urge them up. He looked across the table at Viktor and said, "Again, I am so sorry to steal them away." Cocking his head as if in a moment of realization, he said, "I don't think I asked your name. How rude of me."

"Viktor, my name is Viktor."

"Ah, Viktor, enjoy the wonderful day. There is nothing quite like being in Athens, outdoors, in the bright sunshine, experiencing God's creation. Goodbye." The monk guided Nick and Elena slowly away, pointing to the buildings, stopping to laugh or say something to them. He summoned a taxi, and they all climbed in.

Viktor needed to regroup. How much did this monk know? Who was he meeting tonight? Why did the note he held have the symbol of Imperial Byzantium on it? What was this monk researching? He needed more information to place it in the context of what he already knew: he had copies of letters written by Vasyl Palevych to a colleague in Ukraine while Vasyl stayed in Sitka. Those letters hinted at the wealth of Byzantium and protecting it from seizure by the Revolution, but lacked details. A mistake at this point could be disastrous. His best course would be to let the monk sightsee with Nick and Elena, and Viktor would pick up their trail when they returned to the hotel. He would switch from Nick and Elena to following the monk for tonight.

They were now safe in the cab. Nick anxiously said to Brother Alfanas, "You should not have said anything about your meeting tonight in front of Viktor."

"I wanted him to hear it. I want him to follow me. He will do so because he cannot help it. Even if he suspects it is a trap, which it is, he will pride himself on being cautious and outwitting a silly old monastic who is misguided by his beliefs. You see, I have prearranged with the Department of Cultural Heritage and Antiquities and the Hellenic Police to meet me on Orfeos Street tonight because a stranger named Viktor has offered to sell me a stolen religious artifact that, oddly, is now in my pocket. I think Viktor will be surprised, maybe not pleasantly, but surprised," Alfanas said with a smile on his face.

"Where are we going now?" Elena asked.

"To the Parthenon, as I said. It would not do to have you in Athens and not see the Parthenon!" Alfanas laughed.

So far, Nick had seen more of the world in a week than he had in his prior thirty years. Yet nothing matched the excitement of standing on the Acropolis, surrounded by its renowned architecture and history.

The sun shone, and though it was brisk, Nick enjoyed the day with Elena and Alfanas. For the first time, he felt like a tourist as he snapped selfies at the Parthenon, and texted one or two to Chris: "Sorry, can't send you a gyro to go with the pictures."

Alfanas smiled broadly for Nick's camera, enthusiastically encouraging them to explore in wonder and joy. Too long oppressed by fear and anxiety, without tools to deal with the complexities they had unwittingly stumbled into, would take its toll if left unrelieved.

He didn't want them to worry about Viktor. They might be able to make it to the end of their quest without dealing with him permanently, but they also might have to settle for postponing a future necessity.

On the way back to the hotel, they stopped for supper. It felt good to be out together. There seemed to be more security with three than two, and the worldly Alfanas exuded and imparted confidence.

"What do we do tomorrow?" asked Nick as they waited for food to be served.

"Well," began Alfanas, "as I suspected earlier, we will have a wait until we move on from Athens. I need to hear back from the Metropolitan of Sparta before we head to Mystras. We could go early, but there is no point. Athens holds so much more for young people than Mystras. You will stay here and enjoy it. We will then journey down together."

"What is the Coronation Stone, and why is it in Mystras?" asked Nick.

"Mystras served as a significant Byzantine stronghold and administrative center in the Peloponnese before and immediately after the fall of Constantinople in 1453. The church there, St. Demetrios, is claimed by some ancient authors and tradition to be where Byzantine emperors were rumored to have been crowned. A marble slab now commemorates the spot. That slab is known as the Coronation Stone".

When their supper came, Alfanas asked them not to take too long to eat. He had a long drive and walk ahead of him, and he needed to ensure Viktor didn't get lost in the night. He had arranged his meeting for 9:00 that evening.

They returned to the hotel room with plenty of time to spare. Alfanas stayed for a while and finally bid them a good night.

Alfanas sat for a moment in the hotel lobby, pretending to look at his phone.

The delay actually accomplished two goals: messaging last instructions, and signalling to Viktor that Alfanas was getting ready to leave and Viktor needed to prepare to follow him. Alfanas did not want to lose Viktor.

He would leave his car in one of the parking lots in the Elaionas district. Busy by day as a significant industrial hub, the district is devoid of vehicle and foot traffic at night. It would be the ideal meeting place for a clandestine encounter, either for information or to pass along stolen goods.

Alfanas would take Viktor for a walk, just the two of them—well, maybe one or two more. Alfanas would be in the open, Viktor in the shadows, until Alfanas turned from Orfeos Street onto Agias Annis Street. Then, everyone would be out in the light.

Alfanas received a text message, stood up, grabbed his walking stick, and took off.

He found a large lot to park in, turned the lights off, and struck out on foot. Alfanas needed to walk slowly. Viktor might be good at this game, but like a fish pursuing a fly-covered hook, he would not know until the end that Viktor had swallowed the bait. Viktor would be on his guard and loath to enter the open too soon. Alfanas did not count on him making a personal appearance. His plans took place in the shadows, where Viktor felt secure and aloof.

It was 8:30, and Alfanas was now on Orfeos Street, headed toward Agias Annis Street, but he felt his plans might be astray. There should have been confirmation by now that his fish pursued the bait, but it had not come. He slowed his pace and stopped under a light, looking at his phone. He then looked up and around at the darkness. It was all quiet and calm, but he knew eyes were watching. He relied on eyes watching. He prayed those eyes were watching!

Alfanas dared not take too long under the light. It would not be natural for someone who wanted to have an inconspicuous meeting to pause too long in the light. He moved back into the dark and slowly down the street. Alfanas could now see the intersection with Agias Annis Street. He felt the weight of failure. Could Viktor be that good? He might be better at concealment or discernment than Alfanas expected.

His phone buzzed in his hand. He paused, glanced at it, and smiled. His pace quickened briefly, and he rounded the corner onto Agias Annis Street. As he did so, he heard a whistle cut through the silence.

Brother Alfanas quickly turned and sprinted back in the direction he had come. Across the street were two barely discernible figures in the night, one standing, the other on the ground.

"Good work, my old friend. Here, take this cord and bind his hands and feet behind him. Quickly, I hear feet running." Alfanas slipped the ornate Russian Orthodox cross he had "borrowed" from the Metropolitan's private collection earlier into Viktor's pocket. "Run now; leave him to me." The other shadowy figure ran down the street.

Suddenly, five Hellenic Police officers came running up. Two ran past the monk, who struggled to get to his feet after pretending to work on the knots that bound Viktor. One of the officers helped him up.

"Oh, my goodness, bless you. I am not as young as I used to be," puffed Brother Alfanas, in dramatized, insincere fragility. "I quickly tried to bind him before he could escape."

"Oh, the other man?" he responded to their inquiry. "I suspect a simple passerby who did not want to be involved, or maybe frightened by our violent exchange."

The police took over handling Viktor, who was now regaining consciousness just in time to hear Brother Alfanas as he spoke to the officer, "Yes, officer, this was the man I was to meet here this evening. I am sure he thought it would turn out differently than it has, but he is the one."

It wasn't a lie. He had made a significant effort to arrange this meeting with Viktor. As for the cross, likely, he would never be called to testify, or at least, by the time of the trial, he would be out of the country. The police had caught Viktor red-handed without his having to say a word.

Alfanas knew that in his life, there would be many things for which he would have to account. He did not know how many of them his life's final interviewer and judge would accept as the necessity. He considered them a case of "needs must when the devil drives." For this night's deception, this was such a case. He would take the weight of his judgment when it became due.

Ultimately, he would depend on his judge's grace, even if that should have to wait until the final trumpet sounded, and the dead raised. Alfanas was guilty, yet the world judged him even more harshly than his actions deserved.

Viktor, still bound, looked up first at Alfanas and then at the officer and protested, "Why am I bound? I've broken no laws. Or is it illegal to walk alone at night?"

"You may walk where you will at night in Athens," the officer replied, "but you may not take a stolen artifact with you on your walk." He held up the cross. "We found this in your pocket. Perhaps you have an explanation?"

Viktor stared first at the cross and then at the monk but said nothing. *"All these delays,"* he thought, *"the monk does not know who he is playing with. Now I am angry. Nick has run out of choices."*

The other two officers ran up with the news that they had not been able to capture the third man. Brother Alfanas sighed to himself in relief.

After thanking the officers for their help, sure that the Metropolitan would be pleased, he walked contentedly back to his car. That would keep Viktor busy, but it would be hard to tell for how long. Viktor had connections who could secure his release before any trial or conviction, but that would all take time.

Tomorrow, Alfanas would head back to the Metropolitan of Sparta's office and see about getting the earliest appointment he could to meet with him and arrange for his vigil at the Church of St. Demetrios in Mystras. Viktor might well have helped expedite things since Alfanas helped rescue the Metropolitan's cross; indeed, it might make it easier for him to gain approval.

Brother Alfanas stopped by early the following day. Nick and Elena were eager for news about his encounter with Viktor and what had happened.

"It went well," he began. "I don't think he is permanently out of the way, but I pray that I have sidelined him until after we visit Mystras and are out of Greece. If he has no pull with the authorities, seeing that he is a foreigner, the Greek authorities may be more inclined to keep him in custody to prevent a flight risk. In that case, we will have months before he is free.

However, I would suggest we have several weeks before the authorities complete the initial investigations and the case proceeds to pretrial. It will be there that his influence will step in. My friends are doing what they can to provide numerous leads for the police to follow. When he gets out, he will have to locate and catch up with us. Not impossible, especially with his probable connections, but we now have a little more time."

"That is excellent news," Nick said in relief. "I'm glad I didn't have to run into him on a dark street at night."

"It is good news, but be warned, he will be a formidable foe when he picks up our trail next. Be careful. He is angry and dangerous now." Alfanas paused, sighed, and stood up, leaning heavily on his stick. "I am off again to Sparta. I will petition the Metropolitan as soon as I can get in to see him. Until I get back, I have some things that you must do for me."

"Anything," blurted out Elena.

Alfanas held them both in his stare, one at a time, and, with a smile on his face, he said, "I need you to be tourists until I get back. See the sights and taste as much of the food as you can. Enjoy, relax, and recover. You are now on holiday until I return." He embraced them both and left for Sparta.

While Brother Alfanas did not say precisely how long they would have, they figured from what Alfanas said earlier that it would be approximately five days. Nick jumped on the internet, and between ChatGPT and Google, he had a full touristy agenda laid out. They would start today, Friday, by returning to the Acropolis, where they could spend time in the museum and other ruins they had not had the ability to explore when they were there yesterday, and it gave them a familiar place to start.

They ate lunch at a local taverna in the Plaka neighborhood. And they wandered around the National Garden for a relaxing afternoon. They headed back to the Plaka neighborhood for supper and a stroll.

Nick and Elena had, by this time, grown comfortable with each other. Nick watched her in the National Garden as she cupped flowers and ran her hands across the rough bark of trees. He realized she was the first woman whose company let him forget himself and simply enjoy the moment. For the first time, he thought of her as more than just a traveling companion, but as someone he wanted to be with.

Who knows what the old monk saw between them or how much time he actually needed to accomplish his task, but he would not object if someone suggested that the time for Nick and Elena to spend together would be well worth the investment. Alfanas had a high regard for them. Both age and life experience had taught him not to waste opportunities. He would throw Nick and Elena together with the splendor of Athens, the warmth of the sun, and a healthy allotment of carefree time. Who knows what might grow in such a rich environment?

Over the next four days, they visited sites, shops, and restaurants around Athens. They even spent a day on a tour bus to Delphi. They enjoyed every moment. Nick spoke to both his parents and Chris, who by now was not merely jealous of his traveling friend but more than a little surprised by how casually Nick talked about hopping on planes and driving around strange cities. Chris felt more like a recluse and the one missing out, consumed by the mud of routine when compared to his jet-setting friend.

But by day four, both Nick and Elena were getting anxious about moving on to the next leg of their journey, Mystras. As Monday dawned, they woke up late and had breakfast at the same cafe where Viktor had caught up with them five days ago. In the afternoon, no call came from Brother Alfanas, so Nick and Elena headed out to visit Lake Vouliagmeni, just outside the city, to spend the rest of the afternoon. They visited shops on the way back in before returning to the hotel restaurant for supper.

As they walked through the lobby doors, they recognized Brother Alfanas, in flowing black robes and a cap, coming to meet them.

"Brother," cried Nick, "welcome! I hope all went well in Sparta?"

"Yes, yes, predictably well. But let's eat as we talk."

The host seated them at the table, and Nick and Elena unloaded the events of the last four days. Alfanas could not help but think how much like regular tourists they had become. They excitedly told stories, finished one another's sentences, and leaned into each other to share a laugh or a playful nudge. Alfanas smiled at them and at the memory of a younger him, so long ago, so many cares before. He had known both youth and love, both now blossomed before him.

"I have arranged for us to go to Mystras tomorrow. We will visit the ruins after checking into the hotel. I will start my vigil the next day when the sun goes down, and it will last until the next morning when the sun rises. You will ride in the back seat of the car with me when I go. You must keep yourselves hidden until about 7:00 in the evening when it is dark. Then, carefully exit the car and go into the church.

I will be in prayer, and you must not disturb me. I will not be a liar to the Metropolitan or cheat God of my pledge to him. You are on your own.

Take pictures of everything before you start your study, in order to return everything to the same condition you found it in by the time you leave. Be precise in this task. Return to the car in the dark when you leave the church. You can sleep in the back seat of the car until I come at sunrise. Keep quiet and out of sight. Getting back to the car will be easier said than done. The ruins of Mystras are very scenic. They perch precariously on the mountainside. You should ensure you download the map to your phone as the cell service might not be dependable.

Once we leave, we will head to the Greek restaurant to break our fast together. It is just across the street from the hotel. I can then give you my full attention, and we can go over what, if anything, you may have found. Let us aim to leave Athens by mid-morning. That will put us in Mystras by noon for lunch. We will grab a bite of the continental breakfast here before leaving. With that, I think I will leave you for your last evening in Athens. Good night."

Chapter 8: The Mystery at Mystras

Brother Alfanas took no liberties when it came to arriving on time. He called for Nick and Elena precisely at nine the following day. While not under formal time constraints, Alfanas preferred to be in Mystras by the early afternoon. The trip alone would take three hours, but he wanted his young companions to stay in their tourist relief mode for as long as possible.

The drive to Mystras from Athens would take them through the world's exceptionally beautiful landscapes and seascapes. Just experiencing the trip would be a meditation on beauty and artistry. They would stop here and there along the way, but he wanted them in Mystras and at the Byzantion Hotel by the afternoon.

Once settled in, they would head up to the Church of St. Demetrios together. The gentle breeze, scenic countryside, and small-village feel would be hard to pass up on a sunny day. It would be a good day to begin their explorations with a reconnaissance mission.

Nick took on his new role as a spectator with ease and relief. Brother Alfanas drove, freeing him to take the scenery in. The only ocean he had ever seen was the Long Island Sound. The beauty of the Aegean Sea on the coast of Athens, the pure smell of salt water in the brisk air, and the sunlight through the windshield were intoxicating. Nick wished to forget the entire business with Vasyl and to have a week to explore the shore, to hear the waves crashing and feel the spray that he saw as they drove by. He knew he was missing an opportunity for a richer connection with the natural world.

The thought unsettled him; the ruins loomed not as stones on a mountain but as a summons, one he dreaded yet seemed powerless to refuse.

Yet even as the beauty flowed past his window, the shadow of Vasyl lingered; he could not escape the reality for long, nor really pause it indefinitely.

As he watched the coast pass by, Nick reflected on his past life, feeling as if he existed in two worlds. In his other life, he saw himself as worldly and experienced, living in a progressive country, working in a diverse city, and studying at an Ivy League school. Yet that former life, defined by routine contracts and long commutes, now seemed foreign and detached from reality.

Here, in this reality, in this universal instant, the honest Nick drank in and experienced the actual diversity that New York City only suggests might exist in some other world. The City offered only two dimensions of experience: food and language; everything else was American.

In Greece, he experienced the landscape in three dimensions. The coastline transitioned from the Aegean Sea to the Taygetus Mountains, where the seascape gave way to views of mountain valleys, and the air shifted from sea air to cooler temperatures with the scent of woods and forests. Valleys were present on both sides of the road, and Nick observed the relative scale of his surroundings compared to places like New York City. He lowered the window to feel the breeze and take in the air.

They traveled through towns and villages with histories spanning thousands of years. Both ancient and contemporary architectural styles coexisted within the same space. Nick considered the generations that had constructed buildings from stone, wood, and metal to meet fundamental needs such as shelter, protection, and sustenance. These basic challenges and solutions gave rise to the cities and cultures of today.

They stopped to stretch their legs at Eleftherios Venizelos Square in Corinth. While Elena lived in Istanbul, she had never crossed the border into Greece. She had escaped the congested city of Istanbul for trips into the countryside. As children, her parents would take her siblings and her out of the city for day trips and picnics. She grew up on the Mediterranean, which made her experience, while new, also have a hint of the familiar.

Elena was used to the mix of old and new. Unlike countries with only a few centuries of history, Istanbul has 2,700 years beneath its streets. Each year, modern development reveals tunnels, foundations, and cisterns from the city's ancient past.

Elena had always wanted to visit Greece and the places her faith held sacred, like Corinth. Corinth was old, even by Istanbul's standards. Archaeological finds date back five thousand years. She even had family in Athens, but did not know where they lived. Most of her great aunts and uncles fled Türkiye, or the government had forced them into resettlement due to the hostilities between Türkiye and Greece. They would now have become part of the Rum Polites community in Greece, settled into communities, raised their families, and established careers. Yet, she wondered if they could ever entirely forget centuries of family connections to the land and history of Istanbul. Did Constantinople still call to them the way it did her?

So, for her, this was as close to a pilgrimage as she had ever been on. She, too, felt the overwhelming pull of the natural beauty, especially as it contrasted with her regular life in crowded Istanbul. Other odors inhabited the crowded streets of Istanbul. Elena sensed release from the stigma of being a minority, Rum. Acceptance and freedom hung in the Greek air as they did not at home.

Nick, meanwhile, envied her clarity. He felt like a man caught between shores; he longed to once again be settled in place and spirit, but the tug of the unknown in his lineage and heritage dragged him compulsively forward.

In the center of Eleftherios Venizelos Square stood a bronze Pegasus statue. Elena paused in front of it. She gazed at the neoclassical and modern buildings surrounding the square in an effortless blend of history and modernity. The rich aroma of Greek coffee and grilled souvlaki drifted from bustling cafes where locals and tourists sat, exchanging stories over their drinks. Traditional Greek music hummed softly from a nearby cafe, mixing with the chatter of visitors and the occasional cooing of pigeons.

Fresh sea air from the Gulf of Corinth brought in a hint of salt mingled with earthy rosemary and olive oil scents drifting from the local vendors. Footsteps on the stone pavement and distant traffic add a gentle rhythm to this lively yet serene square, where ancient and contemporary Greece meet harmoniously. She had never considered herself so much a part of what was happening around her and yet so much an individual at peace in her world.

Over the years, Alfanas had stood there or sat on the benches as he both took part and observed life going on about him. Now he wore black robes, but he remembered bygone years of being there in blue jeans and a tee shirt, with young ladies or friends now gone. He had known both peace and joy in this square. A place of past reprieves from intrigue, politics, and his role in the world's struggles. He smiled as he sat there and watched Nick and Elena explore this new world together. No, no, he would sit on the bench. They should explore the shops and try the local food. He would sit and remember other times when his eyes were as young as theirs and the wonder of the world had enticed him.

"But be back in an hour," instructed older brother. "We are only halfway to Mystras."

Once again, the mountains passed beneath them as the landscape streamed past the car's windows. The trio were fast approaching the end of the trip to Mystras, but for Nick and Elena, it also meant the end of their sabbatical from their quest. They would now have to return to tombs, stones, dangers, and mysteries.

They reached Mystras a little after two. At the center of the village of Mystras stood the Byzantion Hotel. Compared to the large cities Nick and Elena inhabited, Mystras Village fit the title: small, quaint and the perfect place to immerse into the cultural and historical ethos of the surrounding Medieval buildings and ruins. Brother Alfanas had been here several times and knew the sites well enough to find his way around without a map or GPS. Nick and Elena were eager to explore the small village and the surrounding ruins. They did not know what to expect, and it was overwhelming now that they were here.

On the mountain summit were the remains of the Byzantine castle and the ruins of Mystras, stretching down the side of the mountain. Nick's first thought was, *"Navigating that in the dark is going to be a challenge."*

92

Before heading out to the church and exploring, they found a cafe, five minutes' walk from the hotel. They ordered three tsai tou voudou, opting to forego caffeine for a local beverage experience. They sat outside in the warm sun to drink their tea, not bothered by the chill in the air. The warmth of the sun and tea added to the fresh air, settling them after their journey.

After their tea, they headed off to find the Church of St. Demetrios in the ruins of old Mystras. Brother Alfanas pulled into the upper car park, purchased their tickets, and descended the steep streets that were more similar to stretched-out stairs than our modern concept of roads.

As they walked, Alfanas explained, "Tomorrow, I have the Metropolitan's permission to park within the upper gate after sundown. This will put you inside the fence and give you some freedom to move. You will need to find your way as best you can in the dark. Google Maps will help you, but you will both need to try to remember the route we will take today. At night, it is perfectly dark here. You can get your bearings by the light pollution of Sparta," Alfanas waved his hand toward the sprawling modern city visible in the distance, "but because the moon is old, you will have little light on your path. No flashlights! There are no lights on the site after dark. Light will draw attention. To succeed, your journey will need both stealth and silence."

Nick had only read about ruins like these, and he found it hard to believe that this was a thriving village until the late 1700s. *The people must have been half-goat,"* he thought to himself. It was quite a climb.

The ruins of old Mystras hung on the mountainside, cut right into it. The architecture blended into the topography, yielding to the determination and creativity of humanity. And when he turned and looked over the valley, the vista overwhelmed him.

The scene stretching out before him revealed the little village and their hotel, as if right below his feet. Beyond a flat expanse stood the city of Sparta. Nick felt he could nearly step off Mount Taygetus and right into the heart of Sparta. He could see for miles.

Low vegetation and heather lined the streets of old Mystras. They could see and smell herbs and evergreens when the gusts died down to gentle breezes of the valley coming up the mountain slopes. Although only a few weeks had passed, Nick recognized that his sense of urban Western superiority actually reflected a lack of appreciation for diverse forms of beauty. He extended his hand towards the valley floor, as if attempting to make a physical connection, before retracting it and acknowledging the moment with a composed smile.

When Nick turned, he found Elena watching him with a smile on her face. He hung his head, almost ashamed, but she rubbed his arm with her hand, said nothing, and looked away as if to both recognize and grant him his vulnerable privacy. The moment passed, he lifted his head again and thought, *This moment was worth everything.* Seeing Alfanas now far ahead, he turned and headed up the road.

The walk through the remains of Byzantine homes and businesses gave way to the main street to the Church of St. Demetrios. The walls and buildings formed somewhat of a courtyard at the Church's entrance. Before the doors, there was an arched porch. The wooden door stood open.

"How quaint," Nick first thought on entering the restored church. He had envisioned a grand cathedral, a gaudy Notre Dame. After all, supposedly, more than one emperor supposedly had used this church for his coronation, yet it seemed small and private. Mystras had been the center of administration for the Despot of the whole Peloponnese, similar to being the capital of one of the American states. Furthermore, it served as the center of authority and power for the final Byzantine Emperor before he assumed the throne. This was a royal village.

Set into the floor, in front of the iconostasis, Nick saw the Coronation Stone. It looked like a flat white marble slab two feet wide by three feet long. Engraved on it was the double-headed Byzantine eagle, the symbol of the emperor who watched over and ruled both church and state. A woven border ran around the edge of the stone. Nick and Elena recognized it as the same image engraved on the four corners of the Evangelion in Sitka. Surrounding this somewhat plain marble slab were nondescript stone pavers. On the surface, nothing seemed to point to what to do next.

Nick could not put into words what went through him as he knelt by the stone, placing his hand on it. Constantine XI Palaiologos touched this stone and may even have knelt on it. He worshipped here and might have been crowned here. History hung heavy in the air, mixing with culture, mystery, and legend.

Nick wondered what would happen the following night. He had this strange feeling, a powerful urge of no longer being a tourist visiting old building, but this place felt like part of his DNA. He could not figure out why, nor how this all connected with the odd secret that Vasyl took with him to his grave. A secret that now called Nick's whole existential identity into question. Who was he? Why was he here? What did all these ghosts want from him, and would they finally speak tomorrow night?

Nick shivered and turned to the old monk as he asked, "Can we go now? I'm cold."

Alfanas had been watching him. His private moments were not entirely as hidden as Nick would have hoped. Alfanas had no answers for him and could only wonder what it must be like to discover that your family lived a life with a mysterious hidden past: Alfanas' skeletons he had chosen to hide a long time ago. But he knew them. When the past would whisper out of the darkness, he knew the incantations to silence them. However, what if the past whispered in your ear, and you felt the gentle tug of a person or place just beyond your ability to connect the pieces, like a word or name you can't remember?

"Yes, let's go. We need dinner and rest," Alfanas said as he placed a hand under Nick's arm to help him up from the floor. "We have accomplished what we needed to for today."

For Nick, the walk back up to the car differed from their descent, because their visit to the Coronation Stone unsettled him. The sun, still as bright, but shadows filled his eyes that its light could not pierce. He felt haunted, as if a strange force had crept into him as he touched that stone. Emperors in purple. Walls under siege. Dynasties of promise left unfulfilled.

"It's all too cold. I wish I had thought to bring my coat," he said out loud as if a coat could warm his disturbed soul.

They had dinner mostly in silence. Both Alfanas and Elena noticed the mood change that had crept over Nick. Neither could understand it. Both chose not to mention it. Nick had drawn into himself, distracted by feelings he could neither understand nor articulate. Elena didn't know quite what to think. Alfanas just looked at Nick, shook his head, and thought, *"The vacation is over, and the weight has once more descended. Well, it will be a mad dash now to the end of this."*

Chapter 9: The Lost Chronicle

Nick remained in his funk the next day. Brother Alfanas had last-minute details to settle with the Ephorate of Antiquities of Laconia, a division of the Greek Ministry of Culture that oversees the day-to-day operations of the Mystras site. So, Nick and Elena had the morning to explore the tourist village of Mystras that had sprung up on the edge of the archaeological site.

A quick walk down to the street brought them to the modern village of Mystras' central square. The morning mists dissipated as the sun rose and a warm breeze blew from the south. As the fog retreated, the familiar ruins emerged, a reconstituted dream from the night, given form to dispel the vapor-shrouded mystery.

But for Nick, the mystery remained. He could still feel the coolness of that stony touch that misted his heart, a haze that heeded not the sun's dismissal. They passed by the little cafe where they had their tea yesterday. In the village square, a bigger-than-life statue of Constantine XI Palaiologos, dedicated in 1978, proudly stood. As he looked at it, Nick thought, *"This really isn't the man who touched my heart yesterday."*

For Nick, this man of copper had a face chiseled by reclaimed ancient history and a physique toned by legend and myth, which belied more the hand of historical reconstruction, if not an invention, than reality. This Constantine, clad in ideals of heroism and unapproachability, missed human fallibility. He seemed too big for Mystras. Yesterday, as his hand touched the stone, he imagined Constantine the man: a complex mixture of human ideals, reality, and, above all, a conviction to live into the role he had proudly inherited.

Alfanas' recounting of Constantine's life echoed a fatalism in his defiance, mixed with a complexity latent in the human spirit when pushed to its limits. Wealth, privilege, ego, and power—yes, characteristic parts of his life—but in the end, he did not cower and flee. He did not see his sacrificed life as folly. Could he have seen it as the future?

Nick eerily connected with his imagined Constantine XI, as the ever-shifting winds of fate drove Nick to … where? Would it be the last stand before a dreadful gate? Not all endings are happy. Yesterday wasn't the first time Nick had felt someone walk on his grave, but this time, the tread seemed heavier and from someone long dead.

By noon, they had walked up and down the main street, sat outside for a cup of coffee, and returned to the hotel, where they expected to wait for Brother Alfanas to join them in the lobby. But already waiting for them, Alfanas greeted them as they entered. The fresh air and sunlight had eased Nick's haunted feeling from last night. Now, anxiety about what tonight might unleash settled like a cloud veiling the full warmth of the sun.

"Let us go for something to eat, and we can talk," Alfanas said, motioning toward the door.

The trio walked across the street to a restaurant for lunch. Seated and having ordered, Alfanas began, "After this, we must rest. I'm glad you spent the morning out. Mystras is a small village, but it holds its own charm. We will have a long night ahead of us. I must be through the gates by about 5:20 if I am to be settled in the church by sunset. You will be huddled in the back seat. I will have candles going, and one of you should keep watch as inconspicuously as you can.

Though no one lives at the site, we cannot tell who might be watching, especially if they see strange lights on the mountain. I must remind you that we risk the reputation of my house and the Metropolitan's trust if we are caught. Do not fail me," he said, his tone heavy with unspoken consequences.

"Can you tell us a little about the history of Saint Demetrios?" Nick asked.

"Yes. It is an old church. It is also a precious structure that has endured only slight modification over the last one thousand years.

The old village of Mystras remained inhabited until the massacres of 1825, which led to its abandonment. It is one of the best medieval sights in the world.

The church itself is but one of several holy buildings in old Mystras. It was built in the 13th century as a metropolitan church. I know it does not look like it now, but Mystras was a special place when the Byzantines lived here. There was a communal egalitarianism that existed in no other place. It would not be uncommon to run into Queen Helena at the market or meet the great philosopher Plethon strolling the streets. The powerful walked the roads with regular folks.

Here, tempered by Roman thought, flourished ancient Greek culture in a brief Byzantine Renaissance, one that would ultimately succumb to the fate of Constantinople, to be lost to the world."

Alfanas' gaze had drifted from his plate out the window into the courtyard where birds sang, and the chill breeze carried the scent of roasting lamb into the streets. Yet his set eyes gazed far beyond the courtyard, into a dark and remorse-filled history. He mourned not only for Mystras but for all of humanity, the kingdoms, and cities lost to conquest, the libraries, and art destroyed by fire, and the wisdom of centuries discarded in moments of violence and greed. *"Humanity,"* he thought, *"is drawn like a moth to the flame of its own ego, blind to the treasures it consumes, powerless over the lusts that drive it."*

Nick detected something more profound than historical grief in the old monk's expression, a profound sadness for humanity's very soul. Alfanas started, sighed, and returned to finishing his lunch. Time slipped away, and he suspected that he and his young new friends raced to protect something of worth from the same fate as Mystras and Constantinople—abuse, or, worse, destruction.

"Come," Alfanas finally said, his tone lighter though the grief still lingered in his eyes. "Let us finish our lunch, return to the hotel, and get some hours of rest before the sun goes down."

Alfanas roused them with a knock at the door at 5:00. He had loaded the car with blankets, food, and water for them during the night. As he bundled them into the backseat of the car and threw old books and papers over them as a ruse to a disorganized academic old monk, they drove off to the ruins to be in the gates before sunset.

As they drove, Alfanas cautioned them again about staying as hidden as possible until dark had claimed the mountain and all the attendants had gone home. Carefully, they should leave the car and walk the path to the church.

"Once inside the gate, you must remain unseen until nightfall. If you're discovered, your quest will end. Move as shadows, silent and swift," he cautioned.

With that, they had arrived at the gate. Because of Brother Alfanas' preparations the day before, the attendants greeted him as a friend, trusted and known, letting him pass with a brief look at the car. Alfanas parked, prayed, and told his two companions, "I am off to my fast and vigil. You are now on your own until tomorrow morning. God be with you." Hearing the car door open and shut, they knew they were alone.

As Nick and Elena huddled together on the floor, Nick thought to himself how bizarre it all was. Fate has a way of weaving a thread of irony in life. Here he was with a woman whose first impression repulsed and somehow fascinated him. Now they were so intimately connected that this time together, with their faces so close that they drew warmth from one another, hearing and feeling each other breathing, seemed so natural and comfortable. They dozed and thought but rarely talked during that time.

Nick felt his phone vibrating in his pocket. He had silenced it and set an alarm for 8:00 to ensure it was dark enough.

"Time to go," he whispered to Elena as he pushed the blankets, books, and papers off them. Brother Alfanas covered the car's interior lights with black plastic to keep it perfectly dark. Nick peeked around, and everything was silent. Elena, on the sheltered side, swung open the door nearest a group of bushes and silently climbed onto the ground by the car. Huddled down, they made their way to the ancient streets that led up the steep slope of Mount Taygetus.

Their descent into the dark was torturous, having to keep close to the ground and off to the sides of the road, tripping over a bush or stubbing their foot against a stone or one of the steps built into the road. When that happened, the noise caused them to pause, stop breathing, and listen to hear anything that might show betrayal or unknown footfalls.

Checking each other as one or the other's imagination fancied a sound that might suggest more than a natural cause, they plodded forward. The rustle of the chill wind through the leaves and over the heather filled the evening with sounds, making it seem even chillier. Night birds called out, and an occasional alarming rustle in the underbrush of a nocturnal rodent on its own nightly business.

They made steady progress toward the church courtyard in the near-complete dark. On drawing near the church, they could see the faint flicker of candlelight out of the windows and through the door that Alfanas had left open just enough to let them pass. They quickly crawled into the dim church and fully closed the door to the night.

Candles placed on the floor flickered in the draft, casting living shadows across the ancient walls as the dim frescos of saints and Savior faded in and out of focus, dodging the shadows of the wandering light. The scent of beeswax filled the air like incense rising to God. Brother Alfanas was prostrate on the floor before the iconostasis in prayer.

Nick felt as if he were trespassing on sacred space and time, eavesdropping on a holy dialogue, silent yet heavy on the air, thick with mystery. He sensed the solemnity of the space. Nick and Elena stayed at the back of the sanctuary, fearing to disturb the divine dance they witnessed. But they were called there; without them, none of this would have happened; they were part of this dance. Neither Nick nor Elena was a leading partner like Alfanas, but they coordinated with the shadows on the periphery.

Nick turned the flash off on his phone. Elena risked enough light from a flashlight for Nick to take pictures of the Coronation Stone and the floor around it so they could later return it to the same condition they found it. Nick took out two soft brushes from his backpack, and Elena covered two flashlights with cheesecloth to make them dim but usable.

Nick started at one end of the stone and Elena at the other. Neither of them knew what they were looking for, but a close examination of the stone or border might reveal a clue or inconsistency pointing to their next move. But the marble slab showed no visible or apparent clue. Alfanas might be able to spot something in the photos they were taking as they cleared the surfaces and sides of the stone, but they could see nothing.

Next, they began working on the stones that paved the floor around the marble slab. The pavers were irregular, oddly irregular.

Once again, they divided up their work. While visiting yesterday, Nick had noticed the pavers. They planned to take their brushes and explore the cracks in the stones to see if anything might suggest a difference in the setting material, saving all the dust in piles to fill the cracks once they were done. It would be a time-consuming and fiddly task. Nick and Elena were prepared to be at it until just before dawn. Nick sighed and glanced over at the black puddle that was the monk on the floor. "I almost envy him," he said under his breath as he started on his first crack.

After working for about three hours, examining deep into the cracks of the stones and the area around the marble, Nick moved over to start on one of the light-colored, smaller paving stones. Halfway through the far edge he noticed something unusual on the side of the stone, maybe an eighth of an inch down from the top surface. On the side of the stone, he could just make out a carved line.

"Elena, I've found something, I think," he whispered, barely to be heard, "come here and take a look."

Elena joined him in inspecting the stone. They both worked on the crack, digging down about an inch before reaching the bottom of the paving stone. With the seam between the stones slightly larger than the thickness of one of their knives, making it an arduous task to remove the sediment, they finally were able to confirm the existence of engravings into the side of the paver.

"Let's clear all around the stone down as far as possible," Nick whispered. "Then we can maybe use a couple of knives to lift it gently so that we can read what is written on the side."

Patiently, they took their time in order to ensure they cleared as much of the debris as possible from all sides of the stone before lifting it. They knew it would be impossible to pry up only one edge without jamming the stone against its neighbors. The paving stones were too close together. They needed to lift the stone evenly from all sides, careful not to chip or damage it. They had brought plenty of small tools, a couple of knives, and scrapers.

With both of them working in unison, they wiggled the stone patiently until they could slip their tools under it. They had to start over several times until they both became accustomed to the weight and the ability to work together. Finally, they were able to lift it high enough to secure first one, then two, and finally, all four sides with either a scraper or a knife beneath it.

Nick wanted the stone secure enough to examine and photograph the side. He hadn't considered moving it out of place. He didn't want to risk debris falling in and destabilizing it so that it rocked.

With the side fully exposed, he could take a photo of the engraving: a shield divided by two crossbars, with the letter "B" mirrored in each quadrant. The design seemed deliberate and purposeful, though its meaning was a mystery to them both. Nick and Elena exchanged confused looks and shrugged. Brother Alfanas would need to examine the image in the morning to see if he could tell them what it meant.

As Nick prepared to lower the stone, Elena touched his shoulder and whispered, "Let's check the bottom; there might be something there."

Nick conceded and nodded. Working together, they both gently turned the stone over. The paver had no further marks on the bottom.

However, in the subfloor, there was an outline where the solid medium used to stabilize the paving stones had a rectangular block of rock, approximately seven inches wide by four inches long, filled with sand.

"I think we should dig it out if we can," Nick whispered. "We will need to work quickly, as the night is getting on."

With a cloth laid on the Coronation Stone, and using their hands as shovels, they began digging out the sand. It went down about a foot, and at the bottom it ended in a solid flat stone. Nick took his brush and cleared away the last of the sand from the bottom.

Once they had excavated the sand, there remained a perfectly rectangular marble shaft with no seam or break except at the very bottom. The bottom revealed a lip on one side, as if a large, square piece of marble were placed there. Nick used his pocketknife to work on both the bottom and top of the marble square. Slowly, it slid out to reveal a compartment.

After taking the capping stone out, Nick put his hand in the compartment and felt something cylindrical, cold, solid, and heavy. He slid it out into the shaft, which fit perfectly, leaving just enough room for him to raise it out. It was made of lead, and on it, it bore two devices: the double-headed eagle and the same inscription as on the side of the paving stone.

A broad smile spread across both their faces as the dim light from their flashlights cast the first light this cylinder had seen in six hundred years. Nick whispered, "I think we found what we were looking for. Let's get everything back as it was and get out of here before it gets too light. We have to have enough darkness to return to the car."

Nick placed the cylinder in his backpack. They reversed the work that had taken them so long. In about an hour, they had everything back together. They eased the last dust back into the cracks of the paving stones and marble slab and returned the area around the Coronation Stone to the same condition they had found it.

Nick stepped back, looked at the photo on his phone, and compared it to the floor, smiled, and whispered to Elena, "Perfect. Let's go."

Nick and Elena strenuously made their way back to the car parked at the top gate, but they made it before any revealing light had dawned. It wouldn't be a long wait for Brother Alfanas to return. They were able to crawl under their blankets, books, and papers on the floor of the back seat, relieved to be in the safety of concealment.

The warmth, ebbing adrenaline, and lack of sleep overtook them, and they fell sound asleep. They didn't even hear Brother Alfanas quietly open the car door, start the car, and pull through the gate. It wasn't until he stopped at the hotel that they woke up.

Alfanas peered over the seat and said, "Okay, you two, wake up and crawl out from under there. It's time to break our fast and share our news."

The weary group walked across the street to a little restaurant. Nick and Elena recounted in detail what they had done and found the night before. Nick left the cylinder in the car, but he had photos of the stone and cylinder on his phone to show Alfanas.

Alfanas took the phone, looked intently at the photos, before he commented, "You both have done extremely well. Finding the engraving on the side of the stone was a good catch. And," looking at Elena, he added, "it's also good that you suggested turning the stone over. I'm not sure I would have been able to get permission for another vigil to get back into the church."

"You do realize, Nick, that you are probably the first person in over five hundred years to have held that lead cylinder. It is a remarkable find."

Alfanas looked at the photos again to let the significance of what he had just said sink in before he continued, "The symbols are plain. The double-headed eagle represented the imperial Byzantine rule of the church and state. The other symbol is called a tetragrammatic cross. It is commonly used and associated with the Palaiologos family. As much as I would love to open the lead cylinder you found and look at the contents today, I think we will wait until we are all rested and fresh. We will only after we recover can we carefully, respectfully, and cautiously open the cylinder. But for now, we should finish and get back to the hotel for sleep."

All three fell fast asleep once settled back in their rooms. There would be time in the afternoon or evening to investigate what they had found.

Chapter 10: The Chronicle of the Last Emperor Begins

Nick and Elena slept restlessly. The lead cylinder rested on the table in front of the window. Nick wondered what it contained and how it would lead them to the next series of clues. To his mind, every step they took along the path seemed only to heighten the mystery of the elusive goal on their journey. Other than lineage and self-discovery, the only real clue came from their enemy, Viktor, who alluded to a secret that Vasyl took to his grave. Was this all about money? Granted, wealth would be nice, but he would give a pretty penny never to see Viktor again. The remembrance of him sent shivers up Nick's spine even now.

Every so often, Nick heard the other bed creak as Elena tossed and turned, finding sleep as interrupted as he did, he guessed. As his mind wandered, Nick realized he had not spoken to Chris or his family in about a week. While not unusual, he tried to check in routinely; his sister would still track his phone, which would have reported his location. Apart from stopping in, he seldom called. With everything going on, he had forgotten to keep them in the loop, which made him wonder if they were thinking of him.

Elena dealt with the waiting in her own thoughts. Because of Nick's restlessness, she knew they were both awake but hesitant to get up. As she spent time with him, Elena found she had grown rather attached to Nick. She smiled to herself as she remembered back to New York and her naïve, unnecessary attempt to manipulate him.

Unbidden, she also wondered where things were leading them. Not that doubt crept in, but the path now seemed less straightforward than when she had planned the adventure out in her private thoughts in Istanbul. She had hoped for a supportive and limited role in the progression of events in which Nick would decisively take the lead with a more straightforward path forward. It all seemed so muddled now. But she liked Nick.

Occasionally, the heater would kick on, releasing white noise into the room so that the sounds of folks in the hallway or outside enjoying the day receded, as did the hushed sounds of breathing, sighing, and shifting in the bed. A soft knock at the door released Nick and Elena from their naps, and they both jumped at the opportunity to let Brother Alfanas in.

"I hope you had enough sleep," Alfanas said as he entered the room, but a note in his voice betrayed a knowing that they probably had not. His black robes rustled and disturbed the still air as he entered. The aroma of incense from prayers gone by and beeswax from the night gently followed him.

"Where is your treasure?" he asked.

"On the table," Nick gestured to the table on the other end of the room, in front of the heavily curtained window.

Alfanas seated himself at the table and carefully picked up the cylinder. He said, "Ah, well, let's see how well you have learned, shall we?" He pointed to what looked like a stumpy cross made to fit into the square. In the quadrants were what looked like the letter "B," but on the left side, mirrored, somewhat resembling a malformed butterfly. "What is this?"

Elena, now looking over Nick's shoulders, her hands resting on them with a casual familiarity regarding his personal space, answered before Nick even focused on what Alfanas pointed to, "A tetragrammatic cross."

Byzantium, relics, and religion were her world. The term may have been new this morning, but she would never forget it. Nick looked up at her as if to say, *"Give me a chance,"* though the words never left his mouth. She squeezed his shoulder, grinned, and winked at him with the intention that he could have the first shot at the next one.

He didn't have to wait long.

"And this one," continued Alfanas, "what is it?"

He pointed to a very familiar symbol for Nick. Nick had seen it first on the cover of the Evangelion, the image in the four corners that brought them to Mystras. He remembered the same image carved in marble on the Coronation Stone. He had this one.

"It's the double-headed eagle signifying the Emperor of Byzantium," he said quickly, as if to do so before Elena.

"Good, very good," Alfanas and Elena exchanged a glance that seemed to appreciate that their young novice had paid attention. "What would these two symbols suggest about this case and its contents?"

"It must have something to do with the Emperor of Byzantium." Said Nick, clearly taking the next turn to provide an answer, "But which emperor?"

"Well," said Alfanas, "I suspect it would be safe to say that it would have to be someone of the Palaiologos line. We are in their domain, and the use of the tetragrammatic cross became as close to a national flag or trademark under their rule of Constantinople. This … this is an imperial treasure untouched for over 500 years. This is a time capsule, which lay in wait for the preordained hour, the right hands, and eyes, to hold and behold it. Look, my hand trembles at the weight of our charge," and indeed his hands shook as he held them out for examination before he continued, "Nick, pass me your pocketknife."

The curtains closed for sleep, now kept out would be prying eyes. They had no reason to suspect that anyone would come along and peer inside, yet a solemn sullenness filled the room, brightened by the glow of the hanging lamp over the table. Alfanas placed the cylinder on a towel to avoid a knife slip or unintentional damage.

He had worked with both documents and artifacts for many years, valuable training to proceed with caution and to cause as little destruction as possible. Slowly opening the pocketknife, closing his eyes for a brief prayer, and then hesitating slightly before carefully touching the tip of the knife to the furthest point away from the historic seals.

Whoever preserved the contents rightly chose lead for the container. It is very malleable at room temperature, has a low melting point for a metal, and can be opened easily without damaging the contents when the time comes. Protected in its marble crypt for over five hundred years, the case looked untouched by time. The hard marble added the strength to resist any crushing blow that would damage the lead and break the airtight seal.

"Airtight," Alfanas took a moment to consider. The air from that vessel had not been free for centuries, and Nick's knifepoint stood poised to disturb what someone highly positioned in the emperor's household and inner circle had placed there. Could it even have been sealed by the emperor himself?

The knife scratched against the cylinder's surface, leaving a faint mark. Slowly, a slit formed, not deep enough to endanger the contents within but sufficient to gauge the thickness of the lead casing. Now confident of its thickness, Alfanas moved with increased precision. Carefully, he cut along the inner edge of the cylinder's end, keeping the blade level with its interior surface as it traveled around the circumference. With the cut completed, he gently worked the edge until the cap separated from the cylinder.

The contents fit the cylinder so precisely that they were revealed when the end fell off: a roll of parchment. Alfanas slid the scroll out onto the towel and put on white cotton gloves to touch it. As he did so, the odor of stale, centuries-old air hovered briefly in the air. Alfanas paused, closed his eyes, and inhaled as if not to let the moment pass unmarked.

"It's written in Greek," said Nick. Obvious Greek lettering filled both sides of the parchment. As Alfanas unrolled, the musty smell continued to linger. He exposed about six inches of the scroll, revealing a header written in red. The ink was crisp, with gold leafing still firmly adhering to the page, even with its first unrolling in so many years. Like a coiled spring, the parchment relaxed its tight coils hesitantly, and Alfanas needed to gently hold it open, hoping it would not damage or rip the scroll. Within the upper left of the header border was the symbol of the double-headed eagle, outlined in red with a gold leaf body, and in the lower right quadrant, a red and gold tetragrammatic cross.

Nick looked at the scroll and saw the words in red:

Η ΙΣΤΟΡΙΑ ΤΟΥ ΕΣΧΑΤΟΥ ΒΑΣΙΛΕΩΣ

Περὶ τῆς Τελευταίας Μάχης Α'

Γράφει Κύριος Μέγας Σκευοφύλαξ Αλέξιος Σακελλάριος, Ἔτους ΚΣΔ'

"What does it say?" Nick asked.

"It reads," Alfanas replied.

"*The History or Chronicle of the Last Emperor*

Concerning the Final Battle 1

Written by Lord Great Skeuophylax Alexios Sakellaris, in the Year 6954.'"

"Alexios Sakellaris," repeated Alfanas, "Elena, he must be a relative of yours … maybe?"

"I don't know. Five hundred years is a long time to track lineage, especially after so much has happened to us. I am sure that, given time, Papa could look it all up, and possibly one day, God willing, we will have that time, but not now. It would make sense that the family pledge would start with him and his agreement with Constantine XI."

But she left unsaid the feeling that came over her at the thought that one of her distant grand sires had written these words. He had seen the inside of the imperial palace in its glory. More than that, because of his title, he worked directly with the emperor, managed the accounts and safeguarded the empire's wealth. He had overseen its defense alongside the emperor. While this was not a letter to her, it was as close as a child gets to a parent, some 25 generations removed.

Some of the puzzle pieces were now falling into place. Still having no clue why Nick and Elena's families were joined at the hip through history, at least Elena's heritage now connected, concretely establishing Elena's connection to the journey fate had them on. To Nick, the scroll suggested Elena had emerged as the primary actor in the progression of their quest, and he looked more like a supporting cast member. He didn't know if he felt relieved or sad as Vasyl seemed to have faded into the background.

"What does this bit mean?" asked Nick as he pointed to the last line.

"It means that Alexios wrote it. It also refers to his title as 'Skeuophylax.'"

"What's that?"

"Μέγας Σκευοφύλαξ," Alfanas read from the scroll, "used in the secular sense, which seems most applicable here, would suggest Alexios Sakellaris as a senior keeper of treasures, perhaps the imperial regalia, or even the arsenal. He would answer only to Constantine XI, and we can assume that he worked closely with him on Tuesday, May 29, 1453, the final and fateful day Constantinople and Byzantium fell. If there is anyone able to recount his last days, it would be he. Notice that this scroll is written a year after the fall of Constantinople: the Byzantine calendar year 6954 equals the Gregorian year 1454."

Alfanas paused as he admired the document on the table before him.

"I had never heard of this Chronicle before. It is likely Alexios compiled it and hid it to preserve the history of his master. He passed along a secret that remained relatively safe until Vasyl and the Russian Revolution appeared. That's when a break in the hereditary transmission line became necessary. Vasyl Palevych, Oleksandr Mykhailenko/Paleon, and Elena, your great-grandfather, must have felt so threatened that they needed to bury a great secret to protect Vasyl's family literally. It is fascinating how they wound and twisted it into legend and history."

He cautiously unrolled more of the manuscript. As he reached the end, he furrowed his brow and shook his head from side to side, and said, "It is unusual to have this type of header on a manuscript of this nature, but it looks like, in our modern terms, this is a partial copy of a chapter from a book. The title of the book is *The Chronicle of the Last Emperor*. The chapter is titled 'Concerning the Final Battle.' But this is section one. Oddly, Alexios broke the chapter up into separate sections for some reason. Section one might reveal all that is necessary, or perhaps section one points to where section two resides, and so on. We won't know until I have time to read the whole thing."

Brother Alfanas reflected for a minute. Contemplating what to do and where to go, he looked at them and said, "I will take this back to my room. Here are the keys to the car. Tomorrow, you must occupy yourselves. Don't sit around here and wait for me. I do not know how long this will take. Go to Sparta and spend the day. When you get back in the evening, we can eat together here. I should be able to make sense of the scroll's contents by then. You will be on your own this evening and tomorrow. Good night."

Without another word, Brother Alfanas wrapped the lead remains in the towel, tucked it under his arm, and cradled the scroll with a tissue wrapped around it in one hand before leaving for his room.

Chapter 11: The Chronicle Reveals

After Alfanas had left, neither Nick nor Elena felt much like going. Their thoughts were both anxious and eager about what Brother Alfanas would learn from the scroll. Nick likened it to Christmas Eve and distracted himself by making plans for the next day's adventures.

He turned to Elena. "Another tourist day in Greece!"

While he sounded cheerful enough, part of him could not escape the twinge of anxiety. On their own, they would be vulnerable. Nick believed that the menace of Viktor dogged them despite incarceration. He must have other eyes watching them.

Nick kept his fears to himself. He turned and asked Elena, "So, I'm going to Google some things to do in Sparta tomorrow. Do you have any suggestions?"

"I have never been there, so no, but I would like to keep things lower key. I don't want a lot of crowds, yet I don't want to be all by ourselves either."

"Hmm," Nick uttered with a wry grin on his face, "was it something I said?"

"No, not you … of course not you. It's just…" her words trembled away into silence.

"Viktor," Nick sighed.

"Yes. It's silly, but it's like I expect him to pop up, even though I know it is not rational." Elena looked away.

As he turned and took out his phone, he said, "We will need to be careful but not paranoid. We don't *know* anything," he dramatically emphasized the word 'know'.

"I don't mind them watching, as long as they don't try to touch. However, I think Brother Alfanas weighed the dangers. He would not have let us go if there were trouble. So, I think we are safe, but you are right about tomorrow. I'll see what I can find online for low-key things to do in Sparta!"

Elena smiled and drew up beside Nick, slipping her arm under his as he searched the internet for things to do in Sparta. With their plans made and the decision to set out early in the morning, they decided on an early night.

The next morning, Nick woke to the soft hum of the heater and the faint light of dawn filtering through the heavy curtains. The room's warmth lulled him, but his mind immediately drifted to the scroll Alfanas had taken the night before.

He rolled over and glanced at his phone. They had a day to fill before the monk's promised revelations. Across the room, already up, Elena tied her hair back as she peeked through the curtains.

"Good morning," she said with a small smile, catching his eyes in the window's reflection. "I thought we should grab a quick breakfast at the hotel and head to the museum. It's not far, and we'll have enough time to enjoy the exhibits before the square gets busy."

By mid-morning, they walked through the subdued halls of the Archaeological Museum of Sparta. Nick enjoyed examining the display of Byzantine mosaics, marveling at the intricate details, while Elena studied a small collection of Byzantine coins. She playfully wondered if Alexios Sakellaris' hands held any of these when they were new and shiny. It wasn't until Nick's stomach growled that they realized they needed to leave.

After a leisurely lunch at a cafe in the central square, where the hum of conversation and the clinking of coffee cups provided a pleasant soundtrack, they drove out toward the Menelaion, the ruins of an ancient Greek sanctuary dedicated to the Homeric king Menelaus.

Leading to the site, a narrow road wound through olive groves and low hills, offering glimpses of the valley below. Few tourists wandered the modest ruins, but the hilltop view was breathtaking—the Eurotas valley stretching to the horizon.

"Imagine the people who have stood here and looked out on this," Elena said to anyone within earshot, as Nick took photos. "The same hills, the same river. It's strange, isn't it? How much has changed, and yet how much would still be familiar to Vasyl or Alexios—the hills and valleys remain the same."

Nick nodded, pocketing his phone. "Strange and … grounding. Like, no matter what we're chasing, this," he gestured to the view, "will still be here when we're done."

The sun dipped low in the sky as they made their way back to the hotel in Mystras. Nick pulled into the gravel lot and glanced at the clock on the dashboard. With a contented sigh, Elena climbed out of the car. For a moment, the tension of the past days seemed to lift. But as they walked toward the hotel door, Nick caught himself scanning the shadows, wondering what secrets the evening might yet hold.

Nick and Elena did not want to disturb Alfanas immediately and returned to their room to wait for him to knock as usual. It would be hard to wait. All day, they had been anticipating returning to hear his report. They had a fun day but wanted answers to their questions more than sightseeing and souvenirs.

As they came down the hall, Alfanas, evidently keeping an eye out for them, opened his door and invited them in. Having fulfilled the customary inquiries into the nature of each other's day, Alfanas directed them to the chairs about the table on which lay the scroll. He thumbed through a notebook as he spoke:

"Well, this is a fascinating document that must not leave Greece or fall into the wrong hands. As I worked on it, I took photographs and notes. We will plan to wrap it up and secure it in the Metropolitan's safe in Sparta now that I have examined it. He will not mind allowing me to keep a valuable under his care until we return."

Nick and Elena exchanged glances when Alfanas said the word "return."

"Yes, yes," he continued, acknowledging their looks of surprise, "we will need to leave Greece and head back to Istanbul, where I think we will find the rest of the story somewhere under the city. Here is what my brief skimming of the scroll tells me.

This section of *The Chronicle of the Last Emperor* recounts the final battle at the Golden Gate and Constantine's heroic defense until a Turkish soldier struck him down. When the sultan's army breached the historically impenetrable outer walls of Constantinople, Constantine reportedly cried out, 'The city is lost, but I live. Long live Rome!' After which, he divested himself of all his royal regalia, entrusting them to your ancestor," nodding to Elena, "Alexios. Alexios sent them to be deposited aboard a secret merchant vessel moored in the Harbor of Theodosius.

In this section, Alexios does not say where the vessel went, but he alludes to his preparations to save what little wealth, royal regalia, and relics remained in the city. Unlike Constantine, Alexios realized that it was only a matter of time before the walls would fall to the powerful cannon of Mehmed II, especially the 27-foot-long cannon known as the Basilica. Alexios looked out from the walls that had stood for nearly a millennium but had not been built to withstand a cannonball 30 inches in diameter. Once the walls fell, the vastly outnumbered Byzantine army would be lost.

But Alexios was a practical man. He had been arranging for this day for years. He was perfectly placed to fulfill his mandate to protect the resources of the empire. With the last of Constantine's regalia secured and the ship holding the most sacred treasures of Constantinople on its way, Alexios rejoined the emperor in the fighting before the Golden Gate.

Constantine had now put on the armor of a regular infantryman. I will spare you the details of the battle. Let us say that it was horrific and grim. Constantine took several hits but kept on fighting. He would give his all in the battle and defense of Rome. Alexios and his three sons fought nearby to protect the Emperor with life and limb. One of Alexios' sons was cut down, but the rest of them fought on until Constantine himself fell.

At this point, none of the Ottoman soldiers knew they had felled the emperor. Alexios and his remaining two sons rushed to defend Constantine's body. They fought off and killed the man who had struck Constantine, lifted the Emperor, and brought him back within the shadow of the Golden Gate, wounded and unconscious but still alive!

It is here that the story takes an unusual twist. Alexios had prepared for several contingencies. Had Constantine fallen at the main Rheios gate, there was a secretive route of transport provided for him or his body to be taken and hidden from the infidels.

But five years prior, Alexios had a vision that he should prepare a secondary way at the Golden Gate, a way that would connect to a vast branching labyrinth of cisterns and water channels that lay under the streets of Constantinople. The underground of Constantinople is steeped in mystery. Whatever Alexios intended to hide, it has remained in the dark, untouched for centuries.

This section of the book does not chart the course they took or tell us anything beyond the fact that Constantine XI was taken via this underground to be cared for at the Monastery of Saint John the Forerunner. That is where this part ends.

But it looks like we are on the trail to find not only the mystery of both your families but also the artifacts that Alexios saved from the plunder of the Ottoman Turks. If Alexios was successful and those artifacts still exist, we could restore to the world the refined, unique culture of Byzantium."

Elena sat quietly, her fingers brushing against the grain of the table as Alfanas's words lingered in her mind. The scroll's revelation had shifted something deep within her. The quest, no longer only about uncovering her family's role in a forgotten history, concerned the legacy and future of her people, exactly why she had traveled to New York. For centuries, the Rum had lived on the edges of the city they once called their own, their voices silenced, their legacy scattered. But what if they could find something here? Something tangible, something undeniable? Something restorative?

Her thoughts turned to the treasures Alexios had hidden away. Byzantine regalia and sacred artifacts weren't just relics; they were symbols of a culture too refined and unique to be erased. Perhaps if these treasures could be recovered, they could give the Rum pride again. They could prove to the world and themselves that their story wasn't over.

She glanced at Nick, his brow furrowed as he stared at the scroll. He had a stake in this, too, though she doubted he fully grasped what it meant to her people. But maybe that didn't matter. He continued to share this journey with her. Together, they might reclaim something far more significant than either had imagined. Elena straightened in her seat, her resolve hardening. Whatever lay beneath the streets of Istanbul, she would see it through, not just for herself, but for them all.

Alfanas then showed them the last photo he had taken of the end of the scroll, and pointing to a piece of the text, he said, "In Medieval Greek, this reads:

Ἐν τοῖς σπλάγχνοις τῆς Χρυσῆς Πύλης κεῖται ἡ μοῖρα τοῦ μαρμάρινου βασιλέως.

In English translation: 'Within the bowels of the Golden Gate lies the fate of the marble emperor.' Remember the legend that Constantine XI Palaiologos did not die but rests, turned into a marble statue buried beneath the Golden Gate, to wait for revivification to lead a new army to reconquer Constantinople.

Whatever that may mean, our next set of answers awaits us beneath the streets of Istanbul. We will need to retrace our steps now. We will go to Sparta in the morning. You will accompany me to the Metropolitan's offices, and then we will head back to Athens, where we will spend the night. Before bed tonight, I will phone the Monastery of Agia Eirini Chrysovalantou in Lykovrisi, Attica. Once we are back in Athens, we must be careful. We cannot be sure that Viktor's friends are not watching the hotels and the airport.

The monastery will provide us with accommodation for the evening and is unlikely to be under surveillance. The next day, we will fly to Istanbul. Elena, do not call your parents. I know it is hard, but we must not expose them to risk if we are followed. Remember and take Viktor's threat seriously. It is bad enough that you met them before at the airport, but at the moment, only Viktor knows what they look like, and probably not who they are.

That is enough information for tonight. We have a long day ahead of us tomorrow, with much traveling. We must be more guarded once we get back to Athens. Good night."

As they settled in for the night, Nick couldn't shake the words from the scroll: 'Within the bowels of the Golden Gate lies the fate of the marble emperor.' They haunted him, lingering like a shadow over what was to come.

Chapter 12: A Dead End in Istanbul

The first rays of dawn had barely brushed the hills of Mystras when Nick, Elena, and Brother Alfanas set out from the Byzantion Hotel. As they loaded their modest belongings into the car, Nick continued to consider what had been discussed the night before. The words of the scroll, 'Within the bowels of the Golden Gate lies the fate of the marble emperor' echoed in his mind, weaving themselves into the fabric of the journey ahead.

Brother Alfanas, seated in the passenger seat, adjusted his robes and directed Nick toward the winding road that led out of the village. While his eyes betrayed a quiet urgency, the monk exuded a demeanor of calm.

On his lap, his hand rested on a brown paper-wrapped package that contained the lead cylinder and scroll. Elena sat in the back seat. Her hands wrapped around a travel mug of tea. She stared out the window, lost in thought as the car hummed along the narrow roads, leaving Mystras behind. Elena could not help but be sad heading home. She loved her parents, but because of Viktor's threat, she couldn't let them know she was coming.

As the countryside unfolded around them, the ride turned out to be quieter than the trip down. The road cut through familiar valleys and hills, but they were returning to danger. Nick glanced at Elena in the rearview mirror. She seemed deep in contemplation. Her lips pressed together as if holding back words. For a moment, he considered breaking the silence, but something about the solemnity of the morning held him back.

Their first stop was the Metropolitan of Sparta's offices, an unassuming stone building nestled in the city's heart. Alfanas had arranged the visit the previous evening. As they pulled into the small parking area, Alfanas turned to them with a faint smile.

"I won't be long," he said. "The Metropolitan has graciously agreed to secure the scroll for us. It is safest in his care until we return from Istanbul. You both may wait here if you wish, but if you'd like to stretch your legs, the cathedral square is nearby," he said as he waved his hand across the street to a large building with a park-like lawn to one side.

Nick and Elena exchanged a glance. "We'll wait," Elena said, her voice steady. "But let's not stay too long."

Alfanas nodded, securely holding the wrapped lead cylinder and disappearing into the building. Left to themselves, Nick leaned back in his seat, letting out a breath he hadn't realized he'd been holding.

"You okay?" he asked Elena, turning slightly to catch her gaze.

She nodded, but her expression softened. "I was just thinking about what Alfanas said last night. If those treasures still exist, Nick … they might change everything for my people. This isn't just about history anymore. It's about restoring something many considered forever gone."

Nick gave a slight nod, unsure how to respond. Her words added a weight to the scroll that went beyond its fragile parchment. He wasn't sure how he felt about what seemed to be a shift in the narrative. The apparent switch from being center stage to a supporting role meant he did not have a target on his back. Viktor needed to be talking to Elena and not to him.

Yet, in a way, the shift made him more anxious than ever. In a strange emotional twist, he would have felt better if he and not Elena were in harm's way, for he didn't want to see her get hurt. They were growing into being more of a couple in Nick's mind: he wanted to protect her.

By mid-afternoon, they were back on the road, winding their way toward Athens. As they approached the sprawling city, the hum of modern life seemed jarring after the peace of the countryside. Yet Nick felt a strange comfort that he frequently felt in New York. There is no better place to hide a favorite tree than amid a forest. They were now back in the anonymity of a forest of humanity. Alfanas directed them toward Lykovrisi, where the Monastery of Agia Eirini Chrysovalantou awaited.

The monastery rose like a serene island amidst the suburbs, its whitewashed walls and red-tiled roofs standing resolute against the cool November air. Bare branches reached skyward, their skeletal forms softened by the golden light of the setting sun. The rhythmic chanting of vespers carried softly from the chapel, weaving a sense of timelessness into the crisp evening. As they stepped through the gates, the world outside seemed to fall away.

Stern stone walls and strong buildings contrasted with the fragile and humble lives of the nuns who dwelt there. The monastery exuded a peaceful strength and assurance that others were watching over them. In their pursuit to guarantee their guests' safety, the nuns didn't care where those guests had come from or where they were going. He smiled inwardly, the image of Julie Andrews retreating to the safety of the abbey flashing in his mind. He hummed "The hills are alive …"—a fragment of Western culture that felt like it belonged to a distant world, but it comforted him.

A nun greeted them warmly, her voice gentle as she guided them to the guest accommodations. The rooms were simple yet inviting, with wooden beds draped in clean linens and icons of saints adorning the walls. Elena lingered for a moment, her fingers brushing the frame of an icon.

"It feels … safe here," she murmured.

"It is," Alfanas replied. "And you'll need your rest. Tomorrow, Istanbul awaits."

The night held a muted and peaceful sleep for all of them. They all accepted the meager portions of food offered with gratitude and slept soundly. Nick and Elena barely recognized Alfanas when they met him at the gate in the morning.

Alfanas had traded his monastic robes for a crisp white shirt, its collar scarcely visible beneath a gray sweater. A tailored black coat and trousers completed the transformation, making him look more like a professor than a monk. Wrapped loosely around his neck, a woolen scarf softened his otherwise austere appearance.

Nick noticed how comfortably Alfanas fit this attire; his clothes, ecclesiastical or secular, were just two sides of the man, each reflecting as accurately his complex character as the other, astride two worlds that so often conflicted.

"When we get to the airport, we must be on our guard," Alfanas said in response to their quizzical looks. "We must assume that Viktor has one or more people looking for us. I do not need to tell Elena what awaits us in Istanbul, but you, Nick, have never traveled to a country where there is overt religious persecution. In both the East and the West, toleration is merely a cover for the lack of acceptance and a transitional form until you come to my truth claim. The only difference is that in the East, it can be deadly. I cannot move freely as a cleric in Istanbul. Street clothes are a must for me until we leave Istanbul.

Remember, Elena, you must not contact your parents. If we are being watched, we don't want whoever is watching us to have any potential leverage over us by using your parents' safety as a bargaining chip.

Once at the airport, we will move as quickly as we can through to the secure area. From now until we are in private places, we must watch what we say publicly. Even behind the security, we can still be overheard."

With those warnings issued from the safety of the monastery, they left for the airport. Nick's insecurity came more from Alfanas' warnings than any observed danger. They were still in the forest at the airport, but some trees might be invasive species trying to move into your space without you even noticing. None of his senses were sending alarms, yet he had an oppressive feeling of danger and vulnerability.

He wondered about Elena but dared not ask her. After all, they were returning to her world, where she had grown up as a minority. He had never heard of the Rum, from the Turkish word *Rûm*, meaning 'Roman,' and referring to the Greek Orthodox believers in Istanbul, until Elena introduced him to the term. He looked at her and wondered, *"Has she just gotten used to hiding that side of herself?"*

Elena did not need the warnings of the old monk. She had lived all her life trying as much as possible to remain in the shadows of Istanbul. The Rum had been pushed to near extinction historically due to state policy and contemporary waves of violence in the twentieth century.

Her brothers had shed their Christian roots to adopt the Islamic trappings that would advance their careers. In theocracies, not what you know but your worldview dictates your place in society, or, at least, what you say you publicly profess that view to be. Elena loved her brothers deeply. She always would. She also understood the sacrifices they felt they had to make to thrive in a world that rewarded conformity.

Yet she mourned what they had lost, what they had given up. *"Soon, they won't even remember what it felt like to believe,"* she thought with a pang of sorrow. For herself, she chose the arduous path to live her convictions, even if it meant hiding in the shadows. To her, faith without conviction was no faith at all.

By the time they had made it through security, boarded, flown, and disembarked, it had taken them over four hours to set foot on the streets of Istanbul. A mix of city sounds, from a vendor to scooters speeding past, greeted Nick on the sidewalk. The air smelled of roasted chestnuts and diesel fumes, a sharp departure from the sanitized vibe of the airport. He felt his foreignness acutely. Every utterance and action betrayed him as an outsider, which meant he would now be more dependent on Elena and Alfanas than ever. He was in a strange world that felt hostile to him.

He couldn't escape the nagging sense that two rival groups were currently seeking to locate and unmask him. On the one hand, he had Viktor and his accomplices, who might now be watching them. On the other hand, he saw how desperately out of step he was with this culture.

Elena drove them around. She knew Istanbul like the back of her hand. Both Nick and even the well-traveled Alfanas were visitors here. Tomorrow, they would start their investigation of two sites they knew about from the scroll: the Golden Gate and the Monastery of Saint John the Forerunner.

Once they had settled into their hotel room, Nick took to his phone to research the two sites they would investigate the next day.

The Golden Gate, once the grand triumphal archway of Constantinople, marked the ceremonial entrance to the city's walls. Built of gleaming white marble and adorned with gilded decorations, it had stood as a symbol of imperial power and victory. Emperors returning from military campaigns would enter the city through this gate, their processions heralding glory and divine favor.

Over the centuries, however, the Golden Gate had fallen into ruin, its remnants buried beneath layers of history and urban sprawl. Today, little more than a shadow of its former majesty, hidden amidst the crumbling remains of the ancient Theodosian Walls, its secrets lost to time and reconstruction.

The Monastery of Saint John the Forerunner, known locally as the Stoudios Monastery, had once been one of the most significant monastic centers of the Byzantine Empire. Established in the fifth century and famed for its strict asceticism and scholarly pursuits, it housed a vibrant community of monks devoted to prayer, study, and preserving sacred texts.

Over the centuries, the monastery faced the ravages of war, natural disasters, and neglect, its grandeur reduced to ruins. Nick read that the surviving remnants, including fragments of mosaics and marble columns, now lay scattered among modern houses. The former monastery's ancient bones weave into the very fabric of Istanbul's living neighborhoods. Legends persisted about hidden passageways and crypts beneath the monastery, their stories tantalizing but unverified.

Upon hearing Nick's report, Elena confirmed what they all suspected: both sites had been extensively explored, built over, or left in ruin.

"There's little left to uncover," she admitted, her tone laced with frustration. "But we'll have to see for ourselves."

Alfanas nodded gravely, grounding them in the reality of their situation.

"We have no other clues. To advance our understanding of the mystery, we need to find the path Alexios used. That's our only way forward."

He paused, his expression softening. "But for now, we must rest. Tomorrow will demand all of our powers of observation. And for that, a good night's sleep will serve us far better than either Google or ChatGPT!"

His unexpected humor drew a faint smile from Nick, though it quickly faded. Especially for Nick's sake, they had dinner in their room. The hotel offered them a fleeting sense of refuge, a small oasis in a city where they were acutely aware of their vulnerabilities: A Christian monk, a woman of the Rum, and an American man stood out in ways that invited scrutiny or worse. While no immediate threat to their lives existed from these realities, each knew the risks of drawing attention. Crude remarks have a way of quickly escalating to something far more dangerous.

As they finished their meal, Nick contemplated the dark underground they sought to access. At least there would be no crowds to scan or read. Something about the dark unknown fascinated him. With those thoughts, he drifted off to sleep.

The day broke overcast and chilly. Nick thought the somber weather fitting and protective as he looked out the hotel window. *"There won't be as many people out and about on such a damp and bitter day,"* he reasoned silently. *"Not a great day for selfies at the tourist sites, but a good day to poke around in holes and crevices with maybe less notice."*

Their first stop was the Golden Gate. Elena advised them to use a taxi due to the area's congestion, limited parking, and frequent altercations. The cab would not be as inexpensive as a bus.

"Public transportation would mean that we would be rubbing up against the native Turk population and be subject to the schedule and stops of a bus." Nick mentioned, "And I would rather pay the $60 round-trip fare than risk the potential hassles of riding in a bus."

"I will request a taxi through BiTaksi for 9:00," Elena said. "That way, we will be at the Yedikule Fortress by 9:30 or so. That is a good time because it will be before most tourists leave their hotels for the day."

By the time they walked from the taxi, purchased their tickets, and made it to the other end of the Yedikule Fortress, where the imposing 5th-century Golden Gate and its two towers formed the Western side of the 15th-century Ottoman fortress, it was mid-morning. Nick stood there feeling small and helpless in front of the massive gate as it towered over him.

One or two visitors were milling about. He heard their faint voices. The city's noises were muffled and barely audible, like a hum in the background, broken only occasionally with a brief horn or siren. Unlike Corinth or Mystras, there seemed to be no pleasant odors, just the smell of old earth and stone. The old stone and brick were weathered rough. Reconstruction aimed to roll back the effects of time, mixed with wars and neglect in various places, hinted at past glories that modernity would never fully reclaim.

"Why are the arches mostly bricked up?" Nick asked.

Elena answered, "It is probably because the Ottomans wanted more control over the entry into their fort, and who needs 30-foot-high bronze doors? But there is a legend that the Sultan feared the rumors that the last Emperor, Constantine XI Palaiologos, did not die. An angel or God turned him into a marble statue hidden underneath the Golden Gate, awaiting the archangel Gabriel's summons to rejoin the battle and lead the victorious procession of the Byzantine army over the occupiers of the city."

"So, Constantine is not buried somewhere around here?" Nick looked around him, as if he might find the place where "X marked the spot."

"No. The Ottoman troops searched for his body, but there is no record of it ever being found. Alexios' scroll tells us that it is because he was carried off." Elena responded, touching his arm lightly.

"My suspicion," began Alfanas as all three of them now gazed at the mostly blocked gate, "is that if the entryway to the underground passage were anywhere inside the gate, we would never find it now. This gate and its three arches have been so reconstructed, built over, and explored that any possible entry is hidden from us. We should look in the North and South towers."

With that, they set off. To satisfy their curiosity, they took a quick look around the gate; they didn't want to risk later remorse that there might have been something they had overlooked. They kept their eyes open for anything out of the ordinary, scanning the cracks and crevices of the stone, but with all the modifications over the years, as they feared, there were no clues to be seen.

Moving next to explore the towers, as the vast tower floor lay under his feet, Nick reflected on their experiences in Mystras and the hidden Tetragrammatic cross. Even with private access and weeks to explore, it would be impossible to investigate so many stones.

"This is pointless," he said exasperatedly as he sat on the floor. "We have no idea what we are looking for, or even if a clue exists! If we had a plan 'B,' now would be the time to mention it."

Alfanas stood in the dim light, stroked his beard, and finally said, "Yes, I think we can do no more here. It was not fruitless. At the very least, we know that this is not how we will find what we seek. I suggest we head to the Monastery of Saint John the Forerunner for the rest of the afternoon. It would be a fool's hope to think that we would resolve this today. We are merely scouting the next steps and figuring out which site to focus on. Deciding comes later."

Rather than take a cab, they walked the short distance from the Yedikule Fortress to the Monastery of Saint John the Forerunner.

Nick's description of the night before didn't prepare them for what they now saw. The remains of the Monastery of Saint John the Forerunner and the surrounding grounds were gated entirely and shut off to them. It gave every appearance of a fortress; it lacked only razor wire. Between every building were thick iron bars and locked gates, contrasting with overgrown and neglected ruins visible through the bars, making inspection impossible from the outside.

Nick turned to Elena and said, "You would think this place was made of gold. Now what?"

"No. It is not that." Elena answered, her hand longingly resting on the iron barrier as if on a protective shield for something too holy to be open to just anyone. "No. These remains are of one of the oldest former churches in Istanbul. Even though it is now the remains of a mosque, it keeps its original essence, which makes it more precious than gold. Its mosaics and artifacts are priceless and must be preserved and protected from vandalism or theft.

We can inquire at the main gate, but it must be Alfanas who knocks and inquires. I am now only a subservient woman and a member of the Rum. Alfanas is a senior male, and unless he makes it known otherwise, is assumed to be Islamic. Because he also speaks Turkish like a native, the caretaker will not question his authority to speak for us."

Eventually, they found the main gate and rang the bell to get the attention of the site's caretaker. Out came an older man, whose state of hygiene and physical appearance reflected the characteristics of the monastery ruins. Nick felt secretly pleased that Alfanas needed to take the lead for them.

"What do you want?" the caretaker asked gruffly.

"My name is Alfanas, a traveling scholar from Uzbekistan. I have come on a pilgrimage to study and worship at the historic mosques of Istanbul. I am especially interested in visiting the remains of the İmrahor İlyas Bey Mosque. May we briefly look at the site?" Alfanas' demeanor was firm but not aggressive. There would be little point in trying to gain access confrontationally.

The old man looked them all over before he answered, "Do you have a paper giving you permission?"

"No," Alfanas sighed, "but we promise to be very quick and…"

"No, no, no," barked the caretaker back into Alfanas' face. They all come to my doors, ringing the bell, 'Let us in. We are special. We will be quick.' Again, no. You go and tell your story to the Republic of Türkiye Ministry of Culture and Tourism. They will get you a paper with permission. You will bring it back here, ring my bell, and then we shall see."

Alfanas opened his mouth to reply, but he had no chance before the other man held up his hand in protest and said, "Oh, just go away." And he turned, slammed the doors shut, and rejoined the ruins from which he had come and looked so much a part.

Alfanas stood still for a moment. His lips pressed into a thin line. "This city," he muttered softly, to himself. "It guards its secrets like a miser hoarding gold." He then turned and looked at his two young friends. "That could have gone better. I could petition the Ministry on behalf of St. Alexander's Monastery in Uzbekistan, but that would take time that we do not have and would likely yield similar results to what we have had today. Let us head back to the hotel and consider, as Nick calls it, 'Plan B,' if there is one."

Sullenly, Elena summoned the taxi to take them back to the hotel near the airport. They were all silent, not needing to ask what the others were thinking about. They were on the verge of reaching the end of the road for the next steps, if not the whole quest.

Nick realized, *"I have quit my job, spent most of my retirement savings, traveled halfway around the world, risked my life with Viktor, and here it ends? Really? I still don't know anything about my family's connection to all of this. It is frustrating and depressing that I could be driving over the answer hidden below the pavement right now, and I cannot get to it!"*

For her part, Elena thought much the same. So much for the hope of the Rum and upgrading their lives. So much for the plight of her own family and their struggles to compromise and survive.

Alfanas' dogmatic, patient tenacity had always paid off in producing outcomes and answers throughout his life. God had aligned the universe to speak so long as Alfanas patiently listened. But now, he heard nothing being said, no next.

Sitting around the table during dinner, none of them had engaged in the apparent conversation of what to do next because there were no answers.

Finally, Brother Alfanas, who had become more like a father figure in their lives by this time, broke the stalemated silence. "Tomorrow we will regroup. I think I shall head off to Istanbul University, where I am a fellow. I will start gathering resources on both sites and see if I can call in some favors to get into the Monastery of Saint John the Forerunner, cutting through all the red tape. I am sorry. This is all going to take a long time. I think Nick should return home until I find something. There is no reason for you to stay here now."

Nick couldn't believe it. Was this really the end? The story hadn't finished; it just hung there, stamped with a shaky "to be continued," and even that felt uncertain. He pulled out his phone, scrolling through one-way flights back to New York. His finger hovered over the "book my flight" button, but he couldn't bring himself to press it. That would mean surrender.

He glanced at Elena. She sat propped against the headboard, knees drawn tight, arms wrapped around them. Her brow furrowed, lip caught between her teeth. She hadn't quit. Not yet. Nick shut off his phone, rolled onto his side, and let exhaustion pull him toward sleep.

Nick lay awake longer than he wanted; thoughts tugged him in two directions. Part of him longed for home, for his parents, for the familiar rhythms of work and routine, for a life without shadows dogging his steps. Yet something deeper insisted he could not leave, not yet. The mystery bound him, unfinished, unwilling to release him. And then there was Elena …

Chapter 13: The Scholar's Path

Elena refused to give up. Her fingers drummed against her knee as her mind sifted through possibilities. This wasn't a puzzle to solve. It carried the weight of her people, her history, and something far larger than herself. She hadn't shaped a plan yet, but a "lead B" already took form. Yes. Where there's life, there's hope. She glanced at the sleeping body of Nick and allowed herself a faint smile. "Now that you are here, I won't let you walk away without a fight. We'll find a way," she promised silently, switching off the light before settling to sleep.

Sleep eventually came, though uneasily.

Nick barely remembered falling asleep, but the previous day's weight clung to him like a shadow. The Golden Gate, the monastery, the curt caretaker—every step felt like walking into a wall. They had nothing, no leads, no progress. He rolled over, staring at the faint light creeping through the curtains, wondering how long their quest would now last. Then came Elena's voice, urgent and determined, shaking him from the half-dreaming sleep he had experienced all night, where his thoughts bordered on dreams.

"Nick, wake up. Come on, we need to go see Brother Alfanas."

Immediately, he sprang up and dressed just in time to follow her out the door, to stand at the old monk's door, knocking.

"What's this all about?" while tucking in his shirt, he asked.

Alfanas had a surprised, if not confused, look on his face as the door swung open.

"What is it? Come in, come in. Is there trouble?"

"I think I have a plan; we will see Papa." She enthusiastically blurted out. Alfanas began to object with the same old warnings, but didn't have a chance to get very far.

Elena interrupted him. "You must listen to me first. As head of the Byzantine Studies Research Center, Papa has spent years piecing together fragments of Constantinople's history."

She took a quick breath and continued. "If anyone knows where to look for forgotten paths beneath the city, it is he. As you mentioned, visiting a university and a library is the most natural way to research the remains and ruins in Istanbul. Once we are on campus, I am familiar with the stacks and offices, which are now dispersed over the campus due to the evacuation; I will get us lost even to the best tracker!

Plus, the entire staff there knows me well, and I can get in to see Papa quickly and quietly. Brother, you have the academics, but Papa not only has the academics and access to resources but also knows folks from around the world and in Istanbul who may be able to help. We will not involve Mama or meet him outside of the library."

Alfanas wrinkled his brow in consideration of her suggestion. Nick looked at him anxiously and risked his opinion. "In my opinion, it's worth the risk. Mr. Sakellaris already knows everything about what we are doing, so we are not bringing anyone new into our confidence. He brought you to us. Who knows what other resources he has to offer now that we are in his backyard? We are at a dead end without him."

"All right. We will risk it." Alfanas accepted.

They quickly got themselves together and headed out to Boğaziçi University, where Elena's father worked.

Boğaziçi University, on the European side of Istanbul, is one of Turkey's most respected schools, with a strong library and a reputation in the humanities and social sciences. Elena's father, Niketas Sakellaris, worked there, giving him access to resources on Byzantine heritage and to the scholars, local and international, who gathered at the university's Byzantine Studies Research Center.

From the street, the Aptullah Kuran Library still looked every bit the stately heart of the campus. Its arched façade and quiet dignity marked it as a keeper of memory. Elena explained that her father's office and the collections had to be moved due to the evacuation. The contents and staff were scattered across other buildings, leaving the library itself silent.

Driving past the library, Elena pulled up in front of a more nondescript hall. One of the exterior doors bore a temporary sign reading "Byzantine Studies Research Center." The trio moved through the doors and into a small office where a receptionist's desk sat between visitors and the temporary collections, reading rooms, and offices.

The receptionist greeted both Elena and Alfanas warmly, bidding them to "Go ahead, in; you both know the way. He's not busy, and I'll let you surprise him!"

The temporary office of Niketas Sakellaris was cozy, but functional. Seated behind a desk, he jumped up, a smile spreading across his face as Elena entered the room. He greeted his daughter with a hug and a kiss, shaking hands with the men. His mood changed from wonder to one of curiosity.

"Elena, why didn't you tell us you were coming? Do you all need a place to stay? Wait until your mother hears you are here!" exclaimed her father excitedly.

"No, Papa, you can't tell her," Elena pleaded, holding his hand. "We kept it from you both because it might bring misfortune to the family. The truth is, we don't know what kind of trouble pursues us, or even if it still follows us. All we have are suspicions. Yes, we were followed on our first visit to Istanbul and Athens. So, we must assume that we are now in danger again. Let me explain to you."

Elena recounted their journey from Sitka to Mystras, this time including Viktor, finding the scroll, back to Istanbul, and their initial scouting of the Golden Gate and the Monastery of Saint John the Forerunner.

"You must stop," her father spoke as he raised his hand. "When we first planned your trip, we had no idea that this kind of danger would follow you on the road. It is too risky to continue. Perhaps if everything returns to normal, this Viktor will assume you have come to a dead end, and it is over."

"People like Viktor do not assume," interjected Alfanas, "and now it is personal for him. He will not pull back until he has spoken to both children. The only way back to normal is moving forward. But we have hit a dead end."

Elena retook her father's hand. "Yes, Papa, that is the only reason we have turned to you. We need your help."

Niketas paced the room, his hand stroking his beard, and finally spoke. "If this is the only way … I'll do what I can."

Alfanas took off the pastoral persona and put on his academic demeanor. Elena and Nick knew him well enough now to recognize the switch, if not to anticipate it. They exchanged knowing looks and little smile with each other.

Alfanas explained, "We must find this path under the city, at least the part from the Golden Gate to the Monastery of Saint John the Forerunner. The Chronicle of the Last Emperor stated that Constantine XI was taken secretly under the gate to the Monastery to be treated."

Pausing, Alfanas took a breath while holding Niketas' gaze. "I am assuming that Alexios connected up to the underground cisterns and watercourses that were a part of the hydraulic system of Constantinople. I suspect the next clue or section of the Chronicle lies under the city. But we must find out how to get access. I would suggest that we concentrate on the area between the two and see if any reports mention the double-headed eagle, tetragrammatic cross, or some passageway, water channel, or cistern that has not been thoroughly explored."

Niketas put his hand up to stroke his beard. "Hmm, there are always reports of findings in Istanbul. Any home improvement that digs a foot deep into the soil of Istanbul risks striking a piece of architecture or archaeology that has hitherto been unknown. People are always finding things. But the Golden Gate is not a good place to start. It has been the focus of much attention over the years."

"But," interjected Elena, "couldn't they have missed something or left something uninvestigated?"

Her father shook his head. "It is not likely. Over the years, sultans have remade it, developers have dug it up, and archaeologists have reconstructed it. Add the earthquake damage, and you have very few original stones left in situ."

He considered the map of Istanbul that hung on the wall. After a deep breath, he went on, "No. Better to focus on the monastery. A team from the Italian Association of Restoration Companies has recently been consulting the university archives. They've been mapping what remains of the original structures, including possible heretofore unreported underground passages that might still connect to the cisterns or hydraulic systems Alfanas mentioned. They were particularly interested in documents and maps related to the Monastery of Saint John the Forerunner at Stoudios as part of their restoration training program."

"How would they locate undocumented passages?" Nick asked.

"The Italians sought to engage the many parties connected to the site, including the Rum. They also surveyed the surrounding buildings that were suspected of having been built on the footprint of the old monastery land. I remember they did report on anomalies they found in a couple of the local buildings, passing the information on to the Department of Antiquities inspectors." As he spoke, Niketas adjusted his glasses, looked at his computer screen, and pushed several keys. "The inspector they talked to is a former member of the Rum Orthodox community and secretly sympathizes with us still, though, to all outward appearances, he is a loyal Islamist."

"What kind of anomalies?" interjected Nick.

"Again, people find a hole in a wall or a crack in their floor," Niketas explained, turning from the screen. "thinking it might be something, and sometimes it is, but many times a crack is just a crack. Mortar it up."

"On occasion, these anomalies reveal more than cracks. There can be a sealed doorway, a carved emblem like the double-headed eagle. But too often, they're ignored or dismissed as structural damage and not fully investigated. I'll contact my friend and stress the urgency. When I hear back, I'll let Elena know immediately."

Niketas paused for a second in consideration before he continued, "If he's willing to help, it will be because of his past, but

136

he walks a fine line, as we all do. If anyone suspects he's assisting Rum Orthodox, future promotions would be out of the question."

"That makes sense," Nick replied. "But if he's still connected to the Rum community, maybe he's been waiting for the right reason to help."

He glanced at Elena, marveling at her quiet strength for all these years. It bothered him to think that others still lived a life so constrained, where every word could be a risk, and still fought for what mattered. Just weeks ago, his biggest concerns had been deadlines and lunch breaks.

They said their goodbyes and left Niketas already on the phone, reaching out to his contact, Inspector Leontios Karamanlis of the Antiquities and Cultural Heritage, Ministry of Culture and Tourism. They would step into another unknown tomorrow, hoping the past would finally speak its truth.

Elena took them to one of the hall's back doors rather than having them leave the way they came.

Niketas hung up the phone and immediately there was a knock at the door.

"Come in."

The receptionist entered the office, closed the door behind her, and, with a concerned tone, said, "It might be nothing, but a middle-aged man came up after Elena had come back to see you, and said that he felt he had recognized some young friends of his who had entered the office right before him. He asked about their names and who they were visiting so that he might connect with them later.

I told him they hadn't given their names, but had shown a signed letter from the dean of Byzantine Studies authorizing them to consult restricted materials in the archives. I asked for his name so I could pass it along to them.

He apologized for interrupting my work and said he would wait outside and surprise them. I thought you should know."

"Thank you," Niketas replied in the best unconcerned tone he could muster. "I am sure it is nothing, but I will tell her. You did the right thing. Just curious, did he look like he was from around here?"

"Yes. He was not a foreigner. He spoke excellent Turkish. In every way, he appeared average."

Niketas fidgeted with some papers. "Thank you for telling me."

"You're welcome. It was good to see Elena," she said as she closed the door.

Nick, Elena, and Alfanas were on their way back to the hotel to figure out how they would kill time while waiting for Elena's father's call, when Elena's phone rang.

"Hello Papa, did you already hear back?" she paused. "Wait, wait, I will put you on speakerphone." She took the phone from her ear so that they could all listen. "Say that again."

"You are being followed," Niketas' anxious voice announced. "A Turkish man asked the receptionist about your names and the nature of your visit to the library. The receptionist did not give him any information. But you must be careful."

"Thank you, Papa. We will be careful, as you should be as well. Love you, goodbye."

"I warned you," said Alfanas, shaking his head, "but I guess we had no choice." He paused briefly before he continued, "Well, our suspicions are confirmed. Viktor has not been idle. We also know that he has at least one accomplice. Are there more?

None of my sources report that he has been released by the police yet. Still, others can act on his behalf, especially if what they tell Viktor suggests we are getting close to something. Now, we also need to act to protect your mother and father, along with this inspector."

He was quiet as he reflected and added, "We should not meet your father at the university again. If we are going into this business, we must try to confuse anyone following us. Let's allow your father time to work behind the scenes. We will take on the persona of tourists and allow Elena to show us the city's famous sights, culminating in a sunset cruise for dinner tomorrow? We should be in public places as much as possible.

They arrived back at the hotel and spent the rest of the day relaxing in their rooms. In the evening, they would have dinner downstairs and discuss the next steps.

After dinner and as the evening settled over Istanbul, Nick, Elena, and Alfanas gathered in the hotel lounge to plan their next steps. Elena had thought about how to spend their time tomorrow and perhaps the next day, if need be, until her father called.

"If we're careful, we can visit some key sites tomorrow. There's so much history here, so many layers to this city's story. It will be a fun adventure that will not aid Viktor at all," she laughed.

Nick nodded, feeling the pull of the ancient city. "Let's make a day of it," he said. "But we will stay vigilant."

Alfanas smiled.

The following day, after a light breakfast of simit and tea from a cafe near their hotel, they set out early to beat the crowds. The trio would visit Hagia Sophia first, its towering dome glowing in the morning sunlight. Nick marveled at the blend of Christian mosaics and Islamic calligraphy that adorned the interior.

"It's like walking through centuries of history in a single space," he said softly. Her passion clear, Elena explained the significance of the mosaics. Alfanas, ever the scholar, added his thoughts on the architectural innovations that had made the structure so enduring.

From there, they made their way to the Blue Mosque, pausing in its serene courtyard before entering. The cascading domes and delicate blue tiles left Nick in awe.

By mid-morning, they walked through the Basilica Cistern, its dimly lit columns reflected in the shallow water below. Nick imagined the labyrinthine waterways beneath the city, wondering how many secrets they held. Elena pointed out the enigmatic Medusa heads at the base of two columns, speculating about their origin.

They had a quick lunch of Turkish delicacies as Elena planned for Nick to experience the exotic cuisine of Istanbul fully.

All the while, Nick continued to feel like eyes were watching him, a feeling he was growing accustomed to. He caught Alfanas scanning the crowds, his cautious gaze confirming his unease.

The Topkapi Palace occupied their afternoon. While the others had seen these displays before, Nick couldn't help but be impressed by the opulent displays of Ottoman wealth and power.

A sunset cruise on the Bosphorus as the sun descended wrapped up their day.

"This is the Istanbul I always imagined," Nick said, leaning on the railing. Elena joined him, her voice soft. "It's beautiful, isn't it? It's like the city itself is alive, breathing with its past and present."

Nick looked at her as she stared out into the setting sun over the city. The orange tones highlight her dark hair and complexion. She had the hint of a smile on her lips, and her face was relaxed as the wind blew back the one or two strands of her hair that had escaped confinement. Istanbul may have been many things to her, some good, some bad, but he could see the love on her face.

Nick took hold of her hand with a squeeze. She looked over at him; her smile widening. Letting go of his hand, she slid her hand up under his arm, leaned her head on his shoulder, and moved her free hand to complete the hug of his arm. It was sunset in Istanbul.

Alfanas, standing a few feet away, gazing out over the water, added, "And like any living thing, it hides its secrets well."

The trio was ready to retreat to their hotel by the time the cruise ended. They walked back quietly, each lost in their thoughts, the weight of the day tempered by the tranquility of the Bosphorus. Safely back in the hotel room, Nick turned to Elena to state the obvious, "We haven't heard from your Dad, yet."

But Niketas had not been idle. The moment he hung up after telling Elena about the mysterious man, he dialed Inspector Leontios Karamanlis.

He recognized the voice of his old colleague and friend answering. "Hello."

"Hello, my dear friend Leontios. This is Niketas Sakellaris. I pray that all goes well with your family and your work."

"Ah, my friend, how are you? How is your family? If I remember my ancient history correctly, your children should now be settling into their own lives and thinking of giving you grandchildren. Yes?" Inspector Leontios asked.

"Yes, they are grown now. The youngest is 21 years old. It is really for Elena's sake that I have called you today," replied Niketas, thinking how nice it would be to have the luxury to keep the conversation at this level, but he needed to go deeper quickly, "It has been too long since we have spoken, my friend. I wish this were simply a social call, but I'm reaching out with some urgency for my family and our community. Elena decided to dig into some family history and legends, and you know how, too often, legend and history blur and fuse in the reality of Istanbul."

Niketas collected himself, recalling the conversation he had rehearsed, and continued, "She is researching a new lead on Constantine XI and a possible connection to the Stoudios Monastery, but she is having difficulty gaining access and information on the site. So, I thought of you and your work with the Italians from Associazione Italiana Restauro."

"Yes, it has been a nice change of pace working with the folks from the Associazione Italiana Restauro. Their survey of the site is proving invaluable. But with any research, they will be protective." Leontios confirmed. "What is she looking for? I cannot grant her access to the site."

"No, no." Niketas quickly interjected. "She does not want to go to the site. She wonders if there are any reports of structural anomalies or possible uncharted cisterns or aqueducts."

"Well, if I remember some of the reports correctly," Leontios paused to consider for a moment, "some things might fit what she is looking for. Some were dismissed as structural defects, but there was at least one that the team suggested would be worth further consideration and excavation. I will need to look it up. Officially, I will need to be present for any action on the information from the work of the Associazione Italiana Restauro team. So, you will be stuck with me if you involve me."

Niketas was silent for a moment or two. "I must warn you that helping us could cause you future problems if you are seen connected with us. We don't entirely know why, but there is involvement from a third party, and we don't yet know who employs him. Plus, unless you are careful, you might get some Rum Orthodox mud thrown on you."

Leontios did not pause or hesitate to respond. "Understood, old friend. We are always careful, aren't we? Do not worry. For old times' sake, I will be glad to help. You were there to help my father accept my new life and the choices that I made for my family. When others of the Rum turned away, you loved me. I owe the peace of my heart, the love of my father, to you. That will be a debt I can never repay. I will review the report today and get back to you later tomorrow."

Late the following evening, Niketas' cell phone rang.

"Good evening, my old friend Leontios. Do you have any news for me?" Niketas hopefully asked.

"Yes, this one is promising. A derelict building is across the road from Stoudios Monastery. I will text you the address. I am calling so late because I wanted to talk to the property owner to see if I could have his permission to investigate further. He has granted me access and will have a key ready for me to pick up when I am ready. The property is currently uninhabited. Windows were broken out, and graffiti is on the walls. I can arrange to meet you at the site at 9:00 A.M."

"That is wonderful news. I will set it up with Elena tonight!" Niketas exclaimed enthusiastically. "I will see you tomorrow."

Nick and Elena had been back at their hotel for about thirty minutes when Niketas called.

Elena's voice sounded a bit tired, but happy with the day she had spent with her friends. "Hello, Papa. Nick is here with me. I am putting you on speakerphone. Do you have any news for us?"

"Yes, I just got off the phone with Inspector Karamanlis." Niketas began. "Earlier, he thought there was mention of one promising anomaly in the reports, and now he has confirmed it. He will meet us there tomorrow morning at 9:00. I texted you the address. Do you want me to pick you up on my way?"

"No," Nick and Elena said simultaneously, but Nick continued, "It is better if you come separately. We will probably be the ones followed. We will try to shake any tag-a-longs we pick up and then meet you. Should we bring anything? Do you have a crowbar in case we need to enlarge an opening? What about flashlights?"

"Do not worry. I will throw some tools in the car's boot and bring flashlights. There is one other complication."

Niketas gave them time to register what he had said and prepare for what he would say next. Then he continued, "Inspector Karamanlis is insisting that he be present for your investigation of the site. As a senior inspector, he obtained permission from the landowner to investigate the landowner's basement. But he must be with you. It's understandable officially, it's his investigation, but it might also draw attention we don't need. Yet, there is the trade-off that he also brings cover to any eyes questioning our legitimacy. I worry for him, but I suggest it will be too late to harm any of us by the time this might come to light. That is my prayer."

"Can he be trusted?" Nick cast a worried look at Elena.

"I think so," Niketas stated, the words hanging in the air. "I think so," he reiterated, a little lower in tone as if he were not entirely confident. "Leontios was brought up in the Rum Orthodox tradition. That he is no longer part of our community has more to do with providing for his family than with our beliefs. He remains a loyal sympathizer. Yes," now with more confidence, "he has always been careful, perhaps too careful, but I'm sure his heart is with us. I trust him."

After hanging up with Niketas, Nick phoned Alfanas and filled him in on the conversation.

Alfanas felt it was better news than they could have hoped for a couple of nights ago and ended with the warning, "Sensing we might need more help, I have reconnected with an old friend of mine willing to drive us when needed. He will help our travels stay private."

They had many things to find peace in. They had a very promising lead to follow up on, and two new people with resources were going to help them in their search.

Nick, however, was worried. He thought Viktor and his allies were getting more aggressive. The interfering monk, according to Viktor, had bested him, but he would not make any errors next time.

Nick fell asleep, wondering how long it would be before they were forced into a confrontation.

Chapter 14: The Hidden Way Revealed

Wednesday began with a cloudless sky. Nick rolled onto his side, peering out of the window whose curtains Elena had drawn wide to coax him awake. Nick stirred, and she came and sat on the edge of his bed. She placed a hand on his exposed shoulder and smiled.

"So, what are you thinking about?"

He returned her glance and smile, rolling over on his back. "I am thinking about home. Mom has already begun shopping for Thanksgiving Day dinner. No doubt she has the turkey thawing in the refrigerator. She loves the holidays. I wonder if I will make it home for Christmas."

She let her hand settle on his chest; her face serious as she empathized with Nick's pain. "I know it is hard for you. I feel bad. Now that I know you so well. It all seemed so romantic when I was inconveniencing a stranger." She no longer made eye contact but wistfully stared at her hand on his chest. "I wish I had left you alone, at peace, simply being Nick Paleon."

Tears formed in her eyes. Nick took her hand in his. Raising it to his lips, he gave it a kiss before moving it back to his chest with his hand over hers.

"There will be other Thanksgivings and Christmases, but this is once in a lifetime. Yes, I miss my family and home, but what I am beginning to learn is that there is so much more to miss. Like all the people I would never have known, Alfanas, your dad, and you. You have all made me glad I stepped out and came along for the journey. I had other options that I could have chosen at any time. When leads ran dry two days ago, I could have gone home, but I have something left to do." With one of his wry little smiles, Nick added, "And look, you finally got me in bed with you."

The smile returned to her face, but the knock on the door stopped her from responding. She patted his chest, brushed the side of Nick's face with her hand, and got up to answer the door.

Brother Alfanas came in and, seeing Nick still in bed, picked up one of the pillows from Elena's bed and, flinging it at him, said, "You lazy bum. It is time you were up! We are supposed to meet at 9:00, but it is already 7:30! We will be picked up at 8:00. My friend will unfortunately need to lead us through the streets and traffic of downtown to make sure that we are not followed."

"Is this friend of yours a monk as well?" asked Elena.

Alfanas laughed. "Oh, no. He is a perfect heathen. No, I lie. He is an atheist. When I met him, we all were. There was not much to believe in life back then. The church and the state were the same. In some places, they still largely are."

"Can we trust him?" Nick asked.

"Yes. I have trusted him with my life and still would. There are certain groups that one belongs to throughout one's life. Undoubtedly, we would still give our lives for each other. Oh, get up and get dressed!"

They arrived in the lobby a little before eight. While they passed, Nick observed a man occasionally glancing up at them, feigning interest in his newspaper. Once they reached the outside door, the man got up and followed them. Nick wondered if this shadowy figure meant to confront, observe, or harm them. Oddly, being able to put a face to the presence eased some of his anxiety. He now knew who he should scan for in the crowd, or at least one of whom to look for. He would not worry about more than one for now.

As they walked out to the sidewalk, a car pulled up to the curb, and Alfanas opened the passenger door and slipped in while gesturing for Elena and Nick to get in the back seat.

Once in the car, Alfanas turned to them and, pointing to the driver, said, "This is my friend. His name is unimportant, so let us call him Sam. Sam, this is Nick and Elena."

Sam turned briefly, his weathered face marked by years of indifference, and grunted an acknowledgment, clearly caring less. He might die for Alfanas, but had little regard for them.

The car lurched out into the traffic without signaling or, to Nick's observation, the driver without looking. Horns blared. Gestures forthcoming. Sam grunted with a clear disregard that bordered on amusement.

"Did you see," began Nick, his voice shaky with fear over the driving but wanting to appear worth dying for, "did you see," he repeated, "that man in the lobby watched us and followed us out of the door?"

"Yes," turning his attention briefly from his friend to Nick. "It is not the first time I have noticed him. I don't doubt that he is the one who inquired at the library. He will not follow us to the monastery. Sam is the best driver in Europe, if not the world."

As if in response to the words of acclamation, Sam hit the accelerator and dove between two cars to cross three lanes of traffic and back to get off the highway at double the ramp speed. Nick felt sick to his stomach.

Elena seemed unfazed by Sam and his driving. She had grown up on these roads with drivers like Sam, who didn't necessarily try to lose people but wanted to get somewhere ahead of somebody else. Sam, certainly an extremist in his auto-manic driving style, had reason today, but most of the everyday traffic did not. If anyone other than in a helicopter tried to follow them, they would be lost by now. Elena, while in the car with him, found herself lost at times, coming on recognizable landmarks, wondering how they got there.

Inexplicably, they pulled up to the derelict property at 9:00. Outside the building stood Niketas and Inspector Leontios Karamanlis. Niketas held what appeared to be a heavy backpack on his shoulder. Nick assumed it held tools and probably flashlights.

Many of the building's windows had panes broken out or had been boarded up, and graffiti covered the exterior walls. The building appeared to be abandoned, neglected, and scary.

As Sam sped away, Niketas took out five flashlights and handed them to Alfanas, Nick, Elena, and Leontios.

Leontios unlocked the door, but before heading in, he cautioned everyone, "Be careful. We do not know what we are walking into. This building has seen better days. There may be loose plaster or missing stairs. If you ask me, we're on the verge of a list of architectural anomalies, most of which are minor issues like floor cracks or plumbing leaks. Such is the story of my life."

Experiencing the inside of the building made them all glad to have other places to sleep tonight. The overcast skies outside amplified the gray gloom that filled all the space. A softer shade of grey inhabited the places the windows were not boarded up, as the light found its way to the floor.

The place smelled. It smelled of mildew and urine. While mostly quiet, they heard the odd scurry of something undead running around in the shadows and occasionally the far-off drip of some liquid oozing through something. As they moved further into the space and down to the basement, the air became more stagnant and humid. In the upper floors, the broken windows let in a breeze; once in the subfloor regions, the air hung undisturbed by anything fresh. The beams of the flashlights pierced the darkness, revealing trash and decay.

Elena remarked first, "This is horrible."

The decrepit building, rather larger than the buildings in the area, presented the team with a challenge to explore every corner of the basement. So they split up. The only visible feature of the space, other than the columns that supported the floor above, interrupted the beams of their flashlights and cast eerie shadows across the floor. But for the brief illumination of their flashlights, darkness reigned everywhere.

The walls, mostly in decent shape, had one or two cracks that showed recent repairs, suggesting a needed deeper inspection of the patching mortar. But they wanted to do a general survey and go back to scrutinize any open cracks first.

They had been in the building for about an hour when Niketas found *the* crack. It had been patched once, but the patching mortar had not adhered to the stone below and had fallen off. Compared to the other cracks, it resembled the Grand Canyon. It gaped about an inch wide and approximately four feet high on the northwest wall opposite the street side of the building. Niketas held his flashlight up to it and peered inside. Amazed, he saw … nothing. No wall, no earth, simply open space that his small light did not define or angle enough off the crack to get any reflection on any surface. Niketas drew closer to peer better through the crack. A cooler, fresher, earthy-smelling slight breeze brushed against his face.

"*Ορίστε! Ορίστε!*" shouted a jubilant Niketas, who, in his excitement, slipped back into Greek to be followed by the English, "Here it is! Here it is!"

Everyone came running over. Nick saw at once that this section of the outside wall differed in its construction from all the other walls. It seemed to be a stucco coat of mortar on stacked stone that had to have been much older.

"Typical," Inspector Karamanlis said, shaking his head. "People build these places without regard for the law or history. What people don't tear down and destroy, they try to cover up and disguise because they do not want the delay or expense of getting our office involved. None of this was reported in the files on this place. While I should formally call in a team to investigate, I think we will do a little more on our own for the sake of friendship." He smiled at both Niketas and Alfanas. "After all, you never know who comes down here poking at these 'anomalies,' now do you?"

The excavation didn't even require the supplied crowbar. The mortar crumbled away in their hands, and the dry-fitted stone moved easily. Soon, they had a hole big enough to squeeze through. Inspector Karamanlis demanded that, as the professional, he should be the first inside to ensure the stability of the revealed void.

"Yalla! Yalla! All is well! Carefully come in." They heard Karamanlis shout from the other side of the enlarged anomaly.

Nick wiggled through the hole and came out in a passageway with a small stream running through its center. The water smelled clear, fresh, and cold to the touch.

Nick shivered as cold water soaked through his sneakers. "What is this place?"

Busy helping Alfanas through, Inspector Karamanlis answered, "This looks like a lost subterranean aqueduct. The city is full of them.

Remember that even ancient cities like Constantinople need to provide fresh water for hundreds of thousands of inhabitants. This meant that a labyrinth of underground hydraulic systems, water channels, cisterns, and drains, was necessary."

"Wow, and they didn't get filled in over time?"

"No need. With the advent of modern piping and drains, there was a natural progression to systems that do not run this deep under the surface. The old structures are still intact, and some wells and cisterns are still in use."

As Nick examined the stonework of the passage, the arch above his head, and the neat lines of the well-laid stone suggested they had broken through a patch of ill-fitted stone, probably a modern repair made during building so that the builders could complete the project with no one knowing archaeology existed on the site.

He marveled that human labor did this by hand, shovelful of dirt by shovelful of dirt. Human muscles lugged stones and worked by candlelight or oil lamplight in the deep dark of the tunnel. He put his hand on a single stone with reverence and acknowledgement of the unknown man who placed it, realizing no one had touched this stone for over a thousand years before him.

The aqueduct ran from east to west as far as their flashlights shone. Alfanas suggested heading west toward the Golden Gate, as it would be the closest. This would take them back to where they might find clues about how Alexios used the passage and where Constantine XI had ended up.

They had gone about thirty feet when the aqueduct opened to a large cavern. The reflection of their flashlights off of the surface of the water suggested that they had probably discovered a lost cistern of the old Monastery of Saint John the Forerunner.

"Everyone, be careful. Don't fall into the cistern. We might have to wait and come back with a boat," concluded Inspector Karamanlis as he and Alfanas investigated from the front of the line, while the others waited behind them in the aqueduct.

"Look," Alfanas said while gesturing with his flashlight, "this must have been some of Alexios' modifications to ensure a way through during high water."

The light hit the water's surface, and about two inches below, a stone walkway led into the cistern's darkness.

"Well, it looks like we will be getting our feet wet!" Inspector Karamanlis chuckled. "Welcome to old Byzantium!" Pointing to Elena, Nick, and Niketas, "You three remain here for now. Alfanas and I will go into the dark waters and return if all is safe. These stones and arches have been here for over 1,000 years. They may not all remain, and they may also not all have remained sound."

Alfanas had an air of serene confidence about him that identified him as a capable person, physically and mentally. Even while the inspector had not known him long, Karamanlis clearly relied on his judgement.

The three left behind watched as the flashlights danced on the water's surface, illuminating ripples that softly spread over the surface of the mostly undisturbed water. Occasionally, they heard "plunk" from somewhere as a water drip from the roof above hit the surface of the pool to ripple across the surface.

Nick guessed they must be toward the upper part of the cistern and speculated about its depth. Nick recollected their visit to the Basilica Cistern. Relatively small by comparison, this cistern still showed signs of the same architectural flourishes and arches, but in miniature.

Set on top of the columns sat Corinthian-style capitals featuring acanthus leaves and ornate floral patterns that peeked out of the dark as their arches continued their long rest and slumber, silently bearing the loads the ancient builders designed them for. Nick wondered if the column bases hiding under the chilly water had the image of Medusa carved into them, eternally holding her breath down in the dark recesses. He shivered considering it.

The two adventurers returned, their lights became bigger and shone on the little group's faces as they drew closer.

"It is all right," said the Inspector as he splashed along, his light fixed on the stones in front of him. "The path is clear, and the stones good, exceptionally good. They are a little slick in several places, so you must be careful. I would not advise you to go for a cool swim followed by a wet walk, so watch your step! Follow us back across."

Nick kept his light trained on the walkway in front of him. He remembered the cold water of his childhood and did not want to visit Medusa in the cold depths.

Gazing into the depths as much as his flashlight beam let him, Nick could not discern the bottom. "How deep is it, do you think?"

He reckoned, at least, it would be over his head, and that criterion alone made it too deep and mysterious for his liking. He wondered if the watcher in the water of Khazad-dûm might winter in Istanbul.

"It's hard to tell," replied Inspector Karamanlis. "It's probably 5 or 6 meters deep. This walkway is different from the typical construction. I have not seen it before."

"It could be a later addition to the original," Alfanas suggested. "Because it is below the high-water level, it would mean year-round access and a straight path in the dark without the need to grope your way around a walkway skirting the water. Its existence would make me think it is probably more like 4 meters deep. Why, Nick? Do you want to dive in and swim to the bottom to find out if my guess is correct?"

Nick laughed nervously. "I hate cold water!" Had the shrewd old monk guessed his anxiety? Elena's warm and confident hand rubbed his back to reassure him.

Elena, her father's daughter, confronted the dark with the venomous resolve of an unconquerable spirit, thrilled by the adventure. These ruins, unseen and unexplored since her ancestor laid these stones, comforted her. These stones, like her people, are strong and resilient. They would not let her down.

A marvel of its time, Constantinople held the allure of a modern metropolis. It sparkled with gold and glittered with jewels. Its royalty dressed in the finest silks, whose beauty surpassed the courts of sultans. The builders of old meticulously crafted every part of a building project. They didn't care if the architecture would be seen by thousands or, well, never seen again by human eyes. God would notice. The highest art of a builder honored God, catching the creator's eye with finials and bases, amusing God by a drowned god squashed by a column, made the attention to detail worth the labor of years. God would see; that's enough.

"It is beautiful," Elena said, as if speaking to herself, "simply beautiful." She touched Nick's back again. "Do not worry; we are being watched by loving eyes, even here. And can't you feel the spirit of Alexios in this place? He is watching too and maybe smiling at his ancestors groping in the dark."

Nick, still anxious, but it comforted him every so often to sense her warm hand on his back. As they reached the other side of the cistern, he let out a sigh of relief. Leaving the deep waters behind, they plunged into the aqueduct that fed the cistern.

No more than ten feet from the edge of the cistern lay a four-way intersection. Opposite them, a stairwell once went up into the darkness. Rubble that must have fallen from the top and now blocked it completely. Two other paths joined from the right and the left, but which belonged to the secret way, and which merely fed the hydraulic system?

"Everyone take a door," Alfanas directed. "Make a full investigation of the stones on the front and inside the tunnel. Brush the silt on the floor away and observe the stones under the water. When we have all done this, we will share what we find and choose our way."

"Do we need to consider the passage we came through?" Nick asked.

"Yes," Alfanas replied, "we will need to get back, and we will also need to note any clues to aid our decision. Remember that those who did not know its construction would have taken this path and probably had not walked it before. There must be a clue to the correct way."

Nick and Elena worked together on the path the group had come down. That left the other three to inspect the different paths. Nick stayed out of the water and left it to Elena.

Elena broke the silence first. "Here it is! Here it is!" she yelled. "Look on the floor, in the water, in the center of the entry. It is the tetragrammatic cross from Mystras."

In the circle of light from Elena's flashlight, in the middle of the clear flowing water, Nick saw the odd small squat cross in its shield. The Greek character beta, β, in the two right quadrants, with its mirrored twins in the left quadrants. He and Elena shared a smile as they recalled that night in Mystras, which now seemed so far away and long ago.

Three more cries echoed in the tunnel; "It's here. It's here. It's here."

"Look for another clue to the way," said Alfanas.

They all searched, but they found nothing.

Inspector Karamanlis rubbed the back of his neck with his hand. "I suggest we need to stop here for the day. I can bring a larger team down to map this place thoroughly. If we choose wrong, we can get lost down here."

At the mention of a "team," Alfanas become noticeably more anxious. The publicity and the delay would derail the entire journey. Helplessly he grabbed Niketas' arm, whispering, "You know what is at stake."

Niketas smiled as he turned his face from examining one of the engravings, turning his attention to the Inspector. "Leontios, my dear friend, whose family is as of my own. You must trust me as never before. Our quest is for the honor of my family. Please, I beg, let us figure this out, and then you can judge the best way forward."

Inspector Karamanlis let his gaze rest on the tetragrammatic cross in his pathway as if deeply considering the request, and his face changed to an expression of interest, progressing to curiosity. He stooped down and brushed the image as if to clear even more silt away. "Yalla! It is small and hard to make out in this light, but the beta in the lower left quadrant is not mirrored! This cross is incorrect!"

Alfanas knelt at the base of the stairwell to examine his cross and reported, "This one, too!"

Elena had not moved from where she had first found her cross. She confirmed that the image carved in her stone was correct. Niketas brushed away more silt from his assigned cross to reveal a correct carving.

"Ah, my daughter, we match! This must be the way. It would make sense. If you were being pursued, the symbols would guide you, but an enemy rushing in the dark could not take the time to discern the clues: a foreigner would not know where to look and what is amiss. Looking down that way, they would not notice the walkway under the water in torch or candlelight, and all the markers would, upon first glance, appear the same. We can move more quickly now that we know the sign. Let's take this opening."

Inspector Karamanlis kept his peace as they walked down the path that headed north in the wrong direction from the Golden Gate; it did so for about thirty feet before shooting straight west.

"We are headed back toward the Golden Gate," Alfanas observed.

They came to one more juncture, but it, too, fit the pattern, allowing them to move quickly in the right direction. The way ended with another cistern, marked with the wrong tetragrammatic cross, and no walkway below the water's surface. On their left, a few steps remained of a walled-up stairway, with a correct engraving on the floor at its base.

"Well," said Alfanas, "it seems like we have found the stairs to the Golden Gate. I am glad now that we did not spend much time there." He put his hand on the stonework. "This was intentionally sealed from this side and, no doubt, filled in secretly on the other side. It would have been impossible to find unless you dug down 10 or 15 feet. The secret way has been intentionally hidden by someone."

They retraced their steps and quickly returned to where they had entered. Inspector Karamanlis suggested they proceed down the East way: "After all, it cannot go that far, and we now understand how to make it through the roadblocks."

Smooth, almost level, and with one junction, they headed east. Like the earlier western cistern, they found a correct tetragrammatic cross with a path of stone below the surface. Other than the discomfort of their feet feeling slightly numb, everyone had become accustomed to the wet and the dark. Even Nick now considered it rather routine.

Inspector Karamanlis led them. Alfanas, followed by Nick and Elena, with Niketas last. He had moved on to thoughts of his own. Nick shifted from anxiety to familiarity as his thoughts shifted to home. He wondered if his dad had managed to get everything out of his apartment and close it up. *"I hope he didn't let that landlord of mine trick him out of my security deposit. I don't trust that guy. He would rob his own …"*

A stone shifted. He grabbed at the darkness, which was empty; he tumbled and splashed into the cold depths of Medusa's lair. His flashlight flew out of his hand and sank to the bottom. At first, he made for it; he needed light, but became confused. Which way should he go? *"Float, you'll go to the surface,"* he told himself. He floated up, and his head hit a stone above him, trapped. He must have swum in the wrong direction, surfacing in an arch or something, and he panicked. The flashlight still glimmered, beckoning him down as his body screamed for oxygen, urging him to take a breath. *"This is how it ends,"* ran through his mind. He would die in the blasted icy water he hated so much!

Suddenly, a light appeared on his right. Nick felt a powerful hand pull him forward and push him to the surface. Four other hands, the hands of Niketas and Karamanlis, hoisted him, coughing and gasping, onto the stone walkway, where Elena held him as tight as she could.

Niketas and Karamanlis turned their attention to fishing the wet monk from the water. Alfanas did not fear what he did not like; the dark, cold water, or death. He had known them all before. Seldom caught either by surprise or without a plan, he had the knack of meeting every dark contingency head-on with a split-second resolve and response.

The moment Alfanas heard the splash, he knew what had happened and barked orders for the flashlights to be trained on the water and directed Elena to thrust hers beneath the water as a guide for him and Nick. He threw his jacket and shoes off, and he jumped in.

Nick shook all over—not from the cold, but from the fear of his near escape.

Elena strove to be strong for him, and she tried to hold back her tears and anxious thoughts about "what if." In fear she held him tighter than she meant to, but he had become more to her than a quest or a people. Yes, the future, somehow she relied on him more and more as her future. Losing him? No, she would rather go home now and keep him safe. The feeling stuck like a stone in her throat as she desperately clung to him in the dark.

Nick had never been so near death before. He thought of his parents and how hurt they would be. Is their quest, no matter the end, worth more than his life? The cold seemed to claim him as he shook uncontrollably in the dank, wet, dark. He also considered Elena and all that they had been through. Her arms now cradling him for the second time, the warmth of her embrace reminded him of being in front of a comforting fire, and he closed his eyes to focus only on her embrace.

"Move him to the other side. Don't let him sit in the water." Barked Alfanas, now safely out of the water himself. The entrance to the marginally drier aqueduct lay roughly ten feet from the far side of the cistern. Elena and Niketas help raise and support Nick as he walked from the threat of the deep water to the safety of the tunnel.

Nick stammered through clenched, trembling teeth: "I-I'm f-fine. J-just a l-loose st-stone. O-oh G-God… I c-couldn't s-see… I c-couldn't g-get out… I th-thought I was g-gone." He looked at the old monk in the light of the flashlights. "Th-thank y-you. Y-you s-s-saved m-my l-life." And he hung his head lest the old monk notice the tears in his eyes.

Nick had always seen Alfanas as the wise, enigmatic guide, but in that moment, he was more, more substantial, braver, and perhaps more selfless than anyone Nick had ever known. For the first time, he wondered how much the old monk had seen and endured to be this calm and decisive in the face of death.

Alfanas smiled, put his hand on the side of Nick's face, gave him a little pat, "You are welcome, and you are not alone in hating cold water. Let's now move on quickly."

Thankfully, the tunnels sheltered them from the open air. The underground temperature is always around 58°F, but still and humid, so the cold would bother them less than being in the open outside, where there would be evaporative cooling. Still, Alfanas knew they would now need to move more quickly to get to the surface and warmth. A quicker pace and physical activity would help Nick and Alfanas to feel warmer by getting their blood flowing through exertion.

The tunnel to the west of the last cistern had dried up, so they did not have to worry about slips and falls on the slick stones under the water. It actually went up slightly and then leveled off. The tunnel ended at a single stairwell. Inspector Karamanlis and Niketas went up the stairs to investigate and had the other three sit and rest.

Nick, Elena, and Alfanas sat on the dry floor of the tunnel. Nick put his head back, and even though he was cold, he felt he could sleep at once. Alfanas and Elena shone their flashlights around the tunnel while waiting for the other two to return.

Alfanas suddenly drew in his breath sharply. "What is that on the wall?"

The other two followed the beam of light to its resting place on a stone at the base of the wall. Engraved in one corner of the stone, they saw the imperial double-headed eagle. Elena crawled over to the stone, and to clear the image for better viewing. She then brushed the dirt and dust off the floor, revealing another correct carving.

"What does this mean? There is no doorway here. The stairwell had a tetragrammatic cross."

"It means there is a closed door we haven't yet opened," replied Alfanas. He got up and began to pace and talk as he paced. "Whatever is behind that door is what we came for. If we investigate it now, Inspector Karamanlis will need to be involved, and what is behind that wall will be in the daily papers and around the world. They will be back soon. Say nothing. We will come back tonight with your father to examine it more closely."

Terror struck Nick at the prospect of having to cross that horrible walkway not just once more, but three times. Of course he would steel himself and do it, even if not looking forward to the experience. In the back of his mind, he also wanted Alfanas to think he was brave. The question of his masculinity had never felt important, but after Alfanas' example, he wanted to impress him somehow. Even if it meant his life, he would suppress his fear and do the next thing.

Voices from the stairwell let them know their comrades were returning.

"Well, some good news, especially for Nick," announced Niketas, "but for all of us. We will not need to go back through the cisterns and aqueducts to return. The stairwell ended on loose-fit stones in one of the ruined walls of the Gate of St. Aemilianus on the coast.

I will call a taxi for Leontios and me to take us back to our cars, and you can call your friend to pick you up here. Once we get into the open, we will restore the stones until a gate can secure the passage."

Sam grunted as the now-damp Nick and mostly dry Elena climbed into his backseat. Alfanas got a nod and an inaudible comment as they tore off for the hotel. Not needing deception, they experienced a calmer ride back to the hotel. Nick and Elena were the first ones out of the car and headed up immediately so that Nick could get warm. They left Alfanas talking to Sam. Nick had showered and dressed in dry clothes again when they heard the familiar knock on their door.

Alfanas had cleaned and dried up as well. It was now early evening. Alfanas pulled out a chair, sat down, looked at both of them for a minute. "I hate to break it to you, but we need to leave in about half an hour. I have arranged for Sam to pick us up and take us to the Gate of St. Aemilianus: the entrance to the tunnel."

Nick reacted out of exhaustion, fear, and anxiety: "Can't it wait?!"

"No, I don't think it can. I know you are tired and drained, but I need you to dig deep, push through, and put yourself second tonight.

Inspector Karamanlis can't officially act for a few days, but he will not delay long in reporting what we have found. We will cover up the carvings and replace the stones. Chances are that this will remain an enigmatic listing buried in a report, filed for posterity. This small hydraulic system will quickly fade into the obscurity of the bureaucracy, which is the nature of all governments. But we must act before other eyes watch and gates are installed and locked. No, tonight is the night. We leave in thirty minutes."

Chapter 15: Summoning the Marble Emperor

Alfanas once again summoned the enigmatic Sam, who performed his auto brake dance on the highways and byways of Istanbul with now audible subtitles in Turkish. Every so often, Elena would grimace, blush, and look over at Nick, patting his hand in embarrassment. Nick appreciated his lack of linguistic fluency in Turkish for the first time during the adventure. As thrilling as Sam's rides are in the light, in the dark Nick found them similar to a ride on Disney's Space Mountain. After the first five minutes, Nick couldn't imagine anyone being able to follow them.

In the middle of the evening, they arrived at the Cerrahpaşa Park. They all, including Sam, got out of the car at the park. Sam opened the trunk and passed what appeared to be something heavy wrapped in burlap to Alfanas. He drove away, leaving them alone in the dark.

Filled with people by day, the park becomes eerily deserted at night. The ample lights from the park and the highway gave them more than enough light to return to the undercut part of the old seawall of the Gate of St. Aemilianus. Nick and Elena kept watch as Alfanas moved just enough rocks to allow him to squeeze into the concealed stairwell, with Nick and Elena following.

Once in the stairwell's privacy, they switched on their flashlights and descended back into the damp ever-night of the tunnel. At the foot of the stairs, Elena began sweeping away the dust and dirt from the floor in front of the stone where they had found the carvings earlier. While she worked, Alfanas examined the stones to determine the best way to remove a few, allowing them to explore whatever might lie behind. If it were a simple stash, removing the marked stone would suffice, but if it led to a larger void, they would need to ensure that they did not compromise the wall's integrity.

"Whatever we do, we must undo without any evidence that the wall has been tampered with," he cautioned, "We do not want to leave any suggestion that this place holds any other secret than a way into more of the subterranean hydraulic system of old Constantinople."

Elena had cleared the dirt from the carvings in front of the marked rock. The stones fit tightly together to form the wall. Alfanas unwrapped the burlap bundle Sam had handed to him and extracted several types of bars, knives, and hooks.

"I figured that we would need some tools of our own tonight and asked Sam to procure them for us," explained Alfanas as he continued to examine the stone with a small bar in his hand. "I think if you take this," he handed a second bar to Nick, "and we worked at it from two sides, we could ease it out of place. Try not to scratch it!"

It was slow going, but they had to remove the stone. The masons of old tapered the inner sides and top toward the back, allowing it to move easily after being pulled out about an inch. With this keystone removed, they quickly created a good-sized hole able to accommodate a flashlight, offering a glimpse into what lay beyond. Clearly, they were dealing with a significant void and not a small stash as in Mystras.

As Alfanas traced the sides with his flashlight, noting that a back wall remained elusive, he concluded they had found an extension to their tunnel. "We will need to remove these three stones to allow us to squeeze through and not risk the integrity of the wall."

Concerned to remove only the stones necessary to create a hole large enough to admit passage but not so large as to collapse the wall, they finally were able to squeeze into the tunnel. They found themselves in a compact tunnel, narrower and lower than the main aqueduct space they had left. It went back about twenty feet and west for another twenty feet before opening to a ten-by-ten-foot small vaulted room. There, in its center, stood a half-height marble statue, bearing the Greek inscription, Κωνσταντῖνος ὁ ΙΑ' Παλαιολόγος, Βασιλεὺς Ῥωμαίων.

"What does it say?" Nick asked.

Elena let her hand drift over the characters. "It says, 'Constantine XI Palaiologos, Emperor of the Romans.'"

The "Marble Emperor" stood wearing the full military gear of an infantryman of his time. He had a medium build with his hand on the hilt of a sheathed sword, ready to defend but not yet at war. Nick placed his hand on the statue's shoulder and looked into the frozen eyes as if they could suddenly come to life. They had found the legend, and he still waited for the summons to return to the city. Nick thought back to the larger-than-life man in Mystras: *What a contrast.*

Caught in a demanding situation, raised in privilege and expectation, with an ego to match both, Nick felt a wave of compassion for Constantine XI. In the end, he tried to do his best with the cards delt him, protecting and ruling a weakened, demoralized city, the sole remains of the mighty Roman, Byzantine Empire. He faced a foe over three times his strength, with walls that were not meant to withstand the innovative technology of gunpowder, but he fought on.

Alfanas placed a caring hand on Nick's shoulder and looked up at the vaulted roof. "We must be under the highway." His touch and words brought Nick back to the present. "We should look for clues about what to do next. Examine the stones and look for our double-headed friends and the cross."

Nick and Elena took to the walls and floor. Alfanas would examine the floor around the statue and the statue itself. After searching the entire room, the walls yielded no further clues, but Alfanas pointed to two familiar symbols. Small and near impossible to find in the dim light, carved into the back of the statue's base were the two familiar symbols they had been following since Mystras.

Alfanas observed the flagstones extended under the base of the statue, not cut around the statue, whose base rested on a footing. The workmen placed the statue directly on top of the pavers. "It is as if one would need to move the statue to get the stone up. I suspect that what we are looking for is under the statue and not under the floor. Nick, you, and I will slowly pry up one side of the statue. We should be able to raise it enough to see what, if anything, is under it."

They worked carefully and slowly together to tilt the statue to one side. They did not want to tip it to the point where it would become off balance and fall, shattering on the stone pavers. When Alfanas took the flashlight and peered in, they had about four inches of clearance under the base. Another lead cylinder, identical to the one they had found in Mystras, lay on the floor and fitted into a recess carved into the base of the statue.

Alfanas grunted and wiggled the cylinder. "It looks like we have now found our second scroll. I think I can slip it out."

As if loath to leave its rest, the base finally released its hold on the cylinder. Now in the full view of the flashlight, the engravings affirmed it as matching the earlier Mystras cylinder. Alfanas handed it to Elena to hold while he and Nick returned the statue to its place.

"All right," Alfanas said in a satisfied tone with a smile on his face, "now back to the main tunnel, fix the wall, and call Sam to get us home. Along the way, I will call your father. He'd love to hear about all this tomorrow and help me read the scroll. That will leave the two of you with a day to yourselves. I would get out of the city and do something. It won't matter if you are followed. I don't think we need to fear what these watchers will do, merely what they see. So, take them sightseeing in the country!"

As they headed back down the small tunnel to the aqueduct, Nick turned to Elena with a smile. "So, where are you going to sweep me away tomorrow?"

She returned the smile. She said nothing except to herself, *"Sweep you away, my little American boy still shines through now and then."* His resilience pleased her. His devilish little smile had come like a ray of sunlight from behind the cloud. Tomorrow, she would try to keep them both relaxed and smiling: two friends on the beach, in the cafes and markets. Walking and leaving care behind them.

"I think I will take you to a family tradition for us growing up, and when we wanted to get out of the city. Mama and Papa would take us to Şile. You will enjoy it there. You will see a side of Türkiye you have not seen before. The quiet beauty of the countryside blends into the sandy beaches and the rhythmic waves."

After squeezing back through the small opening, they returned to stones to their places in reverse order, covered the carving with the loose dirt of the floor, and headed back up the stairs to summon Sam.

Now after midnight, they were all pleased to see the hotel rise before them in the dark. The scroll and Şile would have to wait until tomorrow. They all thanked Sam, who nodded in response, surprising Nick, and drove away. *"We must have gone up in his estimation,"* Nick reasoned. *"At least he is acknowledging our existence."*

They fell asleep the moment their bodies sank beneath the covers, never so thankful to be dry, warm, and safe for the night, especially Nick.

The next morning, Nick woke to the sound of the call to prayer drifting through the thin curtains of their hotel room. Despite the early hour, the energy of a new day reverberated through the city. Today promised a reprieve for Nick and Elena. Alfanas' reprieve would be the joy of working with Niketas on the scroll.

Elena stirred in the other bed next to Nick's. "Morning," she said groggily, rubbing her eyes. "Ready to escape the chaos?"

Nick stretched. "More than ready. I am looking forward to seeing … what's the name again?"

"Şile," she said softly, "It's a quiet town on the Black Sea coast, about an hour's drive. There are public beaches and a lighthouse. It will be a perfect place to escape the city and remain anonymous with the tourists."

Elena drove their rented car more sedately than Sam as she navigated out of Istanbul's labyrinthine streets, following the GPS. The crowds and smells of Istanbul faded, giving way to pastoral scenes of a less hectic way of life in the suburbs and the rural landscapes of Türkiye. Nick noticed a marked contrast to New England not merely in the wandering of goats and sheep but also in the architecture and materials, like terracotta-roofed houses with small patches of flowers and gardens.

By mid-morning, they arrived in Şile. They spent the rest of the morning walking on the beach and visiting the lighthouse. They soaked up the retreat from the crowded streets, airports, and current experience of the cities they had been to.

Nick and Elena had lunch outside at a small seaside cafe. The afternoon lazily slipped past as they casually visited several area towns, attractions, and cafes.

Reluctantly heading back toward Istanbul as the sun dipped lower in the sky. The closer they got to the city, the frenetic energy crept back into their senses. When they reached their hotel early that evening, the streets were alive with evening traffic and the hum of countless lives intersecting.

Alfanas sat waiting for them in the hotel lobby, their expressions a mix of excitement and exhaustion.

"How was the countryside?" Alfanas asked, his eyes twinkling.

Nick glanced at Elena as he answered. "Exactly what we needed. What about you?"

Alfanas gave a wry smile. "Let's just say the emperor's story is far from over. I have supper waiting for us upstairs, and we can talk in private."

When they had returned to the room and could safely talk, Alfanas turned to Elena. "First of all, your father sends his love. He is disappointed that he will not be able to see you again before you leave."

"Leave," cried Nick and Elena in unison.

"Where are we going and why?" Elena beat Nick to the punch yet again.

"We are going to Kyiv next and hopefully last. Your father and I read section II of the *Chronicle*, and we both concur that it is to Kyiv we must go. The small merchant vessel that set sail in 1453 was only the last of several Byzantine secret shipments sailing under the flag of the Venetians that year. Alexios had been planning for a long time to save what he could of the remains of Constantinople's significant heritage. The last thing to be saved, he hoped, would be Constantine XI himself."

"He wasn't killed then?" Nick gasped, "He is not buried somewhere here?"

Pleased with the surprise, Alfanas continued. "Not according to Alexios. He was bandaged and treated at the Monastery of Saint John the Forerunner and in very grave condition, barely holding on to life, but alive when they carried him aboard the ship. Alexios and one of his sons, the eldest, Theodore, journeyed with him. The other son, Michael, stayed behind in service to the Sultan. Michael is the one who sired your family, Elena.

"What about Alexios?" She asked.

"Alexios never returns, but having lost his wife in the siege, he enters a monastery for the rest of his life. Michael was the one who hid the scrolls, filled the stairwell, and covered the tracks. After that, he began the legend of the Marble Emperor, among other legends of the time. According to the scroll we found, which is now in the keeping of your father in the university vaults, Michael was a brave man who endured many hardships to keep the family alive.

This second section tells his story up to nearly the end of his life when he interred the scroll and sent a copy to his brother, Theodore, who joined his father as a monk in service at Kyiv Pechersk Lavra, now known as the Monastery of the Caves in Kyiv, our next stop. Oh, one last thing about Theodore: he was the gatekeeper to the catacombs.

Today, the cave churches and passageways primarily hold relics and are used liturgically; long-term residence in the caves themselves is uncommon."

Nick, feeling like a spectator to a game where he had been benched, asked, "What will we find in Kyiv Pechersk Lavra?"

"Well, the scroll does not say. As did the first section, I suspect it points us to the third section of the Chronicle, which will point us to either a fourth section or a resolution of what happened to Constantine and the remnants of the regalia of Constantinople."

"Did Constantine have any children?"

Alfanas sighed remorsefully. "No. That is a sad chapter in personal history. He was married once when in Mystras, but his wife, Theodora, died during childbirth, after less than a year of marriage. He never remarries or produces an heir to the title of 'Sovereign Emperor of the Romans.'"

"What comes next?"

Alfanas' gaze shifted from the window where he had been looking into the suffering of the past to focus on Elena's question. "Tonight we will rest. Tomorrow, we will go in different directions."

Nick gasped in fear and surprise. "We're splitting up? What about Viktor and his allies? You're going to leave us alone?" Nick felt a knot in his stomach. The thought of being left to their own devices excited and daunted him at the same time, especially with the shadow of Viktor's allies still looming.

"Viktor is still being held. I expect his collaborators will not harm you, but only watch you and report back what they see. They will need to split their resources if we head in different directions. I must prepare the way for you in Kyiv Pechersk Lavra. Things are not what they used to be. It remains under the control of the Russian Orthodox Church. I do not expect everyone will welcome a stranger with open arms. Your visa will allow you to cross political borders without issue. Still, it carries no weight with the abbot. The abbot has ties to the Russian state and may view us with suspicion. We'll need to tread carefully."

"Are we to stay here?" inquired Elena hopefully.

"No. I think I need to get you away from any potential contact with your parents and out of the more critical climate of Istanbul. I think a bus to Ormenio, Greece, will be a good place to park you until you hear from me. It keeps you headed toward Kyiv, but in a field where I have more pull and that is more accepting of the West."

"How long will we be there?"

Alfanas pursed his lips and rubbed his forehead in concern for a moment. "It is hard to say. I simply have the beginnings of a plan, depending on how long it will take my abbot at Holy Trinity St. George Monastery in Uzbekistan to respond. Even then, we will need to work around the curiosity of the gatekeeper of the catacombs. But for tonight, we sleep. Tomorrow, we are back on the road. The road to Kyiv will test us all," his voice lowered. "But if we succeed, we may finally uncover the last chapter of the last emperor's story."

Alfanas' ominous final words echoed in Nick's mind as he closed his eyes to sleep. He replayed the journey to date, and his highlights had to be Mystras and Sparta. Ormenio may be perfectly fine, but he didn't believe that he and Elena would ever escape the shadows Viktor now cast on their journey. Once finished, he might leave them alone, but maybe not even then. Indeed, the road to Kyiv would test them all.

Chapter 16: The Paths Diverge

Wednesday dawned bright and beautiful, meeting the world with the promise of energy and potential: Alfanas moved with purpose, now back in his black robes that swished as he walked, releasing the ever-present smell of incense and beeswax in the soft breeze he created. He always rose before dawn. Nick followed, a little less enthusiastically, his backpack slung over one shoulder, trying to shake the grogginess of too little sleep, enhanced by the habit of not getting up before the sun if possible. Elena brought up the rear, her eyes scanning the streets with a mixture of alertness and anticipation, her thoughts focused on the journey ahead.

Breakfast had been a hurried affair, a piece of simit and strong Turkish tea gulped down as they prepared to leave. Nick and Elena planned on seeing Alfanas board his flight to Chişinău, Moldova, as he began his trek to Kyiv. Their bus didn't depart for Greece until later in the afternoon. To fill the gap, they would spend the time visiting a museum in Istanbul, with a late lunch to follow.

They took a regular cab to the airport. Alfanas figured that Viktor probably had the airport watched anyway, so he would not need to use Sam's skills for this trip. Nick felt a pang of anxiety seize him as the airport emerged on the horizon. He felt a little queasy, fidgeted with his pack, trying to get his mind off the fact that somewhere out there, Viktor's shadow still loomed. Nick could not guess when or whether that shadow would strike again. Now, he and Elena would be on their own.

He looked at the old monk in the front seat and realized how much they depended on him. Nick did not look forward to Alfanas' absence, but they would persevere to meet whatever challenges awaited them.

"You said that the trip to Kyiv would challenge us. What did you mean?" Nick asked.

"I don't know exactly, but I do know that we're going to Ukraine, and we will start setting off alarm bells with Viktor. Russia has always kept a tight grip on Ukraine's independence. Viktor will sense we're stepping into his territory and act fast. I think he will double his efforts to make a personal appearance on the scene," answered Alfanas.

Elena, herself harboring some of Nick's misgivings, looked out the window. "I guess it is no good our asking to go with you? It does not seem right that we are put in the background while you take all the risks."

Elena, ever the optimist, felt she and Nick would be okay on their own. She would wait and see how things worked out. Viktor didn't scare her, but she hated being idle. Surely they would be of more help in Kyiv than out of the picture in a small, unheard-of town in Greece, once more on holiday.

"No. You must be out of the picture and off the radar of associating with me while I prepare things. It will be more dangerous for you to kill time in Kyiv than in Ormenio." He paused silently, reflecting for a minute. "I do not know what is going to greet me as I return to Ukraine. It's complicated for me to go there. There're too many things that might happen. Your safety would be a distraction."

Alfanas turned back to glance at them, his expression calm but unreadable. "I know this is concerning for you both, but I think that it is best with what information we have right now. If all is well, I will send for you. Wait patiently for my call."

They walked with him up to the security scanners and paused. Alfanas looked at them both and smiled. "Do not borrow trouble from tomorrow. Today is enough for both of us. Ormenio will be a good place for you. Resign yourselves to being followed. But the worst they can do is get a picture of you in your bathing suits! Peace, be still. The road ahead may not all be comfortable, but it will all be okay. I will meet you in Kyiv soon." He hugged and kissed them on each cheek.

They looked on as he passed through security and off into the airside of the airport. He did not turn once but kept to his course. Of course, he didn't tell them that even as they worried about themselves and the path forward; he worried for them. He gambled Viktor would remain in jail and not seek to entrust what he surmised to his friends on the outside. While the police held Viktor, Nick and Elana would be safe. Viktor might risk more and sound more alarms if Nick and Elena moved toward Kyiv with Alfanas. All of them moving at once would signal an endgame run to some finish line, and that might have terrible consequences. "No," he assured himself, "this is the best way."

Nick and Elena stood near the departure gates at Istanbul Airport, watching Alfanas disappear into the mass of travelers.

Nick felt more than a little remorse as Alfanas' black robes disappeared into the crowd. "Let's go." Taking Elena's hand, he led her out of the airport.

With time to waste before getting on their bus to Ormenio, Elena wanted to show Nick Istanbul's past glory by visiting the Istanbul Archaeological Museum, a massive complex with artifacts and exhibits spanning the history of Byzantium and the Ottoman Empire.

"Istanbul wasn't just the crossroads of East and West; it was the heart of an empire," she said as they entered the museum. "Constantine I intentionally selected it as the center of the Roman Empire in the fourth century. He never saw it as a new culture, simply a relocation from Rome."

As they moved through the displays and artifacts of stone, gold, and silver, Nick wondered at the level of sophistication and technical expertise. Like almost everyone in the West, he was familiar with ancient Rome but had no direct experience of Constantinople or the Byzantine Empire.

They came to a model of Constantinople at its height before the Christian West occupied and ravaged it through the Fourth Crusade, and Venice pillaged it. It was vast. The massive palace complex put to shame the most expansive buildings of America's Gilded Age. The West came to call it Byzantium to distinguish it from ancient Rome, even though Roman culture and law continued without pause.

Nick examined the dates that stretched back a thousand, 1,500, or more years. "You know, we in New England put plaques on our homes dating back to the eighteenth and nineteenth centuries, thinking they are old and historic. But here, the etched stones whisper down thousands of years, millennial struggles for continuity and tragic consequences of drastic change." He paused momentarily, considering, "And here we stand in the context of all of this. Our families are entwined in the dance of history and fate as the story continues."

"It is the first time," Elena responded, "you have felt the heavy weight of history. I grew up walking among the ghosts of the past, being held somehow accountable for the glory and majesty of this heritage to which so many others would have me feel inferior or ashamed." She paused. "Sometimes, at least here, it does not seem like we stand on the shoulders of giants as much as we are walking in their shadows."

Nick stood with his hand resting on one of the imperial porphyry sarcophagi located outside the museum. The stone had absorbed some of the day's warmth. "I'm glad we came here. I'm feeling more connected to the story that I have stepped into, and I begin to understand a little more of what it must be like for you and the hopes and dreams that motivate you and your people. They were great once. But now ..." He let his voice trail off into silence, unable to find the right words.

Elena gave a faint smile. "Yes, but now? That's the part we're still figuring out. We're still working out."

They had lunch and arrived at the bus terminal on time, ready to be on their way to Ormenio. Crowded but quiet, the trip took about six hours, with one stop between the border of Türkiye and Greece for customs and papers.

That evening, the bus reached Ormenio, and the serenity of the small Greek town contrasted with the pandemonium of Istanbul. A driver from their hotel greeted them, and within minutes, they were at their accommodations.

Once in their modest but comfortable rooms, Elena opened the window, letting in the cool night air. Insect noise and the ability to see the stars underscored they could let their guard down for a while. Alfanas had encouraged them not to care about anyone following them. They could take all the photos they wanted and inform Viktor of how much coffee and baklava they ate, but it would provide no other information.

Nick sat on the side of the bed, rubbed his temples, fell back onto the soft comforter and sighed. "I feel like we've been on the move for weeks. Granted, we have had some good time off, but I'd love to make a final push and get this over with. I feel like a piece of leftover chicken that has been in and out of the refrigerator and reheated more than eaten."

"I think we are all a little anxious," Elena said with a faint laugh. "It is hard knowing that Alfanas is bearing more of the burden while we sit and wait, and knowing that he is right in what he is doing doesn't make the waiting any easier."

Nick nodded, got up, and prepared to go to bed. Their journey continued toward an unknown horizon, with Ormenio serving as an indeterminate pause.

The next three days in Ormenio passed slowly. Nick and Elena found it boring as a reprieve from the relentless pace of their recent travels. On Saturday morning, they woke late; the sunlight streaming through the curtains of their hotel room. There was no immediate plan, no pressing urgency to leave. They allowed themselves a leisurely breakfast at a small cafe near the town square. Nick noticed the local charm of the place in the communal familiarity that welcomed the regulars.

Small and quaint, Ormenio's narrow streets, houses, and terracotta roofs spoke of another era. On their first full day, Nick and Elena explored the village, mapping out places to eat and shop. An old church and a few family-run shops framed the main square. They purchased a few essentials, including bottled water and snacks.

Nick sat on a low stone wall overlooking the valley and nursed a bottle of water. "Do you think Alfanas has made it to Kyiv yet?"

Elena shrugged, her gaze fixed on the horizon. "If anyone can navigate those waters, it's him. But I hope he's safe."

Their evenings were spent at the hotel. On Sunday night, as they sat in the cozy lounge by the fire, Elena pulled out her phone with the text of the next legs of their journey, Alfanas had laid out for them, tracing their next steps toward Kyiv. "I hope he'll contact us soon." She turned the phone off and threw it in her lap.

Boredom had blossomed into unbearable restlessness by Monday afternoon. The stillness of Ormenio now felt heavy with anticipation. Nick had taken to wandering the village, his thoughts swirling as he tried to piece together the fragments of their journey so far and consider where this led next. Elena spent the morning reading, but even she seemed distracted, her usual focus giving way to a muted tension.

As the sun dipped low in the sky, the call finally came. Nick and Elena had come back to the hotel from a walk when Nick's phone buzzed, and the word 'Alfanas' appeared on its display.

Nick held up his phone so she could see the name. "Here we go!"

As Nick and Elena rested in Ormenio, Alfanas started his next challenge. The journey by plane would be the most peaceful hours he would have for some time. Once on the ground, he would need to talk to various people to gain access to Kyiv Pechersk Lavra.

The Kyiv Pechersk Lavra, also known as the Monastery of the Caves, is a stunning and historic Orthodox Christian monastery on a hill overlooking the Dnipro River in Kyiv, Ukraine. Established in 1051, it is one of Eastern Europe's most important religious and cultural landmarks.

The Lavra is a vast complex with golden-domed churches, bell towers, and monastic buildings. Surrounded by gardens and protective walls. But its genuine wonder lies buried beneath the surface: the catacombs. These underground passages, initially dug by monks seeking solitude and prayer, stretch deep into the hillside and house a network of chapels, burial sites, and relics. Many of the catacombs' niches hold the mummified remains of saints and monks, preserved naturally over centuries.

Unlike other catacombs, the caves at Lavra house more than the mummified remains of the monks and saints of the past, but also serve as a place of adoration and worship for the living. In years past, some monks lived in cells inside the caves, seeing little difference between their brethren except that their cellmates happened to be dead.

Today, they are not used as living spaces. But there are also very few times in a day when the caves fall silent and are empty.

The sounds of prayers and the light of candles hold the darkness off until deep in the night, when the darkness returns for a couple of hours so that the tombs rest in peace.

On the grounds of the monastery, Alfanas would try to get lodging as a pilgrim from a fellow Russian Orthodox monastery. He would speak to both his abbot and the Metropolitan of Sparta to vouch for him to the abbot of Kyiv Pechersk Lavra.

The more challenging part would be to escape the political attention of both sides, now focused on the Monastery. "I will have to renew some old alliances, I think," he sighed to himself under his breath.

His flight took him to Chişinău, Moldova, where he boarded the bus for Kyiv. He liked the back seat. It gave him a view of everyone and what they were doing. He recognized a certain man in a white button-up shirt and street clothes, and wanted to keep his eyes and, when possible, his ears on him. He had followed Alfanas everywhere since Istanbul.

That would be a gift from Viktor. "That's fine. He would be at least five seats up from me. He will be able to watch but not hear." Alfanas would make sure of that.

Alfanas settled into his seat for the 12-plus-hour trip, which would put him in Kyiv by about midnight. He would stay in a hotel for the rest of the night, giving him privacy until the morning. But for now, he would wait until the bus left Chişinău to start his calling.

A little after noon, Alfanas had a pleasant conversation with the abbot of the Monastery of Saint George the Pilgrim, his home for the last 14 years. He would immediately reach out to the abbot of Kyiv Pechersk Lavra and vouch for Alfanas as a pilgrim and scholar.

Next on Alfanas' list came the Metropolitan of Sparta. He did not expect any issues with either man, and none arose. They both were eager to work with a pilgrim and a religious scholar. He would give them time to speak with the abbot of Kyiv Pechersk Lavra before he showed up at the monastery seeking to talk to him. If he could stay at the monastery, he would also be able to introduce himself to the gatekeeper, maybe even accessing records of the caves' permanent residents.

He was about four hours from Chișinău and could see the border crossing into Ukraine ahead. It had been fourteen years since he had set foot in the place of his birth. Alfanas' parents had died five years ago, making this a bittersweet homecoming.

Not only could he not go home to see them, and his parents died believing him long dead, but even when they were alive they were probably glad to hear the traitor, their son, a black mark on the family's honor, had met justice.

They could not be told the truth. So they died disowning their son. He sighed heavily as the bus crossed the border. "Yes, Gavriil Novokshonov is still hated by so many. They shouldn't know he is now called Alfanas, let alone that he is a monastic. He must remain dead to all but a few." He smiled. "But those few now run Ukraine."

The bus rolled to a stop at the border checkpoint, its passengers greeted by the sight of armed guards and razor wire fences. Alfanas adjusted his robes, his heart steady but his mind alert. The man in the white shirt rose from his seat two rows ahead, stretching casually before stepping off the bus.

Alfanas followed. He handed over his documents. Alfanas saw himself as a pilgrim returning home; he would have no issues with the border guards. The guard glanced at the passport and then at Alfanas. "Welcome to Ukraine, brother. What is the purpose of your visit?" the guard asked.

"Pilgrimage," Alfanas replied. "To the Lavra in Kyiv."

"All seems in order," the other replied. "Enjoy your time with us. Next!"

Things had to change. Alfanas didn't mind 'white shirt' hanging on to him until now, but he did not want him to follow him to the Lavra. He had to be proactive; the pieces of the game were now in play. Pulling out his phone, searching for a moment to find a number, Alfanas swore he would never dial again. Gavriil used that number last, summoning the owner outside a building engulfed in an inferno from which no flesh would escape. The only charred survivors would be some hardware and the testimony that Gavriil had died. That fire birthed the phoenix Alfanas. Now, these two young people he loved so dearly are on the edge of resuscitating Gavriil, raising him from the ashes that consumed him.

He pressed dial and waited for an answer. "Yes, it is Gavriil. I need some favors for myself and a couple of friends coming in behind me. They are being pursued for some reason. First, I need to know when a man named Viktor, who is being held in Athens, gets released. Second, I need your department to look the other way when I go to Lavra. Any help that you can give us with the gatekeeper would be appreciated. I just crossed the border and will be in Kyiv by midnight. I will talk to you tomorrow. Oh, I am still Brother Alfanas; Gavriil remains dead after this call."

Silently, but monitoring the man in white, Alfanas waited for the other to respond. "No, not at this time. I know that your resources are needed in other places. Just let your folks know that I am … well … harmless," he chuckled a little at this, "and that they should not worry about my friends and me."

Another pause. "Fine. I will call tomorrow."

After putting the phone into the folds of his robe, he returned his gaze to the window. The pieces were now all in play, as the battle moved to Pechersk Lavra.

The big wildcard would be Viktor. Has he figured out Alfanas' identity? If so, he won't be fooled a second time. Did he make a mistake in not taking the children with him? Time would tell. Again he sighed and let an audible vocalization escape: "It is in God's hands."

As he drew closer to Kyiv, everything looked familiar. There are places you never forget. He was young when he last came here. He had lived in the city for ten years. Of course, a lot had changed in both of them. But a lot remained the same.

Arriving after midnight, tired, Alfanas summoned a cab and headed straight to his hotel. Let the man in white watch. He could report nothing except that Alfanas would have a good night's sleep. At breakfast, he would talk to another friend, like Sam in Istanbul, who would ensure the "white shirt" again had nothing to report.

Alfanas did not wake up early the following day. His next stop would be at Pechersk Lavra in the afternoon. Room service delivered his breakfast, and he called his friend at the SBU, the Security Service of Ukraine.

He informed the SBU of his 2:00 meeting at the Lavra to speak with the abbot. Viktor remained in custody by the Greek police, while his friends privately used diplomacy to lobby the court for his immediate release. Alfanas began worrying that he wouldn't have as long as he initially figured.

Alfanas drained the last of his coffee as he stared out of his hotel window over Kyiv with his phone to his ear. "Look, if you have any available assets in Sparta who can monitor Viktor and inform me if he's released and where he's headed, that would be a big help."

There was a pause, and then, "Do what you can. I appreciate the help. One other thing, can you lend me a driver who can lose a man in a white shirt who has followed me from Istanbul?"

"Good, good." … "Yes, 1:30 is fine."

He put the phone next to the empty cup on the table. His attention shifted to Nick and Elena. He hoped they were enjoying their peace. "It is best that they do not know about Viktor for now," he supposed, at least not until Alfanas had any certain news to pass along.

Alfanas lunched downstairs, eating in full view of the man in white. As he finished, he picked up his cup of coffee and sat across from the infamous man in white, who seemed slightly surprised and flustered by the directness.

"Ah, don't I remember you from Istanbul?" Alfanas inquired, his eyes steady and piercing as if searching for answers hidden in the other's thoughts.

"Well, um, I don't think we met," said the other, still trying to figure out what he should do.

"I know we did not meet," Alfanas smiled, "and that is my rudeness. After all, we could have spoken on the bus trip as well. What is your name?"

"Um, Ahmet,"

"Ah, I see," Alfanas smiled even more. "Popular name, Ahmet. You may call me Brother John Smith, a popular name as well. But I see that my ride is here. It has been truly a blessing speaking with you. I am sure we will meet again."

With that, Alfanas drained his cup, rose, and glided out of the restaurant and through the lobby into a compact car that sped away before Ahmet could even react.

Brother Alfanas glanced at his young driver in military garb as he fastened his seat belt. While not quite a Sam, he did well weaving, dodging, and playing with the traffic, making it next to impossible for anyone following to keep up without at least betraying themselves. This trip to Pechersk Lavra would remain off of Viktor's radar. But for how long?

The car slowed as it approached the complex of simple white buildings mixed with the golden domes of the monastery, making the Lavra stand out as it literally caught the rays of the sun or the moon, bouncing and reflecting them off its surfaces. Alfanas had been through its gates before as a younger man, on other business. "Back then," he thought, "it had been a bunch of old buildings like so many others in Kyiv." Yet now, with his vocation realized and embraced, his heart could not help but be moved by the spiritual power long disciplined and channeled within those walls.

He roughly remembered the way to the abbot's office, but he also figured a monk would watch for him and guide him to the abbot. As he walked along one of the many stone pathways through the maze of lawns and gardens, not far ahead, a young monk emerged from a side corridor, his face framed by the faint shadow of a nascent beard.

He approached with a bow and in a muted voice. "Brother Alfanas?" The monk gestured toward a building with high arched windows. "The abbot awaits you in the library."

Alfanas nodded and invited with a wave of his hand. "After you, brother."

The young monk led him through heavy doors that opened onto rows of books on shelves. As they moved silently through the stacks, deeper into the library, the visitors dwindled and fell away, leaving the two monks finally alone, passing through the books.

Near one of the tall windows, the abbot stood, his silhouette softened by the light. He turned, his lined face breaking into a measured smile. "Brother Alfanas, I trust your journey was not too arduous?"

Alfanas bowed as he said, "The Lord bless you, Father. I have traveled many miles to be here, but God has sustained me, and my journey has been rich in spiritual fruit. I look forward to spending time here with the Saints and worshiping with my fellow brothers."

The abbot's gaze lingered on him, a trace of weariness in his eyes. "We will do what we can to accommodate your pilgrimage, Brother. But these are … unusual times. The Lavra does not stand outside the world's troubles."

"Yes, Father," Alfanas replied, his voice steady. He stepped closer, lowered his tone, and met the abbot's gaze. "You have been in my prayers. I know that here, the world should not intrude upon the work of God, but too often, it forces its way in. I am deeply grateful for any hospitality you can extend. By the grace of God, I will carry no trouble to your door."

The abbot nodded slowly, his attention drifting to the window as if burdened by unseen weights. Without looking away, he patted Alfanas' hand and turned to the young monk. "Brother, please find lodging for Brother Alfanas and make him welcome."

The young monk bowed, gesturing for Alfanas to follow. Alfanas turned back to the abbot with another bow. "Thank you, Father. Your kindness is a blessing that fortifies my heart and eases the labors of my journey."

He truly felt compassion for the old ascetic. In a war between brothers, there is no winner. There are varying degrees of losers. His mind drifted back to his time in the Crimea: the faces shifted, but the motivation and means remained the same. Futile power plays and politics.

That is why he chose Uzbekistan and a monastery in a region where Christianity is a minority. He had to get along with the differences. No other choice remained. He caught a familiar look in the abbot's old eyes. A fatalistic look where no good choices remained in the gales of change now sweeping over his community and country. They would all choose sides on which to stand.

Opening the door with a gesture of invitation, the young monk said, "Here is your room, brother. Please let me or any of the brothers know if you require anything."

Alfanas stepped inside a comfortable room. Certainly less so than the hotel he had been in the night before, but in a way, more inviting to his sensibilities. He answered the invitation to simplicity, if not austerity. Spiritually and physically, this reminded him of where he now called home.

The monk stepped back, handing Alfanas a sealed envelope. "Mutual friends asked me to give you this note upon your arrival," he added quietly.

Alfanas accepted the envelope with a slight nod, the wax seal catching the light as he turned it over. His gaze lingered on it for a moment before he slipped it into the folds of his robe.

"Thank you, Brother." The monk bowed and disappeared down the corridor, leaving Alfanas alone with his thoughts.

Standing in the doorway momentarily, patting the envelope through his robes, Alfanas wondered what it could mean. He closed the door and stood with his back against it. "This is too much like old times. Old times I went through great effort to forget and be forgotten." He sighed.

Chapter 17: Brothers Betrayed

As the door closed with a gentle click. Alfanas' first thoughts were about privacy and security. The small room had one door and a window that looked out onto a courtyard. With winter on the horizon, the temperatures had turned from chilly to cold, and life both inside and out had become more muted. The tourists to the monastery had dwindled with the seasonal change, making indoor adventures far more tolerable than wandering the brown courtyards and gardens. Birds, so plentiful in the surrounding gardens and woods in summer, were nowhere to be seen. Not that Alfanas would have noticed them or their absence, the letter in his pocket had his attention and warranted this quick survey for privacy.

With mixed thoughts and emotions, he surveyed his environment. He might be in a community of brothers, who covenanted to have each other's backs, but these were strange days, filled with uncertainty and divided loyalties. Fraternity would not protect him. A surer bet for him would be to trust nobody, not even the abbot. That reality did not stop Alfanas from longing for someone here to depend on. But having been a betrayer himself, he realized that the smiling face of the man who passed him his bread might sell his life in the next breath. These days, too true of brothers either biological or institutional.

Alfanas pulled the envelope out of his robes and looked at it. It appeared to be a plain white envelope with the handwritten words, "Brother Alfanas," sealed in wax applied over gum paste to make any alterations noticeable. The seal bore the *Tryzub*, Ukraine's enduring symbol, impressed in red beeswax.

Alfanas sat on the edge of his bed and carefully opened the envelope, removing a trifold sheet of paper. On unfolding it, he found two sentences: "The bearer is a friend. Call for details."

Alfanas gaze drifted back to the barren landscape on the other side of the window as he thought to himself, *"Clear enough. But I think that I must still wait to trust this new brother."* He returned the letter to the envelope and stuck it in his pocket, where it would be secure until permanently destroyed. He moved to the door and opened it to check the hall, making sure there were no lingering ears or eyes in the hallway. Satisfied, Alfanas moved to the window again. He took his phone from the deep folds of his robes. He hit redial on his recent call list.

A moment passed before he responded to the prompt from the connected call. "Yes, I was handed your note."

He paused for a response.

"He was tall; I would guess around 6 feet. Slender, though it is hard to tell with the monastic robes. Green eyes and dark brown hair. Skin tone was a bit darker."

Another pause.

"Ah, Brother Timos," Alfanas echoed, "it is good to have a friend within the walls. He knows my connection to you? You are sure about him?"

Brother Alfanas nodded as he listened intently to the phone before offering, "Very good. I will seek him out this evening."

Alfanas put the phone back into a pocket deep within his robes. There were no clocks in his room. Living on monastery time, kept for him, he hadn't noticed the hour on his phone, but he guessed by the shadows in the garden that it must be in the middle of the afternoon. He had several hours to occupy himself before the bells summoned all to evening prayers. There would be little time to approach Brother Timos after dinner, before Compline. It would be beneficial to have a compatriot familiar with the Monastery's layout and personalities, but he would need to assess the reliability of this young brother first. Suspicion came naturally to him.

Alfanas set out to explore the Monastery.

As he stepped into the hallway and the door to his room swung shut with a creak and a click amplified by the lack of sound and space, he reflected, *"Old buildings have a voice all of their own."* A hot-water radiator gurgled in some nook or alcove while another distant door joined in the conversation. Alfanas smiled to himself. Everyone had the same goal of not disturbing the silence and of being unobtrusive to their fellows, yet the subtle sounds seemed all the more attention-grabbing as they broke the stillness with the proclamation, "Here I am!"

He descended a short flight of worn stone steps, his eyes adjusting to the dim light filtering through narrow windows high on the walls. As Alfanas traveled further down, it felt cooler to him. At this stage in life, he did not know if such things were reality or due to the waning of the fires of youth, a decreased metabolism. A younger Alfanas had lived in Kyiv many years ago and occasionally visited Lavra, but he had not visited this part of the grounds before. He had been told it housed some of the monks' cells and the entrances to the labyrinthine caves that gave the Lavra its name and fame.

Half-heard conversations haunted these old buildings, conversations always on the edge of hearing. In the contemplative silence he now walked, monks and even visitors toned down their natural voices to a whisper. Normal volume for the world outside would, in this silence, seem like a yell, and a yell would cause everyone to cover their ears as if having been momentarily abused by the sound.

Alfanas turned toward a small wooden door at the end of the hall. It was ajar, revealing a glimpse of the monastery gardens beyond. He stepped out into the courtyard, pulling his robe tighter against the sharp chill of the evening air, which he felt all the more keenly having emerged from the moist heat of the old building. A lone monk worked near the far wall, carefully cleaning up the last fallen leaves and the debris of summer's passing.

Alfanas turned toward a low, arch-covered walkway on the opposite side of the courtyard. It led toward the caves. He hadn't intended to come this way, or had he? Had he yielded to a subconscious urge to dive into the reason he had come here, to find an entrance to the caves? Even though he had no clue which cave he needed to be in? There were two cave complexes at Lavra: the Near Caves and the Far Caves. At this point in his visit, he had no clue where to look.

One of the entrances to the caves loomed before him. It led to the Near Caves. Alfanas paused in front of it. He considered what lay beyond. He placed his hand on the exterior door of the Church of the Elevation of the Cross, pausing for a quick consideration if he should go in. It served as a gateway to an alternate reality where the distinction between the living and the dead became blurred. The caves were a sacred and silent place, carrying a sense of mystery and, at times, unease, as if one were joining in an ongoing millennia-old conversation.

He would have to gain access to them eventually, but that would not happen until he gained the trust of one of the senior monks. The beginning of a plan formed in his thoughts, to be interrupted by a hand on his shoulder and the sharp voice of an older monk. "Brother, you seem lost. Is there anything I can do for you?"

Alfanas, keeping his hand on the wood of the door, turned to look into the ancient face of one of the monks. "Ah, you caught me! I was reflecting and praying to the blessed saints who rest peacefully." His eyes turned from the brother to look at his hand resting affectionately on the door, and with a tone of longing continued, "Saints that I have traveled long and endured much to be close to." He patted the door, letting his hand drop, and returned his smile and gaze once more to the brother.

Alfanas spoke truthfully. A different person had stood in his flesh when last he visited Lavra, but now he understood more. His old self would have been a gawking tourist with a morbid fascination. But for the last 14 years, he had longed to be back on "home soil" and see the birthplace of Northeastern Orthodoxy, where he could venerate the Saints Anthony and Theodosius of Kyiv. He hadn't noticed it before, but he felt cheated. Here he stood on the doorstep of one of the Holy of Holies of his faith, but he must enter it more in pretense than genuine piety. God has a sense of humor, or is it justice for sins past?

The older monk's gaze lingered on Alfanas for a moment, unreadable beneath his bushy brows. His hand stayed on Alfanas' shoulder as if weighing his sincerity. But he smiled as if he understood both the spoken and contemplated aspects of their exchange. So it is with true contemplatives; they see deep and look beyond the surface, even beyond deception.

"Perhaps we can go there together one day. It is indeed a unique place where our brothers sleep. Come, let me show you where we keep the record of their names, all the way back to Saint Anthony of *Kyivan Rus'.*"

The older monk led Alfanas through the corridors and stopped at one whose small brass plaque read "Archives." He drew out a ring of keys, fitting one into the lock, and swung open the door to reveal a room filled with shelves and one or two desks for working at.

The smell greeted Alfanas first as he added to his observations of old buildings; it smelled of old paper, musty and close. *"Not only do old buildings have their sounds, but their individual smells as well. I wonder what a modern department of health would think about some of these places we monks pass our time?"*

He dared not offer such thoughts audibly.

"These," the monk began solemnly, "are the original records preserved as best we can. Some date back to the time of Saint Anthony himself." He gestured toward a low bookcase where ancient scrolls rested in wooden slots behind glass covers, their edges frayed and discolored. "But we no longer consult them unless the task is urgent, and the information needs verification against the originals. They are too fragile for regular handling now that better ways exist to find the information. Come."

Alfanas followed the monk to the far corner of the room, where a computer terminal sat incongruously on a polished oak desk. As the old monk started the computer up, the screen produced a dazzlingly bright light in the subdued twilight of the room. The monk motioned for Alfanas to sit. He leaned over to type a password, his gnarled fingers surprisingly agile on the keyboard.

"All of our records have been digitized," the monk explained, straightening back up. "We do this to protect the originals and ensure the knowledge is not lost to fire or decay, or so the professionals we hired tell us. You will find the same information here—names, dates, locations—all cross-referenced by year, event, and individual." He turned the screen toward Alfanas. "Type the year you wish to search. The rest will follow."

Alfanas hesitated, his fingers hovering over the keys. He felt the tension between wanting to take advantage of the access he had been given and not revealing too much information about his true quest. He wished the monk would leave the room for ten minutes.

"Is there anything specific you wish to find?" the monk asked.

Looking at the waiting screen and not the questioner, Alfanas found himself in a rare place, lost for how to respond. "I … I'm not sure. Perhaps I will know when I see it."

The monk nodded and turned toward the shelves. "You poke around as I do some straightening of these books over here. Some of the brothers have become lax in their dedication to returning volumes to their proper places."

Alfanas exhaled slowly and typed "1453 to 1510" into the search bar.

The screen filled with rows of names, places, and notes. His eyes darted across the entries, searching for anything that might stand out. A name caught his attention: Alexios Sakellaris, 1470. Below that entry another: Theodore Sakellaris.

His heart quickened. The dates matched. Clicking on Alexios' name, he found a brief note:

"Buried in the Far Caves, Section IV, west corridor. Refugee from Constantinople. No official title recorded."

He shifted to Theodore Sakellaris, whose entry contained an obscure note:

"Interred 1501, Far Caves, Section IV. Reported arrival with relics. Origin unknown."

"Relics?" The word sent a shiver down Alfanas' spine. He glanced over his shoulder, but the monk seemed to inspect a log or ledger behind him. Leaning closer to the screen, Alfanas pulled the phone from his robes and took a photo of the screen. No sooner had he done this than the clear, piercing tone of a bell ringing disturbed the silence. Alfanas quickly returned his phone to the folds of his robe.

"Ah," said the old monk, whose attention had once again shifted to Alfanas as he pressed the keys that returned the computer's screen to the login, "that would be the call to evening prayers. I will show you the way. As long as you are here, you will be expected to obey our rules." Alfanas felt uneasy under the old monk's steady gaze. His hardening was no match for the steady years of integrity behind those aged eyes. Alfanas blinked first and looked toward the door. With a gesture, the other invited him to exit first.

Alfanas stepped into the hallway, his mind still racing from what he had found in the archives. The names, Alexios and Theodore Sakellaris, and the mention of relics gnawed at him like a buried ember threatening to ignite. But the steady presence of the old monk behind him kept his focus in check.

As he walked, he recounted the entire episode in his mind. Had the old monk caught him taking a picture of the screen? Had he seen the names he had pulled up? Would he go back and look at a hidden log that Alfanas knew nothing about? He acted hastily when he searched like that. After the fact, he realized how rash he had been. *"None of us is perfect. What is done is done. I will need to be more careful."*

The sound of the bell reverberated through the stone corridors, its tone low and commanding, resonating like a heartbeat through the Lavra. Other monks emerged to form a growing throng. No one spoke, but the rustling of fabric and the soft shuffling of footfalls on the worn stone floors filled the air and joined the conversation of the quiet building.

The old monk guided Alfanas toward the chapel, his hand briefly brushing the shoulder of a younger monk who passed them as though to correct his hastiness wordlessly. Alfanas followed, his steps deliberate, but his mind remained divided between the present, his slip with the records, and what the Far Caves held for the future.

The chapel doors stood open, revealing the glow of candlelight. Inside, the sanctuary was a vision of solemn beauty. Massive icons of Christ Pantocrator and the Theotokos gazed down from their places of honor, their gold leaf shimmering in the flickering light. The scent of incense visibly hung in the air, rising in soft plumes from the censers held by monks standing at the front.

The older monk gave Alfanas a brief nod and gestured for him to join the line of brothers already gathering in the nave. In one long line, the monks stood shoulder to shoulder, their hands clasped lightly in front of them, their faces turned toward the altar. Alfanas slipped into an open space near the back, mimicking their posture and respecting his place as a guest of their house.

As worship began, the chanting filled the space with unearthly tones, smells, and dancing shadows. Alfanas thought of home and the familiar cadence and rhythm of the unified voices. The frescoed dome over his head seemed to shimmer in the candlelight, the figures of angels and saints almost alive in the flickering glow. *"Candles,"* thought Alfanas, *"are living lights that reflect the dance of the Holy Spirit as they cast varying shades and moving shadows across the walls, objects, and worshippers. I pity those who have never experienced the drama, the deep emotive path of living worship."*

For a moment, Alfanas let the tension in his shoulders ease. The thoughts of names and hidden bones seemed to fade back underground. Whatever shadows lingered in his thoughts, in the end, this place is a refuge, a space where the eternal seemed to draw close to the temporal as the portal to heaven opened wide. And yet, how ironic, he was here not as a true penitent but as a man with secrets who sought to uncover truths buried by others.

As they left their prayers for the afternoon, silence reigned, the sound of passing feet and rustling clothes the sole exceptions. Alfanas felt much of the weight and anxiety of the day lifted by the service. With a sense of peace, he headed toward the *Trapeza*, the monastery's dining hall, looking forward to the light meal. The building stood apart from the chapel. Inside, long tables filled the room with ample space for all.

The monks walked in silently, taking their places assigned by age, authority, and office. Near a modest lectern, a younger monk stood at the head of the room, ready to begin the evening's reading. The faint scent of baked bread replaced the odor of incense, and a simple soup waited for them on the tables.

Alfanas took his place at the table nearest the wall, bowing his head as the abbot raised his hand to bless the meal. As the young monk's voice rose, steady and clear, reciting a passage from the lives of the saints, the brothers ate, their movements muted and deliberate. The clink of spoons against ceramic bowls was the only other sound in the hall.

Alfanas looked at the brothers around him. Near the abbot sat the old monk, his guide. At an angle to him, across the table, sat the young monk, Timos, who guided him to his quarters and gave him the note. Several times, Alfanas caught Timos looking at him curiously. They would have a brief chance to connect after the meal, but more time would be available tomorrow.

After the meal, the monks dispersed as they tended to last-minute duties before Compline, personal reflection, and bed. The young Timos lingered behind, waiting for Alfanas to approach him.

Timos spoke first. "Ah, brother, you seem to have settled into our daily rhythm already. I trust you haven't wandered into too many dead ends today!"

Old habits die slowly. As Timos spoke, Alfanas observed his young compatriot's cues: every motion, glance, hand twist, or stance betrayed something about the young man. Alfanas had survived by being cautious, but nothing here betrayed any meaning other than pure interest and perhaps a little juvenile awkwardness with a stranger.

"Yes," replied Alfanas in a steady tone, "the other brothers have been kind in guiding me and helping me to feel at home. I want to thank you for the note that you delivered to me. It would seem that we have some mutual secular friends."

Timos smiled, and his eyes warmed. "Yes. My friendship with the one who gave it to me to watch and pass along to you made me wonder if we were brothers in other ways, too."

"It seems we are." Warmly confirmed Alfanas. "But now is not the time or the place to talk. Possibly tomorrow."

Alfanas' pillow never felt so good. It had been a long day with loaded with information. He couldn't wrap his head around all of it. He lay there, wondering who slept thirty feet under the ground beneath him. Would he meet the author of the *Chronicles of the Last*

Emperor? If he did, what would Alexios or Theodore tell him that would lead them to the next step? He would have to deal with one bigger problem: once he called Nick and Elena, how would he get them into the catacombs without being observed?

He sighed to the silent night. "One problem at a time." Closing his eyes, he fell into a sound sleep.

A soft but firm knock on his door woke him instantly. It had been about three hours since laying down. Quickly he threw on his robes and, opening the door, found the old monk, Father Makar, waiting patiently.

He whispered so that Alfanas alone heard. "It is time to start the Midnight Office. The bell rang to call us; perhaps you did not hear it. But I was hoping you might come with me. I am the eldest of the community, and the abbot grants me leave to worship with the saints in one of the subterranean chapels. You will join me. Follow closely so you don't get lost."

Father Makar's robes cast long shadows against the stone floor and walls as they moved both quickly and quietly down the passage to the stairwell. Down they moved. Down one flight to the ground floor, two to the basement, three to the sub-basement, and thus to a long passage with doors on either side.

Through the second-to-last door on the right into what seemed to be an old storage room, but behind a curtain on the wall was a heavy oak door that creaked as Makar swung it open to reveal yet another set of stairs. As Alfanas stepped through the door, a musty smell mingled with incense, and a gentle breeze of earth-cooled air tried to escape to freedom and, perhaps, light.

Down the two black shadows glided, in the dim light of an old lamp. At the bottom, a long tunnel and yet another door awaited them. The old monk paused. He put his hand on the door and crossed himself.

He raised the lamp to illuminate both of their faces; he was grave and solemn. "Behind here lies a sacred treasure not of Lavra but of Orthodoxy."

He lowered the lamp, opened the door, gestured for Alfanas to go in, and closed the door behind them.

Alfanas found himself in a whitewashed tunnel that led in both directions. They had come to one of the paths of the catacombs beneath the monastery. Directly across from him, in a niche on the wall, a glass casket, in which the silent remains of a monk long dead lay awaiting the last trumpet to sound and be raised, reflected the flickering light of the lamp. His robes were as pristine as the day his brothers laid him to rest. A cloth covered his as if to shield it from any light that might disturb the soundness of sleep.

Down the passageway, they moved. Alfanas close behind as they passed by the sleeping bodies of the saints of Lavra. Passages opened one way and another. Little chapels, whose interiors were mere shadows in the lamplight, sprang up at intervals. They turned right off the main tunnel into one of the small chapels.

Makar handed a book of matches to Alfanas. "Here, take these and help me light the candles. There are several little-known entrances to the catacombs. We monks come here to worship, care for, and always watch over the caves. Over the years, paths from the monastery and other buildings above had been hewn from the stone so the monks would be able to come here both quickly and secretly."

They lit all the candles and began their time in prayer. It took Alfanas a while to pull himself away from the idea that the old monk had shown him the ideal way to get Nick and Elena into the caves. But he recovered from his elation so that both of them were deep in prayer. Alfanas would remember the hours of that night in Lavra's caves as the most peaceful and inspiring times of his life. A time that ended far too soon.

As they blew out the candles in preparation to find their way back once again to the living, they heard a couple of slaps of sandals on the hard floor of the tunnel.

"Who could that be?" whispered Makar. "No one has permission or duties down here until after Morning Prayers."

"Hide your lamp, and we shall see," whispered Alfanas as he removed his sandals and quietly crept to the edge of the darker doorway.

In the utter darkness, he saw the glimmer of a shielded candle. Every so often, its bearer would allow the light to escape more fully into the night. The stranger crossed the entrance to the little chapel. When he needed to correct his course, he let more light flood the tunnel. His hood covered his entire face, but Alfanas would recognize that gait and frame anywhere. He followed it to meet the abbot when he first arrived. It belonged to the lanky Timos, now hunting for them in the dark catacombs.

Alfanas suddenly felt an overwhelming anxiety seize him: could he trust Timos? Did he miss Alfanas at prayer and come innocently looking for him? How would he guess to look down here? Why shield his candle and not call out if his actions were pure? Alfanas would need to prove him true.

The dark shielded Timos, but also hid Alfanas' face, his reaction to Timos escaped the knowing gaze of the old monk. Timos and his candle had gone further down the tunnel or into a side passage.

"The young often wander where they should not. Curiosity is a fire that must be carefully tended, or it burns the wrong things. Let us go now," said the old monk at his side. "I cannot be sure who would be wandering in the caves at this hour, but I will talk to the abbot about it during the day." He uncovered his lamp, and they retraced their steps to the back stairs.

They made it to the main floor of the monastery when the bells rang out for the morning prayers that preceded breakfast.

As the faint light of dawn filtered through the sanctuary windows, Alfanas stood with the brothers in the nave. The chanting of the morning prayers filled the air. Alfanas chanted the words by rote and let his mind wander. Those words contrasted with the unrest he felt in his soul after the early morning encounter with Timos.

His mind replayed the scene in the catacombs. There were unanswered questions. He would need to arrange for answers.

Alfanas forced himself to focus, bowing his head as the abbot stepped forward to deliver the final blessing. The rising sun illuminated the icons in a sudden burst of yellow-orange light that Alfanas found comforting and healing.

As the service ended, the monks filed silently toward the Trapeza. Alfanas joined them, his steps measured, but his thoughts remained restless. He resolved to speak with Timos later to test the young monk's loyalty and perhaps uncover the truth behind his late-night wanderings.

He didn't have long to wait. Timos sought Alfanas out after breakfast. Tugging at the sleeve of Alfanas' robe, he pulled him aside with muted excitement. "Brother, I will be working mopping the monastery floors this morning as my obedience. If Brother Makar has not told you yours yet, as a visitor, you would be forgiven for going to him and asking him to work with me on the floors so we can talk."

"What an excellent idea," agreed Alfanas. "I will seek him out immediately and join you with a mop in hand!"

Alfanas found Brother Makar working in the scriptorium. The steady scratch of pens, echoing an older age of quills, and the faint rustle of paper suggesting a by-gone era of parchment, as the gifted and experienced monks copied and translated volumes. Alfanas's presence drew Makar's attention away from his work. After hearing the request, Makar set down his pen with a deliberate motion and fixed Alfanas with a thoughtful gaze. His brow furrowed slightly, suggesting a concern he wasn't ready to voice.

Makar slowly weighed his words. He leaned back in his chair, the aged wood creaking under him. "Very well ... very well. But be cautious, Brother Alfanas. Young Timos is ... zealous. That zeal can sometimes obscure judgment. Listen to God's guidance more than his words and lean on the skills you have developed in discerning the intents of others."

Makar paused, his gaze sharpening. "We are all flawed, Brother. Light can find entrance in the cracks of men's character, where darkness first resides. Let the Spirit guide you, as it has guided us all."

Alfanas inclined his head, accepting the wisdom at face value, even as his thoughts churned. Makar's words struck him as more than general advice; they conveyed a warning. Did Makar perceive something about Timos, or was this simply the wisdom of an elder who had seen other men's souls falter under the strain of hidden agendas?

"I will remember your counsel, Brother," Alfanas replied, calm and measured. "And thank you for trusting me with this task."

Makar nodded and returned to his work, but as Alfanas turned to leave, the older monk added, "The truth often waits in the silence between words. Listen carefully."

Alfanas had to cross the courtyard to return to the monastery and find Timos, not to mention a mop. As November drew to a close, the cold had settled in, prompting everyone who had no business outside to venture in search of a heated location. But Alfanas found the cold a welcome privacy barrier. Wind rustling in the few dead leaves, still too cowardly to risk falling to the cold earth, supplied the isolated sound.

Alfanas glanced about and called his friend at the SBU: "I have no time to talk. Have someone call me in an hour and hang up. Thank you."

He shivered as he entered the warm monastery again. Timos greeted him with a bucket and mop. "Welcome, brother. The downside of always feeling at home is that there are always chores to pitch in on! Your pilgrimage might well be with the Saints downstairs, but your duty is with the floors and me this morning!"

Alfanas laughed as he took both mop and bucket from Timos and worked beside him on mopping the floors. Despite the opening levity, Alfanas felt the tension as neither of them wanted to seem obvious, yet both needed to get a deeper conversation going. Likely for two different purposes. Timos had his agenda, which remained suspect. Alfanas had to figure out a way to disclose Timos' actual intent.

Alfanas disturbed the silence first. "So, brother, you don't look old enough to have served very long. Have you been to other monasteries before coming to Lavra?"

"No. Only here. It is an honor to serve here. God has blessed my path," Timos tried to look reflective while leaning on a mop. "I grew up outside Kyiv and came here often. My parish priest interceded with the Patriarch of Moscow and all Rus' to help me find a place here. I do not know what His Holiness saw in me, but he instructed the abbot to find room for me. And, well, here I am," he concluded with a shrug and a smile.

Hmm, thought Alfanas, usually when things are too good to be true, they aren't true. Timos' placement here would require more than a lucky break. Larger gears are moving the wheels in the rise of Timos than simple fortune.

Alfanas felt the two gears of state striving against each other in that room, the superpower of the mighty against the supernatural power of the lowly. He now had a good understanding of his situation.

Leaning on his mop, he deeply considered the old walls and doors of the warm room, far more comfortable than the Monastery of Saint George the Pilgrim in Uzbekistan. "Yes, you were fortunate indeed."

Timos' voice interrupted his thoughts of home. "What about you?"

"Ah, my whole service has been at Saint George the Pilgrim," he said affectionately. "We are humble there. We are a minority, but we get along with our neighbors by making an effort. It is not a good thing to always get your way. That means you never have to figure out harder lessons in finding a way. It is not easy, but it is honest. I cannot ask for more." He paused and looked around before he continued, "It is nice here. But I miss home. I have been away too long on pilgrimage. I pray that God will release me soon, and I may return," he concluded as he returned his mop to its rightful place in the bucket.

"Were you always a monk?" The younger inquired.

"No, no. I was a civil servant before I became a monk. A mere clerk behind a desk," Alfanas spoke without hinting at the big lie he had told. He had a learned and natural response he used so frequently that it slipped out now with a genuine tone and cadence, "paperwork and the endless monotony of process and procedure. There had to be more to life than tracking people's healthcare choices. I found that more in serving God in Uzbekistan."

"Ah, I see," Timos exclaimed. "So, were you always known as Alfanas? Did you have a secular name?"

Alfanas had a ready answer to this as well, but he did not get the chance to let the next lie fly. His phone rang. "Excuse me. This is probably the call I am expecting from a colleague who is working on researching one of the saints whom I am on a pilgrimage to honor."

He pulled out his phone and stepped into a connecting hallway, ostensibly to achieve a level of privacy, but making sure Timos overheard him. The caller hung up immediately after Alfanas accepted the call.

"Hello, yes, good to hear from you, my friend. All is well, and I have inspiring news for you. I think I have discovered where the last piece of information we need to put all the pieces together now resides."

Alfanas paused as if listening to someone on the other end of the call.

"Now, Nick, you must make your way here as soon as possible. I have a plan that might see us all home for Christmas."

Another pause.

"Good, good. I will see you in a couple of days. I will continue my investigation of the resources here. Travel safely. Goodbye."

When Alfanas returned to the hall where he and Timos were mopping, Timos had not moved from the same piece of floor he had mopped before Alfanas took the call, moving his mop repeatedly over the same space and with his eyes focused opaquely on the floor, his brow furrowed as he chewed at his lower lip. Alfanas renewed his relationship with his mop with indifference, but inwardly pleased with himself. *Yes. He has taken the bait. Let's see what he does next.*

After a moment of silence, Timos spoke. "Brother, we never finished our conversation about our mutual friends in Kyiv the other day. We should have that conversation while we are assured of a little privacy here with the monks out and about doing their obediences."

"Yes, let's. My friends at the SBU spoke highly of you."

"I will thank them when I see them," Timos said as he moved his bucket with focused attention, "but I can help you. I know the Lavra very well."

"Thank you. I will keep that in mind. But I am making satisfactory progress. I must say," Alfanas paused his mop again and looked Timos in the eye, "it is an enormous relief knowing that there is a friendly face here with my back if I need it. I am delighted that I can complete what I came here for. But thank you for being there for me."

Alfanas continued his mopping. The sounds over the next few minutes were the swish as the mops covered the floor and the plop and squish as they rinsed and came out of the buckets.

Timos forced a chuckle, possibly to relieve the stress, or, more likely, to disarm the situation. "I can remember my first days here. It was so overwhelming. Everyone seemed to have their place, and I lacked a place or authority. It was quite unnerving. And now I am an old hand. I know not only these old passages but the monks who inhabit them. Sometimes," he chuckled again, "I wonder which is older, the building or the monks?"

Silence again.

"So, have you felt fulfilled in your purpose for the pilgrimage to us?" Timos asked as he rinsed his mop.

"Oh, yes," Alfanas responded as he worked on one little dirty spot that turned out to be a natural coloration in the floor. "I came to draw closer to Saint Damian and feel I have found him. I will ask Brother Makar to take me to see him before I leave."

"I can guide you to his relics and," Timos hesitated, "… and anywhere else you might want to go. Is there another place you would like to visit?"

"Ah, that is the question. One never knows where the Spirit will lead when on a pilgrimage. I have friends coming who are also on pilgrimage. I shall have to wait to see what they want to do." Alfanas offered disinterestedly.

"Friends?" Timos inquired with excitement, as his tone rose. "On pilgrimage with you?"

"Yes."

"Do you want me to make arrangements for them? Please, what are their names? I will ensure they are welcomed." Alfanas saw Timos' anticipation and excitement. "Are they here to pay respect to Saint Damian? Are they monks as well?"

"So many questions," Alfanas raised his hands when he got a word in. "No, they will not need to rely on the monastery's hospitality. Their arrangements are made. Their pilgrimage is their own, as is their business. I will not learn their full interest in Kyiv until they come. Until they arrive, I will mop the floor."

Timos looked as if he would explode. His brow deeply furrowed, and his lower lip must have been nearly raw. He had to do something, anything, to bring this back around so that he could be included in their plans and confidences. So close. He didn't want to continue the current strategy of trying to follow this blasted monk around the whole of Lavra, hoping to find something out. That didn't work well last night when he got lost in the catacombs.

"Bro … Brother, I … I know a little about your being here," Timos ventured.

"Oh?" Alfanas responded while thinking to himself, *"Now come to me, my little puppet. Tell your older brother all about it."*

"Yes. The SBU sent me here because they feel that the state has an interest in finding resources that a priest named Vasyl Palevych smuggled out of Istanbul before he died. He had visited here before he went to America. That is why they asked me to help you," Timos concluded as he looked with complete sincerity into Alfanas' eyes.

"Oh, you are good, my friend," Alfanas thought. *"I can't see any deception in your eyes. But it is all an overreach and a lie. The SBU does not know why I am here, and they, frankly, couldn't care less. But Viktor, Viktor guesses why I am here. Perhaps it was how I avoided certain questions or the careful precision with which I acted. He must have pieced together my intentions from the whispers and shadows that followed my movements. Viktor's instincts are sharp, his network far-reaching, and his presence a reminder of the stakes involved. This is a game of cat and mouse, but the question remains: Who is truly hunting whom? Where else would you get that information? Okay, we play a little more."*

"As I said before," started Alfanas as he held the other's gaze convincingly, "it is good that I have someone I can trust. Yes, I think we will start working together tomorrow to dig up the clues I have uncovered. Perhaps by the time my friends arrive, we will have all the pieces together. Maybe you can arrange with the abbot for us to work in the catacombs tomorrow?"

"Yes, I think that can be possible," Timos said with a completely transformed demeanor. "Yes," he said more softly, as if to himself and the floor that had his renewed attention. "Yes, that will be possible."

The bells rang, summoning all to midday prayers. Alfanas, however, felt a knot of unease in his chest, his thoughts lingering on the earlier conversation with Timos and the subtle tensions it had revealed. They cleaned their mops and buckets. Alfanas told Timos to go ahead of him, and he would join him for prayers and lunch. When Timos had gone, Alfanas ducked outside into the cold again to call the same familiar number.

"I think you have a problem at the Lavra. I don't know how deep it goes, but here is what I know..." Alfanas recounted his conversations with Timos, confirming that his handlers had not briefed Timos on why Alfanas might be at Lavra. Both men concluded Viktor had to be behind the information, though neither understood the connection. "I leave it in your hands, my friend, but please act quickly. I need him out of my way."

The rest of the day passed much as it had the day before, with periods of routine mixed with times of rest and exploration. Once again, Father Makar collected Alfanas at night to start morning prayers in the caves. This time, Makar led him to a different chapel in the complex, and there were no sounds of feet on the stone floor to disturb their time of prayer and worship.

Just as the bells summoned them from breakfast to begin their daily chores, a subtle unease had already rippled through the monastery. The distant sound of boots crunching against the frosted earth outside shattered the morning calm, and moments later, the ensuing chaos broke the daily routine as a swarm of agents from the Sluzhba Bezpeky Ukrayiny, Security Service of Ukraine, swept into the Lavra complex. Their stern faces and purposeful movements brought a palpable tension to the air, as if the very stones of the monastery were bracing for the disruption to come. They searched every niche and crevice for propaganda or any sign of aiding the enemies of Ukraine. The abbot called the monks away from their duties to pray as chaos descended on the otherwise peaceful monastery.

The abbot was called out of prayer, and several monks, including Timos, were removed. Timos looked at Alfanas, and his hatred, betrayal, and anger were fully displayed on his face. Alfanas would learn later that a search of Timos' room had led to the discovery of sensitive documents that he could not explain. Alfanas wondered if they had actually been there or if they were a fabrication to get Timos out of the way.

Timos would spend years in another type of cell and confinement with its unique routine and daily chores. That saddened Alfanas. Young and foolish, Timos made some errors, as so many do. Alfanas shook his head. *"There but for the grace of God could have gone I."*

After lunch, the monks returned to their rooms. Alfanas leaned against the door of his cell, his thoughts tangled. "What did I set in motion?" he muttered under his breath before sinking onto his bed, both body and mind heavy with exhaustion. Alfanas sank into his bed, physically and mentally exhausted. It had been a wild three days since he had left Istanbul. So much had happened, and he needed sleep. When he woke up, he would give Nick and Elena a call.

The daily routine hours would be disturbed for the rest of the day. The bell would not summon them to work time, not with all these strangers mulling about. So Alfanas slept deeply until late in the afternoon. He moved to the edge of his bed, took out his phone, and tapped on the contact that read "Nick."

Chapter 18: An Averted Derailment

As the sun dipped low in the sky, the call finally came. Nick and Elena had come back to the hotel from a walk when Nick's phone buzzed, and the word 'Alfanas' appeared on its display.

Nick held up his phone so she could see the name. "Here we go!"

Nick glanced at Elena, remembering how they had been pacing the streets of Ormenio that afternoon, craving direction. Now, they would probably get directions, though they came with a weight they didn't entirely comprehend.

Nick answered on speakerphone.

"Hey, it's about time we heard from you," Nick chided their old friend. "Have you been keeping out of trouble?"

Alfanas smiled at his young friends' playful innocence. If they realized what evil lay outside their doors on a routine basis, but no, let them live sheltered lives as long as they were able.

But what he thought and said were two different things. "Of course. I am an old man. What trouble do older adults get into? How about you two? Is all well? Any problems or concerns during your time in Ormenio? Tell me about anything out of the ordinary."

"We are bored," exclaimed Elena. "We want to get to the next place and figure out what to do next."

"Well, it's good that I called. Mind you, I think it is now okay for you to come north to Kyiv. I suspect that things here are as settled as they can be. It will take two days to get here. I will meet you at the train station and arrange the details of your stay. We will discuss later how to get you into the caves at Lavra. I have a plan for that as well. Any sign of taggers along?"

Nick glanced over at Elena before he answered. "Yes. The same guy as in Istanbul, but he keeps his distance. He knows we recognize him. I feel that we should be waving to each other by now. We seem to be at a stalemate. We tried to shake him off once, more to relieve the boredom, but that didn't work. Should we try again before we get to Kyiv?"

Alfanas thought for a few minutes. By now, Viktor realized that his attempts at Lavra had failed. He would try to get the information from either Nick or Elena. Most likely from Nick, or if he failed to intercept them, he would plot to come to Lavra in person.

"No, don't risk any danger at this point. Prioritize coming here. Viktor is still detained. I can handle him if he comes here."

"I will make the travel arrangements when we hang up with you. I don't see why we can't get started tomorrow—a bus to Alexandroupoli. A plane to Chişinău, and next a long, boring train ride into Kyiv," Nick laughed as he said this. "I will text you the details when I have them."

"Very good." Alfanas paused. "Be careful. This is not a vacation. I must warn you that the closer you come here, the more danger there will be for you."

"Why? What has happened?" Elena asked with a sense of unease.

"I will tell you all about it when you are here. Text me with the details. I would also like to remind you that you will no longer have the cell service you enjoy once you leave Greece behind. There will be times when you will be totally on your own. Don't be anxious; be cautious. And with that, I will let you go to make your reservations. The early bell for evening prayers rang, so I must go. I hope to see you in a few days."

As the phone fell silent, Elena and Nick looked at each other. The weight they had been out from under while in Ormenio fell immediately back on their shoulders. Nick spent the next two hours lining up the stages of the journey, and he texted Alfanas:

> Arrive in Chişinău on Tuesday by late afternoon.
>
> Arrive in Kyiv on Wednesday evening.
>
> :>)

Alfanas texted back immediately:

Good. See you on Wednesday.

;>)

Nick put down his phone and looked Elena in the eye. "I miss the simplicity of this place already."

Tomorrow, they would take a step toward more answers, but closer to a focused malice as well.

The following day, Nick and Elena were on the bus for Alexandroupoli by 9:00. Elena glanced out the window and turned to Nick, taking his hand. She smiled remorsefully and said, "So we say goodbye to Ormenio." She gazed back out the window. "And the safety we have known. I have a bad feeling about all this. But now it is too late to stop. We can't make it go away unless we walk through it."

Their faithful tail held onto them on the bus and through the airport. They expected he would phone ahead to Chişinău or be on the next plane. A quick scan of their fellow passengers on the plane revealed, to their relief, an assortment of self-absorbed, normal travelers. Possibly the next plane would be so late that their tag-along would not be able to catch up to them.

One possibility had not entered their calculation—Viktor had already guessed where they were going and would plan on both being released and getting there before them. Viktor had now learned that Alfanas had sidelined Timos. New information had also reached him. Alfanas had a connection to state security and is not the simple ascetic he appeared to be, but someone who had the ability to outsmart him. While still out of the picture for the moment, Viktor planned to change his status soon.

Nick and Elena reached Chişinău and caught a cab to the train station. They got themselves into their compartment. It would take them 14-plus hours to travel from Chişinău to Kyiv. These would be long hours of nothing to do, nothing to eat, and only the water they purchased before boarding the train to drink. They paid extra for a sleeper to nap, enjoy privacy, and charge their cellphones, making the trip more tolerable.

Nick gallantly insisted on taking the top berth. During the day, the beds collapsed against the wall, and a table with two chairs unfolded, allowing them to sit to read or watch out the window as the rustic Eastern European countryside slipped by. As their trip began, they passed through old towns where the hand of medieval and Soviet architecture left clear imprints.

There were vast stretches of forest and mountain vistas. Nick sighed. He longed for this trip to be free of mystery and intrigue, craving the simplicity of a peaceful journey. He wished for the time and the courage to jump off the train at the next stop and explore. So much of the vast world lay outside the window, speeding by.

His mind returned to the simple days when people didn't chase him, and he sat at the window on his commute to think about the projects at work or what he would have for supper. Outside of his daily commute, the world sped past him, and he had never taken the time to experience or even wonder about it.

The simple things he casually overlooked. There were lives of little senior men and women, children at play, and buildings that told human stories carved in additions, fires, paint layers, and hidden treasures unintentionally left behind like a time capsule that marks a life. He wished he had a cup of coffee.

Nick felt the familiar touch of Elena placing a hand on his arm to get his attention. He didn't turn around. He looked at her ghostly reflection in the window glass. "I need to step out. I will be right back."

Nick nodded and once again resumed his watch of the world sliding by outside. Perhaps someday he may well return. Possibly … he felt a cool draft of air from the door opening and thought to himself, "She wasn't gone long." Again, he didn't turn. As his vision focused on the surface of the glass and its reflection, Nick gasped as he saw Viktor's image reflected at him! He had followed them on the train!

Alfanas read the text on his phone, half expecting it to say: "Safe on train." To his alarm, it read: "Viktor released three hours ago on the way to Chişinău." Alfanas ran from the chapel. He cared little about the trouble he might get into. Once outside, he tried to call Nick's phone. It went straight to voicemail. He texted, but it didn't go through. Nick and Elena were unsuspecting and alone on the train. He could do nothing but hope and pray they would be okay.

Viktor knew what he wanted and how he would get it. He was angry and had had enough of playing games. "So, this little man wants to play in the pool's deep end. Well, we shall see his appetite after he gets thrown in." He had now settled on the questions that Nick needed to answer for him: Where was the money? Why was he involved? Who was Alfanas? Why was the state of Ukraine protecting them all? There would be no more escapes for the impudent little upstart, Nick.

Alfanas would have smiled and rested easier had he known that Viktor had crossed the line and made this personal. You make mistakes when things get personal. But for now, Viktor held Nick in a chokehold to take him to his cabin in the next car, where he could take his time getting every bit of information out of this little idiot.

Nick reactively lunged into fight mode and moved to jump up, but it was too late. Viktor had learned his craft too well. He had Nick from behind with one steel arm around his neck, squeezing tight. Nick brought both hands to that fight, as Viktor anticipated he would. As Nick opened his mouth to yell, Viktor stuffed a wadded-up cloth in his mouth while dragging Nick back over the folding seat and the table. Nick heard Viktor chuckle. "Gotcha, little man. I think you will come with me to the next car so we can talk. No more invitations."

Nick's feet were useless, his whole balance thrown off. With nothing for Nick to grab onto, being pulled backward with no way to get his balance, Viktor had the upper hand. Nick's foot caught on the folding chair as his knee hit the table. With survival in the calculus, he drew both feet up to the edge of the table and pushed with all the strength he had in his legs. The table yielded, ripping from the wall, but not before it had imparted enough resistance to send Viktor uncontrollably backward against the cabin door. With the weight of both men battering the door, it flew open with a crash and a bang. Nick and Viktor tumbled out into the hall.

The surprise had caught Viktor off balance, and his hold on Nick loosened. Nick wiggled free. "Run." He thought, "Where? Anywhere but here," the answer came. He saw the door to the next train at the end of the passage, and he sprang toward it. Too late.

Viktor was back on him. "Not so fast," he grumbled. Nick's antics created a momentary inconvenience, but not a problem. He lifted more than this little American weighed with one arm. Where did he think he was going?

Nick wondered where the rest of the people in the car were. He couldn't cry for help, but certainly they heard the commotion. Why hadn't someone come out to save him or at least to investigate? Had he heard such a ruckus, he would have … done what everyone else does: locked their doors, turned the lights off, told themselves it was none of their business, and tried to act normal. He would have been one of those good people who stood by and did nothing outside of self-interest, but now he needed help and aid.

When Nick and Viktor came flying out of their cabin, Elena stood in the passage outside the bathroom at the end of the car. She ducked into the bathroom and searched around helplessly for something, anything. Finding an unlocked staff storage compartment, she rummaged through its contents. She had very little time. Nick, no match for Viktor alone, or even with her help, struggled to get away as Viktor wrestled to regain control of him. Elena would add little to the fight, but providence might help her surprise Viktor and possibly give Nick a chance to do something.

Nick and Viktor were tumbling around in the hall. Nick flailed desperately as Viktor reasserted control. Viktor nearly lost Nick, but having tripped him by catching hold of one of his fleeing feet, now he had him around the neck again, lifting and choking him simultaneously. He dragged Nick down the hallway like a spider who had caught and subdued its prey, creeping to the center of its web for consumption.

They were heading toward the concealed Elena to get to the connecting car door. Elena stood frozen against the nearest side of the bathroom wall. She had found an old pipe wrench for emergency plumbing and mechanical repairs. It was big and heavy. She was prepared to put all she had into using it on Viktor. "Oh God, oh

God," she screamed inside. "I have one shot. After that, he will kill me."

Exhausted, Nick had no hope or fight left. The cloth in his mouth diminished his free oxygen, and Viktor's arm continued to limit how much air got into his lungs. He didn't have long before being unable to fight or remain conscious. Both hands were pulling at Viktor's arm in a bid to loosen his hold so Nick could draw in more air. Meanwhile, Viktor dragged him backward down the hallway.

"You need to stop this resisting, little man," Viktor hissed into his ear. "You are not changing anything. This is over."

Victor would occasionally glance over his shoulder to ensure there were no surprises. Elena dared not try to peek around the corner to help her judge her timing. She heard them getting closer now, and they were almost at the bathroom door. Elena felt her heart beating in her throat as she raised the wrench. "Oh God, oh God, give me the timing to make this right." She swung with all her strength and weight combined. Viktor had glanced over his shoulder for a check when Elena's blow hit him square in the center of his forehead.

She heard and felt the crack as the heavy, unyielding iron met the organic bone of Viktor's skull and had no choice but to take its blow by fracturing. Viktor let Nick go. Nick fell to his knees on the ground in front of Viktor and pulled the cloth from his mouth, gasping for air, desperate to recover enough strength but still too weak to be more than a limp pile on the floor. Suddenly, Nick heard Elena scream. The biology of survival kicked in again.

Elena had stunned and put Viktor at a disadvantage, but this had turned into a fight for his life. This little girl and an architect would not be the closing chapter on his career, nor would they best his training and determination. That's what training is for—to handle situations like this instinctively. He needed to take care of the immediate threat, Elena, and afterward handle Nick.

Viktor had his hand on Elena's throat, squeezing the life from her, when he felt the full weight of Nick hit him from the side. He released Elena and crashed into the car's side door, which sprang open with age and the unexpected weight of both Viktor and Nick thrown against it. Viktor clung to the open door and grabbed Nick's arm with his other hand, pulling him to the opening. If he had to go, he would take Nick with him.

Elena held onto Nick as he fended himself off the doorjamb with his other hand. Viktor was hanging halfway out the door by now. His head was swimming from the concussion of Elena's blow. Blood had now filled one eye as it streamed down his face, and his other fixed fiercely on Nick. Nick locked his gaze. In that gaze, Nick saw the rage and hatred Viktor held onto, but Nick's inner urge, his instinct, screamed for Nick to save him somehow, not to let go of him. Even as Viktor held onto Nick's arm, Nick's hand grasped Viktor's shirt sleeve to arrest his plunge into the steep embankment of the speeding train.

Viktor held the remains of the door with his other hand. Now, he let go of the door in a desperate bid to grab Nick securely. Seeing the threat, Nick opened his hand, released Viktor's sleeve, and shook his arm free from Viktor's clutch. Viktor was gone. No yell, no sound at all. He simply wasn't there anymore.

Nick's eyes were wide, peering into but not comprehending the darkness outside. He froze with his hand reaching out into the darkness, disbelieving what had happened or his part in it. He looked at his empty hand as the wind blew through his empty fingers. Was he capable of that? Did it make any difference that he didn't take a gun out and shoot Viktor, and let him go, releasing him to fall to his certain death?

It was Elena who pulled Nick in and away from the open door. She pulled at the door, closing it somewhat with its broken latch and sprung hinges. She picked the wrench up and put it back. Nick leaned against the wall, and he shook uncontrollably as the shock reverberated through him. She pulled and half-dragged him back to their cabin. Tied the cabin door closed with twine from the staff storage compartment.

Elena pulled down her bed and sat Nick on it. She threw her arms around him as he buried his head in his shoulder and sobbed. He was still trembling all over. For a long time, they sat there, Nick limply sobbing in shock, all color drained from his face. Elena held him, rocking back and forth, trying to imagine the battle he waged against himself. She reconciled the necessity more easily than Nick. She understood life and death in a less abstract way. Her society delivered justice quickly and powerfully.

"I'm not prepared for this … I … I'm over my head. I just killed a man. I just let him go. I …" Nick finally sobbed. He could count on one hand the times he had killed something bigger than a bug. Nick felt guilty for days after hitting a squirrel with his car. Life has a right to live, and people should not waste it.

And human life. Well, that's a whole other level. He killed a man who had hopes and dreams. A consciousness in the universe, a one-of-a-kind creation never to be again. A man who should have fallen in love if he had not, had a family, and … well … lived. Potential died because he chose to let go.

Nick felt her hand rest lightly on his leg as she leaned toward him, eyes fixed on his.

"Don't, don't do this to yourself. He would have killed both of us if he could have. You have a right to live as well, and what of me? Do I not have a right to a future? No, he chose not you. He chose and gave you no choice. He chose, and now you must bear the hurt if you must, but it is not your fault."

"I want to go home. I want this over. This isn't supposed to be part of the adventure." Nick despaired while avoiding her stare.

Her grip tightened on his leg. The marks of the struggle they had both been through visible on her face, softened now by an anxious compassion for him.

"You don't get to choose the script all the time. Sometimes, you must read the lines given to you and do the next thing. This doesn't end here, you know that."

Nick drew a breath, letting the silence settle, recalling the journey that brought him to this. Life had been simple, ordinary, and predictable back then. A typical sunny morning in New York, now as distant as another lifetime.

Nick felt Elena's arms holding him, his head nestled against her chest. He heard her heart beating, and his body relaxed and stopped trembling. Nick crashed as the adrenaline and shock wore off. Elena slid out from under him and softly laid his head on the pillow. She threw the blanket over him, softly whispering, "Try to rest now. He is gone, and we are here and safe. Sleep."

She took their suitcases and piled them up against the broken door. Should someone try to force their way in by breaking the twine, they would at least have to navigate over the luggage to get to them. She would have loved to stay awake and on guard, but she felt herself succumbing to weariness. The night would have to hold what it may. Neither of them was ready nor built for such challenges. Indeed, she had more resources to handle this violent encounter with life and death than Nick, but the encounter had taken its toll on her.

As a realist with life and death surrounding her, she realized that sometimes, you had to step out of the way. She faced complex choices between necessity and conviction every day. Nick did not have to. "I guess that is a blessing and a curse," she audibly mused as she pulled down the top berth, climbed up, and fell asleep.

The Bukowina rumbled on through the night, clunk-clunk, clunk-clunk, clunk-clunk.

It might have been the familiar sound, the lulling sway of the train, the great wish of going home, or the extreme release that had swept over him, but all night long Nick imagined himself to be napping on his commute home, dreaming the whole adventure on his way home after a long day at work. The last two months of his life were an uncomfortable nightmare from which he could not shake himself awake.

On his imagined daily commute, he suddenly heard, "Gotcha, little man …," he screamed and threw himself from the bed against the opposite wall, tripping and falling over the broken table that hung there. His heart raced, fist clenched, ready to fight the battle all over again.

He looked around the dim room to find Elena staring at him with fear and wonder in her eyes. Confused and disoriented, Nick blurted out, "It's Viktor; he's here … But no, no, he can't be. I let him go, but will he ever release me?" He covered his face with his hands, put his head against Elena's bed, and stood there wondering if he could ever sleep again.

Elena reached over and ran her hand through his hair. Sometimes, you don't know what to say, so it is better to say nothing and just be there. Nick finally sat back down. Sleep evaded him despite the ongoing night. He had recovered but didn't want to close his eyes. He curled up at the end of his bed, his blanket wrapped around him, his head resting on the window. The night slowly slipped away, broken by the occasional pass through a village. Eventually, Elena's gentle, rhythmic breathing informed him that she had returned to sleep. He hoped Viktor had not suffered a night dying in the cold, spared even feeling the blow of hitting the cold earth before he found … sleep.

When Elena woke in the morning, Nick, still curled up in his blanket at the end of the bed with his head still against the glass, at least had his eyes closed. She had not been able to examine him last night, but now she saw the bumps, bruises, and cuts on his body. He had dried blood on his face. She quietly unstacked the luggage from the door and loosened the twine. She glanced back at him before she exited the door. "He should be safe. I won't go far, but I have no doubt the conductor will be curious about the damage."

With that, she left to report to someone that they had been attacked in the middle of the night and had fended off the assailant, but the fight had caused damage to the train and their compartment.

Elena, standing before the damaged car door and describing the assailant's escape to the conductor, saw Nick enter the hallway through the broken cabin door, still wrapped in his blanket. On seeing him, the conductor apologized for the assault. "Nothing like this has ever happened to me on this train before. I cannot imagine it. We have no other cabin to move you to, but I will station a man in this car for the rest of the trip. And we will give you a chain to secure your door."

At the next stop, the police were called, and the medics came aboard the train to clean and bandage Nick. "We will hunt to see if we can find anything on the side of the tracks. I cannot imagine stupidly jumping from a speeding train in the dark," offered the officer.

When the train moved again, Nick felt comforted to be alone with the clunk-clunk of the train and staring out the window, still wrapped in the blanket. He and Elena had talked little and with no depth. He needed the silence to focus on processing the events of the night, but felt a little better.

His phone rang. The caller ID was "CHRIS." Nick silenced the phone and set it back down on the table. He didn't want to talk to anyone right now, especially from his old life, especially Chris. He couldn't have one foot in both worlds. One foot still the naïve young man who was happy-go-lucky and expected the best of people around him, and the other foot in a world where someone could take a life when need pressed. To joke or laugh seemed somehow profane.

Elena watched knowingly. She would not press him with Chris. Nick would find his way in time. He needed to be self-absorbed for now. They would be in Kyiv soon. And he would have so much else to deal with. Brother Alfanas would meet them at the train station, and they would learn if he had successfully secured their access to the catacombs.

Brother Alfanas waited patiently as Nick and Elena's train pulled in. He did not have to see the bandaged and bruised bodies of Elena and Nick to know there had been trouble. Security rushed to the train to inspect the damage and take the report, which Elena essentially gave. Nick, still unable to say much, merely interjected a nod of confirmation now and again. Alfanas called his friend, and security immediately responded by walking Nick and Elena through the station to the waiting area to meet Alfanas.

Despondently, with red eyes and a face lacerated and bruised, Nick walked slowly into the station. Alfanas knew Viktor's handiwork when he saw it. He guessed Viktor had won. Having had his conversation with Nick and now knowing all the information Nick had to offer, Viktor would beat them to the catacombs.

With a worried expression, Alfanas asked, "Viktor?"

Nick threw himself at the monk and sobbed uncontrollably again. The security guards looked away as if to give him privacy. Alfanas had become an island of safety, understanding, and, yes, now, God's potential forgiveness. Alfanas wrapped his arms around Nick and placed one hand on the back of his head, gently rocking him back and forth.

Elena started to explain, but Alfanas hushed her, his eyes conveying a quiet but firm plea for patience as he turned his full attention to Nick.

"I … I killed him," Nick blurted out into the folds of Alfanas' robes, where he had buried his face, "I killed another human being. How do I live with that?"

Alfanas spoke softly solely for Nick's ears. "Trust me, you'll find a way. Listen, it was not in your heart. It does not define you. You did not wake up with the intent to kill someone. Another had to put it there for you. Another chose his death at your hands. God knows this. You had little will or volition in the act. Viktor decided to make it a choice between your life and his. He understood the risks and accepted them. For him, it was a game he lost. For you, it is a violation you cannot forget, for that is the goodness screaming in your soul. Eventually, you will reconcile what had to be with what you ethically wanted, but he is gone. Now, you must do the hard work of letting him go." Alfanas intoned these last words, with each one getting emphasis.

It must have been fifteen minutes before Nick composed himself and pulled away from the old monk.

"Let's get you all settled," said Alfanas, "I have made arrangements for you." He drove them to their hotel. When in their room, he requested Nick lie down and try to rest, assuring him he and Elena would be close to keep him safe. At first, Elena and Alfanas said little to each other, opting to stare out the window or into their phones. After about 30 minutes, Nick's breathing quieted as he drifted to sleep out of emotional weariness, if for no other reason.

Alfanas turned his attention to Elena. "Now tell me what happened."

Quietly, Elena told Alfanas everything that had happened to them on the trip from Chișinău to Kyiv. The old monk looked even older. He placed his hand on Elena's. "You have done well. It took great courage for both of you. You were matched with a foe beyond the physical strength, mental dexterity, and ruthless abandon of both of you. I had hoped that Athens would have delayed him more. Alas, it was not to be."

He got up, walked over to the foot of the bed, and studied Nick. "Poor man. Some men are not prepared for the rough necessities life throws at them. I tried to help him avoid feeling the weight thrown at him by another, but now he must shoulder it. There is no way around certain realities in life, and through is the only course. I will stay the night in the chair. Viktor is gone for us, but might show up for Nick again. You need rest as well. Sleep, I will watch and pray."

"Well," he thought, "we are all here now. Viktor is gone. Lavra is in turmoil with SBU agents, police, and others wandering about. That might yet be a benefit for us. We shall see what tomorrow brings. We still do not know if Timos worked alone or if others are still plotting against us in Lavra. That will be a journey for tomorrow."

Nick and Elena slept until mid-afternoon. Alfanas decided it would be best for all of them to get out of the hotel room for a walk in the city. The three of them stepped out into the crisp Kyiv afternoon, the air sharp and biting with the promise of impending winter. Nick adjusted his scarf, trying to ignore the lingering ache in his muscles and the emotional weight pressing down on him. Elena walked silently beside him, her eyes scanning their surroundings, while Alfanas led the way with the calm assurance of someone who knew the city's rhythms intimately.

Alfanas suggested they head toward Kyiv's central square. "Sometimes, being in the presence of others, even strangers, helps us regain our sense of humanity."

Nick wasn't sure he wanted humanity right now. Still, he nodded and followed. The square bustled with life. Busy with conversations, vendors, smells of food, and families having fun, Nick felt he could never inhabit normalcy again. Alfanas looked at him knowingly. "Time is a master healer," he thought. "But time is one thing we do not have," he sighed.

Alfanas kept the conversation light as they walked, pointing out historic buildings and recounting snippets of Kyiv's history. Nick barely responded, but Elena tried to engage, sensing the monk's effort to create a sense of ease. Yet both she and Alfanas remained mindful of Nick's distance and tried not to overcompensate, hoping for small steps of healing.

Nick didn't reply but turned back toward the square, his gaze distant.

As the sun dipped lower, Alfanas guided them to a small cafe in a muted corner of the main square.

"We need to eat," he said gently. "We need to take care of ourselves. The journey ahead is unknown."

Nick picked at his food and said little. Elena reached out and took his hand. He looked at her and tried to smile.

She squeezed his hand in affirmation and as a nonverbal response. "It's okay. I may not understand what you are going through, but it's okay. We are here together. We will take the next steps as they happen. None of us needs to know the answers right now."

Alfanas watched them quietly, his thoughts turning to the challenges they still faced. For now, though, he let the silence settle between them, content that they were safe for this fleeting moment.

When they returned to the hotel, Alfanas told them enough of what he had discovered and about his encounter with Timos, omitting his role in calling down the raid. He wasn't proud of that, after promising the abbot that he would not bring trouble to his house, which is what he did. Neither Nick nor Elena interrupted him with any questions. After Alfanas had finished, Nick got up and walked to the dark window. Elena remained seated. Alfanas considered both of them before returning his gaze to the black window. Speaking as if to the gathering darkness outside, "Where do we go from here? You both have had very close calls, and I don't know what you are feeling now."

Elena dropped her head. "I need to go on." In her heart, she didn't want to leave Nick behind, and for so many reasons, she felt that would be an impossibility, but she needed to know what lay behind the years of service and the profound mystery they had unveiled. She needed closure. "My family has endured for over 1,000 years, with trauma. Families broken," she sighed, "spirits broken, I owe it to them to go on." She looked over at Nick, who stared out into the night. Not for the first time, she wished she could take away his pain and confusion. She had grown to love him. Surprisingly, she could not see the next step without him at her side. Worry covered her face as she stared helplessly at the top of the table.

Nick released a labored breath and said, "There is a pointlessness to the whole thing. I'm unsure what could add value to what we have seen or become through this journey. But perhaps in the end, something makes sense." He turned and looked at both of them. "I don't think that it has anything to do with what Viktor wanted, money or whatever he was trying to get out of me. That makes no sense when you're dead."

He thought back to his home, to his mom and dad, and the sense of protection and love that had driven him to Sitka, which now felt so distant. He reflected aloud, "I don't think I started this journey with that kind of motivation in mind. Not like my career or even my life until a few months ago, which always seemed like a road leading somewhere someday, not about where I was at the moment. No, this journey has been about discovering who I am, or possibly who I should be, because I'm not thrilled with who I've been, and I don't think I was ever delighted with myself, even back before all this. Come to think of it, there's always seemed to be a pointlessness in my life even then."

He saw them stir as if to come to his aid. "Yup, I know I had to do what I did. Cognitively, I've worked it all out, but relationally, it still feels like a life wasted. And maybe, just maybe, there is an answer buried out there that I need, that we need," he looked at Elena. "I think I need that answer now more than ever." He turned again to the window and looked out into nothing.

Elena stood and walked up behind him, watching him through the reflection in the window. She slipped her hand around his waist. Her little American had painfully grown up, his innocence dead with Viktor. She leaned her head into his chest more to comfort herself than to lend him aid. She hurt for him and for herself. He instinctively placed his arm around her shoulders as they both looked out into the darkness.

In a strange way, he felt stronger than he ever had.

An insightful advisor knows when to let the silence linger and play out in a still room. Alfanas kept his peace and said nothing.

Finally, Nick broke the silence. "There's a part of me that does not want to go on. But that part is weaker than the part of me that is still looking for answers and meaning. That part of me may not want to go on, but it needs to go on to the end of this. I have given up my home, my career, time with my family, and lost a portion of my ideals and innocence to be here, which needs a redemption that can't come from running back home."

"Very well," Alfanas said slowly and softly, "to go forward, we must plan our next steps. Come and sit." He patted both places at the table. "I think the upheaval at the monastery will help us to get you in. Between tourists and SBU personnel, you will probably not be challenged going into the monastery. All the would-be prying eyes are behind bars or fearing for their lives. I will meet you at the Far Cave Bell Tower at 4 P.M. I am afraid you must wait until things calm down, and I am free later in the evening. We can then use the private entrance to the catacombs to get to the Far Caves to look for Alexios and Theodore. I do have a rough map, but the extent of the caves is not fully documented or explored."

"I have to go soon. I cannot spend much more time away from the monastery without arousing suspicion. By the time I return, the brothers will still be out of the quarters, working various jobs. Our numbers are now fewer because others have been detained, and some have gone to other monasteries due to the atmosphere that pervades Kyiv Pechersk Lavra."

They all stood. Alfanas looked at them in turn. He hugged and kissed them on both cheeks, as is customary, and left for Lavra.

When he had gone, Nick went back to the window to stare, but with a relaxed feeling reflected in his posture that maybe came more from resolve than healing. He did not address Elena but spoke more to the vast darkness outside. "There's something about him, you know. He makes you feel better. I don't even know if he's aware that he's doing it. It just happens."

"Yes," agreed Elena, "he is a dear soul."

Nick wondered if he could sleep, but he found that Viktor's face was becoming less focused in his mind. He thought of the Lavra, caves, monks, and saints. He slept soundly.

Chapter 19: Chronicle of the Last Emperor, Completed

The morning light spilled through the curtains of the small hotel room, golden and warm, yet it did little to chase away the unease that had settled over Nick. He sat on the edge of the bed, lacing his boots, while Elena leaned against the window, gazing out at the bustling street below. The city seemed alive with purpose, but for them, the weight of their next step loomed heavier than the clear blue sky suggested.

Elena's voice broke the silence. "We'll need supplies before we go. The Lavra isn't just a church. It's a labyrinth, and we can't afford to wander blindly."

Nick nodded, glancing at the modest list they'd scratched out the night before. "Flashlights, a camping lantern, perhaps a decent backpack. We should grab water too. Who knows how long we'll be underground?"

She turned from the window, her expression steady but unreadable. "And courage. We'll need that as well."

Nick managed a weak smile. "Does the corner store carry that?"

Elena didn't laugh, but her lips curved just enough to lighten the tension. She picked up her bag from the chair. "Come on. Let's get moving. The Lavra isn't going anywhere, but the longer we wait, the harder this will get."

They stepped outside into a crisp Kyiv late morning, the streets already alive with the rhythm of daily life. Sidewalk cafes hummed with quiet chatter, and vendors plied their wares in the cool air. Nick felt a moment of remorse that they could not be a simple tourist couple enjoying the city, but they had more important goals than comfort. Purpose drove them where comfort would not.

After several false leads and dead ends, they finally found a small general-purpose store a little further out of the way than they had planned. It turned out to be small and cramped, due mainly to the large stock of merchandise packed on the shelves. Housewares to automotive, with everything in between. It reminded Nick of one of the old-fashioned New England hardware stores that still existed in a few lucky towns back home. The clerk barely glanced at them as they entered. Elena made a beeline for the back, scanning the shelves until she found what they needed: a pair of durable flashlights, a compact emergency lantern, and a sturdy backpack.

Nick grabbed a couple of water bottles and added them to the growing pile in Elena's basket. "Do we need anything else?" he asked, glancing around.

"Batteries—we can't afford to lose light in the catacombs."

Nick picked up a pack of heavy-duty batteries and handed them to her. "Good call. Anything else?"

She hesitated momentarily, her fingers brushing over a display of pocketknives. "How about getting one of these? Just in case?"

Nick picked up a miniature multi-tool version and added it to their haul.

They paid in cash, and the clerk gave them a glancing acknowledgement as he handed over their change. Back outside, the city seemed noisier in contrast with the muffled tones of the fully packed shelves. Nick adjusted the straps of the new backpack over his shoulder and took a deep breath. "Ready?"

Elena glanced at him, her dark eyes meeting his. "Ready."

Nick texted Alfanas that they were on their way.

The Lavra complex finally loomed ahead of them like a fortress of faith and history. Its golden domes gleamed in the sinking sunlight, a stark contrast to the shadowed purpose that had brought them here. As they approached the gates, Nick felt his pulse quicken.

There was no turning back now.

Elena led the way, her steps purposeful but not hurried. She paused briefly at the entrance, scanning the flow of tourists and pilgrims. "Alfanas said to meet him near the bell tower of the Far Caves," she murmured as she pointed out the way.

Nick followed her gesture, as they both spotted the older man standing apart from the crowd. His dark robe blended into the shadows of the stone archway, but his sharp eyes found them instantly. He inclined his head in silent greeting as they made their way over.

"You have what you need?"

Elena nodded, patting the side of the backpack. "We're ready."

"Good. Follow me closely."

Alfanas led them through the complex, weaving past clusters of visitors and monks. The atmosphere shifted as they descended deeper into the Lavra. The daylight grew dimmer and the air cooler as late afternoon settled in. By the time they reached his temporary dwelling place, the bustle of the world felt like a distant memory.

Alfanas retraced Makar's steps down the ancient stairs to the musty, complete darkness of the sub-basement. It was late afternoon, too early to go down the private stairs and into the complex of the Far Caves. Visitors and monks accessed the holy caves until late in the day.

He gestured to a small room tucked into the corner of the cellar. "You'll wait here until Compline. I'll return for you once the monks have cleared the catacombs for prayer."

Nick and Elena stepped inside, the weight of stone walls pressing around them. The room held only a low bench. Alfanas brought several candles for light as Nick and Elena passed the late afternoon and early evening hours in order to save the batteries and flashlights for later in the night. He gave them a final nod before disappearing back into the labyrinth of halls.

As the door closed, Nick sank onto the bench, exhaling slowly. "Well, here we are. Underground, waiting again."

Elena didn't answer. She sat with her back against the wall near the candle, her fingers brushing over the table. She closed her eyes and surrendered to the calm. As the candlelight flickered and danced across the floor, walls, and both of them, Nick watched her for a moment before leaning back against the wall.

"Whatever happens," he said quietly, "we'll figure it out. Together. Right?"

She opened her eyes, turned to him, her expression remaining soft in the gentle light. "I know, I just hope we're ready for the next step."

She took hold of his hand and placed it in her lap, let her head rest upon his shoulder, and closed her eyes again.

Nick didn't have an answer to that. He sat in the stillness, listening to the faint echoes of the Lavra as they waited for the shadows to open up and guide them. Together in the dark, he realized he was not the man he used to be. Things that were so important once upon a time were now like shadows in his mind.

Part of him missed the innocent boy he of several months ago. The boy who never really thought about life and death, or, really, for that matter, too much about how his life choices affected others. And now, every step seemed to have geopolitical importance. They had been halfway around the world, had fought for their lives, and he had killed a man.

Now, he was in the dim flicker of the candlelight with the only other person who had been through all that with him. Nick had grown to appreciate Elena being there. No, he had grown to depend on her being there. No, to love her. Stretching out an arm and slipping it around her seemed just to happen without a thought. Naturally, it was right. As he pulled her close and completed the circle of embrace, she snuggled into his warm body, and together they fell asleep.

Alfanas had his obediences to complete. Brother Makar assigned him to kitchen duty for the afternoon, but granted permission for him to meet "old friends" visiting the Lavra. He met Nick and Elena, got them settled, and returned to his duties before being missed.

The presence of security in the monastery had made Alfanas overconfident, perhaps even rash. Not all eyes were inwardly focused: his every move since leaving the kitchen had been observed from the shadows and covered by a silence more impenetrable than his own. He may have dealt with Timos, but the gaze of older and more protective eyes now had him in their sights. Those eyes saw the two youngsters waiting and guessed the intent of Alfanas' deception.

Nick stirred slightly as he imagined the faint sound of a door closing echoing through the heavy stillness. His eyes flickered open, adjusting to the dim light of the candle's glow, now sputtering low. Elena, still nestled against him, her breathing steady and soft, stirred as she felt him tense up, but her warmth grounded him at the moment, lulling him from imagination to the peace of dreams. Before drifting off, he felt a pang of guilt for the fleeting comfort they'd found with each other while Alfanas bore the weight of orchestrating their next move. Yet, something else quickly overtook the thought, a faint prickling at the edge of his awareness.

Stirred again, he glanced toward the door, but nothing happened. Still, something lingered—an unease that tightened in the surrounding air. He shook his head, dismissing it as nerves. After everything they'd faced, paranoia seemed a natural companion.

Elena stirred against him again. This time her eyelashes fluttered as she woke. Her voice was soft and drowsy. "What time is it?"

Nick looked toward the candle, its wax pooling in the holder. "It's three quarters past a candle." He joked. "I don't want to move to get my phone out, but it should not be long now. Alfanas said he'd return after Compline." He considered whether he should tell Elena and decided it would be best. "I thought I heard a door, but that could have been my imagination."

She sat up slowly, brushing a hand through her hair. "It feels like the walls are closing in."

Nick managed a wry smile. "If you ever feel like getting back to open spaces, just say the word."

Elena glanced at him, her lips twitching in faint amusement, but her eyes remained distant. "I'll let you know if I ever feel that way."

The latch on the door of their room lifted. They tensed, and Nick quickly blew out the candle, letting the dark cover them. They heard the door creak open, and the dim yellow light of a candle flickered and danced through the opening door.

"It is only me," said the familiar and comforting voice of Alfanas, "I have peeled potatoes until my hands are raw. I think I will be glad to have a break from that duty for a while. It's time for us to go."

They took the flashlights out of their backpacks, and the bright white LEDs seemed harsh and sacrilegious for a setting that had never been exposed to daylight. Alfanas led them a few doors down to the room where a simple curtain covered the door of the private stairs into the catacombs. It creaked open, and even though they tried to shut it silently, it seemed to boom shut in the relative silence. A familiar sound to Nick. It made him think of the sound that stirred him awake, but even if he heard something, it could have been any door in that black silence.

They carefully followed the stairs and adjoining tunnel until they stood before the door that led into the catacombs. Alfanas paused, his hand resting lightly on the ancient wood as he turned to Nick and Elena. His voice dropped to a reverent whisper, the echoes barely carrying in the tight stone corridor.

"You are entering a sacred place," he began, his tone both solemn and tender. "Remember that. Only by the grace of God are you privileged to be here. Here, the dead sleep, and the Saints keep watch. You have nothing to fear. No ghosts walk here. No evil spirit is given even a foothold. Here are your intercessors who struggle for your thriving. They deserve your respect and adoration. Be on your best behavior. This is holy ground."

He paused, bowing his head in silent prayer. Elena mirrored his gesture, crossing herself with practiced grace, her lips moving in a soft murmur of devotion. Nick stood uncertainly for a moment, watching them before bowing his head. He didn't know quite what to think, but Alfanas' words had stirred something in him, a vague sense of belonging to something greater than himself, even if he didn't fully understand it or completely believe it.

Elena understood perfectly the gravitas that Alfanas expressed. She had grown up with the saints' intercession and the wider family presence that icons evoked. For her, the saints were not distant figures but constant companions, interwoven into the fabric of her life.

These were people who had lived for the good of others. Why would they harbor ill will in death? Nick found the idea to be unexpectedly healing.

And then Viktor crossed his mind. He wondered whether Viktor had ever believed in any of this. Was he too, despite everything, part of this family now? The thought gripped him, unexpected and unbidden, like a sharp wind cutting through the still air. Viktor would have hurt him or killed him, given the chance. Yet the idea of Viktor's redemption, of him even finding peace among the saints, did not annoy him, but it unsettled Nick, this thought that grace might extend even to those who had so wronged him. But wasn't that the point? In the end, he would welcome even Viktor's redemption.

He choked back the lump rising in his throat. "Even you, Viktor," he whispered silently. "Maybe even you." As he murmured, he found deep release from the guilt and sorrow that had plagued him. He hoped, no, he prayed that Viktor had found peace at last.

The door creaked open, and the sound amplified in the silence. Alfanas pushed it gently, leaving it ajar to avoid the loud echo of its shutting completely. "Farther toward the front of the caves, there might still be straggling monks present. Some have late duties here, and others keep vigil in the chapels interspersed throughout the complex. We must be careful."

He glanced at his hand-drawn map, tracing its lines with a finger. "Section IV," he muttered, then raised his voice slightly for Nick and Elena. "Let's keep our eyes open so we don't get lost down here. This is a maze of tunnels. Some haven't been accessed in centuries."

Nick let his flashlight beam sweep across the niches and recesses as they moved forward. Each flicker of light seemed to bring another fragment of the past to life. There were niches housing elaborate coffins with plate-glass panels, the faces of saints painted on icons staring back, unblinking in the harsh light. Smaller boxes nestled into the walls must have held the bones of long-dead monks. Lamps sat extinguished in alcoves, their oil long burned away, waiting for the dawn and the reverent hands of devoted monks to light them anew.

Nick found it strange that he felt no discomfort. If anything, a curious peace settled over him as though the shadows themselves welcomed him, a sense that these long-departed souls were not strangers but family. He almost laughed at the thought, but he let a smile break through at least.

"Almost like being on a football field," he mused. *"And here are the crowds, cheering me on to run with endurance to the goal line. They're watching me. They want me to score that touchdown."*

As they moved along, Nick found his hand would regularly skirt the edge of a niche's shelf as a gesture of affection, or thanks.

They were coming near what should be "Section IV" when suddenly a monk with his hood pulled down over his face stood before them, barring the way.

"You have deceived me and betrayed your brothers," said the voice of Makar, "and now you must satisfy me as to why I should not take you to the abbot for expulsion from this place and the order."

Brother Makar had done something nobody had been able to do for many years—caught Brother Alfanas off guard. In the secular world, he clung to the mantra that needs must rule where the devil prowls, but with brothers in his own house, his own covenant sealed by his vow, he would not brazenly lie to his superior. He had not prepared for this confrontation. A traitor he could overpower, even kill him if it had to be, but if the choice were between forcing his way or ending the journey, the journey must end. He could not escape the authority of Father Makar or plead his case. Alfanas leaned quietly against the wall as he considered what to say next.

But he didn't have to speak. Elena spoke next. She had been silent. Her parents had raised her never to interfere with the work of her spiritual leaders, especially as a woman. But she could not let the quest be delayed or ended.

"Father Makar!" She exclaimed, "Blessed be you, my father! How many years have passed! Glory be to God that I see you again. We greatly miss you in Istanbul. As dear as family is, your memory is in our midst. We are here on God's errand and God's work. Would you deny or obstruct the will of God in the fulfillment of prophecy? Would you interfere in the work of His holy agency? If the saints' sacrifice and the Rum's state mean nothing to you, then end our task. Else, hear us, aid us, and reserve to the end to proclaim the final judgment if God is not with us."

"My heart leapt, child, when I saw you in the courtyard with Alfanas," said Makar as he slowly removed his hood. "It has been years since I have been home to Istanbul. But I should never forget a daughter of my house of faith, even though a thousand years should pass. I suspect you have come to meet with Alexios and Theodore. Brother," he said now, looking at Alfanas, "don't think that age has dimmed the eyes that I have in the back of my head, that I would not notice you taking a picture of their resting locations."

He smiled as he continued, "But it was in vain. I hid them. They are not in Section IV. Of course, I recognized the names when I came here. I have known the Sakellaris family my whole life. They are a direct line to when Istanbul was Constantinople, ruled by an emperor, as is my own heritage. But I needed to challenge you and know your intent before I could either assist or thwart you.

When I came to Lavra, they were just names on a scroll that referenced one of the areas of the Far Caves, which was not open to the public and seldom visited even by the monks here. But I explored them. The scroll was old, its ink faded, yet the names stood out as though they were waiting to be found. I knew from the inscriptions that they were refugees from Constantinople after its fall.

We monastics focus on the inward journey of God's Spirit to guide our outward actions. The Spirit of God told my heart that these names were of purpose and intent in a universe of no coincidence. I realized I was a forerunner of God's work, and their resting places needed my protection. So, I made up the registry on the computer.

I am your guide by divine appointment. That should not surprise Elena or Alfanas. After all, it is God's universe to order and maybe even chart a course just for you. If you doubt me, remember this: none of us is here by accident. With every step, every moment, providence has prepared us for this.

Do you want me to take you to them? Or possibly you would prefer to wander and get lost in the dark?" He smiled again, a lightness in his voice that contrasted with the gravity of his words.

Elena took his hand. "I look forward to your guiding us to see my grandsires, as is my sacred duty and right."

"Who could deny a family access to the memory of their ancestors? Follow me."

Makar led them back down the tunnel in the direction from which they had come. A passage led them to a small chapel just before one of the niches. Behind the iconostasis and to one side, they entered another narrow passage. This led to a section of the catacombs not on Alfanas' map.

Three hundred or so feet down, Makar finally stopped, and his light rested on a simple casket, all wood with hand-drawn figures of the raising of Lazarus, fishes, and crosses.

Makar let his hand lightly rest and caress the casket as he said, "This is Alexios." He looked at Elena. "Here sleeps one of your grandsires, who are beyond number. He has watched over you, but now you are here to meet him. The other lies about twenty feet down the passage."

He walked them down to a carved casket of oak. "Here rests Theodore of blessed memory," the old monk said with reverence.

Alfanas noticed that beneath the niche on which the casket rested, inscribed on a marble plaque roughly 18 by 24 inches were the words written in Greek: Θεόδωρος Σακελλάριος Εἰρήνη καὶ Φῶς.

"'Theodore Sakellaris, Peace and Light.' Hmm, an odd-sized plaque for so few words."

Alfanas kneeled down to examine it more closely. He pushed it, but it did not budge. He tried to pull it, but his fingers could not find a grip. "Curious."

Alfanas headed back to Alexios' grave but stopped short. "Elena, tell me what you see in my light?"

Elena followed the beam to the side of the tunnel, and below Alexios's casket a similar plaque had been set into the wall, but deeper, purplish red.

"Porphyry," she exclaimed. "The stone of royalty."

The carving on the plaque read, Ἀδελφὸς Ἀλέξιος Σακελλάριος. Brother Alexios Sakellaris.

Alfanas looked at the stone plaque. Its dimensions were the same as the white marble of Theodore's grave, but it did not fit quite as tightly. He pushed it with all his weight, and it moved a little.

"Nick, come here and help," Alfanas said urgently. "Push with me. Don't push to topple. Push to slide."

Both men now put their full weight into the task, and the stone slowly yielded to their pressure, sliding back steadily until the path was open enough for them to squeeze through.

"I will go first and ensure it is safe," said Alfanas.

Alfanas, flashlight in hand, crawled and wiggled as his broad frame made a tight fit in the narrow space. His body inched until he was about three-quarters of the way in, and then, pop, he was gone.

Nick looked in the hole and could see a light every so often. "Are you okay?" he said in a loud whisper.

"Yes. All is well," Alfanas replied. "The small passage opens to a larger one, about four feet inside, where I can stand. There is a straight way and a tunnel that leads to the right, back toward Theodore. Wait a moment before anyone else comes in. I need to look at the stone to see if we can open it from this side."

Without warning, Alfanas shone his flashlight back down the narrow opening straight into Nick's face, but also to look at the stone channel. The channel sides and top were tapered with a relief around the outer edge on the top and sides that kept it from being fitted into place from the outside. There were no handles or marks on the back. To reseal the passage would have meant they would be locked in the tomb. Alfanas backed himself out of the narrow entrance and shone his flashlight down the tunnel to the right.

"I am going to go a little way down the tunnel to see where it leads. I will be back in a minute or two."

It didn't take him long before Nick could see the flashlight shining down the narrow entrance to the tunnel again, and they heard Alfanas' voice, "It leads to another narrow way that I assume must be under Theodore's niche. This narrow passage is blocked by a white marble stone that must be the back of Theodore's plaque. Nick, you and Makar go back to Theodore's niche. I will try to dislodge the stone enough for you to grab hold of it and help me."

Nick, Elena, and Makar stood before Theodore's casket with their flashlights trained on the plaque. Nick found it disconcerting to hear grunting and groaning emanating from the niche, even though he knew the origin must be Alfanas wrestling within the passageway and struggling with the white marble stone as it shifted from its setting. Still, the sounds seemed to come from the casket. *"It is as if Theodore were wrestling to free himself,"* thought Nick.

The marble wiggled in its place. Slowly, a fraction of an inch at a time, it freed itself from its socket. Like a capstone, the plaque fitted into the wall so that it could only be removed from behind. The top and two sides were tapered in to fit tight, without a seam or edge to pull from. As Alfanas pushed from behind, Nick and Makar were eventually able to grip the stone enough to shift it free. They then pulled the monk into the tunnel.

They helped Alfanas up. He brushed himself off to little effect. "Ah, this is the exit. The other is the entrance. Elena, Makar, and I will use the entrance to access the tunnel. Nick, you will help me replace Alexios' plaque as much as possible from the front, and then you can enter through Theodore's niche. It will be a challenge to push the other stone by myself, but Elena and Makar will bolster my feet, so I have something to push against. Nick will need to guide me when everything is in place."

It took what seemed to be an interminably long time for Alfanas to move the block of porphyry back in place. It seemed all the longer for Nick, who found himself alone in the tunnel, letting his imagination run wild. When the Alexios' plaque finally lined up with the edges of the whitewashed loess of the tunnel wall, he breathed a sigh of relief.

Nick ran down to Theodore's niche and joined his friends in the hidden tunnel. When they finally pulled him through, he found himself in a similar tunnel to the main catacomb tunnels, with whitewashed loess soil forming the walls and floor. The whitewash made the light of their flashlights bounce off the uneven surfaces of the tunnel as shadows seemed to run and dance ahead of them. The white blinded them as if it had been just applied, not subject to years of smoke and the hands of visitors.

They had by now lost all sense of direction and could not tell on what compass point they were heading. Occasionally, a set of stairs would drop them another eight or ten feet down. They could have been anywhere under the East bank of the Dnieper River, even under the Near Caves, when they came on the iron-bound door. They could find no lock on it. Any who found it would be able to defeat a last attempt to secure it, making a lock superfluous if not defeating the one intended to open it.

Alfanas paused at the door for a moment, looking into the faces of his friends. He let his hand rest on the door's wood as a blessing. "Whatever lies behind this door will be the next step in our journey," he said solemnly as his hand moved to the latch and swung the door wide.

The door creaked open, and the sound amplified in the tunnel's silence. Nick felt the air change, cooler, heavier, stale, as though they were stepping into a place where time itself had stopped and the air undisturbed for five hundred years. Alfanas led the way, his flashlight casting long, wavering shadows as the four stepped into the room.

At first, the ornate gold-decorated white marble column in the center of the vast space drew Nick's attention. It rose waist high, its surface polished to a gleaming finish. Right in the center of the column was the double-headed eagle of imperial Roman Byzantium, and on its top lay a hefty, leather-bound book. Its edges gilded and faintly glinting with gold leaf in the dim light. The sight of it sent a shiver through him.

"*The Chronicle of the Last Emperor*," Alfanas murmured, his voice reverent as he stepped closer. "Nick, get the two lanterns you bought from the backpack and light them so we can see better." With the room better lit, they saw other passages off to the left and right. Fitted stones and columns stabilized and supported the added expanse of the chamber.

With the shadows pulled back by the lamps, they could see dimly to the far end of the rectangular space. Drawn with catlike curiosity, Nick followed the beam of his flashlight to the bottommost step of a set of stairs.

There, elevated on a dais eight steps above the floor, stood an empty throne, glinting in the first light to have hit it in five hundred years. It seemed impossibly regal, yet utterly human. The back and armrests were adorned with intricate carvings of vines and eagles, the Byzantine double-headed eagle etched prominently on the crest. Gold leaf still clung to its surface, and a faint patina suggested centuries of quiet endurance.

Nick's breath caught. He had never considered what it might feel like to stand before such a symbol, not just of power but of a legacy he struggled to take it all in.

"Look," Elena said softly, pointing to the walls.

Lining the room, peeking out between cabinets and iron-bound chests, were mosaics. Even in the dim light, they radiated brilliance, scenes of saints and emperors, Theotokos, Mary Mother of God, and the triumphs of Constantinople. The tiles seemed to catch and hold the light, their colors vivid and rich: gold, lapis lazuli, and crimson.

"These mosaics…" Elena's voice trembled slightly. "They must have been taken straight from the walls of Constantinople."

Nick moved closer to one of the cabinets. Its wood was dark, almost black with age, bound in iron that seemed designed for strength and permanence. Though the doors were closed, he could only imagine what lay within. The last remnants of imperial Byzantium—the treasures, documents, and relics—Alexios shipped out of the city in its final years or days. He felt the weight of it all— the desperate hope of those who had packed these things, believing that the empire might still rise again, and the urgent need for Rome to survive.

Meanwhile, Alfanas and Makar had reached the column. With a shared glance, they leaned over the marble lectern and opened the book to its title page. The leather cover gave way with a faint creak, and a faintly musty scent rose from the pages.

"It's all here," Alfanas whispered, his fingers hovering over the delicate script. The title glared back at them: "The Chronicle of the Last Emperor." He let out a slow breath. "The complete *Chronicle*."

As Alfanas turned the pages carefully. The parchment rustled softly, each page an artifact in its own right. He paused as he reached a section near the end, his finger tracing the first line of text.

"Here," Alfanas said, his voice low but steady. "This is where section three takes up the story."

Makar leaned in to look, and his brow furrowed in concentration as they read silently together. The ancient Greek flowed steadily, their murmurs filling the room as Nick and Elena moved closer to listen.

The words continued Alexios' recounting of Constantinople's fall, and how Alexios, with his eldest son, Theodore, risked all to escape with the barely living emperor. It recounted their journey that brought them to Kyiv, and to construct this hidden sanctuary and reliquary. With each sentence, more and more loose ends were finding their resolution as history and legend met in mutual understanding.

Elena reached for Nick's hand, her grip firm. "This isn't just history. It's their story. It's ours."

Nick nodded. He glanced at the pages he could not read, hearing words without understanding. As Alfanas and Makar read on, the throne drew more of his attention. Let the skilled and learned wrestle with the ancient language; he could understand the symbol of power, the silent witness to the authority of what had been and might still come.

Nick left the two Greek scholars, who had found their treasure, to their work, and stepped up onto the first step leading up to the dais, and the weight of his body triggered the machinery for which the Byzantine engineers were so famous. A gurgling sound of water being released and the clunk of long, motionless gears straining with the stresses of age and weight resonated in the chamber. The throne slid back. Slowly, a large block of porphyry rose from under the floor in the vacancy left by it.

Two doors slowly opened on either side of the dais. One held a crown. The other a scepter. Nick, riveted to the spot, looked on with amazement. He dared not move. Elena joined him as the porphyry kept inching until it solidly stopped in place with a last clunk from a hidden cog. Nick glanced at Elena, and they both climbed the steps. Makar and Alfanas watched from their places at the book, but they knew that what Nick and Elena had found would wait until they revealed the answers from the Chronicle.

As the couple mounted the topmost step and walked out onto the dais, the block of porphyry revealed itself as a sarcophagus topped with glass panes. About two feet below the glass, a surface gleamed like a mirror, though Nick swore he saw ripples shiver across it. He went forward to inspect it, and yet again, another step depressed, and more gears could be heard. The surface of the silver lake now boiled as small chains disturbed its surface to lift a secret payload. Nick and Elena stood in hypnotized fascination as a face emerged from the silver surface.

First, the nose, but soon rivulets of silver were running from the eyes down the cheek, and silver-white hair, almost indistinguishable from the mercury, poked through. After about ten minutes, there he was, Constantine XI Palaiologos. Robed in white with platinum embroidery, the Imperial eagle on his chest. Sword unsheathed at his side. He looked ready to stir and bound through the Golden Gate at a second's notice.

Nick looked into the closed eyes of the long-dead Emperor. He placed a hand on the pane of glass and sighed, his breath fogging the cool plates, a fleeting veil between him and the centuries-old face of Constantine XI. Elena looked on from at his side and then went to investigate the scepter and crown.

Nick felt her warmth leave his side, but then he felt the warmth of a presence fill the void beside him. Father Makar had silently moved from the book on the podium, leaving Alfanas with the charge of deciphering the old Greek text of the tome and murmuring the words to himself. The priest said nothing at first, standing shoulder-to-shoulder with Nick. Then, mirroring him, he placed his hand on the glass.

Nick did not turn to look at him but said, his voice hollow, "It has cost so much to get to this point and look into that face. I think of the people along the way who risked so much for us to be here. And then there are the lives of Timos and Viktor, both destroyed, one beyond redemption. Why do I feel so empty?"

Father Makar exhaled heavily, his breath slow and deliberate as though drawing from a deep well of wisdom. "My son, do not wrestle with the redemption of the dead. They are in God's hands, nor with the living whose role in life is still being defined. You stand on the threshold of weighty choices. I urge you to pause and enter the sacred stillness where true wisdom resides. The obvious path is not always the one that needs to be taken. Frequently, the greatest act of courage is not to seize what is before us but to let go of it, for the sake of others and those who will come after. "

Nick's eyes remained fixed on the glass, tracing the contours of the emperor's face. Responding quietly, "It's not for me, is it? The crown, the scepter. I think deep down I knew all along. I mean … I'm not the one. This is not the time for him." He stroked the glass as if he could touch Constantine's hand.

"That is not for me to judge," Makar answered, his voice gentle but firm. "Only the silent whisper of the Divine to a man's soul can guide him to the truth. But consider this: perhaps your calling is not to sit upon a throne, but to restore what thrones have broken. To heal what thrones have shattered, not to rule, but to take the arduous journey of service. The human heart craves the permanence of being a vessel, holding power, wealth, prestige, and answers. But occasionally, the higher calling is to be a conduit, letting a higher power flow through you to fill others where they are empty.

Like it or not, you are part of an ongoing story. Your choice will shape the next chapter for yourself and those entrusted to your care. Be still. No choice, made in good conscience and despite its fruit, is ever truly wasted by providential design."

Nick turned slightly, his gaze falling on Elena, who had moved on to examine the intricate mosaics on the dais walls. "What about her? She believes this so deeply. How do I explain it to her? How do I make her see that maybe it's not the treasure or the prophecy but something else entirely?"

Makar's expression softened, and his voice took on a quiet resolve. "Liberation, my son, comes from God's hand, through His agency. We cannot define or fulfill the prophecies in our ways and call them God's ways. That is the path to pain and suffering. It has always been so. Men like Constantine XI forgot this truism to their peril. Unlike us, God never lives between a rock and a hard place. He sees the story whole while we fixate on single moments, universalizing our justice and solutions as if we could stand in God's place. When we cling too tightly to one chapter, to power, title, or prophecy, we lose sight of the larger narrative."

236

He placed a steadying hand on Nick's shoulder. Its weight gentle but anchoring. "Tell her this: the story of Byzantium does not end in gold and conquest. That was its downfall. Its greatest treasures are found in faith, in sacrifice, in the hope that something greater can be built even from ruin. Speak to her heart, not to her expectations. She will understand if she loves the truth more than the story she has told herself."

Alfanas approached the sarcophagus holding the *Chronicle of the Last Emperor*. His steps echoed in the chamber, breaking the fragile stillness of the moment. Father Makar removed his hand from Nick's shoulder and turned to face him, a faint smile flickering at the edges of his lips as he gestured toward the glass case.

"This is where it ends," Alfanas said solemnly, "but also where it begins. Shall I recount the final chapter of Constantine XI's life?"

Nick glanced back at the Emperor's face. For the first time, he noticed the weary lines etched into it, not just those of a ruler but of a man bearing the culmination of the weight of his choices. Slowly, he nodded. "Yes, let's hear how his story ends. And perhaps we'll find an ending to ours."

Alfanas closed his eyes briefly, steadying himself in prayer before he began, "Once Alexios and Theodore had Constantine XI on board the merchant ship, they set sail for the port in Thessaloniki. While under Turkish control, it maintained a thriving Greek Orthodox community that would have naturally provided a safe refuge for those fleeing the fall of Constantinople. They stayed in Greece for six months to allow Constantine's condition to stabilize, ensuring he would survive the journey, while also letting the dust settle and a new normal return to trade and commerce in the region. This time also allowed Alexios to complete the transport of the Emperor and the last shipment of relics from Constantinople.

Alexios then writes at length honoring his youngest son, Michael, and his sacrifice of staying behind. Alexios never saw or corresponded with Michael again. He wanted to leave no path to follow. You can feel the grief of a father who missed his son. He also lists all the things Michael had to do to cover the tracks of the missing Emperor."

As Alfanas drew a deeper breath, giving Nick a chance to interject. "So, he did survive the fall."

"By what Alexios has recorded, yes. After six months, Alexios, Theodore, and Constantine XI were able to set sail for Kyiv. They sailed up the Dnieper River, disembarking at Kyiv. Alexios and Theodore establish Constantine XI in a small village named Khotiv. It was in Khotiv that Constantine XI Palaiologos lived out the remainder of his life. He became a small property owner who tenant-farmed his land. But his life does take a turn."

From across the dais, listening intently, Elain asked, "Did he use the wealth Alexios saved from the fall to live on?"

Alfanas paused more for dramatic effect than from weariness or need before he continued. "No. He did not want to risk too much of a connection to the fallen city and arouse suspicion. Most of it remains here, but there is a vague reference to a cache stowed away in Venice, in case all else failed. Constantine obtained land through the agency of Alexios, who arranged an alliance with one of the noble Boyar households, securing land, secrecy, and protection. To cement this alliance, Constantine married again. He had two children, a boy and a girl. He named the son Konstantin."

Alfanas reached across the glass sarcophagus and patted Nick's hand to ensure his full attention as he said, "Look at me, my boy. When Constantine married, he could not use his Christian name. He had to take on an alias. From that day forward, he was known as Andriy Palevych. You are his heir."

From across the dais, Elena exclaimed, "That is the link! Alexios, my grandsire, served your grandsire in imperial fidelity and sacrificed his sons to committed service so that the last imperial seed of the last Emperor should not fail. It was you. I knew it was you!"

Alfanas and Makar's faces remained grave, waiting for a response from Nick. Nick continued his gaze into the old emperor's face. At the same time, his face remained fixed and considerate. He felt a strange calm. It is almost as if he knew it when he walked onto the dais. He smiled a peaceful smile of contentment as he thought, *This changes nothing. It still isn't me. It isn't for me. It isn't time.*" He slid his hand from the panes of glass and looked over at the scepter and crown. He walked over to the gold and bejeweled scepter, raised his hand to touch it, and then let it rest on the carved marble pedestal.

Elena had come to his side and whispered, "Take it. It is your birthright. All of this is your birthright. Imagine the world when the Emperor returns! Imagine the seat of New Rome, where it belongs, in Kyiv, where it fled and was welcomed."

Nick looked at the imperial crown of Constantine on its pedestal and walked over to it. It was stunning. He tried to figure out his feelings and what Elena wanted him to feel. What he should feel. His hand stretched out again. He wanted to take it for her, for them, but was that what he should do? His hand faltered again and rested on the pedestal. He looked down at his hand, turned it over and back, and stared at it.

He thought, *"Imagine in a world torn apart by violence, pride, ego, and greed: death. Now, with all of this in the mix—a struggle for a title, a legacy, one more thing to fight over or for—it's all a failed strategy for peace. Maybe Providence has a different plan. It is not me. It is not the time. This is not the way out for humanity. It never was."*

He knew that to take the wealth, to use the power, the fame, the legacy would be expected and as natural as breathing. It is not only what every other person would do, but it has also been done throughout history. Constantine XI chose his title and ego over his people and their good. He died protecting an ideal, but also a privilege. It is what the powers and principalities of this world always see as the way up and out: absolute power has always tempted the human heart. But what about now?

"Nick…" she whispered, coming up beside him.

"Wha … what if no?" he stammered, looking into her eyes with his own wide in wonder, amazement, and resolve.

"What do you mean? It is why we went through all of this, for this moment. What do you mean?!" she protested, her alarm written on her face, which had changed from an exuberant smile to terror and confusion. "But why then? Why did we go through all of this if not for this moment?"

He grabbed both her arms and held her perplexed gaze in his solid brown eyes as he said, "What if this is not for us? What if this is not the time?" He had begun to trust his internal compass more than at any other time in his life, and it pointed home. Not because of fear, not because he longed for what had been, but when he reached out his hand to claim her perceived next, he heard in his soul, *"No, not now. Not for you. I have other plans for you, not to harm you but to bless you. You are a conduit, not the vessel."*

"Honey, think about it. If this were for now, I would need to put on that crown, take that scepter, sit on that throne, and hold and use that sword. It would rattle and swing with all the other swords in play around the world. The world is inherently a mess and divided by chaos. Imagine the shift of power. The idea of the New Rome is centered here and in me. We have tried it that way forever." His eyes detached from hers and went back to the crown. His hands let loose of her arms and grabbed the sides of the crown's stone perch. "What if fate, the universe, even God has other plans than how we have tried to force our peace before?

I don't know the 'why' of it all. But what if, what if," Nick spoke this last iteration with a confidence of a new understanding, emphasizing each word as his eyes slowly shifted back to her, "what if it was never about him," he gestured to the lifeless body. "What if it was all about us? What if this was destiny's way of finding a path for the future? What if we are part of something bigger than crowns and cities? What if we needed to be with each other, not for us, but for some higher purpose we may never see or know we are a part of? What if this was for us? What if something needs to happen that we must say no to this," Nick waved his hand about the room, "and yes to life?"

Nick gestured to the sarcophagus. "He had this forced on him because he didn't have the courage to fail and say no, simply to stop and accept the hand of providence." He looked at the floor, lost in his thoughts.

It took Nick a moment to stir back to life. He placed his hands on both sides of her face. Staring into her brown tear-filled eyes, he said, "What if winning is only that I walk out of here with the girl? What if that is what we are supposed to do? Neither the world nor I need all of this. Let him rest for now. I am *not* his trumpet."

"But…," her protest weakened, and her resolve crumbled. How could she continue to fight him? She loved him.

"I am no longer that little boy you ran into and tried to pick up in New York. I don't have a job. I don't know what we do now. The money from savings and retirement is all but gone, and all this would be so easy a way out, but no. It's not for us. We and the world will be better off without it, at least for now."

Nick let his hands slide down her face to her arms and into her hands. He led her from the dais, and Alfanas and Makar followed his lead. The machinery slowly reversed. The emperor sank slowly beneath the silver lake, and the empty throne glided back into place. The four of them stood in silence, looking at it. Constantine once more slept beneath his throne, awaiting the trumpets' call to join the last battle. Nick looked into Elena's eyes and kissed her for the first time. She fell into his arms, and they clung to each other as deep shadows once again claimed the chamber.

There they stood, the emperor and empress who refused to be.

Chapter 20: A New Rome

Nick stood there, holding Elena as she mourned the loss of the emperor who would not be. To hold her gaze, he took her tear-soaked face in his hands again, as he said, "I have come to love you more than I could have ever imagined loving anyone. You must have known ..."

Alfanas and Makar looked at each other and smiled. They both experienced what it meant to choose the better part and to walk away from something toward the unknown. Alfanas closed the book of the *Chronicle of the Last Emperor* with a resounding snap and returned it to its place.

Slowly and solemnly, they made their way back through the tunnels. They replaced the marble plaque. The two monks led them out caves, both silent but content. They both felt that their proteges had grown up and blossomed rather well, and they were well pleased.

Alfanas and Makar walked them out of the complex and to Alfanas' rental car. Makar kissed them both. "My children, sleep now in contentment. This night has seen the best you have to offer, and no more may be done. Now surrender its successes and failings to the care of One Who Sleeps Not and be content."

Nick and Elena took the back seat, holding each other in their weariness as Brother Alfanas drove them to the hotel. At the curb, he kissed them as Makar had, and added, "We will talk later about the next steps and home."

The energy had completely drained from them. For the first time, they had no reason to get up early the next day, no plans to make. The haunting questions resolved. They fell asleep peacefully, anticipating a new day.

When that day dawned, Nick and Elena had a couple of loose ends to chase down, and family to follow up with. Nick had other considerations on his heart, but the timing would need to be just right …

***

Irina had diligently kept her mom and dad updated every time the arrow on her app would jump to a new country or city Nick was in. She would also include his last instructions, which were that as long as the arrow moves, he is okay and not to worry. But Nick's father, Mike, decided that he wanted updates all the time, so he and Nick's younger brother, who was home for Thanksgiving Day, upgraded his flip phone for a smartphone that would allow him to track Nick's progress in real-time.

The arrow had jumped back to Sparta and remained there for several days. It had been over a month since he had talked with his son. Mike had decided to call when the doorbell rang. The postal worker asked for a signature on a priority mail packet from Sparta, Greece. When Nick's mom and dad opened the package, they found round-trip tickets for a flight from John F. Kennedy International Airport to Athens International Airport, leaving on December 27 and returning on July 10. A note accompanied the tickets:

Mom and Dad, first of all, I love you. Sorry, I haven't been able to keep you up to speed with everything that has been happening, but it was all too overwhelming while it unfolded. Please, please, I need you to prioritize meeting me in Athens and then going down to Sparta. I've made all the plans for your trip. Bring the safe-deposit box key with you when you come. I am fine; everything is fantastic! See you at the end of the month.

Nick

P.S., Mom, bring Christmas cookies, gingerbread. Thanks.

His mom and dad looked at each other. Finally, his mom shrugged and said, "I guess we're going to Athens. I'd better start packing and baking."

Mike kept looking at the letter with confusion written all over his face. "You've got almost a month. I'll pack on the twenty-sixth."

She laughed as she left for the kitchen.

Nick, Elena, and Alfanas were not idle after they left Lavra. They had decided that the best course of action would be to retrace their steps and put all the clues back in place as they traveled. That meant traveling back to Chişinău. At Nick's insistence, they made the trip by bus rather than deal with the memories the train would evoke. Once in Chişinău, they would fly to Athens. Nick had one last thing he needed to do before leaving Kyiv.

He and Elena planned to spend the morning together before getting on the bus. Nick planned to spend some time walking about the grounds of the Lavra. It would always be a special place for him. Knowing that Constantine XI would have looked out and seen a familiar landscape and that Alexios had prayed on those grounds would suggest a meeting place between Nick and Elena's family.

Nick and Elena held hands as they strolled the grounds as visitors. Nick guessed they were roughly above the niche of Alexios, the man who first conspired to bring them together.

He took Elena in his arms as they looked out over the Dnieper River Valley. "I meant what I said in the throne room. I believe that all of this is about us. You and me finding each other. It wasn't random. We are part of a plan, a future that is waiting to come into existence because we are together. I'm glad that our first meeting didn't work out. I wasn't ready for you, and I wouldn't have been able to buy into any other reality than the one I had carefully laid out for myself and my future. I have come to more than love you. I have come to trust you as a friend, and a friendly pit bull," he smiled, "You are someone who completes me." He looked away from her out into the valley. "Someone I would never be able to forget, or get over." He turned back to look at her. "This was for us. What an extravagant universe! And now, with us, something wonderful is possible. Are you up for an exceptionally difficult adventure? Living with me? Would you be my wife?"

His proposal didn't take Elena by surprise. At first, she fell in love with the Nick she imagined would be, the one who would solve all her problems for her and her people. Then, as she became more of a stable influence on their travels, she questioned whether he could ever be more to her. But he had unfolded to her as a butterfly from its chrysalis. Nick had become a part of her. The lightness of his humor no longer hid his insecurity but came from the joy in his soul and the peace he found in the chaos about him. She now loved him because, well, he's Nick.

"Oh, my silly little boy," she said, tears welling in her eyes, "you don't have a job. You don't have a place to live. You are broke because you spent all your money on a woman."

"Yup," Nick confirmed, squeezing her tight.

"I guess you need me more than ever, huh?" she smiled as she said, "So I will bail you out again. I would love to be Mrs. Paleon."

The mist burned off in the valley as they stood as one in the quiet stillness of the morning. Nick then looked her in the eye with a smile on his face, and they kissed as the Saints looked on, celebrating young love. Nick and Elena swore they could all but hear God proclaiming everything good: They may not have the fame, the fortune, the power, and the scepter, sword, and crown remained sleeping in the hands of providential timing, but they lived now in providence realized.

Alfanas thanked the abbot and Makar for their hospitality as Elena and Nick joined them. Once the abbot had gone, they shared the news with both men. Alfanas and Makar exchanged knowing glances with one another, but Makar was the first to speak. "A conduit has its rewards, my children. It is a Christian truism that God sends a baby when He wants to change the world. Such is the sacredness of husband and wife in their role as parents."

Alfanas took a hand from each into his hands and looked at them with a smile. "Finally, you have both come to the true end of this adventure. The release of the Sakellaris family from the bond of fealty is now consummated in the union of the emperor's line with that of the good and faithful servant. You now mutually own, guard, and pass along a hope, a tradition, and a prophecy that yet would awaken. But I don't think the adventure is over yet. It is time to go. Athens awaits!"

Elena and Nick made their plans on the way to Athens. They would be married in Sparta and ask if Father Makar could marry them, with Brother Alfanas standing up for them. Nick and Elena's parents would come to Sparta. Between Alfanas, Makar, the Metropolitan of Sparta, and Elena's father, they could reduce many of the legal barriers, but it would take about a month for everything to be resolved.

Elena returned home to Istanbul with her parents until the wedding. Alfanas would return with Elena to reinsert the scroll from the University into the base of the statue, then proceed to Sparta to live in the monastery until the wedding.

Meanwhile, Nick would stay at one of the hostels in Sparta. They would spend several days in Sparta after the wedding, and then all three would fly back to Sitka to put the key and the Evangelion back where they found them.

"I would like to take a look at this Evangelion," Alfanas responded to their questions about his interest in going to Sitka, "and I think I might also want to see the grave in Bridgeport. But as to why, I will hold off on explaining until we get to Sitka. Focus for now on the wedding."

Elena filled her time with wedding plans. Her parents were disappointed but understood why she could not have the family wedding they envisioned in Istanbul. Free from the specter of Viktor, she told her mom and dad everything that had happened to them, giving some closure to the family's long-held secret.

"So, at last, we know," Niketas said. "The city is lost, but a prince still lives. Long live Rome! To think that the sopping wet fish we pulled from the waters was a prince all along." He chuckled.

"To think that sopping wet fish we pulled from the waters will be your son-in-law," Despina, Elena's mother, corrected him.

Before his parents arrived, Nick explored Sparta and its surroundings further. Nick also had time to reach out to a couple of the area's reconstruction businesses and found one willing to sponsor him for a work visa. His degree from Yale clinched the application.

He intended to work for them until he could start a business of his own in reconstruction and restoration. Between Elena's father and the Metropolitan of Sparta, he would be in good standing to start a family in his ancestral home. He would carefully tell his mom and dad the news when he returned home with them.

Nick and Alfanas managed to talk the Metropolitan of Sparta into allowing Alfanas to have one more night alone to pray in the Church of St. Demetrios in Mystras. After a short time in prayer, he helped Nick replace the scroll, now sealed shut, under the Coronation Stone. The Sitka trip would close the circle. They would return to Stamford via Sitka, replacing the Evangelion on their way through.

The twenty-eighth dawned bright and cold in Athens. Nick had borrowed Alfanas' rental car and had driven up the night before. While he waited for his parents, he paced the landside of the airport eagerly. They knew nothing about Elena or the wedding. He reflected on that for a minute. "Mom's going to kill me. I bet she didn't bring a dress she would agree to be photographed in. Oh well, let's hope that she'll be so happy to see me alive and so stunned to hear I am getting married that she'll forget about the death thing." He chuckled at the thought of it.

A wave of emotion overwhelmed Nick as he saw them come through security. He ran to his mom, tears streaming from his eyes. She held on to him tightly, her tears falling freely as though they were washing away the weeks of worry and distance. Even the stoic Mike's voice cracked as his planned handshake turned into a firm, heartfelt hug. No words passed between them for a moment, only the quiet reassurance of touch and presence.

Finally, Mike pulled back, his voice gruff but gentle. "Did you find what you were looking for?"

Nick burst out laughing, his face lighting up with relief and joy. "Oh, Dad," he said, "I found so much more." He paused, his eyes twinkling. "Wait until you meet her."

"Her?" both parents harmonized.

Nick put a hand on each of their shoulders and kept switching his gaze from one to the other as he said, "I guess there is no easy way to say this than just to blurt it out and pick you up off the floor later. I asked you to come to my wedding. In two days I will marry the woman I told to get lost in New York. That one arrow Irina tracked on her phone represented two lives that, for a month and a half, never left each other's side."

"A wedding!" exclaimed his mom. "I need a dress!"

Once Nick settled his parents in the hotel, they headed off to supper together. Nick spent the whole evening recounting everything that had happened since meeting Elena in New York. The next day, his mother shopped for a dress in Athens. His father fought off her insistence that he needed a suit rather than his dress shirt and pants. They headed out for Sparta in the late afternoon.

The next day, they had breakfast with Elena and her parents in Sparta. Alfanas would join them for lunch in Mystras. They walked through the ruins in the afternoon and entered the old Church of Saint Demetrios. Nick and his dad, another prince of the empire, stood before the coronation stone.

Nick put his arm around his dad's shoulder and said, "Think of it, Dad, Constantine XI, Andriy Palevych Paleon, kneeled here to be crowned. His hands touched this stone. Without him, we would not be. He was here. In a way, he still lives because we live. For us, Rome never died. It lies sleeping in our cells, waiting for the kiss of providence to wake her up, sound the trumpet, and claim the victory."

His father looked at him, gratified to see the man his son had become. He didn't use the words, but he felt what the old monk Makar expressed to Nick, pleased to be a conduit to the young man who stood to his left.

They returned to the hotel in Sparta for dinner. When it came time for dessert, the server came out with coffee and a big plate of iced and decorated gingerbread cookies. Nick's mom laughed as she said, "Imported from Connecticut!"

The early morning light filtered through the small leaded windows of the Cathedral of Saint Spyridon, casting soft, golden patterns across the ancient stone floor. Muffled sounds of traffic and the gentle rustle of robes alone disturbed the quiet of the church, while the faint scent of incense rose toward the vaulted ceiling. The space seemed to hold the weight of centuries, yet it pulsed with gentle anticipation of this sacred moment in the lives of two young people.

Nick stood near the modest altar, flanked by Brother Alfanas, who had donned a simple black cassock for the occasion. Alfanas held the two *Stefania*, delicate crowns of olive branches bound with silver filigree. His serene expression and the way he occasionally murmured a prayer underscored the sacredness of the event.

Nick's parents sat in the front pew, his mother dabbing at her eyes with a handkerchief while his father watched in stoic silence. Across from them sat Elena's mother. Her proud gaze seemed to take in the ceremony and the legacy it honored.

Elena's footsteps echoed as she entered the otherwise empty and silent church, her hand resting lightly on her father's arm. She wore a simple but elegant white gown trimmed in lace, which had been a part of her family's heritage. Her mother had worn it, as had her grandmother. Her dark hair, swept up and back, flowed a few inches below her thin veil. As she reached Nick, her father gently squeezed her hand before stepping back to join the others.

Standing at the altar in his white and gold vestments, Father Makar began the ceremony with a low, melodic chant, his voice resonating in the stillness. The ancient and sacred words invoked blessings for the couple as they started their life together. He anointed their foreheads with holy oil, marking them as a pair united by love, faith, and purpose.

As the ceremony progressed, Nick and Elena each held a white candle, their flames a quiet symbol of light and unity. Father Makar guided them through the traditional exchange of rings, his voice steady as he declared, "May these rings, a sign of endless love, seal your covenant before God."

Then came the crowning. Alfanas stepped forward, his hands steady as he placed the Stefania on their heads, binding them as king and queen of their household, united in purpose and faith. As Father Makar led them in the 'Dance of Isaiah' around the altar, the soft chant of "Rejoice, O Isaiah" filled the church as they took their first steps as husband and wife.

When the ceremony concluded, Father Makar turned to face the small congregation. "What God has joined together, let no man put asunder," he intoned, his voice filled with quiet authority. With a gentle smile, he added, "May your union be blessed, and may you walk together in faith and love all the days of your lives."

Their hands still joined, Nick and Elena turned to face their families. Warm smiles and tears of joy, silent witnesses of the profound sacrament. Nick's mother rose, embracing her son tightly, then turned to hug Elena with a beaming smile. Elena's father placed a firm hand on Nick's shoulder, a silent but heartfelt blessing.

The small group gathered outside the church, where the Spartan landscape stretched out under the afternoon sun, ancient and enduring. The air carried the scent of olive trees and wildflowers. Alfanas stepped forward, handing Nick a small wooden cross, a keepsake to commemorate the day. "A reminder of faith and purpose," he said, his voice calm and steady. "It was hand-carved from one of the old trees in Lavra. May it bless you both and remind you that you are loved."

Elena leaned into Nick's shoulder, looked at it, and softly said, "It is perfect."

Nick nodded, his hand brushing hers as they stood together under the ancient sky. He felt rooted and free for the first time, ready to embrace their shared future.

Nick and Elena enjoyed both days on their own and times spent with others, where both families merged and created memories. Alfanas spent most of his time at the Monastery of the Holy Forty Martyrs of Sebaste. He phoned in every so often to make sure they were okay and if any plans had changed, but he primarily wanted to leave the young couple alone with each other and their families.

Elena's parents left for home on the third. Nick's folks planned to fly home on the tenth. During supper one night, Nick's dad asked about the trip home and what lay beyond.

"We're still discussing what happens next," Nick replied evasively. He didn't want to overshadow the rest of the week with thoughts of their moving halfway around the world. "We'll make definite plans when we get home. I need to get that safety deposit key from you tomorrow. I left something in Sitka that I must pick up on my way home."

Nick retrieved the key from his dad's room on the way out and safely tucked it into his wallet. Elena and he drove his folks to the airport to see them off. Before going through security, they hugged and kissed. Nick's last words were, "It will take us a bit longer than you to get home. We are spending a few more days here. We will be in Sitka for a day or two and then back in Connecticut. Expect us when you see us. We are in no hurry."

Nick and Elena completed the details for their return to Sparta and phoned Alfanas to tell him they were ready to leave. By the next day, they were off to Sitika. On landing, they immediately headed out to the bank to pick up the Evangelion and the key from the safe-deposit box, and then off to the hotel.

Once in the hotel, Alfanas donned white gloves and carefully unwrapped the Evangelion. The ancient book seemed to hum with muted power, its silver-ornamented cover catching the dim light. Alfanas let his fingers rest on one of the Tetragrammatic crosses, his reverence palpable.

"Ah," he murmured as he turned to the last page. His eyes scanned the list of names and places before settling on the last, cryptic line: 'Οὐκ ἐμὲ ἐκσκάψῃς.' He smiled faintly. "Your great-grandfather was clever. This isn't just a warning; it's a directive."

Nick frowned. "A directive?"

"Yes," Alfanas replied, tracing the line with his finger. "It literally reads, *'not me possibly you dig up.'* But look at the construct—Vasyl is layering multiple clues. It's deliberate, a riddle. In essence, he's saying: *not this grave, but the other. Exhume that.* I think it's a call to return to Bridgeport."

Elena tilted her head, her brow furrowed. "Do you think we can even get permission to exhume it?"

Alfanas smiled. "I did some research in Sparta. Given the circumstances and your family's ownership of the plot, there should be no issue. It seems your journey isn't quite over yet."

In the morning, they drove out to the graveyard, reopened the crypt, and placed the Evangelion back in its lead box. Alfanas quickly soldered it shut and put it back in the casket. The door closed with a bang and locked with a click. Nick returned the key to its hiding place in Vasyl's headstone.

Nick looked anxiously around, but Alfanas reassured him. "Don't worry, my young friend, there is now nothing to fear here. You are safe."

At the foot of Vasyl's grave, Nick asked if he could spend a few minutes alone with his great-grandfather. As Elena and Alfanas walked away, Nick just stared at the headstone. He didn't feel he would ever be back to the grave in Sika. He felt this goodbye would be his last opportunity. They had journeyed far together. Nick thought of Vasyl dying in Sitka all alone.

Vasyl died hoping and praying that the clues he had hidden and the sacred trusts he had left would stand the test of time, allowing Nick to find him and claim him, and bring him back into the family, so that his part as a conduit would be known and honored. He had placed many a flower on the graves of his great-grandparents, never feeling the connection, the love he felt now for a man he never met, but who paid such a heavy price so that he would be born.

Nick kneeled on the ground, put his hand on the grave, and rubbed the earth. "Rest in peace, Vasyl. I was coming for you, and I found us now. Love has brought you home. Rest in peace."

All the loose ends were closed. One new lead only needed to be followed up on, and then it would be over. Nick's parents picked them up from JFK. Nick let his mom and dad show Alfanas and Elena around, and he headed off to hire a lawyer to file the paperwork and cut through the red tape at the local county court. He cited the family's ownership of the burial plot and the possibility of historical artifacts being buried there. With no objections from the cemetery or local authorities, the judge approved the exhumation order quickly.

Breaking through the frost in New England in January is usually a task that even a large backhoe could not accomplish without the use of heaters to thaw the ground, but the weather had been mild for winter. Nick, Elena, Alfanas, and Mike were there to watch and wait. It took 30 minutes to reach the cement vault. In another 30 minutes, the vault top lay off to the side of the open grave. A large casket, oak with iron straps wrapping it, lay within the concrete vault. They tried to use the winch the graveyard usually employed to shift caskets, but it could not budge the casket, let alone lift it to the surface. They ended up using the backhoe and chains to bring it up, and then just barely did so. The hearse couldn't hold the weight, so they brought in a truck to load it and took it to a police garage for opening.

Out of respect for the family, Nick's lawyer requested everyone but the coroner and one detective to leave as they opened the casket. The reason for the weight became clear once they had the cover removed: gold *solidi* and silver *miliaresia*, coins of the Byzantine Empire, filled the interior. A sealed lead box lay at the top of the hoard.

"Wow," exclaimed Nick, "one thing you have to say about Vasyl is that he loved lead." And he chuckled.

He took out his knife and opened the box. Inside lay the last will and testament of Vasyl Palevych Paleon. In it, he bequeathed the family legacy and the treasures within the casket, in perpetuity, to Ivan Paleon or his rightful descendant, who solved the clues and unearthed the grave. It also contained a complete history of the family, the deception, and the change of name to 'Paleon.' The contents of the casket were the sole property and inheritance of the Palevych family, secured by a genuine notarial act from Venice attesting to the provenance of the hoard.

Elena came up beside him, put her arm around his waist, and said, "You know it is not ours, even as it was not his. He protected it the only way he could and passed it along to the future he hoped and believed would be. It is not ours; it belongs to the conduits, as Father Makar would say. It is the future's."

He smiled at her. "I know we will protect it, but it will also help the Rum and fulfill a prophecy lived and spoken by a young lady who believed a legend beyond hope. There is enough here to invest and build more than a little hope for home and our people in Istanbul."

It took them weeks to complete and assemble everything. By the time the plans were in place, they had sold or auctioned most of the coins. The remaining coins they secured in safe-deposit boxes. Nick and Elena set up generational trusts to safeguard everything. At about the same time, Nick had received word Greece had approved his visa. He would now have to tell his mom and dad that they would go back to Greece, a place he had really come to consider home.

Nick stopped off at his folks without Elena and found his dad back to 'reading' with his eyes closed. He touched his arm. "Hey, Dad, can you talk for a minute? Can we join Mom at the dining room table?"

His dad had been here before. He braced himself for something both essential and potentially distasteful. They sat waiting for Nick to start.

"You know that the last three months have really been a reorientation for me, and I don't see my life here clearly anymore. I can't return to simply enduring work for a future that isn't today. When we came back to Sparta, I made plans to stay there. I have a job and a sponsor. Elena and I will be settling there to start our family."

His mom looked at the table, considering what to say next. "You know," she started slowly, "when you said that you were going to Sitka, I remember saying to myself that I could be happy for you if you were going to better your life. I knew that I would miss you. I knew I would not want you to go, but if this is 'better,' who could deny someone they love anything better? Don't get me wrong, I hate that you are going. It hurts deep down, but to hold you here because *I* don't want to hurt is not love. You don't belong to us anymore. You belong to her and to the future you both are making." She glanced over at Mike.

His father looked at him, sighed, nodded, and said, "You must make your own life now. Florida is just as convenient as Greece. Although it takes a little longer and is more expensive to get there, it is doable. In a way, I understand that you are, in a sense, going home. When do you leave?"

"We're thinking about another week or so," Nick replied. "I'll try to get the car sold and get rid of some of my other stuff. I don't want to drag too much junk over."

As the days passed, the reality of Nick and Elena's decision settled over the family like a bittersweet fog. His mom, ever the practical one, started collecting recipes she thought might comfort him in his new home. "You'll be able to make these with what you'll find there," she said one evening, handing him a handwritten notebook. "I've even added gingerbread at the back. Just in case."

His father, meanwhile, busied himself with helping Nick prepare for the move. Together, they sorted through the garage, deciding what to sell, donate, junk, or store. "You've got excellent tools here," his dad said one afternoon, inspecting a sturdy level. "Are you sure you don't want to take them with you? They'd probably come in handy in your new line of work."

"I thought about it," Nick replied, his hands buried in a box of old drafting supplies. "But it's just more weight to carry. I'll start fresh there."

His brother and sister each visited before he left, bringing warmth and laughter to what might otherwise have been a somber goodbye. Irina and Elena bonded quickly over coffee and shared memories of Nick's quirks while Alex teased Nick mercilessly about leaving the comforts of home behind. "You're going to miss real bagels and pizza, you know," Alex said with a grin. "Don't come crying to me when all you've got is olives and feta to suck on."

"Trust me," Nick replied, laughing, "I'll take the olives and feta any day."

By the time the week stretched into ten days, they had their bags packed, the car sold, and the few things Nick couldn't part with, they either safely stored in his parents' basement, or sent on ahead. The night before their flight, the family gathered for a final dinner. Nick's mom made it a buffet of his favorite comfort food with a few dishes Elena suggested, blending the flavors of their two worlds. Unspoken emotions filled the air, but laughter and conversation kept it light.

At JFK the following day, the airport buzzed with frenetic energy, but for Nick, time seemed to slow. His mother's arms were around him, her grip tighter than usual, as though she could hold him back from leaving if she tried hard enough.

"You'd better call," Irina whispered as she stepped in for her hug. "I mean it, Nick. Often."

His mom kissed his cheek, slipping a small bag into his hand. "Snacks for the flight," she said, her voice trembling. "And don't forget, you'll always have a home here."

His dad, ever stoic, clasped his shoulder. "We're proud of you. Stay safe."

As Nick and Elena walked toward security, he glanced back one last time, their faces fading into the crowd. The skyline of New York loomed as a backdrop, a reminder of the past. But for the first time, he didn't feel like he had lost anything. He squeezed Elena's hand, gave her a wink and a kiss as he stepped toward everything that mattered.

The Spartan countryside welcomed them with its familiar warmth, the winter sun casting long shadows over the olive groves and ancient stone walls. Nick and Elena rented a small but cozy apartment perched on the edge of the town with a clear view of the Taygetos Mountains.

They spent their first days settling in, unpacking, meeting with Nick's new employer, and exploring the streets of their new home. Nick marveled at how quickly it all felt right. The weight he had carried for years, the sense of not quite fitting in, left him. He felt at peace, surrounded by the echoes of the past and the promise of the future.

Elena also seemed to glow in a way Nick had never seen before. "This feels like home," she said one evening as they stood on their balcony, the twilight painting the mountains in shades of lavender and gold.

Nick nodded, slipping his arm around her. "It is home," he replied. "For both of us."

Nick leaned against the balcony rail, the twilight casting shadows across the Spartan hills. His phone buzzed to life, flashing the name 'CHRIS.'

He glanced at Elena, who smiled and waved him off. "Go," she said softly. "I'll wait."

"Hey, Chris," Nick said, his voice warm as he answered. "Yeah, it's been a while—months! You want to know what's up?" He twirled the ring on his finger, his smile widening. "Well, let me tell you, it all started when a funny thing happened in New York…"

The End.

Appendix

The last ten years of Constantinople's life witnessed one
of the greatest real-life tragedies to unfold on the
stage of human events, as desperate emperors took
futile thrones, wading into the intrigue of east and
west as the Palaiologos family sought to salvage a
remnant of arguably the most noteworthy, long-lived,
and opulent Empire the world has ever known: the
Roman Empire. With the dedication of Constantinople
in 330 AD, Constantine drew the curtain up on the
next act in what had already been a drama in
progress. Rome appeared on the world stage as a
republic in 509 BC, not to mention its mythic origins
dating back to 753 BC. By the time Mehmed II
entered Constantinople, the Roman imperial culture
had endured for over two millennia, one of which was
the thousand years of the life of the Holy City of
Byzantium.

The West and Western Christianity played a role in the
decline of Constantinople and the Roman Byzantine
Empire, the eldest child and protector to the younger
siblings, minor refractions that arose from the collapse
of the Eastern Empire. Byzantium protected the
fragile West from Ottoman expansion, while provoking
the West to shore up the military effort, avert the
collapse of the city, and expose Western Europe's
south-eastern flank to a powerful enemy. The West,
preoccupied with crusades and its ambitions, gave
too little, too late to save the city, even though such
intervention was in its own interests.

This is the tragedy of the last emperor of the Roman Empire, Constantine XI Dragases Palaiologos, who followed his older brother, Emperor John VIII Palaiologos. They were courageous, if flawed, men who genuinely sought to alter the course of history. They were men of faith, trusting that neither the West nor God would abandon the emperor or the city of Constantinople. Attempting to plot, court, and connive their way to keep both title and empire alive, they ultimately faced a final choice to make a final stand or run.

According to eyewitness George Sphrantzes, a member of the imperial court, before the fall of Constantinople and the end of the Byzantine Empire on May 29, 1453, Constantine XI Dragases Palaiologos rallied his men with a speech to defend four obligations: faith, homeland, the emperor, and family. After speaking, the emperor went to the Church of Saint Sophia for prayer and the "divine sacraments." Constantine XI proceeded to the palace, requested forgiveness from his household as he prepared for what seemed to be his final hours. After that, eyewitness accounts fall silent, as rumor mixed with hopeful speculation filled the void, blurring history with myth.

History is a retelling of stories whose details are shrouded in varying degrees of mystery. Constantine XI's character, motivation, and personality, like most humans, were multifaceted and complex. Without a deposition on the record, or the ability to confront the characters with our observations and questions, the accounts leave the modern spectator with the tasks of reconstruction and debate: the raw materials that build careers and foster the imagination of writers and storytellers.

This novel draws upon the heroic memory of Constantine XI as preserved in Rum and Greek traditions, including family legends of those who tended to his body, or not, and safeguarded relics. These stories live alongside the more critical, pragmatic historical assessments, reflecting both the myth and the man behind the last stand of New Rome. The book takes a middle approach, admitting his flaws, yet also suspecting the heroic myth of the martyr.

Whispers and legends took root concerning where, if, and how the emperor had died. Disbelief and grief at the city's passing, as if no one could face the fact that two thousand years of history had truly ended, reinterpreted reality. Fondness and imagination took over. This is where *Paleon: Echoes of an Empire* begins.

The disorder and pain led to whispers that the Empire had not ended. Out of the chaos of the final day, the news spread that neither friend nor foe had found the emperor's body. Accounts had him at the gate of Saint Romanos and the Golden Gate. There were whispers that he may have escaped, while others claimed an angel had carried him to his tomb beneath the Golden Gate, where Constantine XI awaited an avenging angel to call him forth for the final conquest of the city. Later accounts became muddled with the unknown, evolving into the stone or marble emperor myth, among other folktales.

Stories woven with mystery leave a sense of irreverence in how the fall tragically ended. Two thousand years of Roman order, law, and culture reduced to panic, rumor, and an emperor whose fate no one confirmed. Such a legacy deserved more than silence, smoke, and confusion.

The author has drawn on these imagined details in the fictional "Essential Prologue" that begins this novel. One can only surmise what conversations Constantine XI had, and what feelings lay in Constantine XI's heart as he moved from self-interest to duty.

***

The following table is a brief attempt to show how the prologue blends historical events, legendary traditions, and fictional details, illustrating where the story stays accurate to an interpretation of the past and where it steps into the realm of myth and imagination.

Historical Record	Prologue in *Paleon*	Notes
Date of fall: May 29, 1453.	Set during the final night and dawn of Constantinople's fall.	Historically accurate.
Final night: Constantine XI is recorded as having attended a last service at Hagia Sophia, receiving communion, asking forgiveness, and meeting with close advisers.	Portrays Constantine in prayer and contemplation, with Demetrios urging him to flee.	Consistent with historical sources, the adviser's name is fictional.
Decision not to flee: Accounts say Constantine refused to abandon the city, though escape routes by ship were available.	Same choice—rejects fleeing to "foreign shores" despite the possibility.	Matches historical tradition. Motivation? Unknown.
Ottoman bombardment: Intense artillery fire before dawn; defenders at the	Describes booming cannons, chaos at the	Accurate to siege conditions.

Historical Record	Prologue in *Paleon*	Notes
walls braced for assault.	main gate, and defenders falling under attack.	
Final assault: Breach likely and accepted near Kerkoporta or Rhegion Gate; Constantine fought in the fighting's thick and likely died at this gate.	The prologue places Constantine moving between gates, eventually near the Golden Gate in the story.	Gate choice is fictional, connected more to what exists in legend than reality, but plausible in the day's chaos.
Imperial regalia: Constantine casts off his imperial robes to fight as a common soldier.	Dramatically removes regalia, declaring, "Long live Rome!" before fighting.	True to *legend*, but if accurate to deeds, likely done so that his body would be indistinguishable rather than out of any feigned solidarity with the plight of the common soldier.
Death/disappearance: The body was never recovered.	Disappears into the fray, "swallowed by the earth," becoming part of the Marble Emperor legend.	Matching the post-fall myth, the Ottomans did not conclusively identify his body.

Historical Record	Prologue in *Paleon*	Notes
Legend: The "Marble Emperor" sleeps beneath the Golden Gate until the city's restoration.	Legend is explicitly tied into the story and family mystery in the modern *fictional* plot.	Faithful to Byzantine *folklore,* not historically accurate. The legend of the "Marble Emperor" arose from disbelief that the Roman line could end so abruptly. While Constantine XI's body was never found, later folklore claimed an angel had hidden him, turned into stone beneath the Golden Gate, and would awaken when the city was restored. This myth appears in later retellings associated with Doukas' *Historia Byzantina,* as presented in Magoulias' translation (*Decline and Fall of*

Historical Record	Prologue in *Paleon*	Notes
		Byzantium to the Ottoman Turks, 1975). Marios Philippides, in his exhaustive 2019 study (*Constantine XI Dragaš Palaeologus*), examines these traditions in depth, noting their parallels to Arthurian motifs and their role as symbols of renewal in Greek cultural memory.
Theodosius Harbor: Mostly silted up by 1453. Small craft could still use the harbor, but larger trading vessels would not have been able to.		Its use in the story is purely fictional.

Acknowledgments

This book grew from years of reading, listening, and patient encouragement. I'm grateful to the friends and family who believed in Paleon before it had a name; to early readers who prodded me toward clarity and courage; and to scholars of Byzantium and the Rum community who steadied my steps. Special thanks to Allen Stacey, who read the first copy and endured the errors; Kathleen Bailey, who trimmed and directed with a keen eye; Dr. John McGee, for candor and encouragement; Laura (Lori) Gabor who took great notes on changes, and Cyndi and Steve Bailey, whose careful observations helped me finish well. Any remaining mistakes are mine; that there are fewer errors and the story brighter is all because of them.

About the Author

Kregg Gábor is a historian, pastor, and writer. Learn more at https://www.paleonechoes.com.